SWEET ANTICIPATION

He didn't move to kiss her; yet, he was close enough that if she leaned forward an inch their lips would touch . . . and ignite.

Lucas? She didn't realize that she'd said his name aloud . . . not until he answered her.

"Yes?" He moved away slightly and cupped her face with both hands. "You know I want to kiss you."

"Aye, Lucas," she whispered. "Do it. Do it, before I think of all the reasons why we shouldn't."

With a groan, he bent his head while he lifted her chin, and then his warm mouth slanted across her lips with hunger. The hot, searing contact made Meghan's blood rush and her knees weaken.

Lucas lifted his head, ending the kiss too soon. "Sweet," he murmured in a tone that made her shiver. "So sweet . . ."

ROMANCES BY BEST-SELLING AUTHOR COLLEEN FAULKNER!

O'BRIAN'S BRIDE   (0-8217-4895-5, $4.99)

Elizabeth Lawrence left her pampered English childhood behind to journey to the far-off Colonies . . . and marry a man she'd never met. But her dreams turned to dust when an explosion killed her new husband at his powder mill, leaving her alone to run his business . . . and face a perilous life on the untamed frontier. After a desperate engagement to her husband's brother, yet another man, strong, sensual and secretive Michael Patrick O'Brian, enters her life and it will never be the same.

CAPTIVE   (0-8217-4683-1, $4.99)

Tess Morgan had journeyed across the sea to Maryland colony in search of a better life. Instead, the brave British innocent finds a battle-torn land . . . and passion in the arms of Raven, the gentle Lenape warrior who saves her from a savage fate. But Tess is bound by another. And Raven dares not trust this woman whose touch has enslaved him, yet whose blood vow to his people has set him on a path of rage and vengeance. Now, as cruel destiny forces her to become Raven's prisoner, Tess must make a choice: to fight for her freedom . . . or for the tender captor she has come to cherish with a love that will hold her forever.

Available wherever paperbacks are sold, or order direct from the Publisher. Send cover price plus 50¢ per copy for mailing and handling to Penguin USA, P.O. Box 999, c/o Dept. 17109, Bergenfield, NJ 07621. Residents of New York and Tennessee must include sales tax. DO NOT SEND CASH.

IRISH LINEN

Candace McCarthy

ZEBRA BOOKS
KENSINGTON PUBLISHING CORP.

ZEBRA BOOKS are published by

Kensington Publishing Corp.
850 Third Avenue
New York, NY 10022

Copyright © 1996 by Candace McCarthy

All rights reserved. No part of this book may be reproduced in any form or by any means without the prior written consent of the Publisher, excepting brief quotes used in reviews.

If you purchased this book without a cover, you should be aware that this book is stolen property. It was reported as "unsold and destroyed" to the Publisher and neither the Author nor the Publisher has received any payment for this "stripped book."

Zebra and the Z logo Reg. U.S. Pat. & TM Off. The Lovegram logo is a trademark of Kensington Publishing Corp.

First Printing: August, 1996
10 9 8 7 6 5 4 3 2 1

Printed in the United States of America

For those brave men and women including my great grandparents who came to the New World for a better life for themselves and their families . . . and for my grandparents and parents who stayed . . .

. . . and for my husband's ancestors, who came and stayed in America . . . and made it possible for me to find my own special "Irish" man.

One

April 1847

She would not cry.
He was gone, and she was journeying alone to a strange place and a new life. Tears would solve nothing. Huddled against the cold Atlantic wind, her dark auburn locks whipping about her face, Meghan watched stoically as her father's canvas-draped body slipped over the ship's side and into the murky depths of the sea.

She shivered and hugged herself with her arms. Dermot McBride was a good man, and she would miss him, but she would not give in to grief. She was McBride's daughter after all, and he'd hated displays of weakness. Her one last gift of love for the man who'd sired her would be to stand tall and proud, and to spit in the eye of anyone who dishonored Dermot McBride's memory.

Ah, Da, ye almost made it . . . Just a wee bit longer and we would have been home . . . A lump formed in Meghan's throat, despite her efforts to be brave.

Home? she wondered. Would America really feel like home? Until two months past when her father and she had boarded the ship bound for the United States, her home had been Ireland with its green meadows and blue skies.

Meghan frowned. *And with its hunger and disease.*

There was no turning back now, she realized. Whether she liked it or not a place called Delaware in the United States would be home to her from this day forward. Her life would be with her husband-to-be, Rafferty O'Connor, a man she hadn't seen in over a year and a half.

Oh, Rafferty. What will ye say when you learn of me father's death? The two men had been the best of friends. Their small farms had bordered one another; they'd shared the same dreams. But while Dermot McBride had been reluctant to leave his homeland, Rafferty had foreseen the calamity of their future and he'd had no such qualms.

"The damn Saxons," Rafferty had exclaimed, "they care little or not if we live or die! Their only thought is what our people can give them!"

His green eyes pleading, Rafferty had grabbed his friend's arm. "By all that's holy, McBride, look about ye! People are dying. Children! Whole families. Our potato crops have failed us—and when they looked to be a bounty year. With the *Sasanaigh* stealing our grain, how will we survive until the next year?" His gaze had flickered from Dermot to his daughter. "Meggie," he'd said, "we have little enough here as it is, and what we do have is useless to us. I'll not stay here and die! America is the place to be. 'Tis said that a man can make a good life for his family there."

Meghan closed her eyes. "Dear Heaven, but he was right," she whispered, recalling the horrors she'd seen. Their people were dying, and the English didn't care!

Rafferty would grieve for his friend while he cursed the British government responsible.

She sniffed as she straightened her spine. Sadness was everywhere, but Meghan was determined to control hers as other passengers were buried at sea. She stared without flinching as body after body splashed into the mighty ocean.

Dermot McBride, ye'll be missed, she thought. She blinked to moisten eyes that burned.

A fine rain began to fall, soaking the deck and the passengers on board the *Mary Freedom* within minutes. Meghan stood, unmoving, staring at the spectacle of grieving families bidding farewell to their deceased loved ones. A wild wail drew the young Irishwoman's attention to a middle-aged woman struggling to break free of another's hold to get to the enshrouded body that was being shoved over the ship's rail.

Meghan's eyes were dry, but her throat felt so tight that she could barely swallow. *I will not cry.*

She forced herself to think of Rafferty and their new life. As old as her father, Rafferty would be a good husband, she thought, closing her eyes, and she'd be a contented bride. Meghan didn't believe in passionate love, but she believed in a marriage based on respect and friendship to a man she'd known most of her life.

The burials at sea completed, the passengers were ordered by the ship's captain to return to their cramped quarters on the lower decks, and the crew resumed their duties. The sobbing continued, but the sound became muffled to Meghan as the sorrowful family members descended below deck to escape the rain.

Ignoring the officer's command, Meghan moved to the rail, where she stood, staring off across the sea at the dismally dark sky. Her hair was soaked, and water ran beneath her rough, homespun shawl and down the back of her woolen gown, but still she stayed.

Drenched, her chest tight with pain, she gazed, unseeing, over the mighty ocean. If she'd stayed in the steerage instead of the cabin she shared with three other women, could she have somehow saved her father? Would she have seen just how ill he'd been?

"Gerl," a gruff voice said, "what are you doing here?" A strong hand clamped on her arm, yanking her about to face a man whose eyes leered at her from beneath a wide-brimmed tarpaulin. She recognized the hat and pea jacket of a crew member.

His face was shadowed, but Meghan saw his gaze widen as he studied her wet face. She had seen that look in a man's eyes before, and she realized how vulnerable she was with her father dead and none of her kin left to protect her. She swallowed and attempted to pull free, but the man's grip firmed.

"Ah, lass, you should be nice to Ned Fellows. A gerl as sweet of face as you will need someone to . . ." He cleared his throat. "Watch out fer you."

"I need no one," she breathed. "I've me family to—"

"Liar," he growled. "If you've family to care fer you, where are they?" He glanced about the deck, his gaze feral as it returned to her. His study fell to her mouth, lust contorting his features, and Meghan's heart thumped with new fear. She was alone, unprotected. Who would care if this man misused her?

Meghan struggled, and the sailor gave an angry cry and wrenched her close. Cupping her head, he pressed her face into the dirty front of his coat, while his other hand caressed her buttocks.

Immediately, she started to gag. He smelled of whiskey, tar, tobacco, and a man who desperately needed a bath. She tried to scream, but her cry was muffled in the wet fabric. His fingers wove into her hair, and he jerked her head backward until she was eye to eye and nose to nose with him.

"You like it rough?" he said, sounding pleased. His breath was as rank as the rest of him.

"Let me go!" she gasped. "I'm a passenger. Your captain—"

The man laughed. "The captain and I are well acquainted. You might say we're friends—he and I."

"No," she breathed.

"Yes." He tugged hard on her hair, and she cried out with pain. "Yes, my Irish lass. The captain needs me more, you see, and should I want something . . ."

Meghan tried to see beyond her captor. Where were the crew and other passengers? The man was lying. Surely, the captain wouldn't permit the ravishing of a female passenger.

"Mr. Fellows, sir!"

The man grunted and looked up past the woman he held to the young sailor who waited uncomfortably to speak with him. Meghan tried to turn, to speak, but Fellows's grip tightened threateningly. Her scalp burned at the roots of her hair. He jerked her so close that she could barely draw breath.

"Christ, Jamie!" he growled angrily. "Can't you see I'm busy?"

"I'm sorry, sir, but the second mate wonders what to do with the—"

The rest of his words were lost to Meghan as blackness threatened to steal her consciousness. *The mate? Dear God! This man was the first mate!*

The pressure about her back eased, and she gasped as the fresh moist air filled her lungs, nearly choking her.

"Now, sweet Irish, where were we?" Fellows said.

She gazed up at him with a sudden surge of fury. *"Let me go."*

He blinked at her show of spirit and then laughed with delight, a chilling sound that frightened her more than his anger had. From the outer edges of her frantic mind, Meghan heard the tread of feet; someone walked along the deck not far from where they stood. She opened her lips to scream, and Fellows bent and took her mouth, filling it with his tongue.

Bile rose in Meghan's throat while she fought the dizzying blackness that again threatened. She felt his hand at her breast, and she whimpered as his fingers groped and painfully squeezed her tender flesh. The mate refused to relinquish her mouth, and her lungs hurt with the need for air.

He groaned as he continued to violate her with his kiss. Meghan prayed for the darkness to overtake her, welcomed a release from horror, but she could still feel his hands . . . fumbling, invading.

His head rose, but she was too weak to fight. She felt him shift his hold. Then, he was dragging her across the deck toward the dark shadows of sail and riggings, to a place out of sight where a woman could be subdued and violated. He stopped abruptly, and Meghan's mind filled with a silent scream as he shoved her against something hard and lifted her skirt. Cool air touched her legs and thighs, and Meghan cried out and fought to cover herself.

Fellows laughed, stilling her movements with his brute strength, and she felt his weight pressing her to the deck. The mate's breath rasped against her neck as he pried her legs apart, and Meghan screamed until her world darkened.

Suddenly, she was free of his weight, the pressure. She heard angry voices followed by harsh grunts and then the thuds and thumps of men fighting. Rain poured over her prone form. Struggling to sit, Meghan fought to see past the downpour. Her gaze saw two dark blurred forms locked in deadly conflict. The air filled with the enraged cry of one of the two men as he rammed the other into a massive coil of rope.

Meghan started to stand, only to sink back down

quickly as the men fell, rolled in her direction, and scrambled to their feet again. She recognized Ned Fellows as he circled his opponent, a man she'd never seen before.

"You touched my wife!" the strange man said.

Fellows's laughter was demonic. "Yer wife, you say? What was she doing topside without yer protection then?"

"My bride-to-be," the stranger said. The man's eyes seemed to burn fire as he stared at his opponent. He had a startling face beneath fair hair darkened by the rain. Water glistened on his features harsh with anger.

Meghan observed the scene, wondering who the man was, grateful for his appearance, and wondering where his betrothed had gone. Then, the hot black eyes seared in her direction, making her heart thump harder.

"Love," he said, holding out his arm. "Come here."

She stared at him blankly until understanding dawned. For whatever his reasons, the strange man had saved her by claiming to be her intended. It seemed the most natural thing in the world to run to his side. Immediately, the man encircled her with his arm. She felt the heat of him through their wet clothing. Adrenaline pumped through her veins as she stared at the man who'd attacked her.

From the haven of her rescuer's embrace, Meghan saw Ned Fellows's stunned expression and the skepticism that slowly transformed his features. She turned, burrowed her head against the man's chest, and the arm about her tightened protectively.

"Irish!" Fellows said. "You never said you were betrothed."

Startled, she raised her head to glare at him. "Ye never asked me!"

"You seemed willing enough—"

She gasped with outrage, and the stranger gave her a reassuring squeeze, as if telling her that he believed in her innocence and that he would handle the man. "I would thank you to stay away from my intended, Mr. Fellows." His voice was soft with an underlying edge of steel.

The mate stiffened. "And who are you to threaten me?"

"Ridgely."

Fellows paled. "Lucas Ridgely?"

"At your service."

Ned Fellows cleared his throat. "I'd no idea, Mr. Ridgely. I thought she was a common enough wench."

"Oh? Do you often misuse your *common* female passengers?" Meghan could feel the tension in the man who held her. His anger sizzled in the air, fairly scorching the man before him. "Apologize to my fiancée, Fellows," he said, ignoring the man's mumbling excuses.

The mate offered Meghan his hand. "Lass, let me—"

She ignored his apology and his outstretched hand. "May we leave?" she asked her rescuer. She was suddenly weary. Her head and back hurt, and she felt dizzy. "I'm not . . ." Her voice trailed off; she turned her face against the man who held her.

"Are you all right?"

She tried to nod, but the movement was too weak to be reassuring. He stroked her hair. "Yes," he said. "Come. I'll take you below."

Meghan was assailed by dizziness as she and her rescuer reached the hatch to go below deck. She cried out and grabbed hold of the man's arm.

"Are you all right?" His deep voice came from a distance.

She shook her head, unable to respond or focus her

gaze. Suddenly, her rescuer lifted her into his strong arms. Ignoring her weak protest, he carried her down the steps, out of the rain. Cold, she laid her cheek against his chest. He was wet, but warm, and she leaned into his heat.

The next thing she knew she was in a cabin, and he was setting her in a chair. Her trembling was violent as he released her, and she murmured her displeasure at the loss of warmth. The room spun, and she was blinded by bright lights. As if sensing that she was about to faint, her rescuer exclaimed with concern and pushed her forward until her head was between her knees.

The blood rushed to her face, and she struggled to take in air. The blackness receded, and she became conscious of the smell and rough texture of wet wool.

She sat back. "Thank you."

Two

"Don't talk," Lucas said. He studied the wet female before him and wondered what on earth had possessed him to bring her to his cabin. She'd been attacked and was obviously in no condition to be left on her own, he thought. What else could he have done?

Irritation curled in his stomach. It wasn't like him to rescue helpless peasants; why had he done so now? Yet, how could he have ignored her cry for help?

He couldn't allow Ned Fellows to despoil the girl. *But, dear God, what possessed me to claim her as my betrothed?*

His gaze sharpened on the young woman in his chair. It was a wonder that Fellows had believed him; she didn't look like the fiancée of a man of his station.

Her face looked gaunt with dark shadows beneath her blue eyes. Her hair was dark, of an indeterminable color due either to the rain or dirt, he wasn't sure which.

The woman sat, hugging herself with her arms, shivering so hard that her teeth chattered. With a muffled curse for his thoughtlessness, Lucas strode to his bunk and pulled off a blanket, which he wrapped about the girl's shaking shoulders.

"Th-than-kk you again." Her gaze shined with gratitude.

Disturbed by the effect of her glistening blue eyes,

he grunted in response and went to unlock his sea chest. He took out dry clothes for himself from the chest's contents and then dug deeper to the bottom where he'd packed the garments he'd bought in London for his sister. Lucas withdrew a cloak of green wool, which he eyed critically before turning to gauge the Irish girl's size.

He could tell that his "guest" was warmer. She was trembling less violently.

Satisfied that she'd be fine while he shed his wet clothes, Lucas tossed the cloak on the bunk next to his dry garments, before he started to change. He'd pulled off his shirt when he thought he felt her gaze. He turned only to find that he was mistaken. She stared off in space as if reliving the horror of Fellows's assault.

Filled with compassion, Lucas went to her and knelt, bringing himself to her eye level. "What's your name?" he asked gently. When she didn't respond, he touched her arm. She gasped and jerked away, her eyes wide with fear.

He watched her expression change as her nightmare receded and she realized who he was. He was strangely pleased to see her look of fear vanish. It meant that she trusted him.

"I'm sorry." Her voice was husky. "I couldn't help remembering . . ."

"Don't think of it. You're safe now, and Ned Fellows won't bother you again."

She gave a weak smile. "I don't know how to show me gratitude."

"You can tell me your name."

Her lashes fluttered against her pale cheeks. "Meghan," she said, offering him her hand. "Meghan McBride."

Lucas rose to his feet and took her hand, frowning

when he felt its coldness. He rubbed it to restore warmth. She had small hands, feminine . . . hands that had known work. "Meghan McBride," he murmured. He chafed her palm until he felt heat, and then turned his attention to its mate. "You feel like ice. You'll be lucky if you don't sicken."

He heard a sharp inhalation of breath and saw her face change as if she'd just realized that he had no shirt. Wariness entered her expression, and she pulled free of his grasp.

"I won't hurt you, Meghan," he said softly. He gave her a reassuring smile. He offered her his hand again. "I'm Lucas Ridgely."

She stared at his extended hand before she met his gaze. After a moment of hesitation, she shook his hand.

"I don't know what I'd have done if ye hadn't—" She choked up, her blue eyes misting. She blinked several times against tears.

"Don't think about it." He turned away to pull on his shirt. Then, he grabbed a green garment from the bunk and turned to find her staring. She looked away as he approached.

"You need to get out of those wet clothes." He thought that his voice sounded unusually brusque.

Startled, she raised her gaze. Her expression changed as she studied the cloak, and the meaning of his words registered. She nodded. Accepting the garment with a murmur of thanks, she stood and laid it over the back of the chair.

Meghan started to unwrap the now damp blanket and then froze as if suddenly self-conscious.

"I'll take that," Lucas said. He extended his hand for the blanket.

She took off her shawl and then paused in the act

of unbuttoning the front of her worn gown to meet Lucas's gaze warily.

Realization dawned. He set the blanket on the bunk. "I'll wait outside," he said, moving toward the cabin door. "Will you be all right?" At her nod, he left the room.

Meghan's fingers shook with cold as she unbuttoned her wet garment. She could feel her bruised flesh as she took off her gown, but left on her damp shift. A quick examination brought to light several bruises made by the mate's hand; the areas felt tender to the touch.

She reached for the cloak, and Meghan made a sound of pleasure as she held up the garment for inspection. She'd never seen or felt a garment so fine. It was heavy and well made with a hood, a shade of green darker than the rolling hills of her homeland.

Raising the cloak to lift over her head, Meghan stumbled and nearly fell. She lowered the weighty garment before she struggled to raise it again., She was so tired that her arms felt leaden.

The woolen folds fell about her head and shoulders, trapping her for a moment, making it difficult to breathe. She cried out at the lack of air, reliving the terror of Ned Fellows crushing her beneath his weight, stealing her breath. She panicked and fought to be free of her fabric prison. Fear lent her new strength, and she managed to pull off the cloak. Clutching it to her breasts, she closed her eyes and inhaled fresh air until she felt calmness return to her.

Shivering, Meghan opened her eyes and then gasped. During her attack of panic, Lucas had silently reentered the cabin. She was instantly aware that she stood scantily clad in her thread-worn shift. Heat infused her from head to toe. She clutched the cloak tighter and raised it to her chin to shield herself from his view.

"I heard you cry out," he said, looking mildly uncomfortable.

Embarrassed, she didn't reply. Something in the man's dark gaze scared her. "No," she breathed, shrinking away in fear as she saw not Lucas, but the first mate.

Lucas started to approach and then froze when he saw terror in her eyes. "Meghan."

She blinked and refocused her gaze. Reaction set in, and she trembled.

With an exclamation of concern, Lucas moved quickly. He pried the cloak from her fingers and, with soothing words, pulled it over her head, before she had a chance to protest.

The back of his fingers burned against her flesh as he tugged down the edges of her cloak. He adjusted the hood at her nape and then pushed her gently to sit in the chair. "You look as if you're about to faint," he said. "Rest there while I figure out what to do with you."

She perked up. "Do with me?"

He raised an eyebrow. "We are 'betrothed' now, or have you forgotten? If we're to keep you safe, we'll have to continue the act." He bent to pick up her discarded shawl and gown, holding them up with a grimace at their condition, before draping the garments over his sea chest.

His reaction stung. "I'm thankful ye came when ye did," she said, "but there's no need to concern yourself with me any longer. The man won't bother me again."

He fixed her with a hard look. "And the others? There are at least one hundred crew members on this ship. Will you handle them as well as you did the mate?"

She felt herself flush to the roots of her hair. "I'll manage," she mumbled.

Lucas closed the distance between them. She stared at him as she grappled with mixed feelings. She was angry and frustrated with her predicament, and shaken by the way Lucas Ridgely was making her feel. How could she feel safe and protected with him, yet unsettled, too?

"You need my help," he said without enthusiasm.

"I'll be all right."

He cupped her jaw and forced her to meet his gaze. *"You need my help."*

His hands on her cheeks were warm. To her surprise, his expression was gentle. Had she misinterpreted his reluctance to help? "I'm grateful for the offer, Mr. Ridgely."

"Lucas," he prompted with a smile.

Her stomach flip-flopped. "Lucas."

"After all we're betrothed."

She inhaled sharply at the beauty of his male grin. "I'm sorry. I—"

He held up his hand. "No need to apologize. Our engagement was my doing." He sighed. "What a mess! But we'll think of something. For now, why don't you lie down and rest? We'll talk later."

Meghan glanced toward the bunk that looked inviting. She was in his cabin, and that was *his* bed. Dare she stay and sleep as he'd suggested?

She didn't relish the prospect of returning to her own cabin and the company of three other women, especially when one of them was ill.

She peered at him hard. "What are you going to do?" He looked exhausted himself. Had he been hurt in the fight? She didn't think so. Her face warmed at the mental image of his bare chest.

Meghan sat up straighter when he didn't immediately answer.

"I need to go topside," he said. "Don't worry; your virtue is safe."

She felt herself turning several deepening shades of red.

Lucas reached into a cabinet. "Here." He handed her another blanket. "In case, you're still cold."

Meghan murmured her thanks as she accepted the quilt and clutched it against herself. She looked longingly toward the bunk and wondered if she'd hurt the cloak by sleeping in it. It felt slightly scratchy, but heavy and warm; she didn't want to take it off. "The cloak," she breathed.

"I know it's not the most comfortable article of clothing, but you may sleep in it. My sister has others. Your need is greater than hers."

His sister. "Thank you."

He opened the door and glanced back. "Lock the door when I'm gone." He paused. "I'll knock three times when I return."

Meghan followed him to the door.

He paused at the threshold and faced her. "Don't worry, Meghan McBride." His deep voice was soft and filled with caring. "We'll work it out . . . together." And he left.

She swallowed hard as she bolted the closed door. It had been a rough day . . . a rough voyage. But oddly enough she found Lucas Ridgely's parting words comforting. Exhausted, Meghan moved to the bunk and lay down. She sighed and closed her eyes and was immediately aware of a pleasant, woodsy scent on the pillow. Lucas's scent.

Her eyes flashed open and she stared at the beamed ceiling. Her heart beat faster as she recalled how glad she'd been when Lucas had rescued her, the warmth and haven of his strong arms.

Who was this man who had saved her? And why did she feel as if she could trust him?

She exhaled and closed her eyes. The noises on the ship faded as she fell asleep.

Lucas stood at the ship's rail and stared out over the darkened sea. It had been hours since he'd left Meghan in his cabin, and still he struggled with what to do with her.

We need to talk. But the poor woman had been through a lot and talking would come better after she'd slept.

He rubbed his temple, trying to ease the headache that had been steadily building since his meeting with the captain.

Dear Lord, what had possessed him to claim the girl as his future bride? Not just once, but twice!

After long and careful thought, he could understand why he'd done so to Fellows. It'd been an impulsive action to save Meghan from the mate and protect her from future attacks from the man.

But what had made him embellish the tale to Richard Nichols, the captain of the ship?

He scowled as he recalled the conversation. When he'd entered the captain's cabin, Nichols had eyed him with surprise from across his chart table.

"Ridgely," the officer had said. "My steward said you needed to speak with me."

Lucas had met Richard Nichols on numerous occasions in Philadelphia and Wilmington, where his family ties to the shipping industry had thrust them together at dinner parties and other social affairs.

He nodded, noting the tension in the man and wondering at its cause. "I'd like a word with you about Ned Fellows." He saw something flicker across Nichols's expression.

"Fellows can be trouble, I admit, but he knows his job."

Lucas stared at the man hard. "This afternoon Ned Fellows attacked a passenger. An innocent female passenger."

The captain averted his gaze.

"He's done this before?" Lucas was shocked. He felt his stomach tighten with anger. Why hadn't Fellows been relieved of his duties?

"It was never proven," the man mumbled.

"Dear God!"

Nichols met his gaze with a defensive look. "The *Mary Freedom* has been a cargo ship for most of her days and Ned Fellows has been with her for all of them. The last time the accusation was made, the woman was a person of questionable character."

"So you dismissed the matter." Tension filled the ensuing silence.

The captain cleared his throat. "Fellows wasn't the first to have her."

"*This time* the woman's character isn't in question, captain." Lucas paused. "She's my fiancée."

The man looked astonished, and Lucas was pleased.

"I don't believe the owners of this vessel would look favorably on a captain who can't control his men."

"Are you threatening me?" Nichols looked furious.

"Does it sound like a threat?" Lucas's smile was grim. "I'm merely making a perceptive observation."

Lucas saw the captain relax. He sighed and ran a hand through his hair. "I'm not threatening you, Richard. You know me too well for that. But I need to be assured that a woman—any woman on board your ship—is safe from the unwanted attentions of your men."

Richard Nichols rubbed a hand over his face wearily. "I'll speak with him," he said. His gaze sharpened. "But, Lucas . . . guard your fiancée well. Warn her against wandering about the ship without escort."

Lucas frowned at the captain's tone. After a moment during which he'd deduced no hidden meaning, he nodded. "I'll do that, captain."

Recalling the exchange, Lucas realized that he'd acted impulsively again. Whether he liked it or not, Meghan McBride was his betrothed for the remainder of the journey.

He didn't care that Ned Fellows had worked on the ship since its first voyage. Cargo ship or not, the *Mary Freedom* now carried passengers. His time as a mate should be terminated if he was a danger to the female passengers.

Lucas had always thought the captain an amicable enough fellow who had seemed to take his responsibilities seriously. The Morgans, owners of the *Mary Freedom* and close family friends of the Ridgely family, were well pleased with Nichols's performance as a captain. Lucas had never had cause to doubt the man's ability or his word.

But the man's reaction to Fellows's attack on Meghan had left Lucas feeling uneasy. Apparently, the mate had been accused before . . . and acquitted in the commander's eyes.

How many women have suffered at Fellows's hands?

Lucas thought of the young Irishwoman in his cabin. He recalled how he'd felt upon discovering the mate roughly subduing Meghan's struggling form.

"It's one thing to seduce a willing woman," he murmured, "but to take her by force is reprehensible."

Why would anyone force a woman when it was so much more rewarding to woo her?

He turned from the rail and headed toward the ladder. Meghan had had plenty of time to rest. There was still much to discuss. They needed to talk now.

Three

Meghan woke up and, with her eyes shut, listened for the sounds she'd become familiar with since boarding the *Mary Freedom* . . . The sound of Mary Beth's snoring . . . Bridget's whining of feeling ill . . . Mrs. Finn's gentle tones as she soothed the sick girl.

Where was the ring of feet in the companionway or the other noises made by the crew?

All Meghan heard was silence. Her eyes flew open, and she sat up to study her surroundings. The only light in the cabin came from a wall lantern. The flame of the wick cast a golden glow that softened the lines of the rough-hewn furniture in the room. Memories both harsh and good came back to her with a wave of pain. She recalled Ned Fellows's attack and the man who'd saved her—Lucas Ridgely.

I'm in his cabin. She glanced down at the cloak, which had become twisted in her legs and risen to above her knees. It had all really happened! She was still wearing the green garment meant for Lucas's sister.

Where was Lucas? she wondered.

She listened hard to hear over her thundering heart and heard the sounds of the ship she'd missed earlier.

Meghan sighed and lay back. She was safe. She wasn't dead. The ship was afloat, and everything was all right.

Da. She blinked and stared without seeing as she

was overwhelmed by grief for her dead father. Her eyes watered, but she forced away her tears. She had promised to be strong for Da. He was dead, but she was alive, and she'd make the best of things.

I have to get back to me cabin, she thought. How long had she been here? An hour? Two? Her heart skipped a beat. All night?

She sat up and swung her legs off the bunk. Meghan rose and searched for her gown. She hoped the garment was dry; her shift beneath the cloak was no longer wet. She didn't want to put on a damp gown.

She'd spied her dress draped over the end of Lucas's trunk. Meghan touched it and frowned. As she'd feared, it was still wet.

"Ah, well, ye've no choice, Meg," she muttered to herself.

The door to the cabin opened as she struggled to remove the cloak. She gasped as Lucas Ridgely stepped inside and closed the door.

"What are you doing?" he asked.

She flinched at his sharp tone. "I'm changing back into me own clothes." She glared at him. "You said you would knock three times. You didn't say you had a key!"

"Why?"

"Why?" she echoed, puzzled.

"Why are you changing?" he said.

She blinked. "Because the cloak belongs to you . . . to your—"

"I think it looks better on you than it would on me." To her amazement, a smile curved his sensual lips.

She found herself unable to resist his smile. "Yes, well . . ."

"Your gown is dry?"

She shook her head.

IRISH LINEN

"Take the cloak, Meghan. It's yours to keep. I told you my sister doesn't need it."

She gaped at him in shock. "You're giving it to me?"

He nodded.

"Why?" She was overwhelmed; she'd never met anyone so generous to her before.

Her face flamed as Lucas looked down at the woolen garment in her arms. Her back stiffened. "I don't need your charity." She set the cloak on the bunk.

Lucas softened his expression as he met her gaze. "I bought the cloak for my sister. She has more clothes than she can wear in a month. She doesn't need it. You do."

She opened her mouth as if to argue.

"Please." He picked up the garment. "Let me be chivalrous for once, will you? I usually make a poor knight in shining armor, Irish. The least you can do is accept my gift." His smile was coaxing. "As thanks for slaying Dragon Fellows?"

"But—"

He captured her hand and gave her the cloak. "Take it, Meghan." Her fingers felt small and fragile within his grasp.

"Aye," she whispered, pulling her hand from his grip. "I'll keep it."

He grinned. "Thank you."

She shook her head as if she didn't understand his generosity.

"Now about Fellows . . ." he began. He'd thought long and hard on this, and after his meeting with the captain, he'd realized that there was nothing else to do.

Caution entered Meghan's blue gaze. Could he blame her? "Meghan, there's only one way I know, for certain, to ensure your protection," he continued. "As I mentioned before, Ned Fellows is just one of many.

I think we should continue to pretend we're betrothed."

Surprise flickered in her expression. "You would do that for me?"

He nodded.

"Why?"

"Because it's the only way—"

"*No, why would ye help a stranger?* Ye said ye make a poor knight, didn't ye?"

"Yes," he admitted slowly. How could he explain why he wanted—*needed*—to help her, when he didn't understand it himself?

She moved away, looking confused. "I don't know what to say."

He smiled and gestured to the chair. "Why don't you sit down, and we can discuss what to do next."

She obeyed. "Mr. Ridgely—"

"Lucas."

"L-Lucas," she said, sounding breathless. "Ye mustn't concern yourself with me welfare. I'll be all right."

He scowled. "I told not just one, but two of the chief officers on this ship that we are engaged. I can hardly claim otherwise now, can I?"

She blinked up at him with innocence, and he stifled his irritation. "I do appreciate your help . . ." she said.

"But?" He raised an eyebrow.

She looked startled. "Two officers?"

"I spoke with the captain."

"Oh, dear."

"Yes, it does change things."

A heavy sigh escaped her lips. "I'm sharing a cabin with three other women. How am I to suddenly explain the appearance of me fiancé?"

"You're sharing a cabin," he echoed. "Excellent!" He grinned. He'd been afraid she was quartered in steerage with many of the other Irish immigrants. How could he explain away his fiancée staying in such *lesser* conditions than he would live in himself?

She studied him as if he'd gone mad. "I don't believe ye understand."

He saw with surprise the beauty of her blue eyes. Large and thickly lashed, they seemed to draw him into their bright depths. She appeared so much the better for having rested. *Why, she's actually quite lovely!*

"No, Meghan, I think it's you who don't understand." He regarded her with a smile. "We couldn't very well convince the mate you're my betrothed if you're traveling in steerage."

She glared at him, but when he refused to look away, she averted her glance. "Da was in steerage," she mumbled.

Lucas perked up. "Your father's on board the ship?" He sat down on one end of his sea chest, watching her shake her head and stare off into space.

"Me father is dead. Buried at sea early this mornin'."

He felt a rush of pity for her. "I'm sorry." That explained why she was wandering the deck alone.

"You said there were three other women in your cabin," he then said. "None of them are family," he guessed aloud. "Close friends?"

Meghan met his gaze with a half smile. "As close as one can get from living with strangers for nine days."

The slight curve of her lips transformed her features, making her appear beautiful. His breath caught. What would it be like if she grinned . . . or laughed with pure enjoyment?

But then what enjoyment could this Irishwoman have had in her rough, young life?

Lucas returned her smile. "Tell me about them," he encouraged.

"Why do ye want to know?" Her blue eyes regarded him warily again.

"Because I should know who is sleeping with my fiancée."

She gasped. "Mr. Rid—Lucas," she corrected after he shot her a look. "Did ye honestly believe this is necessary?"

Lucas loved her accent, the way she pronounced her *r*'s and her husky tone as she said his name. It was important for him to convince her that she needed to keep up the pretense of their betrothal. For some reason, her safety had become vital to him.

He reached across the distance that separated them to capture her hands. Cradling her small wrists within his grasp, he searched her expression. "I'll not hurt you, Irish," he said softly. "Play my fiancée until we reach American soil, and you'll be safe from men like Ned Fellows."

She closed her eyes. He hadn't realized how tense he was until she raised her thick lashes and nodded. " 'Tis the right thing to do, I'm supposing."

Relaxing with relief, he inclined his head. "It's the only way." He released her hands and stood. "Now, Irish, tell me about your cabin mates."

When Meghan entered her cabin a short time later, her cabin mates greeted her with exclamations of concern.

"Meghan, dearie, we'd feared something dreadful had happened to ye." The oldest woman, Mrs. Finn, looked relieved to see her.

"I'm fine, Mrs. Finn," Meghan replied with a smile. "I was spending time with me . . . betrothed." She braced herself for what was to follow.

"*What!*"

"Your betrothed?"

"He's here—on the ship! Why didn't ye tell us?"

Bombarded by questions, Meghan raised her hand to halt the questions as she sat on her bunk. She felt both physically and emotionally drained after her experience. Rest, she knew, would be a long time in coming this night. Patiently, she told the tale that she and Lucas had concocted between them before she left him, and as expected, the story only heightened, not satisfied, her cabin mates' curiosity.

"Who is he?" Mary Beth asked.

"An American," Meghan replied.

"Where did ye meet?"

"Da and I met him in Dublin." She didn't meet anyone's gaze directly for fear that they would see that she was lying.

The questions continued, and she answered each one mechanically, her head reeling from the day's events.

"Is he handsome?" Bridget said.

She felt her cheeks warm. "Aye."

"Strong?"

She blinked and nearly choked as she answered. "Aye."

Her gaze encountered Mrs. Finn's odd glance, and she looked away, suddenly recalling the day she'd confided in the older woman. *I told her about Rafferty,* she realized with dismay. *But did I mention his name?* Flustered, she wondered what to do and decided to continue the charade.

"He gave ye that cloak?"

"Aye."

As Mary Beth and Bridget exclaimed with awe, Meghan fought impatience. She was tired of all their questions.

"When?" Mary Beth asked.

"What did he say when he gave it to ye?" Bridget said.

"Lasses!" Mrs. Finn suddenly exclaimed. "There'll be plenty of time to talk with Meghan later. Can't ye see that the child is swaying on her feet?"

"But—"

"Bridget Cleary." Mrs. Finn used the tone of voice that no one would dare to argue with.

Meghan searched the woman's expression; and relief stole over her, uncoiling tense muscles. Mrs. Finn might be skeptical, but she wasn't going to say a word.

"Why didn't Meghan tell us about him?" Mary Beth said.

"Meghan and her betrothed had their reasons for keeping their relationship a secret. 'Tis late, and the girl obviously needs her rest. Have ye forgotten how Meghan began her day?"

"Aye," Mary Beth said as Meghan stood and began to undress. "I'm sorry, Meg."

Meghan laid the gown on the end of the bunk and pulled on her only nightdress.

"Aye," Bridget mumbled. "Me, too."

Mrs. Finn raised the coverlet on Meghan's bunk and gestured for her to lie down. "In ye go, Meghan me girl."

She curled into bed, grateful for the respite. "Thank ye," she murmured to the older woman.

Mrs. Finn nodded and lowered the light of the wall lamp until the small cabin was lit by only a muted glow. After a time, the chatter of her cabin mates died down, and the only sound Meghan heard was the creak of the ship's hull and the breathing noises made by sleeping women.

What strange act of fate had made Lucas Ridgely her rescuer?

She thought of Ned Fellows and shuddered. Lucas

IRISH LINEN

was right; Fellows would be after her again if the mate realized that Lucas had lied about their betrothal.

Chilled, Meghan rubbed her arms and then rolled over, drawing the blanket up over her shoulders to keep warm. She closed her eyes and saw Lucas's face, and relived the moment he'd come to rescue her.

She sighed. It would be all right, she thought. With Lucas's help, she would evade men like Ned Fellows. Soon, she'd be in the United States, and the danger of Ned Fellows would be over. She'd be with her real fiance—Rafferty O'Connor.

Meghan tried to conjure up Rafferty's image, but the vision of Lucas kept interfering, consuming her. Then, she thought of Da and how much she missed him. The pain was like a raw wound, and she lay awake, recalling the good times, the happy times, when both her father and mother were alive. When her mother had died, Da had been devastated, but he'd quickly taken control of his grief in order to help his little girl.

Meghan was awakened by the ringing of the ship's bells, signaling the start of the morning watch. Sometime during the night, exhaustion had taken hold and she'd fallen asleep. She opened her eyes and thought of Lucas. "Will I see *him* today?"

She felt a little thrill. She knew that because of their fake betrothal, she most definitely would. And she was pleased.

Four

"Ye're finally awake," Mrs. Finn said, startling Meghan. The woman sat on the bunk built into the bulkhead on the opposite side of the cabin.

Meghan climbed out of bed and started to dress. "Did ye think I was to sleep the day away?" She frowned. "Where are Bridget and Mary Beth?"

"I finally convinced Bridget to go above. Mary Beth is with her."

Fear squeezed Meghan's chest as she sat on her bunk. "Are they alone?"

"They're safe enough. Me late husband's brother is with 'em." The woman stared at Meghan with concern. "What's wrong, Meg? What happened to ye last night?"

Meghan looked away. "Nothing." She stroked the fabric of her new green cloak, recalling the tenderness of the man who'd given it to her. "I met up with me intended is all."

"Meggie girl, how can that be? I thought you were going to your man in America?"

Blast Mrs. Finn for remembering, Meghan thought. "Aye, it was said so," she admitted. "We didn't want anyone to know about us. We wanted to keep our betrothal a secret until we met with his family. But when Da passed away . . ."

"Will we be meeting him?" Mrs. Finn's gaze was speculative.

"Oh, aye." Meghan was nervous about the encounter. What if the others guessed that Lucas and she were only pretending to be engaged?

"What's his name?"

"Lucas. Lucas Ridgely."

"Oh?" Mrs. Finn appeared confused. "Why did I think your man was an O'Connor?"

Meghan thought quickly. "Me da's friend is an O'Connor. Perhaps ye heard me talk of him."

The woman's brow cleared. "Ah, that must be where I heard the name then. Odd, I would've sworn . . . Never ye mind. An old woman's recollections are not as clear as they once were."

Meghan smiled as she tried to control her frantic heart. "Da used to say the same of old men." She combed her hair back with her fingers. "But ye aren't old, Mrs. Finn."

Doreen Finn chuckled. "I've the desires of a girl, Meg, but I've lost the energy."

A knock on the cabin door interrupted their conversation; Meghan held her breath as Mrs. Finn went to answer it.

"Good morning. I'm looking for Meghan McBride."

Mrs. Finn blocked Meghan's view, but she recognized Lucas's deep voice instantly.

"She is here," Mrs. Finn said in a crisp voice. "Might I inquire as to who *you* are?"

"Lucas Ridgely."

"And," the woman exclaimed, "her fiancé!"

Mrs. Finn turned to flash Meghan a grin. "It be him, Meggie girl," she said in a hushed voice that clearly carried to the man. "Lucas Ridgely, your betrothed."

Meghan nodded, unsure how to respond.

"May I come in?" He sounded amused.

"Aye, of course, lad," Mrs. Finn said, making

Meghan gasp. "Come in. Meghan was just telling me about ye."

"She was?" Lucas stepped into the cabin, filling the chamber with his presence. His gaze caressed her, making her tremble. She felt naked in her homespun gown, although she was adequately covered from neck to toe. "Meghan."

"Lucas," she greeted nervously. How could she have forgotten how tall and handsome he was?

He approached and lifted her hands, clasping them with warmth. Her blood heated, and she felt a catch in her throat when he released her fingers and placed his hands on her shoulders.

"Easy, love," he whispered. "We've an act to play. Remember?" And then he was pulling her into his embrace.

Conscious of Mrs. Finn, Meghan forced herself to relax. She leaned against Lucas and was immediately surrounded by his warm, strong arms. He cupped her head, pressing it gently against his chest, and she closed her eyes. It was good to be held by him. She heard the thundering beat of his heart, and felt safe and cherished.

"How are you, Irish?" he murmured. His voice rumbled deep in his chest, vibrating beneath her ear.

She pulled back to gaze up at him and was startled by his tender expression. She drew a sharp breath. "I'm fine," she whispered. He lifted her hair and stroked her nape. Meghan quivered.

"Good girl." His dark eyes glowed, making her pulse quicken.

Frightened by his effect on her, Meghan reeled, suddenly unsure of their dangerous game of pretend.

She pulled from his hold and spun away. "You're here early." She sensed Mrs. Finn watching them curiously. Meghan swung back with a bright smile.

"It's after eleven," Lucas said, his eyes gleaming with amusement.

"After eleven!" she exclaimed.

Mrs. Finn chuckled. "I told ye ye'd nearly slept away the day."

"Aye, but—"

Lucas grinned. "Dreaming of me?"

Meghan grew flustered. Damn, she thought. The man was enjoying this!

"Ye're embarrassing the child, Mr. Ridgely."

"Lucas," he invited the older woman with a smooth smile.

Mrs. Finn was clearly charmed. "Lucas." She beamed as she met Meghan's glance. "I like him, Meg." She paused, and her gaze narrowed assessingly. "Even if he's not your betrothed."

Meghan gasped. "Not my—"

Lucas didn't deny it as he regarded the older woman with admiration. "A brilliant guess?"

Mrs. Finn nodded, looking pleased. " 'Tis not my place to tell your secrets. I'm sure ye've a good enough reason for this role ye're playing."

He nodded. "Meghan was assaulted by a crewman last night," he said, his expression grave.

"I knew something happened. Are ye all right, child?" Mrs. Finn studied Meghan and then speared Lucas with her gaze. "Ye saved her, I take it."

He nodded.

"Then it's our thanks ye have, Lucas Ridgely," Mrs. Finn said. "Ye've decided on the betrothal to keep her safe?"

"As my intended, no man would dare come near her," he said, his tone dark and dangerous.

"And how do we know she's safe from ye?" the older woman asked.

"Mrs. Finn!" Meghan cried.

But Lucas didn't take offense. "I'm not in the habit of forcing females," he said. He grinned roguishly. "I've never had to."

Her lips curving upward with a satisfied smile, Mrs. Finn nodded. But Meghan felt uneasy.

Lucas's gaze fastened on Meghan. "Shall we stroll the upper deck?" he asked. "You're welcome to join us, Mrs. Finn," he said without taking his eyes from Meghan.

She shook her head. "No, I'll be leaving ye two alone. Bridget and Mary Beth will coming back shortly."

"Meghan?" Lucas held out his arm for her.

"I don't know." She felt heat warm her cheeks.

"Come on," he urged softly. "Get your cloak; it's cold out." His gaze narrowed on her a moment, before he said, "I'll wait outside the cabin for you." With a nod at Mrs. Finn, he left.

The room was quiet after Lucas's exit. Meghan felt the intensity of Mrs. Finn's stare as she picked up the cloak and slipped it on over her worn gown. She wondered what the woman was thinking.

"He gave you the cloak," Doreen Finn said.

Meghan nodded as she adjusted the hood. The garment was heavy and warm, and smelled slightly of Lucas.

"The man is generous."

The younger woman inwardly squirmed. "Aye."

"And attractive," Mrs. Finn said.

Meghan's breath quickened.

"And dangerous."

"Dangerous?" Meghan asked. She felt a sudden chill. "How?"

"Ye be an engaged woman. He is a good-looking man." Mrs. Finn's glance was bright with concern. "Be careful of yer heart, Meggie."

Meghan made a disparaging sound. "Me heart is safe enough."

The older woman grunted with derision. "Then ye've a heart of stone, Meghan McBride, for even this old woman felt a tingle when she gazed upon your Lucas Ridgely."

New Castle County, Delaware

"But Mr. O'Connor," the woman pleaded, "I can't pay on our account. You know my husband doesn't get his wages until next Friday!"

Rafferty O'Connor stood behind the counter of the company store, unmoved by the woman's hard luck. "Mrs. Kelt, I only be looking out for Mr. Somerton's best interests."

"But I need supplies," she said. "My children must eat." Her words were breathy, and he enjoyed the sound of them, almost as much as he was aroused by her pretty face and curvaceous form. "Isn't there anything I can do?"

Rafferty smiled, feeling pleased. The woman was desperate, just how he liked it. "Ye're willing to do anything?" He knew his voice sounded more husky than usual, his Irish accent thicker.

She nodded.

"I'm sure we can come to an arrangement that will satisfy the both of us." His gaze swept down to where her breasts swelled beneath the bodice of her muslin gown. Others had accepted the terms of his offer. Forty-nine, he might be, but women, he knew, considered him to be an attractive man with his sandy hair and green eyes. He recalled the wife of his employer, Alicia Somerton. She certainly had liked him. She'd found his solid and muscular form particularly pleasurable during the second week of his employment. During the third week, he'd been taken from the factory and made manager of the company store.

But apparently Mrs. Kelt wasn't as taken by his physical attributes. When he met her glance, Rafferty saw her astonishment and then her resigned acceptance of his terms.

It was nearly time to close up shop. Mrs. Kelt had come late to make her plea when there would be little chance of eavesdroppers. The woman's husband wouldn't be home for at least an hour after the store closed. Mrs. Kelt's timing and desperation suited Rafferty well.

Rafferty skirted the counter slowly to lock the front door, all the while aware of the woman's nervous gaze. He sensed her fear; it teased him, aroused him. His ability to control her only heightened his desire.

When the door was bolted securely, he swept past her to get behind the counter where he opened the door to the back room.

"Mrs. Kelt?" With a smile and a sweep of his hand, he gestured for the woman to precede him.

Mrs. Kelt stood uncertainly in the center of the storage room as he shut the door. He stared at her grimly. "What are ye waiting for?" he asked irritably.

Her hands trembled as she began to unbutton her bodice. The plea in her brown eyes incited his lust, made him swell and harden within his trousers.

She paused in her undressing, her face filled with uncertainty and fear. "Please," she whispered.

He softened his expression as he approached. "I've a new shipment of ladies' hats, Mrs. Kelt." He stopped when he was within inches of her and touched her hair. His fingers were gentle as he unpinned her shining red tresses. He inhaled sharply as her hair unraveled, and he combed the silken strands until they fell thick and glorious to her waist.

"You're a beautiful woman, Mrs. Kelt." His breath quickened as he studied her lovely face. Lust tightened his muscles, begging to be unleashed.

She whimpered, and he growled and kissed her, subduing her with his strong arms as she started to struggle. He devoured her mouth and then lifted his head to gauge her response. "Ye want me to stop?"

He saw her indecision, her desire to escape, but instead of dampening his desire for her, it only strengthened it. He stared, transmitting a silent message. *Ye want to forget the arrangement? 'Tis fine by me, but I'll not sell ye another thing till yer account is paid . . . in full.*

Her eyes bleak, Mrs. Kelt shook her head, giving him the silent signal to continue. With a growl of satisfaction, Rafferty O'Connor took what the woman reluctantly offered.

Before I'm through, she'll be loving what I do to her, Rafferty told himself as he stripped off the woman's clothes.

And the thought cleared his conscience.

Five

The day was bright, a pleasant change from yesterday's rain. White fluffy clouds dotted the azure sky, and the sun felt warm on Meghan's face despite the time of year. She stood at the ship's rail, conscious of the tall blond man beside her.

She thought of their concocted story, how they supposedly met in Dublin, fallen in love after a two-week courtship that had ended abruptly when Lucas had to return to America. Haunted by his feelings for Meghan, Lucas had returned to Ireland, only to find her gone. He had searched until he'd found her in England where he'd proposed and rescued her from pain and poverty, offering her a new life. It was a romantic story, which had touched the hearts of her cabin mates . . . and her. But such things didn't occur in real life, did they? she wondered.

"How did your friends take the news?" Lucas asked, his voice low. It was as if he had been sharing her own thoughts. "Did they believe our story?" He turned from the view of the ocean.

Meghan noted the play of his arm muscles beneath his shirt as he leaned back, gripping the rail behind him. She lifted her gaze to his face and flushed when she saw that he was watching her.

"Mary Beth and Bridget seemed to believe it," she

said. "But I'm not surprised Mrs. Finn guessed the truth."

"Perceptive woman."

She smiled. "Too perceptive at times, I think." She spun and, like him, leaned back against the rail. She watched the industrious crew at work and sensed Lucas's intent study of her. She chanced a glance at him and saw that she was right. His warm gaze slid from her eyes to her lips, and Meghan felt her blood flow with heat.

She swallowed against a suddenly dry throat. "Why are ye looking at me like that?"

He slowly raised his gaze. "Like what?"

A tender smile played lightly about his lips, and Meghan's breath caught at the male beauty of it. He was an extremely good-looking man . . . too attractive for her peace of mind.

"Like ye're trying to see inside me and decide who I am," she said.

Amusement flickered in his ebony eyes. "I know who you are, Meghan McBride. A man always makes it a point to know the woman who's to be his wife."

She gasped. "You know little of me ways."

He looked thoughtful. "True." He lifted his hand and trailed a finger down her cloaked arm. "Won't you tell me about yourself?"

Meghan shivered under his touch. "I know little of yours either."

"Are you cold?" he asked.

She shook her head, refusing to meet his gaze.

"Good." The male satisfaction in his tone made Meghan look at him with surprise before quickly glancing away. The impact of his dark eyes made her senses swim with sensation.

"What do you want to know?" She was breathless.

"Tell me about Ireland . . . about your family."

"I have no family," she said, feeling her loss deeply. "They're all dead now."

He pulled her about by the shoulders until she faced him, staring at his shirt front. Her eyes misted as she valiantly fought tears. "You have me," he said.

Her gaze shot upward. His words had shocked her. *He means as a friend, girl,* she told herself, and was disappointed.

"You don't know me," she whispered.

"I want to know you," he said.

She raised her eyebrows. "Why?"

"Because you intrigue me, Meghan McBride."

"Perhaps I'm married."

He stiffened. "Are you?" His expression cleared before she answered. "No, you're not married . . . or your husband would be with you."

Lucas placed his finger beneath her chin. "But you were traveling with your father." He tilted her face up for his inspection. Meghan felt a tremor as his finger feathered a caress over her cheek.

"Your father was sick," he began in a husky voice, "so you must have been without food for a long time. You sold your land and went to England, hoping to find work of some kind. You'd heard that people, even the Irish, do not go hungry in England."

Her surprise must have shown on her face, because he chuckled softly. "Did you think I could read your mind?" he asked.

"How—how did you know this?"

"Then it's true?" He regarded her with triumph.

"Aye," she whispered.

Lucas sighed and released her. "Your story is one of hundreds of other Irish."

Meghan felt cold without his touch. "And I'm just like all the rest," she murmured, disturbed by his assessment of her life.

"No," he said, sounding sincere. He cupped her face and raised it until she was forced to look into his gaze. She became more physically aware of his masculinity . . . the power and strength of his hands cradling her jaw. He held her gently but firmly, insistently, like he didn't want to let her go.

Surprise flickered in his dark gaze, and she realized with a sense of shock that he was as startled by his answer as she.

A pleasurable warmth invaded her limbs. He shifted his hands to her shoulders. She saw his head bend in her direction, felt the soft caress of his breath on her lips, and she found herself waiting with mind-numbing anticipation for his kiss.

What am I doing? I don't even know this man, she thought. *I am betrothed. What about Rafferty?*

She jerked from his hold with a murmur of protest, and he released her without comment. She was unable to meet his gaze.

"Meghan—"

"No!" she cried. "This isn't right. I hardly know ye." When she finally looked at him, she saw that his smile held promise.

"A matter easily rectified," he said, his lips curved but his gaze was unreadable. "Come." He grabbed her arm. "You haven't eaten and it's close to noon. We'll talk about this later. You must be hungry."

He ushered her with such speed and command that Meghan had no choice but to allow him to lead her away.

Since she and her cabin mates had always taken their meals in their room, it shouldn't have come as a surprise when Lucas took her back to his quarters.

She'd tensed when he'd paused on deck to speak to

a crewman about food, but then she relaxed as hunger took precedence over her wariness. But now, standing in his cabin as he shut the door, she gazed at Lucas with an accelerated heartbeat and the odd feeling of wanting to escape the man's presence.

Her feelings must have shown on her face, because Lucas stared at her with a strange look.

"Lucas—"

"Relax, Meghan," he said irritably. "I'm not going to attack you."

"I didn't think ye were."

"No?" he said, his tone disparaging. "Your face tells me otherwise." He stared at her hard, and flustered, she looked away.

"I'm sor—"

"Don't!" he barked. "Don't apologize!" His outburst drew her astonished gaze. "I understand, Meghan," he said, softening his tone. "I was surprised by your fear." The dark eyes gazed at her with concern. "I don't usually have this effect on women." He paused. "I thought you trusted me."

"I do," she said quickly. Too quickly to be convincing, she realized. And she could tell by his little half smile that he thought so, too.

"Would you rather return to your cabin?" he asked.

"No!"

This time her quick reply seemed to please him. "Good."

A knock resounded from the cabin door. Lucas raised his eyebrows. "Dinner," he said.

He opened the door; the crewman who entered was young. Probably no more than sixteen, Meghan thought.

At Lucas's instructions, the boy set the wooden tray down on the table fastened against the back wall.

IRISH LINEN

"Thank you, Peter," Lucas said as he slipped the crewman a coin.

Peter's eyes lit up. "Thank you, Mr. Ridgely." The youth turned to Meghan. "Enjoy your dinner, miss," he said.

She nodded and watched as he touched his fingers to his cap and left.

The cabin seemed quiet as Lucas shut the door. Meghan's glance swung from Lucas to the food and back again.

The smell of beef wafted up from a plate on the tray to tease at her nose. Her stomach growled with hunger.

"Go ahead, Meghan," Lucas invited softly. "Sit down. The food looks good, doesn't it?"

She inclined her head and then moved toward the table. Suddenly, Lucas was behind her, pulling out a chair for her. She murmured her thanks and waited for him to sit down across from her. To her consternation, he adjusted his seat and sat next to her instead. She was conscious of the brush of his leg against her skirts as he served her dinner.

"Meat?" he asked.

How could the ship's cook prepare meat to be so tasty after storing the beef for days and days at sea? Was the animal freshly killed?

Lucas seemed to read her mind. "Dried meat," he said. "The cook on board is an expert on preparing dried food."

Meghan nodded. She had learned to be grateful for all food. She knew all too well what it was like to be hungry.

The food was good just as she'd known it would be. Were her cabin mates enjoying the same fare? She thought not. Lucas, she decided, was used to having the best and no doubt he'd paid heavily to ensure it.

She tilted her head as she studied the man beside her. Was Lucas Ridgely a rich man?

The notion gave her a moment's pause. It brought home to her again just how little she knew about the man who had saved her.

He ate with impeccable manners, not that she'd ever been schooled in the social rules of fine dining. Meghan scowled. Just finding enough food to survive had been a major concern for her and her father.

"Are you enjoying your meal?" Lucas looked up from his plate to find Meghan studying him. He met her gaze steadily and made several observations of his own.

"Aye," she said. "Thank ye."

He inclined his head, annoyed, not pleased, with her humble gratitude. It wasn't gratitude he wanted from the Irishwoman.

Lucas tensed. What on God's green earth *did* he want from Meghan McBride?

He studied her features. Her eyes were large and blue, so shiny that he felt he could drown in their liquid depths. Her nose was small and pert, and he loved the slight smattering of freckles across the bridge.

His gaze fell to her mouth. Her lips . . . He felt his chest tighten as he watched her take a bite of bread. Her pink lips opened and cupped the thick crusty slice, and Lucas suddenly wanted to be the one her mouth tasted.

Good God! he thought. How could he feel desire for this skinny Irishwoman?

Because, he realized as he looked closer, she wasn't thin really. In fact, the blue gown displayed her shape to advantage. He envisioned her lovely breasts beneath the cloth, soft . . . round . . . and firm.

Lucas felt his groin tighten as he recalled earlier

when he'd hugged her. The feel of those breasts pressing against his chest through the thin layer of her nightgown had startled him . . . and titillated his desire.

Dear Lord, was it because of her breasts that he'd changed his view of her?

Lucas scowled. He'd had his share of women. Why did this one taunt and tantalize him with her innocence? Why couldn't he put aside the desire to have her beneath him in his bed?

She is vulnerable, an inner voice reminded him.

But strong, he thought.

She's been through a rough time.

I won't hurt her, he reasoned. As my mistress, she'll be safe on board this ship. She'll have my protection as well as my attentions.

Mistress! Where did the idea come from? Since when did he start thinking of intimacy in their game of pretend? There was nothing pretend about his desire for her.

Lucas sipped from his glass, anticipating her agreement to his proposition, as he enjoyed the heat generated by the fine wine.

He'd have to approach this matter carefully. He didn't want her to think that he was no better than Ned Fellows. Would she see the difference? Would she understand?

I must tread slowly, he thought. She'll benefit from the arrangement. I've money to spend on her.

Meghan had known hunger and desperation. Why shouldn't she agree to spend a little time with him?

There were approximately seven days left of the voyage. He'd spend the next two days wooing her gently, and then he'd have five full days to enjoy having her in his bed. Maybe she'd even agree to accompany him to Dover.

He wanted her. God only knew why, but it had to be this woman. *Meghan McBride.*

He stared at her, watching her eat, realizing that today he must win her friendship. Tomorrow, he would ease closer to fully winning her trust.

Six

Orange light filled the dusk sky. Gray, gold, and red slashed across the glow in a splash of breathtaking color. But Lucas was studying the woman beside him. Her beauty was more riveting than nature's wonder. His desire for her had grown since he'd first felt the magnetic pull.

"The sunset is beautiful," Meghan murmured.

"You're beautiful," he said in a husky voice. He heard her sharp little intake of breath and was pleased. She made the noise whenever she was moved. He'd begun to notice that he was starting to have that effect on her with each new hour they spent in each other's company.

He would never have guessed that he'd be attracted to the woman he'd rescued. The look in her eyes haunted him, had drawn him in. Her manner was gentle, unassuming, and therein lay the challenge. Clean and dry and with good food that had already filled the hollows in her cheeks, Meghan McBride was a tempting female.

He shifted closer, brushing against her shoulder. She withdrew, but he followed her, and she didn't skitter away.

"Ye shouldn't say such things to a girl," she said.

"Why not?" he said. "If it's the truth."

Meghan's breath caught as Lucas covered her hand on the rail. She should be angry, but she wasn't. She was disturbed, not by his behavior as much as her reaction to his touch.

"Mr. Ridgely, please," she whispered.

"Miss McBride?"

"Have ye forgotten 'tis but a game we're playing?" she asked.

"Is it?"

"Lucas!"

He smiled. "You blush delightfully, Meghan."

Curse her Irish white skin! "I think I should return to me cabin."

"Afraid?" he taunted.

"Terrified."

His expression softened at her frankness. "Am I so fearsome? I thought you trusted me."

"I did—I do," she said. It was herself she didn't trust. She was an engaged woman, and she'd never felt this way with Rafferty, her fiancé.

"Stay, Meghan. I'll try to behave."

She smiled; she couldn't help it. He sounded as if behaving himself would be a battle.

They stood in companionable silence as the sun set and the night heralded a dark sky filled with bright stars.

"Meghan." The soft entreaty made her look at him. "I'd like to take care of you."

She stared at him, her heart hammering. He wanted to marry her?

"I'm a wealthy man. I have the means to give you anything you desire. As my woman, you'll be happy."

Her face filled with heat. *Mistress,* she thought, looking away. He was asking her to be his kept woman! "Ye want me to—" She broke off, unable to finish as she tried to control her emotions. She didn't know whether to be more offended by Ned Fellows's assault or Lucas Ridgely's proposition.

"Meghan?"

"No!" she choked. "I—" She spun to leave, but he grabbed her arm.

"Meghan, I meant no insult." He released her. "I'm a man of means, but I've little to offer a wife. I'm not interested in marriage, but I'm attracted to you—we're attracted to each other."

She bristled. "Ye think too highly of yourself. I'm not interested in ya that way."

"Liar."

"I have a fiancé of me own. In America. I'm journeying to join him."

Lucas's gaze hardened. "You're engaged to be married." She nodded. "And you didn't think to tell me."

Meghan shrugged as she turned back toward the sea. "Our relationship's been a game, nothing more. It didn't seem important."

He grabbed her shoulders and spun her to face him. "Has it?" he asked. His expression was hard. "Has this only been a game?"

"Yes!" she cried.

"Prove it," he said.

"I don't understand."

"Prove it," he demanded. He pulled her closer and kissed her. His lips were hot and demanding. He ravished her mouth and then gentled, trying to coax a response from her.

Meghan, stiff and angry one moment, softened the next as his kiss changed. She moaned as she felt his tenderness, his desire. She clung to his shoulders as she participated in the exchange. Fire shot through her blood, warming her, making her feel dizzy. She gloried in his gentle strength and his passion for her. Suddenly, he thrust her away.

"A game," he rasped. "I think not. There's more between us. Feel!" He caught her hand and placed her fingers over his thundering heart. Holding her gaze, he roughly lowered her palm to his trousers and the hot bulge that pulsated and stretched the fabric to its limit.

With a wild cry, Meghan pulled her hand away. "Don't!" She blinked away tears. He was cruel; how could he be so cruel?

"I deserve to be a wife, not a mistress," she said.

He sighed and released her. "I'd provide for you. You'd want for nothing." He exhaled with impatience. "Who is this fiancé? What can he give you?"

"Respectability! His name."

"Is having his name so important?" Lucas asked. "As my woman, no one would dare insult you. You'd be treated with the utmost respect."

Meghan gave a bark of harsh laughter. "I'm penniless and Irish, Mr. Ridgely. Or have ye forgotten? No one in your social class would accept me as your wife, let alone as your—your—kept woman!"

"They would if I wanted them to."

She shook her head at his arrogance. She held out her hand. "I think we should end this now." Meghan dropped her hand when he didn't immediately take it. "Goodbye, Mr. Ridgely."

In two days, the ship would dock in America. Surely, she'd be safe enough from Ned Fellows and his kind on her own for the remainder of the trip.

But would she be able to survive her encounter with Lucas Ridgely? She'd have to. She had enjoyed his company. It had been nice while it had lasted. But now she would have to go on alone.

"Are ye sure ye won't come above?" Mrs. Finn eyed Meghan from the open cabin hatch, her gaze concerned.

IRISH LINEN

Meghan shook her head. "I'm waiting for Lucas," she said. "But thank ye for asking."

The woman nodded and left, closing the door. Meghan's cabin mates had gone topside with Mrs. Finn's brother-in-law to get a breath of fresh air. Meghan was relieved. She'd spent the morning wondering how she was going to explain Lucas's absence. Lucas had come for her every day since his rescue of her, and the women had been delighted by his attentions.

But now Meghan no longer had to worry about answering her cabin mates' questions. She could say that Lucas had come for her while they were above on the top deck.

She stared at the bunks across from hers. If they inquired why they hadn't seen her topside, she could say that she and Lucas had gone to his cabin to dine and spend time discussing their future plans. Only Mrs. Finn would know that it wasn't the whole truth, and the older woman was romantic enough to hope that something was developing between Meghan and Lucas. Meghan suspected this because Mrs. Finn had made more than one comment about marriage and her concern over the age difference between Mary, a friend of hers, and Mary's spouse. Meghan had wondered whether Mrs. Finn had confided in her to prove a point. It seemed strange that Mary's husband, like Meghan's fiancé, was old enough to be his beloved's father.

Meghan jerked to her feet and began to pace. No, she thought, I'm committed to Rafferty. I must be mistaken to believe that Mrs. Finn could have made such a suggestion.

Lucas. Why did the man have to be so bloody attractive? She paused and scowled. Why couldn't she remember Rafferty's face?

It was good that Lucas had shown his true colors, she realized, before she'd begun to care for him. The last thing she needed was to be swept up in a lot of romantic nonsense.

Meghan tried to garner excitement for the fact that she'd be stepping on American soil for the first time tomorrow. She thought of her father and suffered a pang of loss. But then she recalled Rafferty, her father's best friend, and had a sudden intense desire to see him again.

Her spirits lifted, and she was smiling as she went to answer a knock on the cabin door. It was chilly topside, she knew. Meghan opened the hatch, believing one of her cabin mates had returned for an extra shawl. And she was shocked to see who stood outside the door.

"Lucas!"

"Hello, Meghan." He looked uncomfortable, uncertain, and she would never have believed the man capable of feeling either.

"I thought it was—" She began and then turned away to hide her reaction to his appearance. "—Bridget."

"You're alone," he said.

She swung back to face him. "Yes."

He stepped into the cabin. "We need to talk."

"No," she said, averting her glance. He looked good, too good, she thought, his image imprinted firmly in her mind. It would be better if he left now, before she did something she'd regret, something foolish like falling into his arms and begging him to kiss her again.

He was silent for so long that she wondered whether he'd gone. Meghan glanced back just as he moved closer. Her heart fluttered. Her breath stilled as she met his dark gaze. She had difficulty swallowing as she felt his disturbing power.

"Will you walk the top deck with me?" he asked.

I shouldn't. She stiffened. "Why?"

"You thought I wouldn't come since you turned down my proposal."

She didn't bother to deny it. "Proposition," she murmured, correcting him. Not a proposal. Nothing in his offer had even hinted at a commitment of the heart.

"You were right," he said. "The bogus betrothal was my idea, so let's continue it." He paused, and his ebony eyes searched her face. "What did you tell your cabin mates about us?"

"Nothing," she whispered, frightened by the physical pull she felt toward this man. "They know nothing about yesterday's conversation."

A flash of satisfaction lit up his expression. "Good."

She raised her eyebrows. "Good?" she echoed.

"Because then you have an excellent reason for coming with me."

"Lucas—"

"We must continue our betrothal until tomorrow," he said. "It's only one more day. Surely you can stand my company for a little longer."

Lucas held out his hand. "Walk with me, Meghan."

She stared at his rugged, handsome features and then at his extended fingers. Her pulse picked up its rhythmic cadence as she debated whether or not to go.

Meghan realized that she wanted to be with him. What harm could it cause to spend just a few more hours in his company?

He's dangerous.

No, she told herself firmly. She was engaged to Rafferty O'Connor. She was going to be married to a man she cared for and respected. She wouldn't do anything to jeopardize their relationship.

It didn't matter that Rafferty was over twenty years

older than her, she thought. He'd be a good husband. She wouldn't allow her brush with Lucas Ridgely to ruin her future happiness.

"All right," she said, and he grinned. And his smile did the oddest things to her. It made her tingle all over. It wrapped her in a blanket of warmth and brought her back to pulsating life. How could she regret this small moment of time with him?

Because Lucas Ridgely is lethal. He makes ye feel things that could ultimately hurt ye. She had never believed that passion blended well with love, yet her strange feelings for the man had her thinking . . .

Rafferty was comfortable, safe, and all that a husband should be. He'd always be there for her, while Lucas . . . was unreliable, not interested in commitment or marriage . . . bad for her in all the ways that counted.

Why then was she so happy that Lucas had come?

Seven

The cry of *Land ho!* filtered down to the lower decks, waking Meghan and causing a feminine flurry in the cabin. The *Mary Freedom* hadn't reached America yesterday afternoon as had been expected. It was the second morning after Lucas had invited her to walk the deck, and Meghan had spent many hours enjoying his company, trying to keep herself at a distance . . . and failing.

She'd bundled her belongings into a small sack the day before. She dressed hurriedly, wondering if she'd see Lucas again before leaving the ship. Meghan grabbed her cloak and threw it over her head.

"Meghan?" Mrs. Finn asked as Meghan went to the hatch.

"I'm going above."

"Meghan, wait!" Bridget exclaimed, but Meghan left, hoping to find Lucas on the upper deck, wanting to see him alone for the last time.

A gust of wind assaulted her as she climbed out of the companionway onto the top deck. She raised the hood of her cloak, holding it beneath her chin to keep it in place. The weather was cold, typical for America this time of year or so she'd been told. She shivered while she searched the length of the port side rail for Lucas.

Meghan's spirits sank. Lucas was nowhere to be found. She moved over to the starboard side, silently praying for him to be there. She knew that she was wrong for wanting to see him, but she couldn't help it. The man had rescued and been kind to her. He'd been the perfect gentleman, accepting her rejection of his offer with good grace.

Her heart hammered hard when she couldn't find him. Meghan debated what to do and felt her stomach burn when she decided to check his cabin.

Ye shouldn't be going. You're betrothed to another. Lucas is dangerous. Go back to your cabin and forget the existence of Lucas Ridgely.

Meghan froze on the companionway steps. What am I doing? she thought. "Saying goodbye," she murmured beneath her breath.

Are ye sure? an inner voice taunted.

"Aye," she whispered. "I must thank him before bidding him farewell." If she didn't, she'd be haunted by him for the rest of her married life.

She found Lucas's cabin with no problem—she'd been there at least four times since his rescue of her. Meghan raised her hand to knock and then hesitated before striking the portal. She experienced a moment's doubt. Butterflies fluttered in the pit of her stomach. Her skin tingled at the thought of seeing him again. How would he react to her coming?

Her knuckles struck wood, and she stepped back, trying to steady her uneven breathing. Despite the fact that she'd spent so much time in his company, she was nervous and excited . . . and a little scared.

The hatch opened with a creaking sound.

"Meghan!" Lucas stood, looking surprised but pleased. Meghan's gaze fell on his bare chest, and she fought the urge to look away, even while she enjoyed viewing the naked skin and muscled sinew. A light dusting of hair swirled about his nipples and formed a triangle of gold down over his belly, its point disappearing beneath the waist of his trousers. *Dear God, what must it be like to lie with him?*

She felt herself flush as she forced her gaze up from his stomach. Expecting to see his amusement—although her study had lasted only seconds—she was startled to see desire in his eyes . . . a desire that matched her own. She glanced about to see if anyone was watching and was relieved that no one seemed to be about.

"May I come in?" she said.

He nodded and stepped back, allowing her to pass him. As she moved past him, she got a whiff of soap and tobacco . . . and a scent that she'd come to recognize and enjoy . . . a scent that belonged only to Lucas.

Meghan crossed the cabin and then turned to watch him close the door. Her heart thundered so loudly within her chest that she was afraid that he'd hear it. But when he turned, there was nothing in his expression then, but polite reception and more than a little curiosity in his gaze. No heat in the dark eyes . . . no burning desire. And she realized she must have misread him.

"Did you hear the news?" she asked as he approached. "They've seen land." She thought she sounded breathless, a state no doubt caused by the man's nearness.

Lucas nodded, and she all but flinched as he reached by her to grab his shirt from the back of a chair. He silently studied her as he shrugged into each sleeve.

Now that she was here, she was anxious to say her piece and be gone. What madness made her come? She, an engaged woman, seeking out a single man? "I wanted to thank ye for all you've done," she said in a rush, feeling foolish all of a sudden.

He paused in the process of buttoning up his shirt. "You've thanked me already, Meghan. You didn't have to come here for that."

Her cheeks filled with heat, but she held his gaze. "I—I wanted to say goodbye." She paused, before admitting, "Without others present."

He finished the last of the buttons and looked up. His eyes warmed and then burned brightly with liquid fire. "Why?" he asked.

"Why?" she echoed. The blood rushed through her veins.

He inclined his head.

Meghan searched for a response. "I couldn't say goodbye before the others, because they think I'm going with ye."

Lucas shook his head as he stepped closer. He lifted a hand and touched her cheek. "I wish you were coming with me," he said huskily.

"Don't, please!"

He slipped his hand about her nape and pulled her against him. She gasped; his body felt warm and hard and very much alive.

"Lucas."

"Kiss me, Meghan. Kiss me goodbye like you'll miss me."

"No, I—"

"Shh!" He was so close that she could feel his breath. Soft warm puffs of sweet scented air fanned her right cheek, her nose, and then moistened her left cheek. His head dipped lower, and Meghan froze in anticipation of his kiss. Her pulse raced, and she knew she should be fighting him, but she wanted—needed— him to kiss her one last time.

"What harm could a little kiss do?" he asked. His mouth was a hair's breadth from her lips. "One kiss," he whispered. "Just one small farewell kiss."

She felt a little catch in her throat, heard the sound it made as he embraced her. Meghan inhaled sharply as he tightened his arms. He began to move his hands over her from back to lower spine, and the press of him against her told her of his desire.

She wanted him, too. Lord help her, she could stop him if she chose to, but she didn't want to. "Lucas . . . kiss me."

"Dear God, woman," he rasped, and then his mouth was on hers, sipping from her sweetness like a man long thirsty for a drink. He drank from her lips and demanded more when she responded. "Open your mouth, Meghan." His voice was deep and thick with desire.

She gazed up into his passion-filled face and felt a prickle of uncertainty, of the wrongness of something that for a second had seemed so right.

"Meghan—"

She opened her mouth with the intention of stopping their passionate exchange, but he ventured past her lips with his tongue. And then Meghan was inviting him to continue as she responded with a whimper of pleasure and the dueling of his tongue with her own.

Fire burned through Meghan's blood, blossoming in her abdomen and tingling in her breasts. He thrust gently against her, and she felt Lucas's hardness pressing against her skirt as she made a sound of pleasure that he shared her feelings.

Lucas kissed her neck, and she gasped. His hands slipped to her sides along the outer curve of her breasts, down to her waist where his fingers squeezed gently for a moment before slipping lower.

Meghan moaned as he cupped her buttocks. With his mouth, he worshiped the area exposed above the neckline of her gown, and she closed her eyes as her senses swam with desire.

He straightened and found her lips with his mouth. Slipping her hands to his nape, she clutched his head and kissed him back, glorying in the dizzying, body-tingling sensations that rocked her. He raised his head to gaze at her with longing.

"Meghan," he whispered, "come with me."

She stared back from beneath lowered eyelids, wishing only that he'd continued to kiss and caress her.

"Come with me, Meghan. I promise I'll be good to you. You'll not have cause to regret it."

Reality brought a cold curling in her breast. She shivered and pushed him away. "No," she choked. "I can't." What had she done?

"Can't?" he said, anger darkening his features. "Or won't?"

"I'm betrothed!"

Lucas stared at her with frustration. "You couldn't tell that a moment ago!"

He heard her gasp and felt regret for hurting her. But he wanted her, and the pain of knowing he couldn't have her was killing him by slow degrees. She wanted him; he knew it! Why wouldn't she give in?

Her face was ashen, her blue eyes huge and bright against her paleness. Lucas wanted to take her in his arms and comfort her, but he knew that the gesture would quickly turn to something else. If he held her in his arms again, he wouldn't be able to stop himself from taking her on his bunk. He wanted her in his bed that badly.

"Goodbye, Lucas," she said. Her lips quivered.

He couldn't keep his eyes off her damn lovely mouth. He extended his hand. "Meghan—"

"I have to go," she cried and rushed past him to the door.

"Meghan, wait!"

She froze with her hand on the door, but she didn't turn around.

"Be happy," he said.

She nodded and only then did she glance back. "You, too, Lucas Ridgely," she whispered. And then to his disappointment, she was gone.

Meghan stood at the ship's rail and with tears clouding her vision stared at the dark shadow of land in the horizon.

"Oh, Da," she breathed. "I miss ye so. Tell me what to do!"

She closed her eyes, and moisture fell on her cheek. She hurriedly brushed it away, for she'd made a vow to be strong . . . for Da . . . and herself.

But then she hadn't counted on her involvement with Lucas Ridgely. She was wrong to desire him; she knew it, but yet her body betrayed her whenever he was within distance.

"I shouldn't have gone to his cabin," she murmured. She should have realized to do so would be courting trouble, that Lucas might take her appearance the wrong way.

She felt alone, so alone. Da was gone. Rafferty waited for her in America, but it had been so long since she'd seen him. Almost two years.

And now she fought a physical attraction for a man she'd known for a few days over a week.

Meghan didn't fool herself into thinking she loved Lucas. She barely knew him. He'd rescued her, and she was grateful, but that was all.

Well, not quite all, she thought. She always knew that physical attraction had nothing to do with love. It was the reason she'd consented to marry Rafferty. A good marriage was based on friendship and respect.

Passion often clouded a person's judgment, tricking one into believing that what one felt was love, while actually physical attraction was simply nature's way of reminding men and women of the differences in their bodies.

One didn't need passion to have children. Passion was a temporary state, while love based on mutual admiration was enduring. Hadn't the Bible warned against sins of the flesh?

Dear God, forgive me, she silently prayed. *I've sinned. I've allowed me lust for a man to rule me heart.*

The worst of her sins, she realized, was that for one moment while she was in Lucas's arms, she'd actually contemplated accepting his offer. She'd nearly sacrificed her immortal soul for a few months in a man's bed!

Thank God she'd come to her senses in time.

By early evening, she'd be stepping off the ship onto American soil. Rafferty would be waiting for her. They were a day late in their arrival, but he would have found a place to stay to wait for his best friend and his future wife

As Meghan turned from the rail, a gust of wind caught her in the face, tearing off her hood, whipping through her unbound hair. The tears on her cheeks dried as if she'd never given in to the weakness. Swallowing hard, she fought to pull up her hood and then made her way to the ship's ladder and the comfort of her cabin mates' company below.

Eight

Philadelphia, Pennsylvania

Rafferty O'Connor clenched his fingers about his glass as he lifted it toward his lips. How could he be expected to remain another day? he wondered angrily. He tossed back a shot of whiskey; heat burned a path down his throat and seared his belly. He'd been in this port city for two days now, waiting for the arrival of the McBrides, whiling away his hours at this bloody tavern. He'd need another day to travel back to Somerton Mill in New Castle County, Delaware.

He had to get back to his job at the store; he couldn't afford to wait another hour.

The Irishman squinted his eyes against the sun's glare as he came out of the tavern's dark interior. He checked the docks one last time, hoping for a sight of the *Mary Freedom*. There were several vessels tied up along the shore, but none of them was the ship from Liverpool.

Rafferty scowled. "Sorry, McBride," he mumbled. A man had to report to work in order to keep his employment.

He felt a moment's regret that he'd not be there to greet his dear Meghan when she came ashore. He searched the quay for someone to meet the McBrides, someone who could arrange to take his friends to Mrs. Pridgly's boardinghouse in Somerville where he lived.

He rubbed his stubbly chin as he surveyed a man hawking his wares from the shop across the way. Peddlers pushed carts while others drove horse-drawn wagons; their singsong voices filled the air proclaiming the quality of the goods.

Rafferty scowled as he studied the people around him. There wasn't a soul in sight he'd entrust with Meghan's care, until he spied a youth about twelve years old as the boy ambled by, pushing a cart of apples.

"Boy!" Rafferty called. "Boy!"

The lad stopped, caught Rafferty's gaze, and with an anticipatory grin approached. "Apple, sir?" he said, holding out a red, shiny specimen for the man to examine.

Rafferty shook his head. "Not today." He stopped the lad from leaving. "What's your name, son?"

"Tom, sir."

"Care to make some coin?"

The boy suddenly looked wary. "Doin' what, mister?"

"Will ye be here tomorra as well?"

Tom nodded.

"Me woman's arriving tomorra morn'. She'll be coming on the *Mary Freedom*. Her name's Meghan McBride, and she'll be traveling with her father. I'd like ye to stay today and tomorra as well, until ye can give the lady me note. Can ye do that?"

His expression brightening, Tom inclined his head.

"Here's something for yer trouble," Rafferty said, handing the boy two bits.

"Two levies, sir!" the boy exclaimed. "Thank you, sir."

Rafferty nodded. "If ye help the lady get to Somerville on the Brandywine, I'll see that ye get a full dollar."

Tom's eyes glowed as he caressed his coins. "Aye, sir. I'll do it. I'll see that yer lady gets to Somerville."

The ship docked in Philadelphia late afternoon two days later than expected. Meghan hugged each of her cabin mates in turn, saving Mrs. Finn for last.

"Ye be sure to write me now, lass," the old woman implored.

"Aye, Mrs. Finn. I'll be sure to do it."

"And make sure your fiancé takes good care of ye. I'll be after his hide if he doesn't."

Meghan nodded, her eyes stinging with tears. She knew that the woman had forgotten to whom she was engaged, but it didn't matter. Mrs. Finn cared . . . and Meghan would probably never see her again.

"So ye'll be traveling to Delaware," Bridget said.

Meghan smiled. "Aye, to a place in the county of New Castle. A place called Somers or the like." She had actually enjoyed Bridget's company once the young woman had recovered from being ill.

"Me—I'll be staying in Philadelphia," Bridget said. "Me cousin Sean lives here. He's arranged me employment."

"Good luck, Bridget." Meghan held out her hand. "Take good care of yourself."

The young woman blinked, her eyes overly bright. "I will," she whispered.

The four women stared at each other as they stood on the upper deck. They'd shared quarters for eighteen days. They'd begun as strangers and now were parting as friends, never to see each other again.

"Where's yer intended?" Mary Beth asked.

Meghan felt a jolt. "He's down below, but he'll be comin' up soon."

Someone called Bridget's name. "Sean!" the young

woman called back joyously, recognizing the man who waved vigorously from the shore. She turned back to her former cabin mates. "God go with ye," she murmured, and then rushed ashore, happily greeting the dark-haired gentleman who hurried forward to meet her.

The three remaining women stood quietly together as each waited for someone to come for them. Donal Finn, brother to Mrs. Finn's late husband, came up from steerage. A thin man with twinkling blue eyes and smile lines at the corners of his mouth, he nodded to each lady before addressing his sister-in-law.

"Doreen?" he said. "Are ye ready to go now?"

"Aye, Donal," she replied, and Meghan was surprised to see her blush. Meghan smiled. The man was younger, but Mrs. Finn had admitted that he was even more handsome than his late older brother. And Donal Finn was a kind man . . . and single.

"Goodbye, dearies," the older woman said as she followed her brother-in-law off the ship.

Soon someone came for Mary Beth, and Meghan waited on deck all alone. Her gaze searched the shore for Rafferty. Would she recognize him or would he have changed too much since he'd left Ireland?

No one in her line of vision resembled the man who'd been her father's best friend.

Oh, Da! What now?

The air was cold and nippy, and she wore her cloak—Lucas's cloak. She clutched her small bundle of belongings and wondered what she should do.

She hadn't seen Lucas since their kiss in his cabin. She told herself she was glad, for he was a complication in her life she didn't need. Meghan glanced over her shoulder and then scolded herself severely for looking. What would she hope to gain from one more glimpse of Lucas Ridgely? She should be glad, not disappointed that there was no sign of the handsome man.

Meghan gripped her cloth bundle tighter and started toward the platform that would allow her to leave the ship. *Goodbye, Lucas,* she thought with a pang of longing. She pulled herself together as she stepped onto the gangplank. *Hello, America. Will ye be good to me?*

The feel of solid earth beneath her feet was strange as she stepped off the ship. She'd gotten so used to the sway of the vessel on the sea that it felt odd to be on firm ground. Meghan moved out of the way of other disembarking passengers, her gaze alert for her betrothed. She experienced a growing panic after minutes had gone by and then an hour with no sign of Rafferty O'Connor.

Now what do I do? Where could she go? She had no money or place to stay. *In the name of God, Rafferty, where are ye?*

She was alone in a strange country without coin or friends. She was vulnerable to criminals and thieves, and afraid.

"Meghan."

She spun at the sound of the male voice. Lucas Ridgely stood beside her, eyeing her with concern.

"Lucas!" she gasped.

He frowned as he studied her. "What's wrong?"

She swallowed against a lump, fighting emotion. She'd never expected to see him, and now he was here when she was scared and feeling the most vulnerable.

"There's no one here to meet me!" she cried, panic evident in her tone.

"Your fiancé isn't here?"

She nodded, fighting tears. *No,* she thought, turning away. *I will not cry. 'Tis a sign of weakness!* And she'd promised Da.

"Do you know where he lives?" Lucas asked. His query was as gentle the hand that he settled on her shoulder.

She hurriedly wiped her eyes, before facing him again. "Somerton or Somerville—I don't know . . . I have to think!" What did she remember from Rafferty's letters? He worked for a company that made paper. Paper and cloth.

"They make paper."

"Somerton Mill along the Brandywine Creek?" Lucas sounded surprised "I know where it is. I'm passing that way; I'll take you there."

"Ye will?"

He smiled, and she basked in the warmth of his grin.

Meghan experienced doubt. *I shouldn't go with him.* What if Rafferty came and she wasn't here?

They stood on the wharf with people all about them, but Meghan's thoughts were with Lucas and how she wanted to go with him, but was afraid. She wondered why Rafferty wasn't here and prayed that nothing serious had happened to him.

"I don't know what to do," she admitted. "What if me fiancé comes?"

Suddenly, a young boy with an apple cart rushed up to them. "I'm supposed to find a lady," he gasped, "but my mam kept me late. Now I think I've missed her!"

Lucas placed a hand on the youth's shoulder. "Who are you looking for?"

"Meghan McBride," he said. "My name's Tom."

Meghan inhaled sharply. "I'm Meghan McBride."

Tom looked at Lucas and raised his eyebrows. "You her father?"

Lucas chuckled. "Do I look old enough?"

"Nope."

"Me father's dead," Meghan said. "Died coming across the sea."

"I'm sorry, miss," the boy said.

Meghan nodded, unsmiling. "Thank ye," she whispered. Feeling Lucas's regard, she looked up, met his dark gaze, and saw the compassion there.

"I've a message from Mr. O'Connor."

Meghan stiffened. "Where is he?" she asked.

"He couldn't be here," Tom said. "He was here, but he had to leave." He reached inside the pocket of his grubby shirt and pulled out a crumpled piece of paper. "He gave me this to give to ya."

Meghan took and unfolded the note. The only thing written on the piece of paper was Rafferty O'Connor and another name. "I don't understand," she said.

"Let me see it."

Lucas scowled after reading the paper. "For God's sake, what is that supposed to mean!" He turned to the boy. "Did he say anything else?"

"Just that he had to get to Delaware."

"It must be his work," Meghan murmured. "I hope he hasn't lost his employment."

"I doubt it," Lucas said. "I've met Mr. Somerton. He seemed like a decent enough fellow."

Tom shifted on his feet. "The man said there was coin in it for me if I got you to Somerville, miss."

Lucas dug into his pocket and pulled out a gold coin. "Here you are," he said. "I'll see that the lady gets home."

The boy's eyes widened. "A quarter eagle, sir? But Mr. O'Connor—he said just a dollar!"

"A reward for finding us, Tom."

Tom beamed at his one-dollar-and-fifty-cents bonus. "Thank you, sir."

Lucas nodded and, when the boy had departed, placed his arm about Meghan's shoulders. "Come. I'll hire us a carriage."

Meghan was stunned by Lucas's generosity. He must

be rich, she thought, recalling the boy's overjoyed expression. She'd entertained the notion of his wealth before; why then did his actions surprise her?

"I'm sorry," she said, allowing Lucas's arm to remain. "It seems that fate has you rescuing me again."

"Fate," he said. He shook his head. "Pleasure, Meghan, not fate. It's my pleasure to see that you reach your destination. After all we've been through, I'd hate for anything bad to happen to you now."

He called and waved to a crewman from the *Mary Freedom*, who left and returned later with Lucas's sea chest.

"Wait here while I arrange for that carriage." Lucas smiled to reassure her.

She nodded, her heart palpitating within her breast as she watched Lucas walk away. She immediately felt the loss of his company, recalling how vulnerable she'd felt until his arrival only moments ago. He was back beside her within minutes with a smile on his face and a man leading a horse-drawn conveyance by the animal's reins.

After seeing his trunk loaded in the back of the vehicle, Lucas tossed in Meghan's small bundle, helped her into the carriage, and climbed in to sit beside her.

"How far is it to Somerville?" she asked, hiding her surprise that he would be driving.

"About twenty-five miles or so," he told her. "We'll travel some distance and then stop to eat at an inn."

Meghan bit her lip. Twenty-five miles! Would they make it to Somerville this night? She had no money for dinner, and she didn't want to take his charity. What if she needed a room?

Lucas glanced over at her and stared hard, before setting his gaze back on the road. "I can afford our dinner," he said as if reading her mind.

She raised her chin. "I'll repay you," she said. She looked ahead, firming her lips.

"Don't be absurd."

She turned to glare at him. "I'll not take your charity again, Mr. Ridgely."

He scowled at her. "The cloak wasn't charity, Meghan. It was a gift."

After several seconds of thought, she nodded and relaxed. "Thank ye."

"Now was that so hard?" he asked. A smile played about his sensual lips as he returned his attention to the horse. "Let me buy you dinner, because it pleases me to do so."

"You're very kind," she mumbled beneath her breath.

Lucas chuckled. "I heard that." He flashed her a grin. "It's easy to be kind to you, Miss McBride," he said, much to her pleasure.

They left the city streets for a bumpy country road that wound its way through fields and woods that had already taken on the rich hues of autumn. Meghan thought of the bustling dock in Philadelphia and decided she liked this scenery more.

The muddy and rutted condition of the road made their pace slower than Meghan thought was necessary if they were to reach Somerville that evening. She glanced at Lucas and saw from his frowning concentration that he seemed concerned, too.

But still the time and distance passed pleasantly until the sun set and the sky began to darken. Declaring that it was the supper hour, Lucas steered the carriage through a huge dip in the mud into the yard of a roadside inn. Meghan was glad, for her stomach was beginning to churn with hunger. Or was she nervous at the thought of not continuing the journey?

As Lucas helped her step down from the vehicle's

step, Meghan eyed the old building with curiosity and pleasure. The public house was obviously a structure from another time. Built of stone, the building appeared to have been added to, as evidenced by the separate entranceway with its own porch and the different roof level of the edifice attached to the main house's left side. The inn was quaint and welcomed Meghan as she absorbed the scenic beauty of a house nestled among trees bright with the season's reds and yellows. Boxwoods planted near the two porches filled the air with their pungent, pleasant scent.

"This inn is over a hundred years old," Lucas told her. "The Pattersons refurbished the place, before opening it up again to the public."

She nodded. She felt like she was stepping back into a time when the public house had been a stop for the weary traveler seeking food and a night's stay. How many people had sought refuge here from the cold and the wind? How many travelers had been comforted by the warmth of its hearth?

"The food is particularly delicious," Lucas said, his gaze moving from the house to her smiling face.

"I'm glad," she said. "I'm hungry." And he chuckled.

Meghan's mouth watered as she anticipated a meal. It'd been the evening before since she'd eaten, and she'd been too excited to break her fast with her cabin mates that morning.

Lucas secured the horse, and then with a warm hand at her back, he guided Meghan up the porch steps and inside the front foyer.

The atmosphere within the eighteenth century inn was one of comfort and peaceful quiet. The staircase in the foyer curved upward to the second floor, its mahogany handrailing dark against its white painted spindles. An Oriental rug covered the wooden floor that was obviously well cared for. A vase of flowers sat on a table polished to a high sheen. Her gaze wandering left, Meghan caught sight of the next room and a portrait of a distinguished-looking gentleman that hung above the fireplace.

She studied her surroundings with pleasure until someone came to greet them.

"Lucas!" A tall, thin man came forward from a room at the back of the house. "It's good to see you again."

"John," Lucas said, offering his hand. "You know I can never resist passing through without sampling some of Anne's cooking."

The innkeeper's eyes fell for a brief moment on Meghan. "You'll be staying the night?"

Lucas nodded. "I'm afraid we'll not make our destination this night. It's too late to continue. The roads are terrible."

John agreed. "We've had three full days of rain the early part of the week," he said.

Her heart thumping, Meghan shot Lucas a surprised look. Why hadn't he said something to her sooner? Her skin began to tingle as she realized that he was just being reasonable. It was late, and the road was in deplorable shape. For them to travel at night would not only be foolhardy but dangerous.

Still, she had no money. How could she expect Lucas to pay for two rooms?

He would have to, she thought. She certainly wasn't going to share with him!

Lucas knew that he'd surprised Meghan with his intention to stay, but he had considered their options, and staying at the Pattersons' presented the safest and wisest thing to do. He drew Meghan forward to meet his friend. "Meghan, this is John Patterson. John, this is Miss McBride. Meghan McBride. I met her on the *Mary Freedom*. We're traveling together."

He felt Meghan tense. "I'm afraid her fiancé left her stranded in Philadelphia."

"Oh, you poor dear!" a feminine voice exclaimed, and a short woman with an ample bosom hurried forward to greet her guests. "Good day to ya, Lucas," she said quickly, before turning her attention to Meghan. "Who do we have here?" she asked.

Lucas performed the introductions. The woman was John's wife, Anne Patterson, with hair the rich color of chestnut. Anne wore a gown that was neat, well made, and protected by a white apron. She wiped her hands on her apron before she extended one to Meghan, who accepted the greeting.

"Are ye hungry?" Anne asked.

Meghan nodded, her eyes widening at the woman's accent. "Ye're from me homeland," she said. "Where?"

Anne smiled. "County of Cork." The corners of her mouth rose higher when she heard Meghan gasp. "Aye," she said softly. "Me grandmother spoke of the McBrides." As she talked, she gently urged Meghan toward a lovely part of the room where a table sat near a back window. She paused and glanced back. "Aren't ye coming, Mr. Ridgely?" she asked.

Filled with amusement over Anne's mothering of Meghan, Lucas nodded and followed closely behind with the woman's husband. His enjoyment of the situation grew as he continued to eavesdrop while he waited for Anne to move so he could sit down.

"Ye said yer da passed away?" Anne was saying.

"Aye," Meghan said.

"Oh, ye poor lass! Come to America all by yerself! Why it must have been a frightening experience for ya."

Lucas stifled a smile as Meghan met his gaze and blushed. "Meghan is a strong woman, Anne."

IRISH LINEN

Anne spun suddenly as if just remembering that he was there. "Oh, for certain, she must be!"

"Allow Lucas to be seated, wife," John Patterson suggested softly. "The man's recently crossed the sea as well."

The woman nodded and moved aside, and Lucas was able to sit across from Meghan. Anne clucked and fussed over the two, seeing that they were comfortable, before leaving to prepare their meal.

John stayed behind for a moment to apologize. "Anne means well, but she can be a bit overbearing."

The sight of Meghan's smile nearly took Lucas's breath away. "Your wife's lovely," she said. "She reminds me of me late mother." She blinked several times and then looked down at her place setting, before lifting her gaze "Made me feel welcome, she did."

Lucas nodded, his gaze on Meghan. "You don't have to apologize to me, John. You know how I feel about Annie."

With a few murmured words about helping his wife and seeing to their rooms, John poured each a glass of water, then left, leaving Lucas and Meghan alone. The dining hall was quiet, but not uncomfortably so. Lucas's explanation of their situation followed by John's assumption that they would need two rooms instead of one made Meghan relax and study the common area.

Like the foyer, the room welcomed her with warmth. A fire burned on the hearth, and the flaming wood crackled and popped, occasionally shooting sparks as a log readjusted itself. Wooden tables, able to seat one to several diners, were set up about the room in a way that allowed the guests the most comfort and enjoyment of their meal. But even as she became absorbed in the contents of the room, Meghan was extremely aware of the man seated across from her.

"Do you like gardens?" Lucas asked, intruding on her thoughts.

"Gardens?" she echoed.

"Plants? Flowers?"

"Aye," she breathed. "I like flowers."

"Take a glance out that window then." Lucas leaned close, and she was conscious of his nearness as he pointed past her glass toward the carefully arranged shrubbery outside. "It's not as colorful now as in the spring and summer, but it's impressive." She could smell his clean scent. A curling heat started in her midsection and spread lower. She forced her attention to the outside.

The garden was breathtaking to Meghan. Shrubs had been planted in short, evenly spaced rows and in an attractive square border around an herb planting. Bright orange and yellow mums added a splash of color to the rows of green.

"It's lovely," Meghan said, remembering the freshly cut flowers in the front foyer.

"As Anne is?" he teased, and she blushed. "A lovely woman with a lovely garden, eh?"

She nodded. "You're poking fun at me," she accused.

His smile vanished. "I'd never do that, Meghan. I think too much of you."

Her heart began to thud harder as she looked away to refocus her gaze on the garden. The sky was a dark backdrop streaked with gold and orange from the already set sun. Meghan decided she liked America.

"Does Anne grow vegetables, too?"

"Yes," Lucas said after a moment's hesitation. "She grows and cooks them to make her delicious side dishes."

Something in Lucas's tone made her glance his way again. "Lucas, about the room—"

IRISH LINEN

"We can't leave, Meghan. You must realize that."

She looked down at the table. "I know, but—"

"I can afford it," he said. He made a sound of annoyance. "We've been through this before."

Her gaze met his. "It's just—how can I ever repay you?"

"Have I asked to be repaid?" His tone rumbled with the threat of anger.

"No—"

He grabbed her hand. "I want you, Meghan. I admit it, but I'm not intent on exacting payment!" He released her fingers and sat back, shaking his head. "I want to see you safely to Somerville . . . that's all. I want you to be *safe.*"

"I'm sorry," she whispered. Hearing him openly discuss his desire for her had made her gasp, but then his words that followed had made sense. And she believed him. He'd never given her cause to doubt him.

"But if you'd like me to cancel one room . . ." His voice trailed off softly.

"Don't! Please," she cried in a whisper. "You promised!" And then she saw his teasing expression.

His eyes danced with mischief. But then he gave her a crooked smile that made her wonder if he had, in fact, been joking.

"Did I?" he said. "Ah, right, I promised to behave, didn't I?" He drank from his glass of water. "Tell me about your fiancé."

Meghan was taken aback. "Why?"

"Because I'm curious."

She didn't want to talk about Rafferty and their betrothal. Not when she was here with Lucas. It'd been a long time since she'd seen her father's friend. It was hard at times to remember what Rafferty looked like.

Lucas seemed determined to pursue the subject, so she sighed and relented. "I've known him all me life," she said, hoping he'd be satisfied enough to put an end to the discussion.

"You've known each other since you were children," Lucas said.

Meghan stared down at her empty plate. She'd known Rafferty since she was a child, but to her, Rafferty had always been a man. "Yes," she lied.

"Is he attractive?"

Her stomach turned over. "Yes," she said after a brief pause.

"I see." Something in his tone drew her attention. "Why are you asking me this?" she asked.

His gaze held hers, deep and dark with banked passion. "I want to know about my competition."

Meghan frowned. "There is no competition. I'm an engaged woman. Rafferty and I are going to marry, so please stop suggesting otherwise!"

"You'd be happier with me."

She pushed back her chair and stood. "Is that why ye brought me here? So that ye could change me mind?"

"Sit down, Meghan," he commanded. "I've already told you why we're here."

She plunked back onto her chair. "I told ye I'll not be beholden to ya. I'm grateful for your help, but I'll not let it change how I feel."

His voice was soft and sultry when he spoke. "How *do* you feel?"

"Like you're pressing me," she hissed. "I love Rafferty, and I'm going to marry him. Nothing ye can say or do will change me mind!"

"Is it me that concerns you?" he said so quietly she almost didn't hear him. "Or are you worried about yourself?"

Meghan glanced away. Was it Lucas's actions that

worried her? Or was it her own weakness and response to him?

"You've made your choice, Meghan. I understand this." He grinned. "Can't blame a man for trying, can you?"

She stared at him as if he'd suddenly gone mad. "You're crazy," she said, voicing her thoughts.

His smile was crooked. "Crazy for you."

"Lucas."

"I apologize, Miss McBride. I promise to behave myself from here on." He placed his hand over hers where it lay on the table, and Meghan was startled by the contact. "And I want you when you're willing, not because you feel beholden to me."

She pulled her hand from under his. "I'm not interested."

He raised one eyebrow. "Aren't you?"

The arrival of John with their meal saved Meghan from having to lie again.

Nine

Lucas kept his promise. He was the perfect gentleman throughout the meal, and the subject of Meghan's fiancé never came up between them again. They spoke of light topics . . . the weather in Delaware and about Dover, which was in the center of the state and nearer to Lucas's home. Soon, they had consumed their meal of baked chicken, vegetables, potatoes, and pie, and John was there to show them to their rooms.

As she followed the two men, Meghan found the second floor as inviting as the first. John led them to the end of the hall and opened the door.

"This is your room, Miss McBride," the innkeeper said. "I hope you'll be comfortable here."

"Thank ye." Meghan peered inside and had no doubt that she'd be comfortable. The room was impressive and feminine with white walls accented with pillows and items in several shades of pink. A rose chintz counterpane topped the high-post tester bed. A floral pattern hooked rug in rose, blues, and greens on a background of ivory protected the wooden floor while adding beauty. There was a dressing table, a chair, a chest of drawers, and a washstand, all of cherry wood that gleamed with beeswax polish. In the center of the wall directly opposite was a door. She wondered briefly where it led, and then decided that it must lead to the attic.

Her attention went back to the massive bed. She had never slept in a bed so fine, and she found herself looking forward to the prospect.

"It's a wonderful room, Mr. Patterson," she said. "I'm sure I'll be enjoying me stay."

"John," he said with a smile. "My friends call me John."

"John," she repeated, and grinned.

Suddenly, the innkeeper seemed uncomfortable as he turned to Lucas. "Anne insists that I give you your favorite room."

Sensing a new tension in Lucas, Meghan followed the direction of his gaze to the door on the far side of her room. She shot him a puzzled glance. *Your room is through there?*

Interpreting her look correctly, he gave her a slight nod.

"If you're uncomfortable with the room—" John began.

"The room will be fine, John," Lucas assured him. He addressed Meghan, "I stay in the same room whenever I come to visit."

She watched with racing pulse as John walked through her bedchamber to the door that she'd thought led to the attic. The innkeeper opened the door to reveal another bedchamber obviously designed to accommodate a man.

Lucas stepped inside and pretended to look around with satisfaction, but his thoughts were concerned with Meghan's reaction to the news that he'd be spending the night so close. He avoided Meghan's blue gaze; yet, he could feel her confusion, her trepidation. Murmuring all the right responses to John, he inspected the room and then returned to where Meghan stood.

"I'll get our belongings," he told her in a quiet voice. He was angered by her look of uncertainty, but he wasn't angry with Meghan. He was irritated with Anne Patterson for insisting he take his usual room.

John's apologetic look as the man had spoken about the room kept Lucas silent. He would not only hurt but insult the Pattersons if he suggested moving to a different bedchamber. John and Anne had simply been trying to please him.

He and Meghan would just have to make do for the night, Lucas decided. No easy feat, he thought, to be so near her when he wasn't allowed to touch.

He followed John down the hall and stairs, then outside, leaving Meghan alone to her worry about his sleeping in near proximity.

He could understand how she must feel, for he felt it, too. How could he sleep with only a single connecting door separating their bedchambers, and when the door had no lock?

Perhaps we should have gone on to Somerville, he thought. *Was it any less dangerous to play with fire?*

Sleeping so close to Meghan, recalling the taste of her lips and the warmth of her silky skin, he would definitely be tempting the devil in himself.

As he thought of Meghan's fiancé, Lucas's blood began to burn. How could the man have left Philadelphia without her? Employment or no employment!

It didn't matter that the man hadn't known about her father's death. There was no excuse for the stupidity that must have driven the man to hire a twelve-year-old youth to see that his fiancé and future father-in-law—two strangers to America—reached Somerville over twenty miles away.

Rafferty O'Connor was not worthy of Meghan, Lucas thought as he removed Meghan's small bundle from the back of the carriage.

Despite what Meghan believed, what she'd said, deep in her heart she must know this!

Why else would she have responded to me with so much passion? He was experienced with women, but he wasn't that good.

He rummaged through his sea chest and pulled out a fresh change of clothes. *But how can I get Meghan to admit that she would be better off with me . . . better off without Rafferty O'Connor?*

He couldn't do a thing, Lucas realized. He'd promised Meghan he'd behave; and to Meghan, behaving meant abandoning all of his attempts to convince her to change her mind.

Damn! He'd never concerned himself with a woman like this before! What was it about Meghan McBride that was so special?

Why was he so desperate to have her in his bed?

Trembling with the thought of having Lucas behind that door, Meghan sat in the upholstered chair and stared without seeing. Suddenly, the prospect of sleeping here was frightening. Suddenly, she wished they'd braved the dark and dangerous road, which seemed far safer to her than sleeping this close to Lucas's room.

She rose on wobbly legs to check the condition of the connecting door. What she found didn't please her. The doorknob worked perfectly, so the door would close shut, but there was no key, no lock, nothing to protect her from the wild and churning feelings that made her fear she'd step past the threshold sometime during the night.

Lucas was right, she thought. It wasn't him that concerned her as much as her own response to him. She enjoyed his company more than she should. She had tasted his kisses and been unable to forget . . . *Lord help me, I'm an engaged woman. Please help me to be strong.*

She opened the door and stared at the room. This was the room where Lucas stayed often; she moved in to take a closer look, wondering what it was there that had first attracted Lucas's pleasure.

A sound in the hall drew her attention, and she hurried from Lucas's room. She made it to her window before Lucas called to her as he tapped gently on her bedchamber door.

She was shaking so badly when she went to open the door that her hands shook on the knob, and it took her longer than normally necessary to turn it. Finally, she managed to swing open the door, and she stepped back to allow Lucas to enter with their belongings.

"A good thing we decided to stay the night," Lucas said after greeting her. He set her bundle on the bed. "It's raining."

Meghan didn't answer him, but watched as he turned from the bed and readjusted his own things in his arms as he straightened.

He captured her gaze. "Meghan—"

"I know," she whispered, feeling as if the lump in her throat was strangling her. "It's good that we've stayed. I know that."

Moving until he was within feet of her, Lucas touched her cheek. "I wouldn't do anything to hurt you."

Her lashes flickered as she looked up. "Ye may not wish to, but—"

"There's a door that closes," he told her, stroking her skin with his thumb. There was something in his expression that tugged at her heart, that urged her to comfort him, but she didn't. "Close the door, and I'll not venture past."

"You won't?" Her reply was on a breathy puff of air.

Lucas shook his head. He dropped his hand from her cheek abruptly and headed toward his room.

"Lucas!" she cried when he'd gone into his room and she thought he would shut the door. He stiffened and turned. "I believe ya," she said softly. "I trust ye."

He regarded her for a long moment, before his lips formed a half smile. "Then you trust in me more than I do." He laid his garments over a wooden chair and then swung back to find her still watching him.

"I'll not be closing that door, Meghan McBride," he warned. "Unless you've a liking to tempt the devil, then I suggest you take the initiative."

The look in his dark gaze and the gruff sound of his voice had her hurrying forward to take his suggestion.

Somerville, New Castle, in Delaware

The bell on the shop door tinkled as someone came into the Somerville store. Rafferty's head rose from his book of accounts.

"I'll be right out," he called from the back room.

There was no answer, but he wasn't concerned. He scribbled a few marks, closed the ledger, and went to the front room. His gaze widened as he saw who it was.

"Hello, Mr. O'Connor."

"Mrs. Somerton!" he gasped, his face reddening. "I didn't expect ya here. I wouldn't have kept ye waiting—"

The woman was blond, beautiful, and built, Rafferty thought, like an angel sent down from heaven to comfort a man of sin.

"That's all right," she said in her soft, husky voice. "I didn't mind waiting. Mr. Somerton and I appreciate when our storekeepers are careful." She gave him a flirtatious smile that made the blood flow hotly between his legs.

"You'd like something from the stock?" he asked, uncertain as to her reason for being here.

She nodded, and Rafferty came out from behind the counter, ready to help the woman find whatever she needed. It was unusual for the mistress of Somerville to purchase her own supplies.

Mrs. Somerton wandered about the room, checking the shelves as if looking for something special. "I don't see what I'm looking for, Mr. O'Connor. May I check the stores in the back?"

"Of course, Mrs. Somerton," he said, following her to the door to the back room.

The woman went to the shelving built onto the back wall, rummaging through boxes of food goods, piece fabrics, and tools, while Rafferty watched her with puzzlement.

"Is there something I can get for ye, Mrs. Somerton?" he suggested tentatively.

She closed the door for privacy, and Rafferty waited for her to confide what she needed. Mrs. Somerton flashed him a look before approaching to touch his arm. He faced her with surprise.

"Rafferty, it's been so long," she breathed as she slid her hands down his muscled chest.

His groin throbbed as she pressed her lips to the pulse at his throat. "Now, Alicia?" he gasped, realizing her intent. "Here?"

"Yes, Rafferty. *Here. Now.*" And she began to tug open his shirt buttons.

Ten

It was late. The house was dark, and the rain beat softly against the window glass in a rhythmic sound that normally Meghan would have found soothing, but not this night. She lay in bed, staring up at the white tester of the bed, her thoughts on the man in the next room.

I'm an engaged woman. Why can't I forget him?

Because no man had ever made her feel so special, so physically and emotionally aware of him.

She rolled onto her stomach and cradled her chin on her hands. What would have happened if they'd met under different circumstances? In Ireland, by chance . . . would Lucas have been as intent to bed her?

A mental image of him in bed in the next room flushed her with heat. Several times she'd fought the urge to go to the door and take a peek, but each time common sense had kept her away.

The last thing she needed was to carry the actual memory with her. How could she marry and live with Rafferty if she kept remembering Lucas . . . the way his golden hair fell on his forehead and curled about his ears . . . the way he occasionally rubbed his temple when he was deep in thought?

Gasping with desire, she flung herself onto her back. Dear God, she wanted to feel his hands on her . . . to experience his kisses and to know the full force of his unleashed passion. But would Lucas allow himself to let go? He was a careful man; could a woman ever make him lose control?

Lord in heaven! What was she thinking? She was a betrothed woman with Catholic beliefs. She had no business having such sinful thoughts!

"Our Father . . ." she prayed, *". . . forgive me my temptation . . . and deliver me from evil."*

Evil, she thought. How could sharing the man's bed be evil?

" 'Tis a sin outside of marriage, me girl," an inner voice said.

"Aye," she whispered, closing her eyes. "Aye, but I want him anyway."

A sound at the connecting door made Meghan freeze. She heard it again—the gentle turn of the doorknob.

It was difficult to pretend she was sleeping as she heard the *click* and realized that Lucas had opened the door. She forced herself to breathe deeply and evenly. She couldn't control her body's reactions as his footsteps creaked on the wooden floor before they were muffled when Lucas reached the carpet.

She sensed him near the bed, and her heart pounded so loudly she thought he surely must hear it. But he said nothing, so she continued to feign sleep and waited for him to leave.

A long moment passed, and he still hadn't moved. Meghan prayed harder for him to go as she fought the urge to confront him, to throw back the covers and invite him to join her . . .

Rafferty. She was engaged. She silently said another prayer and waited.

"Meghan?" Lucas's whisper affected her like a shot in the dark.

She opened her eyes wide. "Lucas!"

He wasn't as near as she'd first thought. He stood near the edge of the bed table, studying her where she lay.

She lifted herself to her elbows as he moved closer and stepped into the soft light that drifted past the open curtains of her room. He wore nothing but a pair of trousers that hugged his thighs and calves. Inhaling sharply, her gaze fastened on his sleek, muscled chest. His skin gleamed in the faint light. Meghan's fingers tingled with the itch to touch him.

She sat, clutching the sheet to her breasts, and met his dark gaze. "Lucas, what's wrong?"

"I can't sleep."

His deep voice sent ripples of pleasure down the length of her spine. "Is it the rain?" she asked.

He shrugged. His eyes glowed in the darkness. "I thought I'd pilfer something from Anne's pantry." He suddenly looked like a little boy, confessing a transgression he'd yet to commit. "I didn't mean to disturb you," he said softly. "I was just . . ." His voice trailed off without finishing.

She sat straighter. "What were ye going to say?"

Her heart pumped as she waited for his answer. She could see his features enough to watch the play of emotion. She felt strange . . . wildly exhilarated and anticipatory, yet scared, too, of her newly awakening feelings.

"Lucas?"

"Would you like to come?"

Meghan blinked. He wanted her to help him steal some food! It was the last thing she'd expected him to ask her, especially after his previous, bold pursuit of her. She had anticipated a renewal of his offer to bed her . . . to feed and clothe her . . . and give her a home. Not a home with him, but somewhere close by.

His kept woman.

Instead, he acted like a young boy begging a friend to be his accomplice in mischief. The idea lightened her mood and appealed to her.

Meghan grinned. "Aye," she said. Lucas and the Pattersons were friends; she didn't think the innkeepers would mind them helping themselves from their larder.

She started to get up, only to stop, suddenly self-conscious of her state of dress. She wore only her thread-worn shift, that was thin and too transparent.

He seemed to understand. "I'll wait for you in the hall."

She nodded, and once he'd closed her door, she hastened to pull on her gown.

Lucas was standing in the hallway, a few feet from the door, when Meghan exited the room. He gave her a conspiratorial grin, which she returned. An oil lamp had been left burning with lowered wick to gently light up the corridor.

Meghan was startled to see the light. She flashed Lucas a look that questioned.

"Anne leaves a light burning when there are guests," he whispered.

But the expense, she wanted to say, but didn't.

Again, Lucas seemed to read her mind. "It's barely burning. John will come at dawn to extinguish it."

They snuck, like two children, down the curving staircase to the foyer below where there was another burning wall sconce.

Lucas knew where the pantry was located, and he led the way as if he'd made the trip a hundred times in the past.

"Ye've done this before," she whispered.

He froze, turned, and held his finger to his lips. "The Pattersons," he mouthed, while he pointed to the door of a room. Meghan's eyes widened.

Lucas's head tilted as he listened for sound, and then he waved her to follow him through the door to the kitchen and to the back of the work area until they came to the pantry.

They found bread, a plate of cookies, and a bowl of apples. Lucas grabbed some cookies and shoved them into Meghan's hands. Then, he picked out two large, shiny apples and tucked them in his left arm. Next, he selected two glasses from a top cabinet. With his arms full, he slipped past Meghan, and with a nod of his head, instructed her to follow him once again. He stopped in the common room, shifting his burden, to take a bottle of wine from a cellarette.

Soon, they were climbing the steps to the second floor, and Meghan listened for sounds that they'd been discovered. She released a pent-up breath once they'd reached the safety of her room without waking their generous hosts.

Lucas set down the glasses, apples, and bottle of wine on her bed. He pulled the wing chair nearer to the bed and then cleared off the bed table by the headboard and moved it between the edge of the bed and the chair. "Sit down, Meghan," he coaxed softly, "and we'll share."

She gave a soft, nervous laugh, before she sat on the bed while he took the chair, the food on the bed table between them.

The cookies were delicious with a lemon flavor. The apple was juicy, succulent, and sweet. It was a new experience for Meghan, sharing food with a man in the middle of the night . . . and she decided that she liked it.

Lucas grabbed the bottle and opened it. "Wine?" he offered.

"Won't Anne and John miss that?" she asked breathlessly. She felt tingly and off balance in Lucas's presence. Dare she risk drinking a glass of wine?

His smile was sensual and most decidedly male. "The Pattersons usually leave a bottle in my room."

She was surprised. "You stay here often?"

He nodded. "Since I first stopped here five years ago, I've found it hard to stay away." Without waiting for her consent, he poured her, and then himself, a half glass of the dark liquid. "Sometimes I just stop for dinner on my way through. Other times—more often than necessary, I'll admit—I spend the night."

Had he shared stolen meals in the middle of the night with other women? she wondered. The notion bothered her.

Then, Meghan noted how his lips curved in a soft smile as he stared at some point beyond her shoulder. "Beth loves the place, too," he said, and her stomach muscles tightened. He met her gaze. "Beth is my sister."

Her stomach unclenched, and she smiled back.

"Here." He picked up a glass and held it over the table. His eyes gleamed as their gazes held while she accepted the wine.

Her skin tingled at his look. Her blood flowed, spreading warmth and a prickling sensation. She took a tentative sip from the glass and found she liked the wine's taste. Meghan swallowed a second and then a third, and felt heat slide down her throat with each disappearing mouthful. She closed her eyes as she fought the effects of the wine and her attraction to the man seated across from her.

"Are you all right?" Lucas asked.

IRISH LINEN

She opened her eyes and nodded. "The wine," she said, her Irish brogue thickening, "it's vera good."

A glimmer of amusement brightened his ebony eyes. "I'm glad you like it."

She jerked her head *yes* and experienced a swimming sensation that made her set down her glass and grip the table edge.

"Meghan—"

She heard Lucas's concern. "I'm fine." For some strange reason, she felt light-headed and weak all of a sudden. A reaction to the wine?

Frowning, Lucas set down his glass, rose, and came around the small table. "Perhaps you'd better lie down."

His hands gripped her shoulders and gently swung her to lie down. She could detect about him a wonderful, wildly intoxicating woodsy fragrance mingling with the faint odor of wine on his breath. But most of all, she loved the scent that was entirely male, pleasant, and instantly recognizable to her as belonging to him alone . . . a scent that stirred her emotions as well as her physical desire for him.

Meghan felt the effects of the wine and Lucas's nearness drugging her senses. She eyed him from beneath lowered lashes as he straightened and moved the table back to its original position beside the bed. Seeing his intention, she fought back panic.

"You're exhausted," he said, turning to face her. "I'll leave you to sleep."

She didn't want him to go. "No! Please, I—" She gazed at him, appalled by her entreaty, but unable to conceal her need.

He froze, his gaze glittering, his jaw taut, as he stared down at her on the bed. "Meghan—"

"Sit here a minute, Lucas, will ye?" she asked, trying to sound casual. She padded the edge of the bed beside her, knowing that she was playing with fire, but uncaring of the danger. She waited with held breath for his decision.

He hesitated before lowering himself to the bed. "This is crazy," he breathed, lifting a hand to touch her hair.

"Aye," she said, unable to deny it. But they weren't doing anything wrong, she reminded herself. Merely talking . . . as friends.

But when Lucas tangled his fingers in her hair and twirled the silky strands before tucking them behind her ear, she didn't feel like merely his friend. She closed her eyes on a silent sigh of pleasure as he continued to stroke and caress her scalp.

His touch was soothing. There was nothing sexual in his actions . . . only comfort . . . until Meghan opened her eyes and saw him leaning down to kiss her lips.

Her niggle of guilt disappeared as his mouth brushed hers in a contact so quick and innocent that the kiss could have been exchanged by friends.

"Good night, Meghan." He started to rise. She grabbed his arm.

"Lucas," she whispered, aching.

He groaned and then lowered his head a second time, capturing her mouth in a kiss wild with desperation and need.

When he straightened, Meghan gasped and caught him back to her, this time taking the initiative. She kissed him with abandon, her fingers entangling in his hair as she clutched his head. Lucas responded with a shudder, deepening the kiss with the invasion of his tongue.

Meghan's world spun; her body pulsed and vibrated with never before sensations. Lucas filled her senses . . . his touch . . . his taste . . . his scent . . . and the ravaging glory of his mouth.

With gasping breath, Lucas gazed into her eyes before lowering his mouth to her neck. He trailed kisses beneath the collar edge of her gown, while he cupped and fondled a feminine breast burgeoning to life.

"Meghan," he murmured, his voice thick with passion.

"Aye," she said. She couldn't help herself from wanting him, although somewhere in the back of her hazy mind she knew that to want this man was wrong.

Driven by a pulsing need so great he wanted to possess her quickly, Lucas captured a cloth-covered nipple, wetting and tugging on her breast hotly. He was hard, never before had he been this hard or this desperate to bury himself in a woman's warmth. The blood had gathered between his legs, making him uncomfortably anxious to take her. Meghan's little whimpers and cries drove him higher up the pinnacle of desire, and he lowered his head, trailing his mouth down her fabric-clad belly.

He was driven to explore further, lower to the place where he knew her gown shielded her moistening femininity. He spanned her hips with his hands and held her while he gently nuzzled her sensitive area.

"Lucas," she gasped, moving beneath his hands.

"I know," he said hoarsely in understanding.

He ran his hands up her sides to her breasts, palming and rubbing the tips, before he moved to the buttons of her gown. Meghan was wild and sweet under his hands as he unfastened her garment and helped her to slip it from her shoulders. She wore a shift that revealed more than concealed, and he could see her swollen, pink nipples ripe from his attention.

"God, Meghan," he whispered, "have you any idea how lovely you are?"

She stared at him, and he saw the way her throat worked as she swallowed. "I'm not beautiful," she began.

He nodded. "Yes, you are," he said, while he lowered the collar edge of her chemise to expose one tight-budded breast. "How can you think you—this—is not beautiful?" he asked in a thick voice.

Her eyes glistened with moisture. Lucas's throat tightened as he studied her, and his feelings for this woman frightened him with their intensity.

She was beautiful and vulnerable. *And engaged,* he thought, releasing her breast. Closing his eyes, he fought the lust that strained his loins and made his staff hard and ready for her. If he took her now, she'd despise him later. He didn't want her hatred; he wanted . . . *what?* He wanted her in his bed, yes, but he wanted her for more than one stolen night.

"Lucas?" She sat up, feeling his withdrawal, covering her breasts with her arms.

He saw her confusion. "I should go."

Her throat worked; a bleak look entered her blue eyes. "I see," she whispered.

"No," he said, "no, you don't." He stood abruptly, spun from the sight of her nakedness, and rubbed his nape with a trembling hand. He gathered his composure enough to face her again.

"Lucas, what's wrong?"

He inhaled and exhaled sharply before answering her. "I want you, Meghan, but you've already had my offer. Nothing—this—" He swept a hand over her on the bed. "—won't change things."

Meghan's face paled with her understanding. "I see."

"Do you?" he asked raggedly.

Her stomach burning, Meghan nodded and then grabbed her gown, holding it to her chest like a shield.

"Ye are willing to bed me, but not wed me. Isn't that what you're saying?"

His expression gave her the answer.

"I'm sorry," she whispered, mortified by her wantonness, feeling ashamed. She'd been the one who'd invited him to stay. It was her fault that Lucas had nearly taken her. She shuddered as her lashes flickered closed. Dear God, what had she been thinking—her an engaged woman!

Lucas spun back to the bed, regarding her with a flaming look that told her that he was struggling hard to be honorable. "I promised myself that I wouldn't touch you."

She felt impelled to say something. "It wasn't your fault . . ." Her voice trailed off. What more could she say—that she'd invited his kisses, his touch? It was true, but to admit it would only make the situation more impossible. She was going to marry Rafferty.

"I'd best go," he said.

She nodded, her throat tight, knowing it was the right thing for him to do, but still her whole being silently screamed for him to stay.

"We'll leave at first light," he said brusquely. He hesitated and then asked more gently, "Are you all right?"

She swallowed. "Aye." But she didn't feel all right. She felt as if she'd bared her soul and it had been ravaged beyond hope . . . past the redemption of sin.

The tension grew and there was a lengthening silence.

"Well, good night then," he said, breaking the quiet. He'd schooled his features, and she was unable to gauge his thoughts. "Sleep well."

She didn't reply as he went to his room and shut the door.

Sleeping would be long in coming if at all, Meghan thought, her throat tight.

"Good night, Lucas," she murmured, and the tears she'd never allowed herself to indulge in after the loss of her father fell silently and unchecked down her cheeks.

She was alone.

She felt guilty.

She wanted a man who wasn't her fiancé.

Eleven

The sun was high in the early November sky, but the wind was brisk, buffeting the carriage and howling through the cracks in the vehicle's sides. Huddled within her forest green cloak, Meghan shifted closer to Lucas for warmth.

It wasn't until an hour later that Lucas steered the carriage onto a narrow road that seemed to disappear into the forest. But as the horse pulled the conveyance along the dirt path, the lane continued to open up before them. A cloud covered the sun for a moment, and the darkness added to the air's chill. Meghan peered through the window to gauge her surroundings as the sun broke clear again.

Glancing to the right, Meghan saw, through the trees, a glint of sunlight reflected off a ribbon of water paralleling the roadway. The river ran for a distance where she could see it before disappearing off in the opposite direction.

Suddenly, buildings loomed ahead and to the right as Lucas maneuvered the carriage along the lane. Meghan realized they'd entered a small village.

"Where are we?" she asked.

"We've just entered Somerville. There's the Somerton Mill," he said, pointing to a large factory building off in the distance.

"We're here?"

He nodded. "The name on the note—it must be your fiancé's boardinghouse."

"Aye, I suppose so." The reminder of her fiancé gave her mixed feelings.

"Down there," he said, gesturing toward a house off in the distance, "is the Somerton residence. The workers generally refer to it as the Big House."

She tilted her head to study Lucas. "How do you know all this? I thought you lived at Windfield near Dover." He'd told about his Kent County home during the journey.

"I do," he said with a smile that sent her pulse racing. "But I've an aunt in the area. Not in Somerville, mind you, but still on the Brandywine River several miles from here. In Delaware, the Somertons and my aunt are considered neighbors."

"I see," Meghan murmured, but she didn't, not really. In Ireland, she'd been able to see Rafferty's cottage in the distance, over the open green meadows.

"You said your fiancé works at the store?" Lucas asked.

"Aye." Meghan's heart had begun to thump faster. She had reached her destination, and Lucas would be leaving her. She'd probably never see him again; the knowledge created an odd little ache in the center of her chest.

Lucas had stopped the vehicle, and he glanced over to study her, his expression unreadable. If he was disturbed by his leaving her, he apparently wasn't going to let her know. "You have Rafferty's note?" he asked.

She nodded and silently gave it to him.

He bent his head to read, and Meghan took pleasure in watching him, even while the fact of their parting caused her pain.

"Pridgly," he read aloud. "I'll get out and ask that

gentleman over there if he knows someone by that name."

He jumped lithely from the carriage and spoke briefly with a man in the shadow of a porch roof. Lucas returned within seconds, obviously pleased with what he'd learned.

"It's that house over there." The structure to which he pointed was linked to another one to its left that had been built similarly, a simple two-story house with four windows across the top floor and three on the bottom with the door. "The owner is Amanda Pridgly."

"It's lovely."

"Yes, it is," he agreed. Something in Lucas's tone drew her gaze to him, and she saw that he'd lowered his guard. He was studying her, and not the house, with a look that made her face flush with heat.

"Lucas," she breathed. She leaned toward him with parted lips.

There was a brief awkward moment after he stared at her mouth and then turned abruptly away.

"Let's go," he said. "Your fiancé is waiting for you."

The muscles along his jaw worked as Lucas *clicked* to the horse, and the carriage started to move again. Neither said a word as he reined in the horse before the house and stopped the vehicle.

Her stomach churning with the knowledge that the time had come for him to leave her, Meghan turned to face him. She extended her hand. "Thank ye for everything," she said. She heard the catch in her soft voice, and she fought the urge to cry.

Lucas ignored her hand, hopped out of the carriage, and came around to her side. With a smile, he reached up and assisted her down. Her heart skipped a beat as he set her on her feet. She was aware of his heat, his scent, and the dark intensity of his gaze when their bodies brushed while he lowered her to the ground.

Meghan had only her small bundle of clothes so there was no reason for him to see her to the door, but Lucas insisted.

"I've brought you this far. I'll see you the rest of the way," he stated in a tone that brooked no argument.

Meghan balked. "I don't think it's wise." What would the landlady say to see her with a man other than her fiancé?

Lucas's mouth tightened. "You're right, of course."

She felt a lump of dread clog her throat as she watched Lucas turn abruptly and climb into the carriage.

"Have a good life, Meghan McBride," he said softly.

She nodded, fighting tears, and wished him the same. But as she watched when he started to pull the carriage away, she cried out to stop him. "Lucas! Wait!"

He pulled on the horse's reins, halting the vehicle, and glanced back. Meghan ran to him and offered him her hand. "Can we not part as friends?"

He stared at her hand so intently that she was afraid that he was going to reject her.

Then, he shifted his gaze, and she felt the impact of flaming black eyes. "Friends," he said, mimicking her speech pattern. "Aye."

Her chuckle of amusement sounded strained. "Thank ye," she said with quiet sincerity. "I'm grateful for all you've done."

He gave her a half smile. "It's not gratitude I want from you, Meghan McBride," he said, as he took her fingers and raised them to his lips. His mouth seared the back of her hand, making her tremble, before he released her. "But then you know that."

"Don't." She closed her eyes, fighting to control her emotions. "How am I expected to be happy with Rafferty when ye say such things?" she whispered.

"What?" He tensed. "What did you say?"

She pulled away. "Goodbye, Lucas." She forced a smile.

His gaze flamed as he studied her. "Meghan—" He started to lift his hand and then dropped it again. "If you should ever change your mind . . ."

"I won't," she said, perhaps too quickly.

He didn't move, but stared at her unnervingly. She wanted him to go, yet she wanted him to stay.

"Please don't make this more difficult," she said.

He inclined his head, his expression unreadable again. "Be happy."

She nodded and then turned away. Meghan felt her stomach lurch as she heard the carriage pull away, and realized that never again would she see Lucas Ridgely. But she didn't look back. She knew it would hurt too much to see the carriage—and the man—heading down the road until it disappeared.

She turned toward the house that waited. Her knock brought a maid to the door, who left her alone to wait in the foyer.

The interior of the boardinghouse was pleasant and bright, but Meghan was in no mood to appreciate it. She studied her surroundings, feeling more lost and alone than ever before. She missed Lucas already. How was she going to get over him?

A middle-aged woman came into the hall from a back room and approached.

"I'm Mrs. Pridgly. May I help you?" The landlady was thin and reedlike. Her graying dark hair was pinned back severely, making her features appear austere. She seemed pleasant enough as she inspected Meghan from head to toe, but Meghan had the feeling that her polite manner was forced.

Meghan refused to be intimidated. "I'm looking for Mr. Rafferty O'Connor," she said. "Does he live here?"

She saw a flicker of dislike in Mrs. Pridgly's expression before the woman hid it.

"I'm his fiancée. I'm newly arrived to America."

The landlady's expression seemed to thaw. "Why, you must be Meghan McBride."

"Aye," the young Irishwoman breathed. "Is he here?"

Mrs. Pridgly shook her head. "I'm afraid not."

"But he lives here," Meghan asked, wanting to make certain she hadn't misunderstood.

"Why certainly, dear." The landlady gestured for Meghan to follow her as she climbed the stairs. "Mr. O'Connor has secured a room for you. If you'd like, one of the maids can get your things for you after I've shown you your bedchamber."

Meghan paused and glanced down self-consciously at her meager bundle of belongings. "That won't be necessary," she said.

Mrs. Pridgly had stopped on the steps to wait for Meghan to catch up; and as the younger woman did so, the landlady patted Meghan's arm. "Come then, dear. I imagine it's best to travel lightly. Rafferty can always get what you need later."

The room was on the southwest side of the house. The afternoon sunlight flooded the chamber through two windows and fell across the rose pattern print of the chintz bed cover. Directly inside the door against the wall to the right stood a washstand with a white porcelain ewer and basin. There was an upholstered chair, a dressing table with mirror, and a fair-sized chest of drawers that could hold more clothes than Meghan had ever dreamed of owning.

Rafferty had been right, she thought. America *was* a land of blue skies and vast riches. But would she be happy here? Her heart thumped. Without Lucas?

"Breakfast is at seven, supper at six thirty," Mrs.

Pridgly was saying. "We have dinner between noon and two, a simple meal of warm bread and pastries, and when in season we have fresh garden vegetables and fruit." The woman went to a window and showed Meghan how to close the drapes.

"Milly keeps the rooms dusted and swept, but I'll expect you to pick up your own belongings. I've got little enough help without you expecting any of my girls to be your lady's maid." She barely paused for breath before continuing. "Mr. O'Connor will be home by five-thirty, after the store closes. You, I imagine, will be getting back near enough to the same time."

The woman stopped to stare at her. "Now I know that you and Mr. O'Connor are betrothed, but I'll allow no—" She cleared her throat. "What I'm saying," she said with a businesslike air, "is that I expect you to keep to your room and Mr. O'Connor to keep to his."

Meghan blushed and mumbled her agreement.

"Good." Mrs. Pridgly was suddenly friendly again. "It's wonderful to have you here."

"Meghan, please," Meghan invited.

The landlady's smile grew. "Meghan, I hope your journey wasn't too diffIcult for you and you'll be content here." She frowned. "Your father—he's not with you."

Meghan's throat tightened as she shook her head. "Me father died on the journey."

The woman clucked with concern. "I'm so sorry to hear that." She approached and placed her arm about Meghan's shoulders. "Then you've only Mr. O'Connor now."

Meghan nodded. Mrs. Pridgly released her.

"Well, if there's anything you need," the woman said. "Anything at all, you come to me."

"I don't expect I'll need to bother you."

"Ah, well, good then." Mrs. Pridgly eyed Meghan's length. "Have you eaten?"

"Aye."

"How about a cup of tea then?"

Meghan admitted that she would enjoy a cup of tea.

"You take a moment to freshen up," Mrs. Pridgly said, "while I put the water on the stove to boil."

The door to the company store jingled as it was opened and shut.

"Afternoon, Rafferty."

Rafferty O'Connor glanced up from his accounts and saw the father of one of the workers from the paper mill. "Good day to ye, Henry," he said with a nod. "I'm ready to close the shop. What brings ye in at this hour?"

"I thought you'd be interested to know that our new tenant's arrived at Mrs. Pridgly's." Henry Beaton leaned against the counter and started to touch the merchandise lined up for sale.

"Did ye see them?" Rafferty scowled as he attempted to straighten Henry's handiwork. He looked up in time to see Henry shake his head.

"Talk is it's a gentleman and a lady. They arrived in some fancy carriage, and the woman's got a green cloak."

Rafferty frowned. "That doesn't sound like the McBrides."

The older man shrugged. "Ma'be, ma'be not," he said. "Man left. Woman stayed."

"Did ye see the lass up close?"

Henry shook his head. "As I said, didn't see her at all. George Carn did. He was sitting on Ted Clacks's porch when he saw them drive up."

IRISH LINEN

The Irish storekeeper snorted. "Carn is blind in one eye and can barely see with the other!"

"Ah, I'd say he saw clear enough, all right. Talked with the man hisself. Then 'e went inside to ask about the new lady and guess what Pridgly told 'im?" Henry paused and smiled like he enjoyed baiting Rafferty. "The girl's Irish all right. Newly come on the *Mary Freedom*. Only the man who brought her was too young to be the girl's father."

Twelve

Beth Ridgely burst from the house, squealing with excitement, as her brother alighted from the carriage and gave instructions to a groom about the horse and the conveyance. "Lucas!" she cried. "You're back!"

Lucas turned with outstretched arms in time to catch her in a hug. "Elizabeth, you're a sight for my weary eyes," he said. Leaving Meghan had shaken him. The odd little pain grew at the sight of his sister. Overcome with emotion, he lifted her high and tightened his hold until Beth laughingly cried out for him to let go.

He released her immediately, apologizing as he set her back from him. Brother and sister exchanged grins.

"It's been forever since you left," Beth exclaimed, encircling Lucas's waist with her arm. They walked together toward the front entrance of their aunt's large stately home.

"England is not exactly across the county," Lucas said. He smiled. "Did you miss me?" His sister's eyes were the color of cinnamon that glowed with inner warmth. She hadn't changed much in the two months he'd been gone, Lucas thought, except to grow more lovely in her smiles.

She wrinkled her nose at him. "Did you bring me a present?"

He thought of Meghan's green cloak, that had been

IRISH LINEN

meant for Beth, and felt a pang of loss so deep it shocked him. The garment was much better suited to the slip of an Irishwoman with blue eyes . . .

"It's all right," Beth said, sounding sincere. "I was only teasing."

"I've not come empty-handed," he replied, his expression soft as he met her gaze. Beth looked feminine and grown-up in a house gown of dotted blue fabric. Her hair was bound loosely at her nape, but with curls left to dance near each rosy cheek. She wore a white lace cap upon her shiny tresses, but she loved hats, pretty frilly hats with ribbons and flowers and lace. "I've brought you a book," he said, "and a new bonnet."

"Oh, Lucas." She beamed at her brother with pleasure.

Lucas climbed the steps and opened the door for her. "How's Aunt Flora?"

"She—"

"What's the matter?" a sharp voice called from inside. "Can't an old woman answer for herself?"

Flora Gibbons appeared from the shadows with a stern face. She was a short woman with pure white tresses secured in a chignon. Several tendrils of hair had escaped from their restricted confinement, softening her features. Flora's eyes were dark against her pale coloring, and her skin looked soft and much younger than her sixty-one years of age. Her two-piece gown of lilac and dark lavender-striped silk gave her an air of stately refinement. Pinned near her lace collar was a handsome cameo brooch.

"Still as cranky, I see," Lucas said with affection.

The woman's eyes twinkled as she regarded her nephew with warmth. The corners of her mouth twitched upward. "I'm glad you're back."

Lucas released Beth to embrace his aunt. "I missed

you." The scent of roses clung to Flora's soft cheek as he kissed her.

She sniffed as she stepped back. "I just bet you did. Probably thought of me for the first hour after you left anyway."

He laughed. "Well, that's not true, and you know it. It was your business as well my own that I was handling in London."

"All went well? You found the equipment?"

Lucas nodded. "I think you'll be pleased."

Aunt Flora started to question her nephew further when Beth stopped her. "Later, you two. There'll be time enough for business after Lucas has rested and we've visited for a while."

"When did the ship dock?"

"A few hours ago," he lied, not wanting to explain where he'd been.

"Why, you must be exhausted!" Aunt Flora said.

"I sailed across the ocean," Lucas teased. "I didn't swim it."

"Never you mind," the old woman replied. "I'll see that supper is ready after you've changed."

Lucas glanced down at himself with wry humor. "Change into what?"

Beth giggled when Aunt Flora slapped Lucas's shoulder. "Get moving, boy."

"Yes, Auntie Flora." He exchanged amused glances with his sister.

The house smelled faintly of oil of turpentine, an ingredient in several of his aunt's favorite receipts for household polishes. The essence mingled with a floral fragrance that emanated from a bowl of dried blooms on a nearby table. The appearance and scents of his aunt's house welcomed him home with a feeling of comfort and familiarity.

Lucas started up the steps and paused. Glancing

back, he smiled. As usual, the walls had been scrubbed to maintain their original bright white, and the tile floor in the foyer shone with a shiny radiance that would make any mistress proud. "I see, Aunt Flora, that you've been keeping your servants busy."

"Damn right!" the old woman retorted. "Isn't that what I pay them for?"

Beth chuckled at the byplay between nephew and aunt. "It's good to have you home again, Lucas," she said.

His features softened. "It's good to be back," he said with the realization that he meant it. He was glad to be home in Delaware again.

And as the image of a red-haired woman with eyes of glistening blue invaded his thoughts, he wondered what she was doing. His jaw tightened. He couldn't help being curious about Meghan's reunion with her fiancé. Was she happy? Had the meeting gone as well as she'd hoped?

Meghan was dozing in bed when a knock woke her. Her first thought was of Lucas. Fortunately, the man spoke before she called Lucas's name.

"Meghan," a deep familiar voice called. "Meghan, me girl, are ye in there?"

"Rafferty!" she breathed. "Oh, aye, Mr. O'Connor," she replied more loudly. She climbed from the bed and hurried to throw open the door.

"Rafferty!" she cried. At her first glance, she thought he looked older, but yet the same. She grinned upon seeing his crooked smile and launched herself into his arms. "Dear God, it's ye. I've wanted so much to see ya."

His thick arms surrounded her without hesitation in

a bearlike hug. "Ah, Meggie, I've waited forever for ya. Ye and yer father."

At the mention of her father, Meghan pushed back from his arms. She saw Rafferty's gaze scan the room.

"Where is he? Where is Dermot?"

Meghan swallowed against a lump. "Da's dead." She touched his arm. "He died coming across the sea."

Rafferty's face whitened. "God in heaven have mercy," he said. "Dear Lord, Meghan, ye came alone."

She nodded and was unable to blink away the tears that blinded her. "Raff, I miss him." She turned away to rub her eyes and moved toward the bed. She spun back to face him, choking with emotion. "What are we to do?" she said hoarsely.

Rafferty's grief became anger. "Damn 'em!" he exclaimed. He closed his eyes as he fought tears. "Oh, me friend," he whispered, "why did we wait so long?"

Meghan understood his anguish. She approached and put her arms around him. "Don't ye be blaming yerself."

" 'Tis not meself I'm a-blaming!" he roared, throwing off her arms. She gasped. " 'Tis the bloody *Sasanaigh!*"

She jumped back as if stung. She'd known he'd be angry, but the hatred within him frightened her. He was in America now; shouldn't he have risen above the depths of this animosity? There were no more Saxons to hurt him. His life was better now. Hatred could eat away at a person, she thought, if one allowed oneself to become obsessed.

"But, Rafferty, we're free of the English," Meghan reminded him.

Rafferty breathed deeply several times before he seemed to get himself under control. "Aye, Meggie. We're free of them . . . at last." He gave her a half smile.

Relieved, she said, "I've missed ya."

His smile grew as he gazed at her with affection. "I've missed ya, too." He grabbed her hands and stepped back, holding out her arms as he inspected the changes in her. "Ye look well, Meghan, all grown-up."

She nodded. "I'm as healthy as a horse." She felt a lump form in her throat as she studied her old friend. It was so good to see him. His hair had a tad more gray in it, and there were a few added lines in his freckled face, but otherwise he appeared unchanged.

"There were times I wondered if I'd ever see ya again."

"Aye," he breathed, drawing her into his arms.

She felt warm and safe as he wrapped her within his solid embrace. "Thank ya, Rafferty O'Connor. Thank ya and the good Lord for bringing me to America."

He gave her a squeeze and then released her, blinking back tears. "So," he said, "how do ye like your new home?"

Meghan glanced about, feeling pleased. " 'Tis a lovely bedchamber."

"We'll have a cottage of our own when we marry."

She looked down at her feet. "And when will that be?" Her heart began to thud as she thought of Lucas and realized that she'd never again know his touch.

"Yer father just died . . . and he was me best friend," he said, and she experienced relief as she met his gaze. "After a time, when we've had a chance to grieve."

"Oh, Rafferty," she said, unable to control the rush of tears. For all her promise to Da, it seemed that she was always fighting the urge to cry. "You're a kind and generous man." *And I don't deserve to marry ya.* Unbidden came thoughts of Lucas.

"We've a lifetime before us, Meghan McBride," her fiancé said evenly. "I can afford to be generous."

She noticed that his grin didn't quite reach his eyes. Had he guessed she had second thoughts?

"Aye, Mr. O'Connor," she murmured. "Marriage is for a lifetime."

And she knew she should have been pleased by Rafferty's patience and understanding, but she wasn't, for the words *marriage* and *lifetime* were ringing ominously in her brain.

Meghan was uneasy. Rafferty had changed in a way that wasn't physical, and she didn't know how to deal with him anymore. For four days now, she'd seen little of her fiancé. He rose at dawn to go to the company store and returned barely in time to eat supper. He was polite and outwardly attentive whenever she saw him; yet, there was something odd about his smile . . . and a look in his eyes that greatly disturbed her. But as long as his work kept him away for hours on end, she realized, there'd be little or no time to ease her fears or to discuss what might be bothering him.

She stood at the window of her room and gazed into the yard. She felt restless, dissatisfied, in her new homeland. Except for the journey on board ship, she had little experience at being idle, and she wanted—needed—to do something. Even on the *Mary Freedom*, she'd found plenty of things to occupy her time.

During her first two days in Delaware, she'd rested and regained her land legs, but the days since then had been too uneventful and allowed her too much time to think . . . and remember Lucas Ridgely.

Yesterday she'd found herself searching for Mrs. Pridgly in the hope that the woman could offer her something useful to do in the house. Mrs. Pridgly had been horrified; she'd allow no paying guest to do servants' work. Knowing that it was pointless to argue,

Meghan had gone outside to wander about the yard and garden, until she decided to shop at the store and visit Rafferty. Last evening Rafferty had brought home two serviceable, storebought garments for her, one made of printed cotton and the other of dyed muslin. She'd never expected him to buy her ready-made clothes. She was skilled with a needle. If she had some fine fabric, she could have sewn a nice gown.

As it was, the gowns Rafferty had purchased didn't fit her right, but Meghan didn't have the heart to tell him. It had been a long time since she'd seen the sparkle of pleasure in Rafferty's green eyes, like the one he'd had when he'd given her the new gowns. She'd thanked him with a hug and then carefully hung her two new dresses on a wall hook in her room.

If I can get hold of some thread, she thought, *I can alter the garments.* Delighted with the idea, Meghan went back into the house and upstairs to gauge how much thread she'd need.

When the maid, Milly, summoned her to lunch, Meghan ran down the steps, feeling lighthearted.

There were four other paying guests besides Rafferty and herself boarding in the home of Widow Pridgly. And all but Rafferty, who was at work, and Paul Whitehall, who was ill, were seated at the table eating their midday meal when Meghan entered the room and sat.

"Good day to ya, Mrs. Pridgly," she greeted. "It's a fine day, isn't it, gentlemen?" she said to the others.

"You almost missed dinner," the widow said.

"I apologize, Mrs. Pridgly," Meghan replied. "I wasn't feeling well this morning and slept in."

The woman's face softened. "Next time I'd appreciate it if you'd send word down with Milly. You're feeling better now?"

"Aye." Meghan smiled. "And I'm a-starving for your cooking." Pleased with her plans, she was anxious to share her excitement with the others and learn the whereabouts of the store.

Mrs. Pridgly beamed. "Well, that's fine then. Henry," she said, addressing an elderly gentleman to her right, "pass Miss McBride the stew."

"Don't burn yer tongue, young woman," Henry warned with a scowl.

Meghan smiled her thanks as she accepted the bowl from the man's gnarled, shaking hands. She had met Henry Beaton at breakfast the morning after her arrival. He was an endearing old man for all his gruffness, so were the other gentlemen in the house—George Carn and Paul Whitehall. Mrs. Pridgly also leased a room to the new community school mistress, Miss Thomas.

The anticipation of seeing the store and buying thread finally prompted her to ask about the store. "Can ye tell me where the store is?" Meghan blurted out, during a lull in the conversation about the coming change of seasons.

The silence that followed her query gave her the uncomfortable feeling that she'd said something wrong. The notion was reinforced when she saw Henry Beaton and George Carn exchange looks.

"Did I say something wrong?" Meghan said when no one answered her last question.

"No, dear," Mrs. Pridgly quickly assured her. "May I ask you if you plan to visit Rafferty?"

Meghan frowned. "Aye," she said. Of course, she wanted to see Rafferty. He was her friend and her betrothed. Why wouldn't she want to go? "Well, I'd hoped to see him there, but—"

"That wouldn't be wise, young woman," Henry piped up, and George Carn mumbled his agreement.

"I don't understand," Meghan said. She only wanted to purchase some thread, for God's sake.

"Mr. Somerton doesn't like Rafferty to be bothered with visitors during work hours."

Suddenly, Meghan understood. "I wouldn't bother him. I need to purchase some . . . items." She wasn't going to tell them that she needed thread to remake the gowns Rafferty had bought her.

"Ask Rafferty to bring whatever you need home for you," Mrs. Pridgly suggested. "You don't know the Somertons. It'd be better if you spoke with Rafferty first before you visited him."

Something underlying the woman's manner made Meghan uneasy. "I wouldn't be wanting to make trouble for him."

Mrs. Pridgly seemed relieved. "That would be best, dear."

Later that evening, Meghan sat on a wooden bench in the garden and eyed the rows of newly turned earth where Henry had planted flower bulbs for next spring. *So much for having something to work on,* she thought with dismay.

The sun had disappeared on the horizon, but a saffron glow remained to light up the night sky. Gazing at the expanse of ground yet to be tended, Meghan wondered if Mrs. Pridgly would allow her to plant her own small area in the garden.

And then she remembered that the garden was Henry Beaton's domain. How could she take away the one thing that possibly made the old man feel useful?

She thought of her life back in Ireland, when she had toiled from dawn to dusk in the house and vegetable garden. She'd not known what it was to have time for leisure. Now she had so much leisure time she didn't know what to do with it!

"Oh, Da," she whispered. "I wish ye were here. You'd know what to do." She smiled through tears as she pictured her father getting the better of Mrs. Pridgly.

"Meghan?" Greeting her with a smile, Rafferty watched her from a short distance away. "All alone with only the flowers for company?"

Her own smile held sadness. "I was thinking about Da."

Pain flashed in Rafferty's expression, and Meghan moved over on the bench, feeling an instant kinship with him. She patted the seat beside her, and he moved closer and sat. Here was her father's best friend, she thought, the man she was to marry. She'd left Ireland on the other side of the sea, but she still carried her memories with her. And Rafferty O'Connor was Ireland and a part of her father, together in one solid form.

She reached for his hand. "I miss him," she said.

"Aye," Rafferty whispered, his Irish brogue thick with shared pain. "The bugger could always make me laugh when I became too serious. Yer father would say to me, 'O'Connor! Ye must stop and take a good, laughing look at yerself! Do ye want the bloody Sax'ns to get the better of ya? Laugh first and laugh hard, and ye'll beat the cruel bastards at their own game.' "

"Aye," Meghan said softly, "I remember." She smiled. "He always did think ye were too solemn for your own good."

He shifted his hands so that his large fingers engulfed hers. "Meghan, there's something I have to tell ya," he began hesitantly.

"Aye, Rafferty, what is it?" she asked. Was he finally going to confess what bothered him, what had changed him?

Rafferty gave her hand a squeeze before he let go and stood. "I've got employment for ya, Meghan." He took several steps and faced her.

"What?" It was the last thing she'd expected to hear.

"Aye," he said. "I've found ya work. You'll be working for Mrs. Somerton. Ye should have no trouble at all, for the lady is kind and generous. A girl could do worse than to work in the Big House. Some might even say it's a plum job."

"Employment?" she breathed, startled but not displeased. "What have I been hired to do?"

"You're to be Mrs. Somerton's personal lady's maid," Rafferty said with apparent pride in what he'd accomplished for his betrothed. "And ye are to start your position tomorra morning at first light."

Thirteen

The Somerton residence was a breathtaking sight to Meghan. Lush lawns surrounded the spacious three-story home. A large porch flanked the lower level of the newly renovated structure; additions had been built onto the sides and the rear of the house in no particular plan or symmetry. Constructed of stone smoothed over with a coat of white-washed mortar, the Big House had dark green shutters on the upper levels and white shutters on the porch-level windows.

Ordinarily, Meghan would have been content working in such magnificent and impressive surroundings, but then she hadn't taken into account the nature of her employer.

Rafferty had told her that she was to be Mrs. Somerton's personal maid, but that had changed when the woman, after one long hard look at Meghan, had apparently found her new servant wanting.

"Can you do anything useful?" Alicia Somerton had inquired in a sneering tone within seconds of their meeting.

"I can sew. My stitches are neat and even."

"Really?" Alicia's eyes had lit up with interest. "If I put you to altering a gown for me, can you do it?" Her tone suggested that she had little faith in Meghan's abilities as a seamstress. She had regarded Meghan's restitched but simple clothing with disdain.

"Aye, I can do it," Meghan had answered pleasantly enough. "Me mother turned a fine stitch and she taught me well." She wasn't going to judge the lady by their first meeting alone, she'd decided. It was possible the weight of the woman's duties had put a strain on her good humor.

But after two full weeks in the Somerton household, Meghan decided that her first impression of Alicia Somerton had been the correct one. Mrs. Somerton was a beautiful, but mean-spirited woman with nothing better to do than create havoc in her servants' lives. And Meghan had tolerated just about all she could stand from her.

Meghan did her work in different areas of the house, whatever room that had struck Alicia's fancy on any given day. Several times Meghan had to bite her tongue when she'd been forced to move to a different floor and drag all her work tools with her. One day Meghan had to transfer the sewing box and three full-skirted fancy gowns which needed repairs from the third floor, where she'd been sewing the day before, to the morning room on the first floor. The arrival of visitors a short time later had made it necessary for Meghan to move everything back upstairs again. When she'd learned that the visitors had been expected, Meghan had been livid, but had hidden her feelings well. A glance at Alicia Somerton's malicious expression had confirmed what Meghan had suspected: the woman had been playing her nasty games again.

She was in Mrs. Somerton's sitting room, altering a gown that looked entirely too young for the woman. Mrs. Somerton had insisted on wearing the garish garment for a neighbor's dinner party that was fast approaching, and Meghan was certainly not the one to tell her that altered or not the frilly-laced pink gown with ribbons and roses would look ridiculous on a woman of her increasing age. Alicia Somerton, Meghan guessed, was thirty-nine, and sensitive about the issue. Meghan smiled as she tacked on a piece of loose lace. Perhaps she should hint about the youthful appearance of the dress . . .

A loud crack from the other room had Meghan setting aside her work, as she recognized the sound. Mrs. Somerton had hit one of the chambermaids again. Bristling, Meghan hurried from the sitting room to the nursery where Lynna had been collecting bed linens, and she paused at the threshold to observe.

As expected, the young maid stood before her employer, her face red, valiantly holding back tears.

"I told you to leave the boy's bed, Lynna!" Mrs. Somerton scolded sharply. "If the boy can't use the chamberpot, soiling his bed instead, then he can lie in it!"

Lynna hung her head as she clutched the wet sheets to her chest. When her gaze fell on the little boy who sat facing the corner, Meghan was barely able to control her temper. Fingers clenched into fists, she advanced into the room.

"Is there something I can help ye with, Mrs. Somerton?" she said, her voice deceptively soft.

The blond woman spun and stared at her. "Oh, it's you, Meghan." She gave her a cursory look. "No," she said, "you're not needed here."

"Are ye sure, Mrs. Somerton?"

"Have ye finished with my gown?" she asked, sounding annoyed.

"No, Mrs. Somerton," Meghan said.

"Then I suggest you get back to work!"

But Meghan didn't move. She was tired of the way the woman treated her staff of servants, slapping and scolding them for some minor or trumped-up infrac-

IRISH LINEN

tion. And she was most incensed by the way Alicia treated her own son.

Believing Meghan had gone, Alicia had promptly gone back to berating Lynna. Angered beyond caution, Meghan stepped forward and intervened.

"Mrs. Somerton, the girl was only trying to protect your son," Meghan said. The woman stiffened before slowly turning around. "Children are easily hurt."

Alicia's face registered shock and then rage at Meghan's boldness. Her mouth worked as if she were trying to speak, but was unable.

Unconcerned of the consequences, Meghan gestured for Lynna to leave the room and then gave her employer a sweet smile.

"How dare you!" Alicia sputtered. "You insolent, filthy Irish lowlife! I want you out of my house. Do you hear me? *Out of my house now!*"

"It will be my pleasure to leave." Meghan executed a respective curtsy that made her former employer's teeth snap with anger. "Good day to ya, Alicia."

"I know I shouldn't have hired you!" the woman shrieked. "But you were Rafferty's betrothed, so I gave you a chance!"

Meghan left the room without answering, passing Lynna as the maid hurried in to comfort her employer. "Lynna, no!" she called, trying to stop her.

To her dismay, the maid stopped but only to glare at her. "Now you've gone and made matters worse, Meghan McBride," the girl said. "You'll waltz out of here as uncaring as you can be, while the rest of us have to stay to endure what you've left behind!"

"But I was only trying to help—"

"We were all doing fine without your help," Lynna hissed. The maid then hurried into the nursery to comfort her employer and no doubt protect a young boy from his mother's anger. As she descended the stairs, Meghan could hear Alicia Somerton's continuing tirade against her.

"My God!" Alicia was shouting. "What on earth can he see in her! Why, she's an ingrate! She'll be sorry she left here, but it's no more than she deserves!"

"Now what will you do?" The housekeeper, Mrs. Wilt, stood in the foyer and studied Meghan with pursed lips as the young Irishwoman came down the stairs. "Where will you work?"

Meghan's heart skipped a beat as she realized the consequences of what she'd done. "I don't know," she confessed softly.

Alicia's shrill voice could be heard at the top of the stairs.

"You'd best leave now, girl, before the Mrs. sees you," Mrs. Wilt said. "You wouldn't want your fiancé to be fired, too."

Meghan was horrified. "She'd do that?"

Mrs. Wilt gave her a look that mocked Meghan's ignorance.

"Curse it, girl!" Alicia Somerton could be heard scolding another servant. "I told you not to sweep that way. You've missed a spot!"

"How do you stand to work for that woman?" Meghan asked the housekeeper as she headed toward the door.

"I've my family to feed and clothe. I haven't a choice," Mrs. Wilt said.

And Meghan wondered if she wouldn't regret her own choice.

"How could you do it, Meghan?" Rafferty exclaimed. " 'Twas a perfectly good position of employment, and ye've lost it! What in heavens possessed ya to anger the woman!"

IRISH LINEN

Meghan was taken aback by Rafferty's reaction. She'd never seen him so angry before . . . except with the *Sasanaigh*. "She's cruel, Rafferty. She's mean to the servants and to her own child. I couldn't stand by and watch it happen one more time. I couldn't!"

"Ye're not in Ireland now, Meghan. Ye're in America, and ye must learn to be silent even when ever'thing inside ye says otherwise."

"She was humiliating her son!"

Rafferty shook his head. "Ye've a heart of gold, but ye cannot take on all the troubles of the wee ones."

"I can't simply stand by and watch, Rafferty."

"Ye must learn to!" he bellowed, startling her.

"Rafferty," she exclaimed, "I'll not take your shouting at me!"

Something flickered across his face before he schooled his features into an expression of apology. "Forgive me, Meggie," he said softly. "But can ye understand me concern?"

"Aye," she whispered.

"I don't like the notion, but ye'll have to work at the textile mill downriver. It's the only other employment within miles that isn't hired by the Somertons."

Textiles? she thought. "Cloth?" she said aloud, and Rafferty nodded.

"Cotton," he said. "Let's hope that ye'll be hired by the Gibbons Mill. The only other employment within miles, Meghan, is the black powder mills upriver."

Meghan felt a rush of excitement. She knew about the making of cloth. It was a craft taught to her by her dear, departed mother. "Is it far? How will I get there?"

Rafferty sighed. "If ye get the job, I'll try to arrange transportation for ya." He touched her cheek. "Meg, I'm only thinking of yer welfare."

"I know," she said with affection. "Thank ye, Mr.

O'Connor." She regarded her late father's best friend and felt a wealth of liking for him. Rafferty was solid and stable, she reminded herself. She could always count on Rafferty.

"Meghan." His voice suddenly became intense as he slipped his hand to her shoulder. "Soon, ye'll be me wife. It'll be me job to take care of ya. Ye and I have been friends for years. Ye trust that I know what is best for ya, don't ya?"

As Meghan nodded, her heart thumped with alarm. She didn't want to think about marriage yet. She needed to adjust to America. She needed the time to mourn. "Aye, Rafferty, I trust ye. But ye must know that this life is all new to me . . . the land . . . the people." *I'm not ready to marry!*

An image of Lucas Ridgely came to mind, and she fought the way her senses swam whenever she thought about him. She had been doing well, managing to put Lucas from her mind for long periods now. But he was back in her thoughts . . . and in her heart. What was she going to do?

She should marry Rafferty and forget the man who had rescued and kissed her. Rafferty was dependable and would make her a good husband, while Lucas . . . Lucas's intentions were not honorable. He didn't want a wife. Why was she foolishly longing for something that could never be?

"I need time before we marry," she found herself saying.

"I know ye do, Meghan," Rafferty said, sounding annoyed. "I've waited two years for ya to come, working and saving to bring yer dear father and ya across the sea."

She blinked back moisture. "I'm sorry."

"I don't say it to make ye feel bad, Meggie. I wanted ye to know that I, too, miss yer father. Not a minute goes by that I don't think about me best friend," he said. "Is it so wrong to want to love and protect his daughter?"

Meghan shook her head.

"I've waited this long for ya; I can wait a while longer." Rafferty gave her a slight smile. "But not too long, Meggie. Yer father would approve, ye know that."

Would he? she wondered. Thinking back, she recalled the time the betrothal arrangement was made. Rafferty had been grinning when Meghan had come into the cottage at her father's summons, but Dermot McBride had looked . . . composed.

"A few months to get used to me new life is all I need." But would a few months really make a difference? she wondered. "There's me new employment to consider," she told Rafferty.

His eyes narrowed as he tried to read her thoughts. "Something's bothering ya. What are ye not telling me?"

"Nothing," she said. "I'm telling ye what I feel." She inhaled sharply before releasing her breath. "Raff, what are a few months in a lifetime?"

Rafferty's mouth curved crookedly. "I said I would wait. You're important to me, Meg. Ye must forgive a man for getting anxious to have his bride. Ye can have a few months, for I'll have ya for a lifetime."

Lifetime, she thought. Why couldn't she envision a lifetime with Rafferty?

Fourteen

The village surrounding the Gibbons Mill was much like Somerville, but the buildings and grounds seemed more friendly to Meghan. It was late November, and Meghan felt the bitter cold as she left her residence for the millwork. Small cottages and other workmen's homes built to share exterior side walls had been constructed along a road paralleling the creek, not far from the mill buildings which housed the machinery. A covered wooden bridge spanned the waterway, allowing the workers easy access to both sides.

Meghan steeled herself against a gust of wind as she headed toward the five-story mill building. She'd procured her employment two days past while Rafferty had waited outside for her in a borrowed carriage. She'd been interviewed by the mill foreman, Mr. Simmons, who was pleasant as he outlined the position and its wages.

There were over one hundred seventy-five people employed at the mill, more than half of them women. Many of the workers lived on the property, boarding at the homes of widows or workers' families. Meghan's new home was a room in a house run by Patricia Rhoades. Patty, as Meghan was told to call her, was a widow with three male children, all over the age of thirteen. Two of Patty's sons worked at the mill in the carding room, while the youngest helped the groom in the stables. Meghan had met the Rhoades boys, who apparently resembled their late father with their red hair and brown eyes.

Today would be Meghan's second day in the village and her first day on the job. She hurried to the office to meet the overseer in charge of the weaving room. Familiar with the basic hand loom, which she'd learned from her mother, Meghan was to start by helping the weavers.

Each floor of the mill building housed a different phase of cotton cloth production. From the bottom level where the picked cotton was sorted and prepared to the uppermost floor where the finished cloth was stored and bagged until it could be transported to the dye house.

Meghan was put in the capable hands of Mari Bright, a friendly young woman, whose smile and disposition matched her surname. The looms on the fourth floor were enormous, much larger than any Meghan had ever seen. At first, she was put to work tying knots and keeping the weavers supplied with thread from the third floor. When a worker had trouble with a broken thread on her loom, it was Meghan who rushed in to help, performing the task without being instructed.

Meghan liked the work, but not the overseer, Mr. Phelps. There was something about the man that bothered her. Perhaps it was the way some of the other girls cowered whenever he was within distance. Whatever the reason, Meghan didn't like him.

Her first personal contact with him came at the end of her second day when he approached her, offering her her own loom. It was a position that many workers in the spinning and dressing rooms coveted, a job with more pay.

That night, Meghan accepted the position and then returned to Patty's boardinghouse, excited with the prospect of higher wages. When she told her new friends about Mr. Phelps's new job offer, they didn't share her enthusiasm, and Meghan's excitement waned.

"What's wrong with taking the position?" she asked them at the dinner table. "I thought it was a good one."

Betsy, her roommate, exchanged glances with Susan Morgan, another boarder, before replying. "It is a good job, Meg," she said. "It's just Mr. Phelps . . ."

"What about him?" Meghan saw the people at the table glance briefly toward Priscilla, Susan's roommate. Priscilla's face appeared more pale than usual, but she otherwise looked composed. Betsy, staring at the girl, seemed unwilling to finish her statement. "I don't understand," Meghan said. "Tell me."

Susan smiled at Meghan. "It is a good position, Meghan, and I'm sure you'll do well."

"Just be careful," Betsy warned.

"Careful? Oh, with the machine," Meghan said with sudden understanding. "I've experience with a loom. I'm sure I'll manage."

"I'm sure you will, dear," Patty said firmly. "You're a capable young woman. I'm sure you can manage anything."

Then, suddenly, the tone of conversation changed, as everyone picked up and shared Meghan's excitement. Meghan retired for bed that night, feeling as if she'd done the right thing in taking the new job.

The next day Meghan began her new position as a weaver. The work was hard, but she didn't mind, although she had to remain at her station all day. A worker in the spinning or dressing room was allowed to leave her station for an hour or more to escape the fabric dust and humidity for fresh air. Some simply

IRISH LINEN

went outside the building, but many used the opportunity to perform personal tasks at home.

Meghan enjoyed working on her prettily painted machine in the wide, high-ceiling weaving room with its bright white walls. Her loom was near a window, which allowed in the afternoon sunlight. The air on the floor was cleaner, free from the heavy cotton dust generated from spinning or dressing the thread.

That night, after a hearty meal shared with Patty, the woman's sons, and Patty's other boarders, Meghan went up to her attic room, changed into her nightgown, and flung herself onto her bed. She stared at the ceiling beam and thought about her day as a weaver with satisfaction. A short while later her roommate, Betsy Long, came in to bed, and the two women talked about the mill, their fellow employees, and Meghan's impression of her new job. Soon, they fell silent, and Meghan drifted to sleep. The next thing she knew it was five in the morning, and she hurriedly dressed for breakfast before beginning her third day at the mill.

When the bell rang, signaling the end of Saturday and the work week, Meghan stopped her machine and tidied up her work area. The sun had set in the night sky, and the weaving room was lit by a series of oil lamps suspended from the high ceiling, away from the danger of igniting the cotton cloth.

As she reached for her cloak, Meghan heard the other girls in the weaving room chatting happily about their next day off.

After five days of employment, Meghan was tired. Her muscles ached in places that until now she'd been unfamiliar with; her feet were sore and slightly swollen from standing for long stretches at her loom. But she felt good about her position and the wages she'd earned. Although she wouldn't receive her pay until later in the month, she felt rich. It was a heady sensation to have money and know that you wouldn't be left out in the cold to starve. If she became efficient enough to manage not one but two weaving looms, Meghan knew the money would be well worth the hard hours of concentrated work.

"Meghan."

She turned to find the overseer near her loom, inspecting her day's production. "Mr. Phelps," she said, approaching him with a smile. "Thank ye for me new pos—"

Her words died as the man turned from her machine. "Would you come into my office please?"

A feeling of dread settled within her breast as she nodded and followed the overseer into a small office at one end of the weaving floor. Had she done something wrong?

Mr. Phelps closed the door, blocking out the conversation of the weavers as they shut down their machines for the day.

"Is there a problem?" she asked.

He turned from the door and smiled. "On the contrary, young woman, you've done an excellent job during your first week here."

"Thank ye," she said politely. She didn't care for the intense way he studied her.

"You like your lodging?" he asked.

"Aye, Patty is a fine woman. I've no complaints. Betsy Long and I get along well enough in the same room."

"Good." Mr. Phelps looked pleased. "After a week or so, would you consider taking another machine?"

Meghan couldn't control a rush of pleasure. Who would have thought she'd be grateful for more work? "Aye," she said, "if you think I can handle it."

"I know you can handle it, Meghan," he said with a grin that made her uncomfortable. He approached her and laid a hand on her shoulder. "I'm glad you enjoy your position here, Meghan," he purred as he turned her and trailed his fingers down her arm.

She stood in shock that he touched her. "Mr. Phelps—"

"Mathew," he invited.

She bristled. "*Mr.* Phelps," she said, "I would appreciate it if you would unhand me."

Surprise flickered in his gaze, before he regarded her with anger. "You had better not speak to me in that tone, woman." He didn't remove his hand; he shifted it to rest on her hip.

"I said let go of me!" she hissed, twisting to break free of his grasp. "You've no right to touch me!"

His mouth tightened as he stared at her. "You forget yourself, Meghan McBride. You are my employee. It is by my word and my word alone that you have—*and keep*—your job."

Meghan shivered as she kept her distance. "You're threatening to release me?"

He stared at her hard. "Have I said that?" He skirted his desk and sat, leaning back in his chair. "A word of advice, *Irish*woman—I don't know how things are in your country, but here in America it's always wise to be friendly to your employer." He smiled slowly as he raked her with an insolent gaze. "Without me, where do you think you'd be?"

Meghan was silent as distress warred with fury. She wanted to hit the smile right off Phelps's smug face, but he was right. She needed this job. Rafferty was upset when she'd lost her last position. The only other employment, he'd said, was the black powder mill downriver. It was a dangerous job, one she was unfamiliar with. She liked working at Gibbons Mill, and she liked the people. *All but Phelps.* And the overseer hadn't actually done anything to her, had he . . . ?

"I apologize if I misunderstood," she said. It was the closest thing to an apology he'd get. She didn't think she misunderstood him, so in her mind, she wasn't apologizing.

He rose from his chair with a smile that appeared more genuine. "I understand that you're new here. If I've offended you," he said, much to her surprise, "then I'm sorry."

She was thinking about the incident and Phelps's startling apology as she left his office and started for home. The man had said he was sorry! Had she misread his look and intentions?

He'd stared at her breasts! she realized. Anger lent a new snap to her steps. No, she hadn't misread his intentions, nor did she believe that his apology was genuine. But position or no position, she wouldn't stand for such behavior from the man again.

"Hold on, Meghan!" Susan Morgan called as the young Irishwoman left the building and headed toward Patty's. "Why are you hurrying?"

Meghan opened her mouth to tell her the truth, but then decided not to make an issue of it. After all, there had been no harm done. And she needed the job and the pay. "I'm hungry," she improvised as she slowed her steps and waited for Susan to catch up.

"Me, too," the girl said. "I wonder what Patty's cooking." She didn't wait for Meghan's answer, but asked, "So how do you like your work as a weaver?"

A stiff breeze swirled about the yard, taking Meghan's breath away, making her answer slow in coming. Meghan held the edges of her hood tight to her chin. "I thought it'd be terrible adjusting, but it wasn't," she said loudly to be heard above the wind.

At eighteen years of age, Susan had a face with the ripe fullness of a farm girl, who had benefited from the fresh air, hard work, and good food. She leaned in close to Meghan. "Catherine Brown was put out when you got a loom," she said. "But then Catherine is annoyed by everything that doesn't benefit Catherine."

"Catherine?" Meghan couldn't place the face.

Susan shivered as she clutched her coat. "She works in the spinning room. Has her heart set on weaving, but Phelps won't use her." She huddled closer to Meghan so that she could lower her voice. "Catherine's all thumbs when it comes to weaving," she said conspiratorially. "She barely gets by with spinning. She started as a doffer and hardly managed to do that!"

Meghan smiled at the mental image of Susan's words. A doffer's job was to change spools in the spinning room, replacing full ones with empty ones as the thread was spun and collected from the machines.

"I haven't met Catherine," Meghan said.

"You'll get to know all of us in time," Susan replied. "I work in the dressing room, and you know me!" She laughed as if she'd told a joke. "Of course, you and I, in a sense, live together."

Meghan nodded and increased her pace when she spied Patty's house ahead. Susan easily kept in step with her.

"You'll be going to church service with us tomorrow morning?" Susan asked as they reached Patty's steps.

Meghan shook her head. "Me fiancé is coming for me this night. I'll be going to church with him, I suppose. It's the only day we have to spend together."

"Oh, you poor dear, how awful for you to be separated from him," Susan commiserated. "You must miss him terribly."

Meghan mumbled an appropriate response. Actually, she hadn't given Rafferty much thought this past week. She'd been too busy working and adjusting to life at the mill. She felt a prickling of guilt as lately she'd been thinking of Lucas again. Too much, she knew, for someone betrothed to another man.

Then, her thoughts returned to her experience with Phelps, and she felt a shiver of revulsion. What would she do if he touched her again? Should she mention it to her friends? To Rafferty? No, she thought, not unless it happens again.

A week later, Meghan felt quite comfortable with her new life. Bad weather this last Sunday had kept Rafferty from coming to take her to Somerville, but she didn't mind. She enjoyed the company at Patty's much more than Rafferty's of late. Raff seemed irritable whenever she spent the day with him. She preferred the easy, laughing camaraderie of the women boarders over her fiancé's long periods of angry silence.

After a month at the job, Meghan was in charge of three looms. The hours were long and there were times when Meghan wished for a free day to lie in and read, but she was grateful for the work, the money, and her new friends. Mr. Phelps had kept his distance, and relieved, Meghan had begun to wonder if she had, in fact, misread the man's behavior toward her.

Susan had been helping her, during the evenings, to improve her reading and writing skills. The young woman had been fortunate enough to have attended a country school near her parents' farm with classes taught by the local Methodist minister's wife.

Today was the day before Christmas. Everyone at the textile mill was excited about the holiday. Patty Rhoades had been baking for three days in preparation for the special two days of feasting. Patty's son James had gone off into the forest last evening for holly and evergreens for the great room and second-story parlor. When Meghan had risen early this morning and gone downstairs, she'd noticed the house was filled with the fresh scent of pine.

IRISH LINEN

Meghan had saved a portion of her first weeks' wages for gifts for everyone at Patty's along with a special present for Rafferty. She wanted to repay her betrothed for his kindness in bringing her to America, but knew there was no way she could repay him for all he'd done.

As she set out to work at 6:00 A.M., Meghan recalled her last visit to Somerville and the increasing feeling she'd had that something was bothering Rafferty. When she'd tried to talk with him, he'd been uncommunicative, even angry at her attempts to question him, until she'd threatened to stay home the following weekend if he didn't shake out of his worrisome mood. Rafferty had put himself out to be charming and cheerful after that, and Meghan was able to enjoy his company for the remainder of her stay. But the memory of his earlier behavior still bothered her.

Meghan was the first in the weaving room, but not the mill, when she arrived to start the day. On her way to her station, she'd spoken briefly to those she'd come to know and smiled a hello to those she hadn't met. The weaving room was on the fourth floor of the factory. All three of her looms stood, side by side, near the window on the building's south side. The day had hardly begun, but there was enough light to see without the oil lamps.

She went quickly to work, for she had set a goal for herself, and she wanted to finish it by the end of the day.

While she'd rather have spent the holiday at Patty's, she'd be spending it with Rafferty. Her intended would be coming before supper to take her back to Somerville and the cold, now unfriendly atmosphere of her former home. Now that she worked and lived near the Gibbons textile mill, Meghan had to share a room at Mrs. Pridgly's with the woman who had taken up residency in her place. Miss Doddleberry snored, often keeping Meghan up well into the early morning hours of the next day. And the woman was messy with her belongings, dropping her clothing on the bedchamber floor, wherever she had happened to undress. Meghan missed Betsy, her quiet, neat, and warmly considerate roommate at Patty's, whenever she was in Somerville visiting.

That morning, Meghan was the first to start up her power loom, and soon the floor hummed with the noise of operating machinery. She felt happy and anxious about the holiday herself as she listened to Ellie Trundle talk with Kitty Mason about their plans for Christmas. Her thoughts drifted again to Lucas. What would he be doing this holiday? Would he be spending it with his sister? Meghan loved her cloak and couldn't forget the man who had generously given it to her. Did he ever think of the woman he'd once rescued? Where would she be now if she'd accepted his offer and become his mistress?

Her mouth curved with amusement as she checked her thread. Certainly not in a mill, making cloth, she thought. No, if she was with Lucas, they'd be . . . She felt her cheeks warm as she envisioned what she and Lucas would be doing together this early in the morning. She recalled the heat of his kisses . . . his bare flesh. She sighed and then scolded herself for such wistful thoughts.

"Meghan?"

She was startled from her reverie. "Mr. Phelps!"

He nodded toward her loom. "Get Kitty to watch that for you and come into my office."

"Yes, sir," she said and approached Kitty with the request.

Meghan wasn't especially concerned when she entered Phelps's office and, at his invitation, sat before

IRISH LINEN

his desk. The man opened a desk drawer, extracted a box, and then handed it to her.

"Merry Christmas, Meghan," he said.

Her gaze transferred back and forth from the box to the man's face. "I don't know what to say," she murmured.

He smiled. "Why don't you open the package before you say anything," he suggested.

With trembling fingers, she took the box and carefully opened the lid. Inside the wooden box lay a beautiful cameo brooch that was much too expensive and certainly inappropriate for this man to give her. "I don't understand."

"You're a good worker," he said, rising from his seat.

She frowned as she stared inside the box. "Mr. Phelps—" She gasped, for he was suddenly there by her side, leaning against the edge of his desk.

He straightened, and she shoved back her chair and stood.

"I can't accept this," she said, extending the box, but keeping her distance.

"Why not?" His eyes gleamed as he held her gaze.

"Because it's not proper—"

He grabbed her extended arm and dragged her against him. She cried out, struggling, as he kissed her, and the box fell to the floor.

Meghan whimpered against his mouth as she fought to be free. Her hands were trapped. She tried to kick him and bring her knee up, but he was stealing her air . . . and her strength.

His head lifted, and he studied her with satisfaction. Meghan caught her breath and then jerked, spitting fury, from his arms. "Don't touch me!" she hissed. "I told you never to touch me."

He appeared surprised by her outburst. "And I

warned you about your attitude toward me! Do you wish to lose your position?"

"Go ahead!" she exclaimed. "Release me. No employment is worth enduring your touch!"

"Irish bitch! Go to hell."

She opened the door and glanced back. "It seems I'm already there, thank ye," she said with a new calmness. Then she left his office, slamming the door behind her.

The noise made by her exit drew glances from the workers nearby. With stubborn determination, Meghan returned to her looms and began to work. She wouldn't allow Phelps to intimidate her! Would he follow her and order her to leave, causing a scene?

When Phelps didn't appear, Meghan relaxed. The man hadn't actually fired her, had he? Could he fire her? Or did a dismissal have to come from the owner of the mill?

Fear kept her nervous for the rest of the morning, but Phelps kept his distance. Once, she saw him watching her, but he didn't approach or order her to leave. *Ha!* she thought. *On what grounds can he release me?*

His threat had been nothing but a bluff designed to get her to cooperate and "be nice" to him. Meghan glanced about the workroom, studying the women workers' faces. How many others had he intimidated into following his will?

Meghan sought out Mari Bright when the time came to break for the midday meal. "May I speak with you a moment?"

Mari, who had been talking with another worker, nodded. "You've done fine work today, Veronica," she said to the other girl. "Keep it up." Then, she waved Meghan to a private area in the corner of the work room.

"Mari—"

"It's Phelps, isn't it?" the woman said.

Meghan blinked with surprise. "Aye, but how did ye—"

The woman looked away. "It's happened before."

"To you?" Meghan asked.

Mari shook her head, but her gaze skittered away.

"Who?"

"One of the girls."

"Only one."

Mari sighed. "All right. It's happened more than once."

"I don't understand," Meghan said with anger. " 'Tis not right! Why is the man still here then?"

"Who's going to get rid of him? Me?"

"Has someone told Mr. Simmons?" Meghan's fists clenched against her skirts. "Why is such behavior tolerated?"

"I don't know if Simmons has been told," Mari said quietly. "W—everyone is afraid to lose their employment, Meghan. Our jobs are important to us. Each one of us is expendable. We have expenses . . . families."

Meghan had heard Mari's slip of the tongue and saw the desperation in the young woman's eyes. Mari, she realized, had been one of those bothered by Mathew Phelps. "There must be something we can do!"

"What?" Mari said. "What can you or I possibly do?"

The Irishwoman grew thoughtful as her gaze went beyond Mari to the workers who had lingered before leaving. "I told Phelps to release me. I said I'd rather lose me position than to endure his touch!"

"You didn't!" Mari exclaimed, sounding impressed.

"Aye, I did." Meghan turned back to meet Mari's gaze. "And I'm still here." She smiled as a thought occurred to her. "I may lose me employment yet, and it wouldn't matter a wit to Phelps, but what if all of us stay together in this? What if we all refuse to work unless Phelps ceases his behavior or is dismissed from the mill?"

Mari's face glowed with excitement as she pondered Meghan's suggestion. "It might work. He could afford the loss of one of us, but not all of us," she said. "Why didn't I think of that?"

Meghan's expression softened as she eyed her friend. "Ye were vulnerable and scared." Her blue eyes sparked with anger. "Just how Phelps wanted ye."

"I'll speak with the others," Mari said.

"Aye, he'll not get away with it again!"

That afternoon, Mr. Mathew Phelps asked the young woman who worked at the station next to Meghan's to come into his office. When Kitty Mason refused to go, the man was startled for a moment before he said something in an undertone that Meghan wished she could hear. Kitty glanced in Meghan's direction, and the Irishwoman gave her a nod of reassurance.

"You can speak to me here, Mr. Phelps," Kitty said, loud enough for Meghan and several others.

"The matter is a private one," the man insisted.

"I'm sorry, Mr. Phelps, but I'll not go into your office."

Mari Bright, who was monitoring the floor, moved to Kitty's side. "Is there a problem, Mr. Phelps?" she said.

The man glanced from one woman to the other, before dismissing Mari. "Kitty, if you wish to keep your position, you will follow me into my office immediately."

"Perhaps I can help," Mari said.

"When I want your help, I will ask for it, young woman," he snapped.

Meghan shut off her machine and approached the small group. "What is wrong?"

Phelps glared at Meghan as if the whole incident

was the Irishwoman's fault. "You! Get back to your loom."

"I will not go back to me loom, nor will any of the others, unless ye change your attitude and your behavior," Meghan said.

The man sputtered. "You're being insolent!"

"And you're a lecherous old man," she returned politely.

A ripple of laughter sounded about the room, and the man realized that all of the workers had stopped production. His face turned red with fury. "What is the meaning of this?"

"We're tired of your filthy hands on us!" Meghan said.

He looked shocked by the accusation as he glanced about the workroom and the women staring at him. "You've misread my intentions," he sputtered.

"Have we?" Mari said. "I think not."

"Get back to work," he ordered, "or you'll all be without position or pay."

The women glanced at each other, and then one by one, they turned on their machines until only Mari, Kitty, and Meghan were left standing idle.

"Meghan," Kitty said.

"Do what ye think is best," Meghan said with a sigh. "I still believe he won't release us. He needs us too much."

"You're right," Mari said. She faced the workers. "Stop your machines," she ordered. "He'll not release any of us, because he can't lose us all. The mill needs us!"

The machines on the weaving floor were silenced.

"Mrs. Gibbons, there's trouble at the mill!"

Flora eyed the young man who'd come to the house

at Mr. Simmons's orders. "What's wrong?" she said. "Has someone gotten hurt?"

The lad shook his head. "Mr. Simmons said to tell ya that the women upstairs have shut down their looms."

The woman exchanged a look with her nephew. The two had been going over the business account books.

"Would you like me to handle it?" Lucas asked his aunt.

She nodded. "Thank you, Lucas. I'll be over as soon as I finish up here."

Lucas rose from his desk chair, stretching as he stood. His gaze rested on the messenger, who stood waiting anxiously to follow Lucas back to the mill. "What happened?" Lucas asked as he gestured for the lad to precede him.

"I don't know, sir."

"But the women have shut down the machines," he said.

"Yes sir," the young man replied. "All I know is that they've refused to work."

"Well, we'll see about that," Lucas grumbled as they exited the house and crossed the yard.

Fifteen

The weaving room was buzzing with nervous conversation from the women workers on the floor. Meghan stared at the stairs and wondered whether or not she'd done the right thing. She was sure that Phelps had gone to see Mr. Simmons. What if she'd guessed wrong? What if Simmons dismissed the whole lot of them? She'd be responsible that these women and their families went hungry.

Her stomach knotted. She knew all too well about hunger. Dear God, what had she done!

Meghan turned to the woman beside her. "Mari, perhaps ye should start up your machines."

Mari shook her head. "No, Meg, you were right. We shouldn't have to endure Phelps's behavior."

"But what of your families?" Meghan said with anxiety. "What if I'm wrong and ye all lose your positions?"

The woman smiled softly as she rested her hand on Meghan's arm. "Better to lose our jobs," she said with sincerity, "than our self-respect. Besides, Flora Gibbons and her nephew must be fair people."

Meghan swallowed, and her gaze swept the occupants of the room. Self-respect wouldn't feed a family in the long winter months ahead. These women would think differently about their decision if they had known hunger as she had.

The level of sound in the room increased as the

women shared their excitement and tales of their experiences with Phelps. A young man appeared at the top of the stairs and called for the workers to be quiet.

"Meghan McBride," he said when the noise had settled down. "Where is the Irishwoman, Meghan McBride?"

"I'm Meghan McBride." Her heart racing, she stepped from the group, drawing the man's attention.

He stared at her for a moment. "Follow me please. Mr. Simmons is waiting to see you in his office." He turned abruptly and started down the stairs, apparently expecting her to follow without incident.

Some of the women called out to Meghan as she followed the young man.

"It'll be all right, Meghan."

"We're with you, Meg, if you go, we will, too!"

Their words made her feel worse instead of better, for she felt responsible for the welfare of these women and their families.

The young man was quiet as he led her down two flights of stairs. He spoke as they neared the mill foreman's office. "Mr. Simmons has called the owner," he said. "I thought you should know."

She acknowledged his warning with a nod, before he left her to enter the room alone. Her chest tightened as she raised her hand to knock on the office door.

"Come in!" Simmons's voice boomed.

His tone made her flinch, and her stomach flip-flopped as she reached toward the doorknob. The door was jerked from her hand by Mathew Phelps who eyed her with a smug expression as he slowly moved out of her way.

"Miss McBride," Simmons said, "come in. Phelps, shut the door."

The triumphant gleam in Phelps's gaze gave Meghan

new courage. The man was lecherous, and his behavior shouldn't be tolerated, she thought. Her resolve wavered for only a second as she studied George Simmons, who had treated her with a measure of respect, despite her factory inexperience and her Irish blood. According to Rafferty, most people in America were prejudiced against the Irish.

George Simmons studied her with a gauging look. "Sit down, Meghan," he said softly.

Meghan sat, conscious of Phelps's presence behind her.

"Mr. Phelps has made some serious charges against you, young woman," Simmons said. "He says that, because of you, the workers have shut down their machines."

"Aye," she said. " 'Tis true."

The head foreman appeared stunned by her admission of guilt. "Why?" he asked. "Why on earth would you jeopardize your position?"

Phelps had approached Simmons's desk, and Meghan flashed him a look.

"Hasn't Mr. Phelps told ye?" she said.

"He said that you refused to come into his office."

" 'Tis not true," she said. " 'Twas another worker who refused . . . but with good reason."

"Whatever the reason, Miss McBride," George Simmons said irritably. "You shouldn't have told the women to shut down."

"It was all her, George," Phelps said. "She's been trouble from the day she came. She needs to be dismissed."

"Mr. Phelps, Mrs. Gibbons's nephew and I will decide—"

The door to the office opened, interrupting the foreman.

"Simmons, Flora sent me. What's the trouble?" a man said as he entered the room.

Meghan felt the blood drain from her face as she recognized the deep voice. *Dear God in heaven. It was Lucas!* Lucas Ridgely was her employer's nephew! Her thundering heartbeat nearly drowned out all sound. She felt light-headed and had difficulty drawing breath. From a distance, she thought she heard George Simmons explain the situation in the weaving room and her part in it.

"Mr. Phelps claims that this young woman is behind the others."

"This woman is responsible for everyone shutting down their machines?" Lucas said with disbelief.

George Simmons nodded. "Apparently. I've only begun to question her, when you came in. Would you like to have the honor?"

"Most definitely," Lucas said, "I'm anxious to know this paragon of a woman who can disrupt the entire operation of the mill."

Meghan bristled at his tone. She knew he was unaware of her identity, for she'd yet to turn around, but he had no right to sound so scathing. He didn't know the workers' reasoning. How dare he condemn her without hearing her story first!

"What do you know of this, Phelps?" Lucas said as he approached Simmons's desk. Meghan steeled herself for his outburst upon recognizing her, but welcomed the challenge.

"I think it might be best if Mr. Phelps leaves," George Simmons said, his gaze transferring from Meghan's face to the weaving room overseer. "Phelps?"

The man scowled. "But, Mr. Ridgely—"

"Phelps . . ."

"Fine!" he said angrily. He paused at the door.

IRISH LINEN 155

"Don't you believe a word she tells you! She's a liar and rebel, that's what she is!" He then left the room.

Lucas regarded George Simmons with an even look. "Why did you make him go, George?"

"I didn't like Phelps's expression, Lucas, and I thought you'd like to get to the truth of this without his interference."

"I do," the younger man said. For the first time, Lucas's gaze settled on the woman in the chair; and he experienced a jolt, then a rush of warmth. It was Meghan McBride! He fought the urge to pull her from the chair and kiss her senseless . . . to ask her why she was here. *Dear God, it's Meghan* . . .

"Take my seat, Lucas." George Simmons rose and offered him his desk chair.

"Thank you, but I prefer to stand, George," he said gruffly. Lucas moved to lean against the foreman's desk. Crossing his arms, he studied the woman whose bent head prohibited him from seeing her face. Oh, but he didn't have to see her face to see the brightness of her eyes and the pink fullness of her lips. He wanted to shout for joy. Meghan . . . He thought he'd never see her again.

Suddenly, the implications of the situation registered in his brain. He saw the tension in her, and his joy dimmed, as he realized that she was the culprit at his aunt's mill. Why did Meghan convince the workers to stop cloth production?

Lucas scowled as he studied her. He wouldn't— couldn't—allow his lust for Meghan to affect his judgment.

"Do you realize you could lose your employment?" Lucas said, staring at her bent head. He saw her nod. "What's your name?" He couldn't let on that he knew who she was.

She glanced up and met his gaze. "Me name's Meghan," she said mockingly. "Meghan McBride, and I've done nothing that isn't justified."

Anger made him flush with heat. She glared at him with fury-laden blue eyes, and he felt his own frame stiffen as it occurred to him that this woman had lied to him about her fiancé. And she had caused trouble at his aunt's mill. And—damn it—he hadn't been able to forget her.

"Is that so?" he drawled. "What could possibly justify shutting down an entire level of operation?"

Meghan gazed into Lucas's dark eyes and experienced a twisting in her stomach. This man had asked her to be his mistress. What will he say when he learns that the reason everyone had stopped working was because another employee had been much too forward with her?

"Ye can blame Mr. Phelps," she said, her look daring him to challenge her.

"And what exactly did Mr. Phelps do?"

"It's not what he did as much as what he wanted to do," she said, furious with his tone.

Lucas raised an eyebrow. "Miss McBride, suppose you tell me exactly why you caused such trouble?"

"The women workers are tired of Phelps and his lecherous behavior toward them!" she burst out. "It's been happening for some time, but they feared losing their positions to do anything about it."

She felt satisfaction when she saw his face register surprise then displeasure. "Are you saying that the man's been using his position to proposition the women workers?"

Meghan could tell by his voice that he found the notion unbelievable and unacceptable. "Aye," she said quietly.

Lucas turned to the overseer. "What do you know

IRISH LINEN 157

of this, George? Have any of the workers come to you before?"

Simmons shook his head. "No, this is the first occasion I've heard such a tale."

Meghan stiffened at his choice of words. " 'Tis not a tale I'm telling ye, Mr. Simmons. Ask any of the other women!"

The man narrowed his gaze. "Perhaps I should do that."

"Meghan—" Lucas began, and then she saw his face change as if he'd realized that he'd almost revealed that they'd met before. "Miss McBride," he corrected himself, "we'll speak with Mr. Phelps on this matter. If he's guilty of such behavior, we'll handle the matter."

"Speak to the women, Mr. Ridgely," she said. "Ye don't honestly expect Mr. Phelps to admit to any wrongdoing, do ye?"

"Mr. Ridgely will handle matters in his own way, young woman," George Simmons said. "I suggest you keep your advice and return to your floor. I want you to see that the women start up their machines again. It's Christmas Eve, and they'll want to go home to their families knowing they still have employment."

"And if they refuse?" she asked.

"See that they don't refuse, Miss McBride," Lucas said.

Fortunately for Meghan, the women agreed to start up their machines after she'd explained that the matter was being handled by Simmons and Lucas Ridgely. Meghan could only hope it was true. No man should be able to threaten a woman with the loss of her employment because she wouldn't cooperate and enter a "relationship" with him.

The room was noisy as the workers began to use

their looms. Meghan went through the motions of starting up her own machines, but her mind was on Lucas Ridgely and their disturbing reunion. Lucas had been angry and scathingly biting. He certainly wasn't the gallant gentleman who'd respected her wishes and went on his way.

Her blood pumped harder as she thought of how well he looked . . . how handsome. No man had a right to look that good! He'd reentered her life just at a time when she'd nearly forgotten his appearance.

Liar. She hadn't forgotten a single feature of his, only minimized in her memory the strength of his effect on her. But one look at him again—even in anger—and her body responded of its own accord.

"What time will she come?" the young woman next to Meghan asked another, pulling Meghan from her thoughts.

"In time for our dinner," Kitty answered.

"Will we have cider again, do you think?" Ellie asked.

Meghan glanced over in time to see Kitty nod. "And pastries," the young woman said.

Ellie's face brightened. "Oh, her cook makes the best sweetmeats!"

"Who are ye speaking of?" Meghan asked, her curiosity getting the better of her.

"Mrs. Gibbons." Mari Bright had come up from behind Meghan with a crate containing several spools of thread. The young woman smiled. "Mrs. Gibbons herself comes on the day before Christmas with food and goodwill for all her employees."

Meghan shifted uncomfortably. "Mrs. Gibbons must be a kind woman to be so generous." Would the woman still come after the incident on the weaving floor? Meghan hated to mention her concern that the weavers would be disappointed.

IRISH LINEN

A short time later, a flurry at the stairway drew Meghan's gaze in time to see Mrs. Gibbons's arrival on the fourth floor. The woman smiled as she called out to her workers. Mathew Phelps rushed forward to help the woman with a tray of pastries, but the lady apparently wanted the honor of carrying the treats, for she wouldn't relinquish the heavy platter.

Apparently, Flora Gibbons wasn't too angry that she'd forget her weavers on Christmas Eve day. Anticipation rose within Meghan's breast as she waited to see if the woman would say anything about the halt in production earlier.

She studied the woman and felt grateful to Mrs. Gibbons for her decent wages and independence. She didn't believe that her employer would condone behavior such as Mr. Phelps's. Did Mrs. Gibbons know what happened? Would her nephew tell her the truth if she asked?

Flora Gibbons was a small woman, but she carried the tray easily to the table near Meghan's station. The woman eased her burden down on the wooden surface and then turned to face her employees with a smile.

Phelps quieted the commotion among the workers caused by their employer's entrance. "Ladies," he said, "Mrs. Gibbons would like to address you."

The talk silenced but the whir of the machines continued to fill the room.

"Tell them to stop the looms, Mathew," Meghan heard her employer say.

"Ladies, stop your machines."

The machines stopped within seconds of the request, for the second time that day. The ensuing silence filled Meghan with anticipation.

"Good morning, ladies," Mrs. Gibbons greeted.

"Good morning, Mrs. Gibbons, "the workers returned in unison.

Flora grinned. "It's so nice to see such happy faces on my employees. It means you're glad to be here." She paused, and Meghan's heart thumped hard as she wondered whether the woman would mention the incident that morning. "Of course, the knowledge that you have the next two days off may have helped form those smiles, eh?" Flora continued.

A titter of nervous laughter was followed by another that was more genuine.

Relieved by the woman's words, Meghan chuckled.

"Those of you who were here last year may remember the *savoy* cakes I brought for you."

Murmurs in the room confirmed the memory.

"I'm afraid there will be no savoy cakes this year." Flora raised her hand to silence the sighs of disappointment. "Mrs. Riker thought it inappropriate to have the same sweet cake for two years running, so we've made shortbread and sponge cakes for you instead."

Appreciation swelled about the room with soft exclamations.

"Now, in a few minutes, Mr. Phelps here will be helping Mr. Gosier and Mr. Franklin carry up three more trays of assorted treats. Of course, what good would treats be without a cup of sweet and delicious cider to wash it down with?"

Flora's gaze fell on Meghan, who couldn't help but grin at her. The woman's manner was warm and giving, and Meghan liked her.

The woman turned to her overseer. "Mr. Phelps?"

The man nodded and then disappeared down the stairs. As soon as he left, Flora Gibbons spun to address Mari Bright.

"Mari," she said, "I'd like you to introduce me to our new employees."

"With pleasure, Mrs. Gibbons," Mari Bright said.

Mari introduced Meghan first since the Irishwoman

was the closest. "Mrs. Gibbons, this is Meghan McBride."

The woman eyed her speculatively. "So you're the one who caused all the commotion this morning," she said.

"Mrs. Gibbons," Mari began, "it wasn't Meghan's fault."

Flora tore her gaze from Meghan to look at Mari. "Is that so?"

Mari nodded.

"I see," the woman said. She glanced back to study Meghan carefully. "You're been here several weeks I'm told. Long enough that I should have met you before." She tilted her head without releasing her gaze. "We must talk after the holiday."

"Aye, Mrs. Gibbons," Meghan said, her face flushing.

Suddenly, Flora smiled and extended her hand. "Relax, girl. I'm not an ogre."

Meghan swallowed and then nodded. "Thank ye, Mrs. Gibbons."

"For what, Meghan?"

"For me position and decent wages," she answered so softly she could barely be heard.

A look of concern entered Flora's expression. "Was the famine very terrible over there, in Ireland, for you?" she asked.

Meghan nodded, surprised by the woman's perception. "Because of it, I lost me da on the passage over," she said huskily. Then her voice became lighter. "But I'm alive and I thank God for that."

Flora looked thoughtful. "A woman with your experiences would hardly jeopardize her employment for no reason," she said.

"No, I wouldn't," Meghan agreed. Her employer left to greet the next worker. She stood for a moment, watching Flora Gibbons as she moved from one weaver to the next, speaking to each woman with care and concern for her well-being.

No, Meghan thought, *Flora Gibbons would be appalled to learn of Phelps's behavior toward the women workers.* But the question was: Would her nephew tell her? Or would he ignore the situation, because he was a man?

Meghan's whole being reacted when Lucas Ridgely arrived on the fourth floor a short while later. He came up the steps, carrying a barrel of cider.

Her first instinct was to run and hide. She was too angry, too affected by his presence. But where could she escape? Her looms were too close to the activity; she'd have to wait for everyone to gather about the food and hope she could sneak off and—*what*? This was her place of employment; she couldn't leave!

She grew calmer as she saw that Lucas hadn't noticed her yet.

"All right, ladies," Flora Gibbons said. "Please help yourselves."

Immediately, the noise level of happy chatter increased in the room as the workers came forward to eat.

The food looked delicious, but Meghan was no longer hungry. Her stomach was a mass of fluttering butterflies. Several workers jostled her as they brushed past, but she had eyes only for Lucas. She took the time to study him. His golden hair that curled near his ears. His sensual lips that were curved in a grin as he set down the barrel and spoke with his aunt. He wore a white shirt that stretched tautly over his broad chest and shoulders, and knee breeches that met the top of his black leather boots. He radiated energy and possessed a male confidence that attracted, Meghan saw, many of the women on the weaving floor. She couldn't move nor drag her eyes from his magnificent form.

"Meg," one girl said, "don't you want to get in line? The food's awfully good here."

Meghan forced her gaze from Lucas to smile at the young woman briefly. "There's no need to haste, Caroline. There's plenty of food it seems."

Caroline gave her a grin. "Plenty enough to have seconds," she said, before she headed toward a group gathered away from the crowd on the far side of the weaving room.

Meghan's gaze returned to Lucas, and her heart tripped as she saw him glancing leisurely about the work area. She retreated several steps and silently prayed that he wouldn't see her. His smile as he watched the workers' pleasure triggered memories of their night at the inn.

He looked the same, only better, Meghan thought. His white linen shirt collar was partially unbuttoned, drawing Meghan's attention to his throat. She inhaled sharply as she recalled the way he'd looked and felt like beneath her fingertips that night at the inn . . . all warm, muscled, and hard.

He turned just then and his gaze swept over the area where she stood, seeming not to register her, until she saw him stiffen before he swung back to stare at her.

She saw anger light up his onyx eyes. Meghan fought to breathe as he began to make his way to her side, his expression determined. Her heart thudded and seemed to drown out all sound. And then she heard his deep voice.

"Meghan, I need to talk with you."

No preliminary greeting. Just raw anger left over from their last encounter in George Simmons's office. She blinked up at him. "I don't want to talk to you!" she hissed, turning away.

He grabbed her arm, his fingers hurting. "Don't be an idiot, Irish. If you want me to do something about Phelps, then we're going to have to discuss it."

"Why?" she said. "So that ye can throw accusations? Question me character?"

Suddenly, his expression changed, softened. He smiled, and his eyes seemed to stroke her, bringing alive the memory of his touch . . . his kisses. A tingle began at the base of her neck and frissoned down her back.

"It's wonderful to see you again," he said in a sudden shift of mood, "but I'm surprised to see you here."

"Aye." She didn't smile. She was trembling so badly it was all she could do to answer him.

"Please, Meghan," he whispered. "We need to talk." He grabbed her arm and started to take her aside.

She resisted and glanced about hurriedly to see if anyone was watching. What would an observer think to see the strange byplay between a lowly weaver and the nephew of the owner of the mill? Fortunately, no one seemed to be staring; Meghan relaxed and allowed Lucas to move her away from her holiday-spirited fellow workers.

Lucas stopped and released her in an area within sight of her station. Meghan was glad. Anyone who happened to glance their way would see them as two strangers engaged in polite conversation, she thought.

"You work here," he said with amazement.

"Aye," she admitted. " 'Tis good employment." Her chin rose. "I'm not ashamed of it."

He scowled. "How long? How long have you been laboring here?"

"About one month and a half."

"A month and a half!" he exclaimed. His frown darkened. "I don't understand. I thought you were joining your fiancé. Did you lie to get rid of me?"

"No!" she gasped as he caught her hand. "I didn't lie to ye. I did join me fiancé!"

"What are you doing here then, working these long hours?" He seemed upset more by the fact that she was working at all.

Meghan's expression softened. "Lucas," she said, "did ye think I wasn't going to work in America? Ye saw all of me riches. Rafferty has done what he can, but 'tis simply not enough."

"You should have stayed with me," he said darkly.

She experienced angry heat. "And be your mistress?" she said. "No, Lucas. I'd rather work. At least here me position is an honorable one."

He tensed and his eyes flashed with fury. "Honorable? So honorable that you've set the weavers to stopping production?"

"I told ye, I had good reason!" she cried. She felt someone staring and glanced over to see the spinner, Catherine Brown, watching her and Lucas speculatively. Meghan's eyes narrowed. Catherine had been jealous of Meghan's position in the mill from the first. It wouldn't be wise to give the girl any fuel for malicious gossip. She lowered her voice. "Ye can believe what ye want, Lucas Ridgely, but I've done nothing wrong! Mayhaps ye should look to your own soul, before ye condemn others!" She spun and walked away.

"Where are you going?" he asked, looking disconcerted. "We haven't finished our discussion."

She met Lucas's gaze and was nearly lost. *He's dangerous, Meghan me girl,* she silently reminded herself. *Get away from him now!*

"It wouldn't look good for me to speak with ye overly long," she told him. "I wouldn't want the others to think I got me position because I know the owner's nephew."

"But you didn't know that she was my aunt, did you?"

"Of course not!" Meghan said, incensed by his comment. "Ye know that and I know that, but there are others here who would like nothing more than to see me gone."

Lucas scowled. "Why?"

She blushed. "Because of me position and me pay." She pulled from his grasp. "I've got to get back to the others. *Please, Lucas!*"

"I want to speak with you later," he said, ". . . after you're done here."

She shook her head. "I'm sorry, but Rafferty is coming to get me this eve. 'Tis Christmas."

His voice was a low growl. "Meghan—"

"No, Lucas," she said, "whatever ye have to say it can wait until after Christmas." And then she left him to approach the table of food, although she longed to stay and learn what he had to say.

To her relief—and disappointment—Lucas kept his distance for the rest of the afternoon. Meghan sat on a bench near Mari Bright, listening to the young woman's plans for the holiday. But her mind and her body were ever conscious of the attractive, golden-haired man across the room.

Flora Gibbons came up to Mari and Meghan to wish them a happy Christmas again and to praise them for doing a fine job at the mill.

"Mari told me you're very good at weaving, Meghan. It's wonderful to have you here at Gibbons Mill." She turned to Mari. "Mari, you're always a delight. I know full well that you've frequently managed to end a disagreement among my workers."

Mari beamed. "Thank you, Mrs. Gibbons."

Flora nodded. "The two of you must see Mr. Pennismart downstairs," she said to both women. "He'll pay you your wages plus a little extra as token of my appreciation for jobs well done."

Meghan gaped at her in shock, considering the circumstances of the morning; and Mari prodded her with an elbow.

"Thank you, Mrs. Gibbons," both women said simultaneously.

"You're quite welcome, dears." Flora Gibbons smiled and waved toward the food. "Now will you please eat up the pastries before Mrs. Riker is insulted?"

Mari groaned. "I've eaten enough to feed a whole stable of horses."

Meghan chuckled. "Not even another helping of chocolate cream?"

Mari rose from the bench slowly. "Ah well, perhaps I can fit in one more spoon of chocolate," she said, her eyes twinkling. "After all, it's light on my tongue."

Rising to follow, Meghan laughed. "Why don't ye take an extra spoonful to bring home for later?"

Lucas heard Meghan's laughter and felt something tighten within his chest at the rich sound. *Vixen. Temptress.* It had been seven weeks since he'd left her in Somerville, seven weeks of being unable to banish her from his mind. Not even his return to his Kent County home nor the many hours needed to catch up on business accumulated during his two months' absence had helped him to forget.

Now he was back in New Castle County for the holiday with his sister Beth and his parents, James and Mary Ridgely. He'd known it'd be difficult with Meghan only a few miles away, but he hadn't expected to see her here.

She works for Aunt Flora! And according to Simmons

and Phelps, she was trouble. His lips then curved into a reluctant smile as he recalled the way she'd stood up to him. Studying her from across the room, Lucas had to admit that she looked well, better than when he'd last seen her. Working at the mill had been good for her, he realized.

Meghan wore her hair pulled back into a knot at her nape. Her dress was plain, of gray muslin with a white collar and a full white apron worn probably, he thought, to protect her dress from the cotton fibers.

He saw Meghan finger the surface of one of the looms and guessed that the machine was hers. His chest tightened and a feeling of possession swept over him, so strong that he wanted to shout out that Meghan didn't belong here. She belonged with him, in his house in Kent County, dressed in fancy clothes, her dark red hair brushed to a gleam and adorned with freshly cut flowers.

What he wouldn't give to have her in his life . . . in his bed. For how long, he didn't know, but he didn't think he'd ever tire of her.

Was it true that Phelps had been forward to some of the women? To Meghan? He felt anger toward Phelps, compounded by understanding of the man's desire for the Irishwoman. He scowled. If it were true, he'd ensure that the man could never get near her again!

If it were true? Damn, what if Meghan had lied about this as she had about living in Somerville? Then again, why else would the other women have followed her lead?

He was here for a fortnight. Tonight, Meghan would leave for Somerville to be with Rafferty, but she'd be back in three days—or so she'd said.

The constriction in his chest eased. There was no way they could avoid seeing each other again. This

IRISH LINEN

matter of Phelps and the workers needed to be resolved, and he didn't know why but he was sure that Meghan wouldn't run from the situation and abandon her fellow workers. Not the Meghan McBride he knew.

"I wouldn't want the others to think I got me position because I know the owner's nephew." Meghan's words came back to haunt him, causing him a moment's pause.

He still wanted Meghan McBride, he realized as he watched her. He wanted her and was going to do everything he could to bed her and make her his. Lucas didn't understand men like Rafferty O'Connor, who allowed himself to be separated from his fiancée, who forced a woman to work and live several miles away. If he were O'Connor, he'd never allow a mile's distance between himself and Meghan.

Lucas scowled. Something was wrong with Meghan's relationship with her fiancé. There had to be. Believing this, he felt justified in pursuing Meghan for himself. He couldn't forget her response to his touch . . . nor his to hers.

Could a woman be in love with one man and yet respond so passionately to another?

Lucas didn't believe so. He refused to believe it. And he would make Meghan see that she'd be making the biggest mistake of her life if she married Rafferty O'Connor. Somehow he'd convince her that she could find happiness for a time with him.

Sixteen

"Meghan, are you certain that your fiancé is coming for you?" Patty asked.

Meghan turned briefly from the window to meet the woman's gaze. "Aye, so he said," she murmured, preoccupied with the lights coming from the big house up the hill. She scowled as she recalled her encounter with Lucas in Simmons's office. He'd made her feel like a criminal when she'd done nothing wrong! Her eyes narrowed and the lights from the house shimmered and then blurred. Would he handle Phelps as he'd said? Or would the vile man's behavior go unpunished once again, leaving Phelps the opportunity to proposition or bother some other young woman worker?

"It's late," Susan said, interrupting Meghan's thoughts. "Come away from the window and join us."

Meghan frowned as she obeyed. Where was Rafferty? *Was* he coming to get her? she wondered. It was Christmas Eve; of course, Rafferty was coming. Hadn't he promised?

The residents of the house sat in the great room. There were chairs about a small table in the corner and a sofa and an armchair before the fireplace. Patty had brought out some cookies, and Susan along with her roommate had made eggnog. The scene looked inviting to Meghan as she sat beside Susan on the sofa.

Her gaze strayed to the window, and she caught sight of a snowflake . . . and then another. " 'Tis snowing," she exclaimed.

"I wouldn't expect Rafferty to come if it's snowing," Susan said. "It's dark, and the road will be slippery."

Nodding, Meghan had to agree. She leaned forward to warm her hands at the fire. She could feel her friends' gazes on her.

"He'll surely arrive tomorrow," her roommate said with assurance.

Meghan smiled. She didn't mind being here for the holiday. But it wasn't like Rafferty not to show when he'd promised to come for her.

She silently prayed that nothing terrible had happened to him. Whatever had caused his delay she hoped it wasn't anything serious.

The man rose from bed, and a soft white hand grabbed his arm, hauling him back against the rumpled sheets.

"Don't go," the woman said.

Rafferty was drawn to the lady's smile. Alicia Somerton shifted the covers, exposing two full rose-tipped breasts. "Please, Raff," she said, cupping and lifting the fleshy mounds in an offering to him.

"Alicia," he growled, feeling himself grow hard. "I have to go. Your husband—"

Alicia snorted. "Michael is too concerned with his damn mill to pay any mind to me."

" 'Tis Christmas Eve," he said, begging for her understanding. "I promised to get Meghan."

She scowled. "The little fiancée. Dear God, Rafferty, what the hell do you see in her?"

"She's the daughter of me friend."

"Ah, yes . . . the poor darling daughter." Her eyes

gleamed maliciously. "Tell me you see her as a little girl. Kiss me and prove to me that I'm the woman you desperately need."

She had dampened her lips with her tongue. Rafferty stared at her moist mouth, wanting again to taste it. His gaze dropped to her breasts that she rubbed and stroked, titillating his desire, making her nipples rise and his loins ache with the need to bury himself deep inside her again.

"Alicia," he gasped. Rafferty grabbed her hands from her breasts, replacing them with his own. He roughly caressed her, enjoying the way her eyelids lowered as she moved with pleasure. He lowered his head to suck a sensitive nipple before transferring his attention to its twin.

There was something extra exciting about Alicia Somerton. She was wild and eager to indulge in sexual games. She loved to play anywhere, to follow whichever direction he decided to take with her. And she'd taught him a few moves he had never tried, but had found wildly exhilarating once he had.

"Alicia," he muttered, "ye are so lovely." He licked and nipped each of her breasts until she cried out, clutching his head in a spasm of ecstasy and then she was begging him to mount her, and he willingly obliged her.

They rocked together in animal heat, gasping, moaning until they reached the pinnacle of pleasure and lay in the pulsing aftermath, struggling for breath.

Rafferty studied the woman beneath him, knowing their time had to end for a while, before they suffered the consequences of being discovered together.

He enjoyed having sex in Alicia's bedchamber, almost as much as he loved burying himself in Alicia's soft, responsive body. The lush, expensive surroundings added to the sexual thrill, as did the danger of his being there. He felt he belonged in such a bed with its rich draperies and thick feather-tick mattress, with its white counterpane and soft, fluffy pillows.

He wasn't sure what had motivated Alicia to drag him into her bed. She was rich and powerful in Somerville. She had a handsome husband, who by all accounts was the envy of every other man for miles. Yet, Alicia had turned to him—a forty-nine year old Irish peasant with a thick chest and a thicker accent.

Rafferty grinned. *And a thick rod betwixt me legs.*

Since she'd literally stumbled into his path in Philadelphia, his life had taken on a new meaning. He'd had no idea when he gently picked her up from the road, when she'd stumbled, and brushed off the dirt from her skirts that she'd repay his kindness tenfold. He enjoyed Alicia, and she rewarded him for his attention handsomely by using her influence with her husband. He'd been offered a job at the mill; later, after he and Alicia had become intimate, he'd been given the position as manager of the company store. The more he pleased Alicia Somerton, the more impressed her husband seemed to become with Rafferty's efficiency at his employment. Rafferty smiled. His situation here in Somerville suited him just fine.

"Alicia, it's getting late. Your husband—"

Her eyes flashed open. "Go then. Go to your little peasant."

Rafferty felt a stirring of unease. It was Alicia who had given him the money to send for Meghan. He'd never thought Alicia would become jealous of his fiancée. In fact, it had been Alicia who'd suggested that his marriage to Meghan would provide the perfect cover for their present arrangement.

"I have to go, darlin'," he said softly, "but if I could choose, ye must know I'd rather stay." He stroked her breast to prove that he had trouble keeping his hands off her. "Alicia, surely ye haven't changed yer mind about me marriage to Meghan. We'll be able to continue our activities right under Somerton's nose without raising suspicion." He grinned as her nipple hardened beneath his fingertips. "Alicia . . ." he pleaded for her understanding. He felt his manhood stiffen as she stared at him hard.

She sighed, her chest heaving beneath his fingers as she released her breath. "You're right," she said. "Go."

He bent down and replaced his fingers with his mouth. He suckled her a moment before he lifted his head. "Mmmmm. Delicious." He flicked her cheek lightly. "Thank ye, dear lady."

She purred and then rose up on an elbow, dropping the covers to below her thighs.

Rafferty's gaze fell to the dark blond, curling thatch of hair between her thighs. "When will Michael be gone for a time?" he asked hoarsely. He gave in to the urge to touch her.

"I'll come for you," she promised, her green eyes glowing.

He grinned with sexual intent. "I'll be waiting." He stood, releasing her, dressed quickly, and went to the window. "Damn!"

"What?" she said. "What is it?"

He could hear her concern . . . her fear, but saw by her face that she was sexually excited by it.

"It's snowing."

She fell back against the bed, looking disappointed. "Damn," she said, but for a different reason, and Rafferty couldn't prevent his chuckle. Suddenly, her face brightened. "You'd better stay. It's too far to travel to Gibbons Mill in this weather."

Rafferty shook his head. "I've no choice. I have to go. It's Christmas Eve, and I promised to be there."

Alicia's green eyes flashed fire. "Do you always keep your promises?"

"Always," he said. "When it suits me," he added slyly.

She laughed. "Go, but hurry back. I'll be thinking of you . . . of this." She cupped herself, grabbing his attention and his desire.

Rafferty groaned and closed his eyes. "God, Alicia, ye know how to make a man ready when he shouldn't be."

Her chuckle followed him out into the hall. A quick glance down the corridor in both directions assured him that the servants were absent, and he hastened down the stairs and out into the night.

Anger curled in his stomach, burning Lucas's insides as he thought of Meghan McBride. He leaned against the window edge and stared outside. The chit had refused to find the time to talk with him! Didn't she know that he could release her from the mill? He scowled, and his right hand tightened on the wooden trim until his fingers whitened. Damn it, but she knew he wouldn't fire her, and that was what irked him to the point of fury—that Meghan knew he still wanted her.

The thought occurred to him that he could use her position as leverage to take her to bed. Lucas straightened and folded his arms. No, he'd be no better than Phelps, if Phelps had actually done what she'd accused him of doing. Simmons was still investigating the matter. Meghan might have lied. But why? What good could possibly come from her lying?

"Lucas? *Lucas!*"

Turning from the window, Lucas held back his anger and softened his expression. "Beth, I didn't hear you come in."

"Obviously," his sister quipped. She had entered the room carrying two glasses filled with a creamy drink. She looked beautiful, her dark hair unbound and flowing down her back. The green plaid of her gown darkened the cinnamon brown of her large, expressive eyes. Those eyes of hers gazed at him with concern as she approached him.

"I called you several times," she said. "What's wrong?"

He offered her a half smile. "Just daydreaming."

"It must have been a nightmare," she replied. "You looked fierce when I entered." Beth handed him a glass. "Mother's eggnog," she said.

Lucas accepted the holiday drink with a murmur of thanks and stared into the ivory liquid. After several moments, he moved to again gaze out the window.

"Is it still snowing?" his sister asked. He heard the swish of Beth's skirts as she joined him near the glass.

"It's stopped, but the sky looks dark. I think that before the day is over, it'll snow again," Lucas said without turning.

Beth spun and caught her brother's shoulder. "What aren't you telling me, big brother?"

He dragged his gaze from outside to focus on his concerned sister. "What could there be to tell?"

She sighed with exasperation. "You're being obtuse." She released him and moved to a chair. She sat and then regarded him through narrowed eyes. "You've not been the same since you returned from England," she said. "Did something happen there?"

He shook his head. Not in England, he thought, but on the voyage home. He had a mental image of Meghan, and he caught his breath as he fought the strongest urge to find her and lay claim.

"You're lying, Lucas," Beth accused.

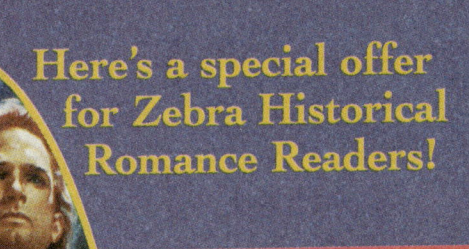

Here's a special offer for Zebra Historical Romance Readers!

GET 4 FREE HISTORICAL ROMANCE NOVELS

A $19.96 Value!

Passion, adventure and hours of pleasure delivered right to your doorstep!

HERE'S A SPECIAL INVITATION TO ENJOY TODAY'S FINEST HISTORICAL ROMANCES— ABSOLUTELY FREE! *(a $19.96 value)*

Now you can enjoy the latest Zebra Lovegram Historical Romances without even leaving your home with our convenient Zebra Home Subscription Service. Zebra Home Subscription Service offers you the following benefits that you don't want to miss:

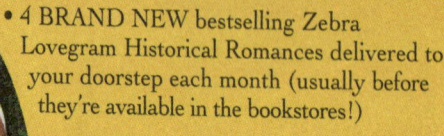

- 4 BRAND NEW bestselling Zebra Lovegram Historical Romances delivered to your doorstep each month (usually before they're available in the bookstores!)
- 20% off each title or a savings of almost $4.00 each month
- FREE home delivery
- A FREE monthly newsletter, *Zebra/Pinnacle Romance News* that features author profiles, contests, special member benefits, book previews and more
- No risks or obligations...in other words you can cancel whenever you wish with no questions asked

So join hundreds of thousands of readers who already belong to Zebra Home Subscription Service and enjoy the very best Historical Romances That Burn With The Fire of History!

And remember....there is no minimum purchase required. After you've enjoyed your initial FREE package of 4 books, you'll begin to receive monthly shipments of new Zebra titles. Each shipment will be yours to examine for 10 days and then if you decide to keep the books, you'll pay the preferred subscriber's price of just $4.00 per title. That's $16 for all 4 books with FREE home delivery! And if you want us to stop sending books, just say the word....it's that simple.

It's a no-lose proposition, so send for your 4 FREE books today!

4 FREE BOOKS

These books worth almost $20, are yours without cost or obligation when you fill out and mail this certificate.
(If the certificate is missing below, write to: Zebra Home Subscription Service, Inc., 120 Brighton Road, P.O. Box 5214, Clifton, New Jersey 07015-5214)

Complete and mail this card to receive 4 Free books!

YES! Please send me 4 Zebra Lovegram Historical Romances without cost or obligation. I understand that each month thereafter I will be able to preview 4 new Zebra Lovegram Historical Romances FREE for 10 days. Then if I decide to keep them, I will pay the money-saving preferred publisher's price of just $4.00 each...a total of $16. That's almost $4 less than the regular publisher's price, and there is never any additional charge for shipping and handling. I may return any shipment within 10 days and owe nothing, and I may cancel this subscription at any time. The 4 FREE books will be mine to keep in any case.

Name _____

Address _____ Apt. _____

City _____ State _____ Zip _____

Telephone ( ) _____

Signature _____
(If under 18, parent or guardian must sign.)

LF0896

Terms, offer and prices subject to change without notice. Subscription subject to acceptance by Zebra Home Subscription Service, Inc.. Zebra Home Subscription Service, Inc. reserves the right to reject any order or cancel any subscription.

A $19.96 value... absolutely FREE with no obligation to buy anything, ever!

ZEBRA HOME SUBSCRIPTION SERVICE, INC.
120 BRIGHTON ROAD
P.O. BOX 5214
CLIFTON, NEW JERSEY 07015-5214

AFFIX STAMP HERE

Here's a special offer for Zebra Historical Romance Readers!

GET 4 FREE HISTORICAL ROMANCE NOVELS

A $19.96 Value!

Passion, adventure and hours of pleasure delivered right to your doorstep!

HERE'S A SPECIAL INVITATION TO ENJOY TODAY'S FINEST HISTORICAL ROMANCES— ABSOLUTELY FREE! *(a $19.96 value)*

Now you can enjoy the latest Zebra Lovegram Historical Romances without even leaving your home with our convenient Zebra Home Subscription Service. Zebra Home Subscription Service offers you the following benefits that you don't want to miss:

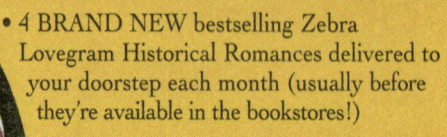

- 4 BRAND NEW bestselling Zebra Lovegram Historical Romances delivered to your doorstep each month (usually before they're available in the bookstores!)
- 20% off each title or a savings of almost $4.00 each month
- FREE home delivery
- A FREE monthly newsletter, *Zebra/Pinnacle Romance News* that features author profiles, contests, special member benefits, book previews and more
- No risks or obligations...in other words you can cancel whenever you wish with no questions asked

So join hundreds of thousands of readers who already belong to Zebra Home Subscription Service and enjoy the very best Historical Romances That Burn With The Fire of History!

And remember....there is no minimum purchase required. After you've enjoyed your initial FREE package of 4 books, you'll begin to receive monthly shipments of new Zebra titles. Each shipment will be yours to examine for 10 days and then if you decide to keep the books, you'll pay the preferred subscriber's price of just $4.00 per title. That's $16 for all 4 books with FREE home delivery! And if you want us to stop sending books, just say the word....it's that simple.

It's a no-lose proposition, so send for your 4 FREE books today!

4 FREE BOOKS

These books worth almost $20, are yours without cost or obligation when you fill out and mail this certificate.
(If the certificate is missing below, write to: Zebra Home Subscription Service, Inc., 120 Brighton Road, P.O. Box 5214, Clifton, New Jersey 07015-5214)

Complete and mail this card to receive 4 Free books!

YES! Please send me 4 Zebra Lovegram Historical Romances without cost or obligation. I understand that each month thereafter I will be able to preview 4 new Zebra Lovegram Historical Romances FREE for 10 days. Then if I decide to keep them, I will pay the money-saving preferred publisher's price of just $4.00 each...a total of $16. That's almost $4 less than the regular publisher's price, and there is never any additional charge for shipping and handling. I may return any shipment within 10 days and owe nothing, and I may cancel this subscription at any time. The 4 FREE books will be mine to keep in any case.

Name _____

Address _____ Apt. _____

City _____ State _____ Zip _____

Telephone ( ) _____

Signature _____
(If under 18, parent or guardian must sign.)

LF0896

Terms, offer and prices subject to change without notice. Subscription subject to acceptance by Zebra Home Subscription Service, Inc.. Zebra Home Subscription Service, Inc. reserves the right to reject any order or cancel any subscription.

A $19.96 value... absolutely FREE with no obligation to buy anything, ever!

ZEBRA HOME SUBSCRIPTION SERVICE, INC.

120 BRIGHTON ROAD

P.O. BOX 5214

CLIFTON, NEW JERSEY 07015-5214

AFFIX STAMP HERE

He raised an eyebrow. "Am I? Then tell me what you think happened while I was away."

His sister relaxed and took a sip of her drink before answering. "A woman," she said. "You met and fell in love with a beautiful woman, but she was unavailable. It was tragic. You were forced to love and worship her from afar."

Lucas's short bark of laughter vibrated throughout the room. "You've been rereading that copy of Brontë's *Jane Eyre* I brought back for you."

She blushed, and he chuckled.

At the deep sound of his amusement, Beth smiled. "That's better," she said. "It's Christmas Eve. No one should look so glum on the night before Christmas."

"Actually, there was a problem at the mill today." His expression sobered.

"So I heard." Beth looked interested. "A weaver organized the others into turning off their looms." She held his gaze steadily. "Why?"

"She claims that Phelps has been bothering some of the workers."

"I believe it."

Lucas was surprised by his sister's response. "Why?"

"Because the man is strange," she said. "I've caught him staring at me with a strange look that gave me the shivers."

"He didn't try anything?" Lucas was incensed that the man had been too forward in his behavior, and if proved, he'd make sure Phelps would be unable to get within feet of Beth or any woman again. *Especially Meghan.*

"No, he wouldn't dare," she said. "He knows the consequences if he did. What will you do if you find out the woman was right?"

"I'll see that the man is fired."

"Good." Beth rose to her feet. "Mother and Dad are in the parlor. Will you come?" Her gaze pleaded.

He studied the shelves of books and felt a reluctance to leave the comfort of this room. "Where's Aunt Flora?" he asked.

"She's in the kitchen, fussing with the servants."

Lucas smiled. "Fussing with the servants" meant that Aunt Flora was dispensing gifts and granting the kitchen staff tonight and tomorrow off. "I'll be in shortly." He heard his sister sigh with relief, and his gaze sharpened. "Mother being difficult again?"

"Is there ever a time when Mother is not being Mother?" Beth said in answer.

Lucas approached and gently chucked her under the chin with his knuckles. "Smile, love. We'll get through this."

"Without the sisters or the parents coming to blows?" she asked cryptically. Flora Gibbons and their mother were siblings, but they were as different as night and day. And their father and mother's relationship was difficult at best.

"Now I didn't say that."

Beth's snort was full of derision and very unladylike. "What would I have done if I didn't have you," she said, "or Daddy." She shuddered at the thought of being brought up by their mother alone.

Her brother's smile was both sad and gentle. "But you have us both, so stop worrying about it." He understood her dismay. He hated the arguments between his mother and father. His parents' relationship had made him distrust the validity of love and marriage. Years past, after a particularly terrible fight between James and Mary Ridgely, Lucas had sworn that he would not suffer the same life. To be alone had to be preferable to living and arguing with a shrew. Why had his father married his mother?

"What do you suppose Daddy saw in her?" she asked, her thoughts apparently mirroring Lucas's.

Lucas thought of his socially upstanding, prim and proper mother and recalled the long-ago beauty of her face and smile. He saw a glimpse of what his mother had been, before discontent had soured her and made her difficult to understand. He thought he understood what had first drawn his father. "Mother was a beautiful woman once," he said.

Beth's eyes widened. "Beautiful—Mother?"

"I remember when I was very young . . . when she smiled the whole room seemed to light up." He gave his sister a smile tinged with sadness. "I guess she was happy then."

"I wish she was happy now," Beth said as she preceded him out the library door.

Lucas sighed as he followed her to join his family. "I do, too," he said with great feeling. It was a shame, he thought, that his sister had known only discord in his parents' household. He had escaped it somewhat when he'd moved into the plantation's caretaker's cottage. It was his now, and with its small interior rooms came a measure of the peace lacking in the big house.

But his peace had been disturbed since Meghan's entry into his life. Would he ever get to bed her and be free of her? He sure as hell was going to try!

Seventeen

Meghan sat in the darkened bedchamber in Somerville, listening to Miss Doddleberry's snores. It was early Christmas morning, well before dawn. She'd been unable to sleep since retiring to her room hours ago.

Rafferty had eventually arrived at Gibbons Mill well past the supper hour, when she'd all but given up hope of his coming. He'd been quiet, but not irritable as he'd steered the carriage back to Mrs. Pridgly's. He'd offered some mumbled excuse about why he was late that Meghan didn't understand, but oddly enough she didn't care. By the time they'd reached Somerville, there had been little time for them to talk, before Mrs. Pridgly suggested everyone up go to bed. All the residents followed her lead.

The boardinghouse parlor was decorated with holly and pine, but it didn't seem as festive to Meghan as it did at Patty's. As she stared at the ceiling of the bedchamber, she thought that the house lacked something. What was missing here that made her time spent at Patty's more enjoyable?

She remembered the warmth generated by the people who lived at Patty's and the pleasure they'd shown when she'd given each of them the small gifts she'd made: linen handkerchiefs for the women, new stockings for the boys.

Then she thought of the things she'd brought with

her . . . a new set of sewing needles for Mrs. Pridgly, some cookies and donuts for Henry, George, and the other tenants. Thanks to Patty's generosity and help in the kitchen, Meghan had gifts for everyone at Mrs. Pridgly's, too.

For Rafferty, she had a special Christmas gift—a gold fob for the watch that Rafferty always carried with him, the watch that had belonged to his father. It had cost her a full week's pay, but Meghan didn't mind. She was grateful to Rafferty for all he'd done for her.

She realized she must have fallen asleep when she was awakened by the sun and Miss Doddleberry, who made enough noise in the room to wake Mrs. Pridgly downstairs. Meghan's head pounded with a dull ache as she blinked and then eyed the woman with whom she shared the bedchamber.

"What time is it?" she asked.

Miss Doddleberry gave her a scolding look. "It's six past. Why are you still abed?"

Meghan's teeth snapped, but she was silent. *Why do ye make noise when ye sleep like the working machinery at Gibbons?* she thought.

"Merry Christmas," she said with all the politeness she could muster.

The woman sniffed. "Merry Christmas," she said insincerely.

Voices in the corridor signaled the awakening of the entire household, and Meghan threw back the quilt. She had taken to sleeping in the chair after her first night's experience staying with Miss Doddleberry. The woman not only snored while she slept, but she thrashed about.

Rising to her feet, Meghan rubbed her throbbing temple.

"Head hurt again?"

To Meghan's surprise, the woman's concern seemed genuine.

"Here." Miss Doddleberry dug inside the top drawer of the bureau chest and handed Meghan a folded paper. "It's headache powder. My grandmother's special blend." When Meghan hesitated, the woman pushed it into Meghan's hands. "I suffer frequently," she admitted. "This helps me."

Meghan stared at the folded paper. "I wouldn't want to take all of your medicine," she said.

The woman brushed off Meghan's concern with a wave of her hand. "I know the receipt. I can make more when I need to."

"Thank ye," Meghan said, warming to the woman. In a moment of a shared experience, the animosity between the two eased.

Miss Doddleberry moved to the door. "I'll tell Mrs. Pridgly you'll be down shortly."

Murmuring her thanks, Meghan set down the powder to be taken downstairs at breakfast and dressed. She suspected that Lucas Ridgely was actually the cause of her recent headaches. The man had done nothing but disturb her sense of well-being from the first moment she'd looked up in his ship's cabin and met his gaze. Well, she didn't know how she was going to solve matters. The confrontations between them weren't over yet. She needed the mill job, but she wouldn't suffer a loss of self-respect to keep it. The throbbing in her head intensified. She didn't want to deal with Lucas Ridgely, but circumstances were forcing her, and she'd just have to make the best of things.

By the time she joined the others at the table, her head hurt so badly, she could barely tolerate noise.

"Meghan, what took ye so long?" Rafferty asked.

"You poor dear!" Mrs. Pridgly exclaimed, causing Meghan to wince. "You look terrible."

Meghan tried to smile, but the effort made her feel worse.

The women at the dining table began to fuss, rising to pull out a chair for her while scolding the men for not taking the initiative, and pouring Meghan a cup of tea.

"Did you take the powder?" Miss Doddleberry asked.

"No," she whispered. She pulled the folded paper out of her pocket and poured some into her tea. She could sense Rafferty's irritation mingled with concern as she tentatively took a sip of the medicine-laced tea, but she didn't care. She had enough to worry about without her fiancé.

"Please," Meghan pleaded when the others continued to fuss over her. "Don't worry about me. I'll be fine."

The diners settled back to finish their breakfast; and although Meghan didn't feel like eating, she took two of Mrs. Pridgly's hot cinnamon buns.

She sipped her tea and nibbled on a bun, listening to the conversation at the table, and soon the pain in her head began to diminish.

Rafferty turned to her when they'd finished eating. "Are ye feeling better now?" he asked.

She nodded. "Aye. The pain has lessened some."

He frowned as he seemed to study her more carefully. "What brought it on, do ye think?"

Meghan shrugged her shoulders. "I don't know," she lied. It was the long night in the chair with little sleep, her thoughts troubled by her anger toward—and her attraction to—Lucas Ridgely.

"I'm glad ye're feeling better," her fiancé said, placing his arm about her shoulder.

She had to force herself not to pull away. Rafferty

had been touching her more and more lately, and she was uncomfortable with his change of behavior.

But you're going to marry him, an inner voice reminded her.

But it doesn't feel right, she thought, disturbed by the revelation and the knowledge that as her husband Rafferty would have the right to touch her whenever he desired . . . and more intimately.

She swallowed hard. The idea had never bothered her before. Why did it now?

Lucas.

Meghan experienced a shaft of pain. She'd never experienced passion until Lucas had kissed and touched her. She hadn't known what she'd been missing.

It wasn't that she was ignorant of a man's lust, but she'd never really thought of it in connection with Rafferty. He was solid, dependable . . . like Da, she thought. And what she'd once shared with Lucas hadn't been just lust, it was more, she thought, recalling their shared moments eating "stolen" food. She'd enjoyed the simple pleasure of just being with Lucas . . . until she'd learned what a misguided cretin he was.

Rafferty escorted her into the parlor where the residents of the house had gathered to exchange gifts. Meghan glanced at the man beside her and was uneasy with the thought of becoming his wife.

But what choice did she have? She had promised to marry Rafferty. He had worked hard to send for her. She owed him a lot, and she was grateful.

But was marriage too high a price to pay?

She'd become betrothed to Rafferty because she had wanted a safe and solid husband. Her decision hadn't been based on any gratitude or sense of loyalty. It had been a wise one, she'd thought at the time.

But Rafferty was a different man than the one she'd known and felt affection for back in Ireland. He was often preoccupied and angry. That quick flash of fury she'd glimpsed when he'd learned she'd lost her employment at the Somertons had upset her. It still disturbed her, more than she'd previously allowed herself to admit.

Rafferty left her side to search under the sofa, rising within moments with a small trinket box and a boyish grin.

Meghan couldn't help smiling. His grin belonged to the man she'd once known. Perhaps the real Rafferty was still there, only weighed down by his worries.

He came to her and led her to sit on the sofa. Then, with an expectant look in his green eyes, he handed her the wooden box.

"Merry Christmas, Meggie," he whispered, leaning to kiss her cheek.

She was overcome with a rush of emotion. "Thank ye, Rafferty," she said huskily.

"Open it," he urged.

His excitement transmitted itself to Meghan, raising her level of anticipation. She studied the box and then opened the carved lid. As she stared at the box's contents, tension coiled inside her, and she couldn't speak. There, nestled within a bed of velvet, was a ring, a circle of emerald stones that glistened with green fire.

" 'Tis your betrothal ring," he said, sounding uncertain. "I couldn't give one to ye before now."

She met his gaze and saw a vulnerability in him she'd not seen before.

"Try it on," he urged.

No, her mind cried. *This isn't right. Ye don't really want to marry him.* "Where did ye get this?" she breathed.

A look of anger entered Rafferty's gaze. "I came by it honestly, if that's what ye're asking."

"No, no, I didn't mean that," she said quickly. "It's just that it's so . . . beautiful . . ." In a gesture of apology, Meghan lifted the ring from the box and reluctantly placed it on a finger of her right hand. The coil in her chest tightened as she studied its effect. "I don't know what to say."

Tell him you'll not marry him.

Tell him he'll always be a good friend, and for that you'll always love him, but that there needs to be more between a husband and wife.

Meghan was surprised by her thoughts. From her—someone who never believed in romance and passionate love.

"A simple thank ye will do," Rafferty said with mild irritation.

She forced a smile that she hoped appeared genuine. "Thank ye, Mr. O'Connor."

She must have sounded sincere, because his expression lightened. "Ye're more than welcome to it, Miss McBride," he said, and then he kissed her . . . on the mouth . . . in a room full of people.

Meghan wanted to protest, to pull away, but she submitted because he was her fiancé, and she'd yet to make a final decision about their relationship.

The kiss was quick and without feeling for Meghan. When he bent his head a second time, Meghan stifled a shiver of revulsion brought on by the moist, insistent clumsiness of Rafferty's mouth.

As he pulled away, Rafferty looked happier than she'd seen him since she'd come to America, and she suffered misgivings. Murmuring that she had to retrieve Rafferty's gift, she stumbled upstairs to her bedchamber and rummaged through the bottom drawer of the dresser.

Tears pricked her eyes as she pulled out Rafferty's gift, for her mind was filled with Lucas's—not Rafferty's—image. She couldn't forget how glorious it had been to be kissed by Lucas. Rafferty's kiss failed miserably by comparison.

Oh, Lucas, why did ye have to come back?

She blamed her seeing him again for her discontent with Rafferty. If Lucas had not reentered her world, she'd have been happy to marry Rafferty, she told herself.

Or would she?

She had found one excuse after another to put off her wedding. She'd been honest in her feelings when she'd asked for time to get over her father's death, and Rafferty had understood. But with his gift of the ring, Rafferty was reminding her of their commitment. He'd given her time, and she had a dreaded feeling that he was getting impatient.

Dear God, what am I going to do?

Rafferty offered marriage.

Lucas had offered her shame as his kept woman.

Rafferty's kisses were lifeless.

Lucas had promised passion and ecstasy beyond her wildest dreams.

Rafferty loved her.

Lucas only desired her.

And why did she have feelings for a man who doubted her word? She was physically attracted to Lucas Ridgely, despite her anger.

Was she mad?

Could she marry Rafferty knowing how she felt about Lucas?

She was a fool for being tempted by physical lust. She'd lose her reputation as Lucas's mistress. Despite her desire for him, she could never take up such an offer from a man.

She needed to forget Lucas and marry. As Rafferty's

wife, she'd have her self-respect as well as the children and family home she'd always hoped to have.

But at what price?

Meghan sobbed into the silence of the room. *I don't know what to do!*

Wouldn't it be better if she remained alone?

She wiped her eyes and straightened her appearance. For someone who had vowed not to cry, she seemed to be doing a lot of it lately, she thought.

With Rafferty's gift clutched in her hand, Meghan left to rejoin the others.

She couldn't decide today. She was still Rafferty's fiancée and she would play the part as if it had been destined for her all along.

She'd allow nothing to wipe away the smile from Rafferty's face or to ruin her first Christmas in America, her new home.

Eighteen

The Gibbons Mill weavers returned to their looms, buzzing with excitement over the last days' holiday celebration. Meghan smiled and made all the right replies to her fellow workers, but her cheerfulness was forced. Her holiday had been disturbing, not joyful, to her.

She turned on her looms and kept herself busy working, while her mind replayed the events of Christmas day. She'd tried hard to enjoy her time with Rafferty; and for a while, in the afternoon, she actually had. Henry had an old fiddle, which to Meghan's surprise, he played with amazing ability. Rafferty, buoyed by the music and the holiday spirit, had gotten up and danced like he and Meghan's father had done in the early days . . . before the potato crops had failed and brought poverty, hunger, and disease.

Henry, apparently having learned an Irish ditty or two from one of the Irish mill workers, played a jig to which Rafferty not only danced but sang the words. Meghan had laughed and clapped her hands with the others until Rafferty had pulled her to her feet; she'd stumbled through the steps that she'd never quite been able to master as a young child.

Pleasantly winded, Meghan and the others had then shared a Christmas supper that, Meghan had to admit, rivaled any meal that had been cooked by Patty.

That Christmas night, Meghan had fallen asleep in

the chair immediately, pleasantly exhausted by the dancing and revelry. But hours later she'd been awakened in the early hours by a disturbing dream.

She'd been too keyed up with her reaction to the dream to go back to sleep. Miss Doddleberry's snores hadn't helped matters. Restless, Meghan had risen and moved her chair closer to the window to stare out into the night. The sky was clear and star-studded. A light blanket of snow had fallen since she'd retired for the evening, and she caught her breath at the beauty of the winter night. The moon glistened on the white-kissed tree branches and on the snow-laden roadway.

At first glance, it had been difficult to tell where the yard ended and the road began, until she saw the dip in the land that outlined the edge of the dirt carriage path. And as she'd studied the night, she'd trembled with the feelings brought on by the dream, for her sleep visions had been filled with Lucas . . . and how he'd come to her after she'd married Rafferty, begging, pleading with her to be his wife.

His declaration of love had been all the more disturbing to her upon awakening, for Meghan knew that in reality Lucas would never care enough, want her enough to make such a claim. And certainly not on bent knee!

In her dream, Meghan had consented to leave Rafferty for Lucas. She'd braved the scandal of leaving her husband to be with Lucas, but after enjoying her in his bed, Lucas had tired of her quickly. Pregnant with Lucas's child, Meghan had found herself alone in Philadelphia, struggling to survive, but no one would hire a woman big with child—especially an Irishwoman. Rafferty, heartbroken at Meghan's betrayal, heard about Lucas's abandonment of her, and he came searching for his wife. He found Meghan in a ramshackle old house, working as a housemaid for a man of questionable character. Rafferty rescued Meghan and took her back to Somerville to live with him. But while she shared his bed, she no longer had his respect or affection . . . a matter Rafferty had no intention of rectifying, as punishment for leaving him.

Meghan had a home and a child, but she'd lost Rafferty's affection and her own self-respect. She had to be content with only Rafferty's lust and a child who resembled his father—the man she'd lost and sacrificed everything for.

"Lucas," she murmured, feeling her old longing for him overwhelm her as she moved to check the smooth running of each loom. "I must forget ye."

In the early darkened hours of the day following Christmas, Meghan had made the decision to marry Rafferty. It was the right and only thing to do, she'd realized, to keep her self-respect and her heart intact.

Her heart intact? Love? Was that why she couldn't stop wanting Lucas Ridgely? Because she loved him? No! She couldn't be that insane!

She knew she'd made the best decision about Rafferty. She needed to get on with her life, forget such foolish girlish fancies.

Yet, why did she feel so disheartened?

"Meghan." Mari Bright interrupted Meghan's painful musings. "You're quiet this day. Did you not enjoy your holiday in Somerville?"

Meghan realized that she must go on and be happy with her decision and her life. "It was a fine time," she said. She held up her hand to display her new ring. "Rafferty gave me this."

Mari gasped. "It's lovely!"

" 'Tis my betrothal ring," Meghan said. She was still uncomfortable with the obvious excessive expense of the ring, and where Rafferty had gotten it.

The woman called out to the other workers to come

and see Meghan's ring; and as the day progressed, each one drifted over to admire the ring as their time and work load permitted.

"Mother of God!" one girl exclaimed. " 'Tis beautiful beyond all. I wish me intended had such riches to spend."

The young woman's comment only made Meghan feel more uneasy about the ring. Where did Rafferty purchase it? Surely, such jewelry wasn't available at the Somerville store? He'd said he'd come by the ring honestly, and she had tried to believe it, but couldn't. Yet, she realized how little she knew about Rafferty's finances. She'd assumed he'd made modest wages; he'd been so adamant to see her employed. It had taken him two years to save the cost of her and her father's passage to America. Could Rafferty have earned enough money to buy her an expensive betrothal ring since?

Immediately after that thought came guilt. She had no reason to doubt Rafferty. He'd given her so much. Besides paying for her voyage, he'd outfitted her with two new gowns. If she knew so little of his finances, it was her own fault. Had she asked him about money? Perhaps he was still paying for the ring? She was his fiancé; she had a right to know and to work to help him.

Rafferty had pretended to be pleased when she'd given him his Christmas gift, but she could see in his expression that he wasn't. And she hadn't asked him why until he'd taken her home last night. She'd learned then that he'd sold his father's watch after he'd come to America. He'd needed the money enough to sell something precious.

Disturbed by her thoughts, Meghan shut off her machines, gathered her cloak, and went out into the night without waiting for Susan or one of Patty's other girls. She'd gone only a few yards when she felt someone grab her arm. Heart thumping, she turned and faced Catherine Brown, the spinner who'd been watching her and Lucas in the weaving room on Christmas Eve.

"Catherine." At first, she'd been afraid that it was Phelps, perhaps furious with her for stirring up a fuss at the mill. The man had been absent from work all day, and the rumor about the floor was that the man had been suspended from the floor until his behavior had been investigated. But none of the workers had been called into Mr. Simmons's office to be questioned. Her relief that it wasn't Phelps made her smile at the woman.

"You think you're better than the rest of us," the woman said with a snarl. "I saw you talking with Lucas Ridgely. If you think you'll get an increase in pay by playing up to him, you're mistaken."

The smile left Meghan's face and she stared at Catherine in shock. "I don't know what you're talking about—"

"What did you say to him, McBride?" Catherine said angrily. "When you left him, the man couldn't keep his eyes off you. You must have said something!"

"He asked me about me work is all." She could feel her face drain of all color.

The other woman laughed harshly. "I'm sure," she said. "Don't think you'll keep the man's interest, *Irish*. Lucas Ridgely is an attractive man. He can have any woman he wants in his own class. You'll never be rich or woman enough for him."

"You're wrong about this, Catherine. I've no interest in Mr. Ridgely," she lied, "and he has none in me." She felt raw, exposed, and she hoped the other woman couldn't see it.

The spinner looked unconvinced. "Mrs. Gibbons doesn't put up with girls who are immoral, McBride."

Meghan bristled. "Then I suggest ye look to yourself," she snapped, "for I've done nothing to be ashamed of." She raised her eyebrows. "Can you say the same?" Then she spun on her heels and strode away.

By the time she reached Patty's, Meghan felt a tightness in her chest. The raw nerve exposed by Catherine's accusation had been replaced with her anger. How dare the woman speak to her like that? If she wanted to speak with Lucas Ridgely, then she would do so—and anytime she desired!

Catherine Brown can go jump off the mill building roof for all I care! Hadn't Susan warned her about Catherine? She mustn't let the woman bother her!

But as the evening wore on, Meghan's anger faded and turned against her, and she felt shaky and vulnerable again. She had lied when she'd told Catherine that she wasn't interested in Lucas. She had promised herself she'd marry Rafferty, yet she couldn't forget Lucas . . . The fact of Phelps's absence at the mill that day had led Meghan to believe, to hope, that Lucas had believed her after all and done something about it.

Late that night as she stared up at the ceiling at Patty's, Meghan wondered what she would do if Lucas asked her to be his wife. But did her answer really matter? Lucas was gone. Rafferty was her fiancé, and she owed him her new life.

But would her gratitude to Rafferty sustain her for the rest of their married lives? Would she be happy with Rafferty—after experiencing a taste of heaven in Lucas's arms?

She sighed and closed her eyes. She'd find out in the years to come, she realized.

When she finally fell asleep, Meghan dreamed not of her marriage to Rafferty, but of a man with golden hair and gleaming dark eyes. When she awoke the next morning, she had a heart made heavy by the reality of her life. She rose, dressed, and prepared for another workday.

Meghan received a summons to see the head foreman in his office just before the midday dinner hour. The day had started badly when she saw Phelps back at work on the weaving floor. So much for her faith in Lucas Ridgely. Ignoring the odious man, she shut down her looms and, then, fighting her feeling of trepidation, she descended three flights of stairs to George Simmons's office.

They are going to dismiss me. They've decided I've lied, and I'm the one they want to leave, not Mathew Phelps. She wanted to rant and rave at the injustice of it all, but she remained outwardly calm as she knocked on the office door. The door swung open immediately.

"Miss McBride," Mr. Simmons greeted her without a smile, which increased her apprehension.

She nodded. "Mari Bright said ye wanted to see me," she said as she took his invitation to step inside the office.

The mill foreman shut the door before turning to answer. "Sit down, Miss McBride."

Meghan sat as instructed and placed her trembling hands on her lap.

"Miss Bride—" he began as he skirted his desk and sat in his chair.

"Ye've decided that ye don't believe me," she said. "That's why the man is back at work."

"There is no one to substantiate your story."

"Ye've not questioned anyone!" she burst out.

"Don't you be raising your voice to me, young woman!" he barked back.

"Ye are calling me a liar, and I'm not to get angry?" She eyed him as if he'd gone mad.

"I've a generous proposition to make to you; I suggest you listen and keep quiet!"

"A proposition like Phelps's?" she dared, and was immediately sorry when she saw how his mouth worked and his face turned a bright shade of red.

"Why you little ungrateful—!"

"George!" boomed another male voice. Neither Meghan nor Simmons had seen the door behind them open.

"Lucas!" he said, looking uncomfortable.

"It doesn't sound like you're offering her the job."

The man scowled. "She hasn't closed her mouth long enough to allow me to," he said.

"I'll take care of it then," Lucas said.

"Fine, I'll be happy to leave you alone with her." He rose and left, looking more than happy to oblige.

Meghan was slightly mollified by the way Lucas's mouth tightened at Simmons's behavior and the man's tone when he'd said "her."

"Meghan," Lucas said as he took Simmons's chair.

"Lucas, I don't know what kind of position ye have in mind, but I'll not stay where I'm not believed." Anger had stiffened her frame until her muscles hurt.

His dark eyes narrowed as he regarded her intently from across the desk.

"What makes you think I don't believe you?"

"Simmons said—"

"George Simmons is entitled to his own opinion. The matter isn't over yet; we're not done with Mathew Phelps."

"But none of the workers have been questioned."

Lucas frowned. "But I thought—" He stopped. "Never mind, it will be taken care of," he promised.

Meghan felt herself relaxing. "Then why am I here?" she asked.

"My aunt has a special request for you."

"Mrs. Gibbons?" Meghan echoed.

He nodded.

"How can I help her?"

"By entertaining me?" The twinkle in his gaze was mischievous.

She gasped with outrage, got up, and headed toward the door.

"Wait!" He rose quickly to hurry around the desk and grab her arm. "Sorry, bad joke I'm afraid."

"Very bad," she said, shaking under his touch.

He released her. "I said I'm sorry. I can see you're not up to a little teasing." His mouth had formed a half smile, but his amusement wasn't in his eyes.

"No." Her reply was short and strained.

Lucas's gaze flickered, and then he became all businesslike. "My aunt needs some stitching done, and she thought you'd be just the one to do it." There was no softness to his features as he held her gaze. "You sew, don't you?" he snapped.

"Aye," she said, regarding him with confusion. "But how did you know?"

"My aunt has a gown to be altered," he said, ignoring her question. "Can you do it for her?"

"But what about me work at the mill?" Had her accusations caused her to lose her employment there? What of the good wages she earned by running three looms?

"We'll—she'll," he amended upon reading her expression correctly, "pay you for both positions."

"You'll be paying me for me work at the mill while I sew the gown?"

He nodded.

Meghan was surprised by the woman's generosity, especially since Flora Gibbons knew about Meghan's part in the disturbance in production at the mill on Christmas Eve day. "I don't know . . ."

"Meghan, take the position," he said gently, "until we get everything at the mill straightened out."

She bristled as realization dawned. "Is this a bribe not to cause more trouble here?" She felt a frisson of warmth when he touched her arm, a reaction she didn't want to feel or notice.

It was his turn to get angry. "There's an easier way to ensure that, isn't there? My aunt could simply fire you, and be done with the whole mess. Instead, she has offered you a better job."

Meghan flushed. Put like that, she sounded like a rude ingrate. "I'll take the position." She paused. "And I'll do a good job for her."

"My aunt will be happy to hear it."

And ye? Meghan wondered, her gaze narrowing on his satisfied expression. *How do ye feel about me working at the house?* But before she dared to ask, she was astonished to hear him thanking her with sincerity.

"I—and my aunt—appreciate this, Meghan."

She gave him a crooked smile. *Why?* she wondered. If she'd been nothing but trouble, why would he want her around? Her heart tripped. Because he still wanted her? "Tell me, Lucas, did I really have a choice?" she asked after she'd paused as she turned to leave.

He looked startled by her question. "Of course," he said.

Damn, she thought. *I should have declined the offer and kept to me weaving looms and away from this man and his family.*

She must be mad to tempt the hell fires of fate. For if he did still desire her, the lure of the devil would be harder and might be much too strong for her to resist.

Damn his good looks! Meghan thought. And curse her for her continued weakness for him.

Nineteen

"I'll not be returning with you to Windfield," Lucas informed his family.

"What?" Beth said. "Why not?"

"Lucas, you can't stay in this house forever," his mother said, sounding put out, and his sister rolled her eyes. "James, tell your son that he must come home!"

"I'll not tell him anything, Mary," her husband said. "He's a grown man."

"You've never taken my side, have you?" Mary accused, and then an argument ensued that had both of the couple's children wincing at the harsh tones and epithets that neither man nor woman tried to conceal.

Lucas intervened by addressing his father. "There's nothing immediately pressing for me at home, is there?"

"No, of course not. Not for a month at least." James Ridgely shot his wife a mean glance before turning back to Lucas. "Stay as long as you like, son. Just be back in time for the spring planting."

"James!" his wife objected.

"Never you mind, Mary," James replied sharply.

"I want to stay, too," Beth announced.

Flora Gibbons, Lucas's aunt, had been amazingly silent through the whole exchange. She spoke up now. "No, Beth. You know I love having you, but you've been here long enough. Why don't you come again after the spring thaw?"

"But—" the young woman began.

"No buts, Elizabeth," her brother intoned. "I'm staying to help Aunt Flora. There'll be no time to coddle or entertain you."

Beth looked crushed. "Is that what you think—that I'm a child to be entertained?"

His expression softened. "No, you're anything but a child."

With tear-glistening eyes, Beth turned her gaze on her aunt. "Aunt Flora—"

"Lucas is right, Elizabeth. We have to attend to business matters. I'll have little time to spend with you."

Beth's shoulders slumped with defeat.

"What is wrong that my children choose to neglect their mother?" Mary Ridgely cried.

Lucas sighed. "We're not—"

"They're not neglecting you, Mary," his father interrupted in a gentler tone than he'd used with her before.

"But James—"

"Lucas is a grown man," James reminded her again. "He's done more for us than any parent has a right to ask of a son." He regarded his son with warmth. "We've got no right to complain or dictate." His voice had sharpened during his last words as he turned back to his wife.

"Beth," he said softly, "I'd like you to come home with me and your mother. You're becoming quite a young woman. Soon, you'll be leaving with a husband of your own. Is it wrong for me to be selfish of the time left with my little girl?"

Beth's brown eyes misted. "Oh, Daddy," she said, "of course, I'll come home."

"Dear God!" Mary cried, seeming oblivious to the

emotional scene being played out by father and daughter. "Spare me this nonsense!"

James's mouth tightened as he raked his wife with a telling glance. "Mary, I suggest you remember your place here."

"Place!" she cried. "I've got no place it seems. Not one in which I'm welcomed!" The threat of another fight hovered in the air.

Lucas had had enough. "Please, no more arguing." Was it any wonder he refused to wed, when he'd been a witness to the travesty of his parents' marriage? "What time will you leave tomorrow?" he asked his father, drawing the man's attention from his wife.

"Immediately after breakfast," James replied.

Lucas nodded and thought with guilt that he'd be glad to see his parents go. These holiday occasions with his family in attendance could be trying at times. He needed the time away from his parents. He wished he could keep Beth here with them, but Aunt Flora was right—they'd be too busy to entertain her.

"Aunt Flora," he said, drawing his aunt's attention, "may I have a private word with you?"

Flora nodded; and ignoring her sister's whining protest, she followed her nephew from the parlor and down the hall to the library. Lucas closed the door and then faced her.

"I've spoken with Mr. Simmons," Lucas said without preamble, "and he's agreed to release that young woman, Meghan McBride, to come and alter your green gown."

The woman's eyes flashed with satisfaction. "Good."

"What made you choose that particular girl?" Lucas asked, watching his aunt closely.

Flora Gibbons stared back without wavering. "Mari Bright has been singing Miss McBride's praises since she first came to us weeks ago. It's obvious she's skilled with cloth. I made a few inquiries and learned that she's as proficient with a needle." She paused, and a twinkle of mischief entered the woman's eyes. "And the girl has spirit."

"Because of the incident on the weaving floor?"

"She got everyone to shut off their machines," his aunt said. "It takes spunk to jeopardize your employment to make a stand. It's obvious to me that she needs and likes her position. Whatever caused her to risk losing it must have been important to her."

He felt the tension leave him. His thoughts had been running along the same lines as his aunt's recently. He'd been startled when his aunt had approached him with the matter of hiring Meghan as a temporary seamstress. It wasn't like Flora not to make her own arrangements. His gaze narrowed. It still wasn't like her. Had Aunt Flora guessed he had . . . feelings . . . for Meghan? Had she perhaps seen the two of them talking in the weaving room Christmas Eve day? No, he thought, that was ridiculous. His aunt's interest in Meghan's sewing skills was genuine.

Heat warmed his insides. Meghan would be in Flora's house daily . . . within his range. He'd be able to see her, talk to her, whenever the desire took him.

He frowned as he suddenly saw their offer of employment from Meghan's point of view. After the way George Simmons had treated her in his office, could he himself blame Meghan for being wary of her new position? He'd made his intentions toward her known from the start, believing it was best to be honest. He still believed that, but he realized that he'd done little to try to win her.

Behave be damned, he thought, recalling his conversation with Meghan. He had behaved as he'd promised . . . on the road and at the inn, but this was his territory now and he'd be damned if he didn't play the game by his own rules. He still wanted to bed her, but he wanted her to desire it, too.

Meghan McBride. His lips formed a smile. *I'm going to kill you with kindness. By the time I'm through, you'll find me irresistible.*

It wasn't fair, he realized. But then life wasn't fair, was it. His father had married the woman he loved, and she'd become a shrew to be tolerated for the rest of his life.

He wouldn't make the same mistake, Lucas vowed. He would marry eventually, but there would be no desire . . . nothing to make him vulnerable to his wife. Marriage would be strictly a business arrangement.

Thinking of Meghan made his stomach tighten and caused a throbbing at the base of his shaft. He desired her more than he'd ever wanted a woman. He would take her to his bed, pleasure her, and when they tired of their relationship, he'd give her all the money she needed to see that she wouldn't have to work for the rest of her life.

She wouldn't have a hold on him like his mother had on his father. He'd gift her with everything . . . but his heart.

"Did you give her the ring?" Alicia Somerton shifted up on her elbow as she stroked her lover's arm.

"Aye."

"And?"

Rafferty reached over and caressed her cheek. "Meghan loved it." He grinned as his hand slipped to her breast. "You have exquisite taste in jewelry my love."

The woman made an unladylike sound. "It was given to me by a friend. I had nothing to do with choosing it."

"Well, it worked perfectly. Meghan was charmed. Mourning or not, she'll be ready to marry me soon."

Alicia regarded him without expression. "Lass?" Rafferty asked, disturbed by her look.

A dark gleam entered her green eyes. "Why do you have to marry *her?*" She spoke of *her* as if she was loath to say Meghan's name.

The Irishman sighed. "We agreed that I should marry. Meghan was me fiancée long before I met ya. She's the best choice, ye know that." He leaned over and drew her nipple into his mouth, laving it with his tongue. His head lifted, but he continued to stroke her with his long fingers.

"She's a child. I've no desire for her," he lied.

In truth, his lust for his young fiancée had intensified with each day. Since she had come to Somerville, he'd not bedded another . . . except Alicia, but then he'd never give up Alicia, not even after he and Meghan married. Alicia Somerton had given him everything he owned, and she could so easily take it all away.

His mind worked quickly. He had to keep Alicia happy; he could keep both Alicia and Meghan happy, he thought with arrogant confidence, without anyone being the wiser of their true relationship.

"Lynna saw you leaving the other night," Alicia said.

Rafferty's hand stilled on her breast. "What did ye tell her?"

Alicia's smile was cruel. "Lynna is no one to worry about, I can assure you. I told the little chit that we were going over the books."

"And she believed ya?" The last thing he needed was for Alicia's husband to discover that he was being cuckolded. Rafferty's gut lurched when she shook her head.

"I doubt it, but it doesn't matter." She grabbed his hand and instructed him to continue his fondling. "You see, Lynna needs her job desperately. Her mother is dead, and her father is ill. It's the only employment that will keep her and her family from going hungry."

Rafferty squeezed her breast tightly in reaction until she cried out, and his touch immediately softened to a caress. He knew what it was like to go hungry. It was a feeling he'd never forget—or forgive. He hated that Alicia had used food—or its lack—to manipulate one of her household staff. "I don't like it, Alicia."

She curled an arm about his neck and rubbed his nape with teasing fingers. "Lynna will be fine, Raff. I know how to treat my employees," she purred. "You should know, my dear. You're the perfect example of my generosity and goodwill."

Eyes narrowing, Rafferty wondered if Alicia had just threatened him. But then she was stroking him while nibbling and tonguing his ear, and all of his thoughts disappeared with the increasing, raging spiral of his lust.

Meghan felt butterflies in her stomach as she stared up at the huge Gibbons mansion. Nerves tingling, she fought back her fears. Do I knock on the front door, she silently asked herself, or do I go around to the servants' entrance? She was hired help. She skirted the house and rapped on the back door.

A middle-aged woman responded and eyed Meghan carefully. "Yes?"

"Me name's Meghan McBride, and I've been called by Mrs. Gibbons," Meghan said.

Recognition flickered across the servant's face. "Come in, Meghan McBride. I'm Mrs. Riker, Mrs. Gibbons's cook."

Meghan studied the woman's flour-coated apron and smiled. "Aye, I can see you are." She grinned. "I'm pleased to meet ya. Ye cooked all the wonderful treats at Christmas."

When the lady looked surprised, Meghan explained. "I work in the weaving room at the mill."

Mrs. Riker beamed. "You enjoyed my lemon cakes?"

"Aye, they melted in me mouth, they did."

The woman waved Meghan further in the kitchen. The room smelled of wonderful scents . . . of baking bread and roasting meat. "Sit yourself down, and I'll make you some tea. Then, I'll find Mrs. Gibbons for you."

"That won't be necessary, Mrs. Riker," Lucas said as he entered the room. "I'll take Meghan up to my aunt." He paused to flash a devastatingly handsome smile. "After we share some tea."

Mrs. Riker obviously saw nothing unusual with Lucas drinking tea in the kitchen, for she immediately went to put on the kettle. Then, with a grin, the cook placed a plate of pastries on the table directly in front of Lucas.

"You share, you hear?" she warned him good-naturedly.

Lucas laughed, and Meghan's heart beat faster at the rich, musical sound "I promise."

Meghan tensed as Lucas handed her a plate and then offered her a pastry. The memory of their late night snack was sharp in her mind . . . and what had happened afterward when Lucas had kissed her and she'd responded wildly . . . wantonly. As Mrs. Riker set out two cups and saucers, Meghan could almost taste the flavor of Lucas's lips.

Lucas seemed unaffected by her presence as he chatted easily with Mrs. Riker while they waited for the water to boil and then the tea to steep. Meghan had trouble keeping her gaze off him. It had been some time since she'd sat across the table from him, but the sensation wasn't new . . . only different after their exchanged kiss at the Pattersons' inn.

His blond hair had been combed into place with a hint of macassar oil, no doubt used to try to tame its tendency to curl. His sideburns were shorter than most men's and he was clean-shaven, while the gentlemen of the day wore moustaches or clipped beards.

She studied his jaw and had the wildest urge to run her lips over his smooth skin. He caught her staring, and warmth spread from her neck upward. She averted her gaze, only to be drawn back with fascination to look into his sparkling ebony eyes.

"Are you hungry?" he asked.

She shook her head.

"Could have fooled me," he whispered for her ears alone.

Ignoring his remark and her flushed face, Meghan bit into a pastry and found it delicious and sweet.

"Here you go, dears," Mrs. Riker said as she poured out two cups of tea.

"Eat and drink up, love," Lucas murmured while he held her gaze. "You're going to need all of your strength to get through your day here."

It was as if he'd read her mind—and her heart, which didn't help her state of mind and didn't bode well for the remainder of her time here.

Twenty

Mrs. Gibbons appeared delighted to see her. Meghan greeted the woman with a smile; and then with Lucas by her side, she followed her employer up the staircase to a sitting room on the second-story level of the house.

"I'd like you to make a new set of drapes for this room," Flora said, drawing Meghan's surprise.

A quick glance at Lucas told Meghan that he was as startled by his aunt's revelation as she. "I thought you wanted a gown altered," he said.

The woman waved the notion aside. "The gown can wait. The drapes in this room are too glum for my taste." She went to a sewing table along one wall and fingered a folded length of fabric. "Can you do this for me, Meghan?" she asked.

"Aye," Meghan assured her. "I'll be glad to." She moved to touch the material. " 'Tis lovely cloth."

Flora smiled. "I had it specially printed at the mill for this room." She lowered her voice to a whisper. "The pattern is one that was designed by my late husband. This will be the only printed cloth. I never thought to use it before . . . until now."

Meghan heard the emotion in her employer's voice and chanced a look at her nephew. Lucas was regarding his aunt with a soft expression that made Meghan's insides melt.

The older woman cleared her throat and gave

Meghan a brief smile. "Lucas will help you remove the old drapes."

"But I thought—" Lucas began.

"I can manage—" Meghan said simultaneously.

"Nonsense!" Lucas's aunt declared. "Lucas, you've been working too hard at my accounts these last few days. You can certainly use some time off from them to help Meghan."

Meghan refused to meet his gaze. The thought of him working by her side made her nervous . . . and yet it pleased her, too.

Flora had moved to the window, and now she gave Lucas instructions on how to remove the drapes. Then she began to address her seamstress. "Meghan?" she said when the young woman didn't respond.

Meghan glanced over and flushed. "I'm sorry, I didn't hear what ye said." Her gaze slammed into Lucas, whose dark eyes twinkled as she approached. She shot him a silent reproving look, and his lips curved with amusement.

"I said that the style of the old drapes is fine," Flora said. "There should be everything you need here. If you run out of thread, you can let Mrs. Riker or one of the housemaids know." She paused to grin. "We have plenty of cotton thread."

Meghan shared her grin. "Aye."

Flora's gaze ran the length of Meghan's serviceable gown. "Did you make your dress?" she asked.

The Irishwoman shifted uncomfortably. She'd restitched the gowns that Rafferty had purchased for her, but they were plain, not at all like the garments that Flora Gibbons wore. "Actually me fiancé bought it for me," she confessed. "I had to alter it, but—"

"Your fiancé?" Flora seemed startled. "I didn't know you were engaged." A furrow appeared on her brow. "Is it one of my workers?"

Did she see her employer's gaze slide briefly to Lucas? Meghan wondered. She shook her head.

Lucas's voice boomed into the ensuing silence. "He works in Somerville, Auntie."

This time there was no denying Flora's surprised glance toward her nephew.

Lucas's facial muscles tightened at the subject of Meghan's fiancé. He stared at his aunt with speculation and wondered why the existence of Meghan's fiancé should bother his relative.

Meghan looked uncomfortable, and Lucas couldn't blame her. Why should it concern his aunt whether or not Meghan was betrothed?

His eyes narrowed. Unless . . . But no, the idea was too ludicrous to make sense, he decided. Meghan McBride wasn't someone his family would approve for him. She was not of their class. Odds are Aunt Flora was simply worried that she might lose a good worker.

"Meghan is not ready to leave your fold yet, Aunt Flora," he said, testing his theory.

His aunt laughed and seemed to relax. "I hope not." Her gaze studied Meghan intently. "There are still matters at the mill that Meghan and I need to resolve."

"Matters?"

"Yes," the woman said. "I want to know why Meghan felt the need to stop production."

"It's being investigated," Lucas said quickly, uncomfortable with his aunt delving into such matters.

"By whom?"

"George Simmons . . . and me," Lucas replied.

"Handle it yourself, Lucas." When Lucas looked at her with surprise, she explained, "I can trust your findings will be honest ones."

Sensing Meghan's uneasiness with the conversation, Lucas agreed and then suggested that Meghan start

IRISH LINEN

work. She seemed tense to him as Flora showed her where the sewing supplies were kept.

Soon, Aunt Flora left the room, and he and Meghan were alone. He hated to know that she was uncomfortable in his presence. He wanted to regain the relaxed camaraderie they'd shared on the ship . . . and then later again on their journey to Somerville. The way it was before he'd lost reason and got carried away by lust.

Meghan was pulling things out of the sewing table drawer when Lucas came up behind her.

"Meghan."

She jumped. She had known he was still in the room, but she hadn't realized that he was so close. *You're a liar, me girl,* she silently told herself. *Ye've known every movement, every breath, that he's made since he greeted ya in the kitchen.*

"I apologize for that awkward moment with my aunt," he said, surprising her.

She faced him. "Neither your aunt nor ye has anything to apologize for. It's her mill."

He sighed, and it seemed as if the tension had left his large frame. She gazed up into his handsome face, and the brightness of his smile stole her breath away.

She blinked and then averted her gaze downward. *Why, God, did I have to fall for this particular man?* Was his aunt right? Would Lucas report honestly and see Phelps punished for his behavior? Wanting to believe it, she felt her guard lower toward this man.

She felt his fingers on her cheek. She lifted her chin, and with the gentlest caress, he tucked a stray lock of her hair behind her ear. Meghan closed her eyes, moved by his tenderness, and the hollow feeling she'd felt for so long began to fill up again with warmth.

"Meghan," he murmured.

Her eyes met his. "Lucas, this is mad. I should have

stayed at the mill. We're courting danger with me being here."

His mouth twisted into a tender half smile. "Contrary to what you may think, this was my aunt's idea, not mine." He bent his head until she could feel his breath whisper against her mouth.

"I could have denied her request," she admitted, unable to keep herself from leaning toward him. She was caught in his spell, a web of magic that stroked and caressed her with heat . . . and caring.

There was something genuine about Lucas Ridgely, she thought. Something good and kind and true. She didn't believe for one minute that he played a poor knight in shiny armor, as he'd said. He had rescued her how many times now? Twice? Three times, she realized, although she didn't want to recall the third when he'd saved her from being a willing wanton.

He didn't move to kiss her; yet, he was close enough that if she leaned forward an inch their mouths would touch . . . and ignite.

Lucas? She didn't realize that she'd said his name aloud . . . not until he answered her.

"Yes?" He moved away slightly and cupped her face with both hands, sensitizing her cheeks. He shifted his fingers lower to rub his thumbs across her lips. "You know I want to kiss you."

She swallowed. "Aye."

"And you want me to, don't you?" His dark eyes held her gaze.

Her eyelashes fluttered closed briefly. "Aye," she confessed with a rasping breath.

Still, he didn't immediately kiss her. He stared at her mouth while his fingers and thumbs caressed her lips, and she gloried in his tenderness, even while she experienced an urgent desire.

"Meghan." His gaze searched hers.

"Aye, Lucas," she whispered. "Do it. Do it, before I think of all the reasons why we shouldn't kiss."

With a groan, he bent his head while he lifted her chin, and then his warm mouth slanted across her lips with hunger. The hot searing contact made Meghan's blood rush and her knees weaken.

Lucas lifted his head, ending the kiss too soon. "Sweet," he murmured in a tone that made her shiver. "So sweet . . ."

And then he captured her mouth with a gentleness that brought tears to her eyes. She leaned closer and sighed with pleasure when his arms surrounded her. He stroked her back, while he used his mouth to caress her lips. He trailed a path across her cheek and nibbled on her ear.

"Lucas," she begged. She wanted more . . . to feel his hands, his mouth on her breasts.

"I know," he whispered. "I feel it, too."

She could hear the increased rate of his breathing. It mirrored the rasp within her own chest.

Suddenly, Lucas stiffened, and it was then that Meghan heard a sound in the corridor.

"Later," he promised. He released her with a smile of regret and a look that rocked her.

As the haze of magic began to dissipate, Meghan's reasoning powers returned with an awakened sense of horror. She'd known it was dangerous to have him near, but she hadn't realized how dangerous. There was no denying that she had invited his kiss. She spun away from him, berating herself for her lack of control, as she pretended to be busy with the folded cloth. Her face warmed as she thought of her behavior.

What was it about him that stole her reason along with her breath?

A wave of guilt hit her hard; she grabbed onto the

edge of the fabric until her knuckles whitened and her fingers ached.

His hands closed over hers, gently easing them from the cloth. "Don't fret, Meghan McBride," he said. "I can tell how your mind is working, but it's my fault more than yours."

Her gaze shot to gauge his expression. His dark eyes and the curve of his mouth hinted at self-reproach. She wanted to tell him the truth, to take the blame for what had just occurred between them, but shame kept her silent.

"Think about this, Meghan, when you're with your Rafferty," he said through tight lips. He pulled her into his arms and kissed her deeply before he set her away. "Now about these drapes . . ."

Meghan's mouth throbbed with the imprint of his kiss. She heard her thundering heartbeat as she followed Lucas to the window and attempted to gather her composure enough to get on with the work at hand. Lucas's high-handed attitude started to make her simmer with anger. "How are ye and Phelps different?" she dared.

He froze in the act of taking down the first set of window drapes. Then he turned slowly, his frame taut with tension, and then climbed down to place them over the edge of a large mahogany desk. He faced her then, his gaze mocking. "The difference, Meghan McBride, is that you like it when I kiss and touch you."

He ignored her gasp and returned to work. "Do you need anything else?" he asked harshly after he'd taken down the second and last pair. The tension was so thick it nearly choked off their breathing air.

She shook her head.

"Then, I'll be helping my aunt at the mill. If you find you need some more thread, tell Mrs. Riker."

Which means don't come to me, Meghan guessed. She

agreed to his terms and then set to work, as if dismissing his presence, which she actually couldn't do. She heard him leave, and at the sound of the closing door, she released a shuddering breath. With trembling fingers, she touched her mouth, recalling the pleasure brought on with his tender kiss. His third and more demanding kiss had aroused her physically; his gentle kiss had tugged on her emotions and her heart. And then she had gone and said something nasty to him, because she was afraid of her feelings . . .

Confused, Meghan fought the urge to follow Lucas and call him back. Then she felt guilt, for she hadn't been thinking of her fiancé from the first moment she'd seen Lucas downstairs. Lately, her only thoughts and desires during each wakened and sleeping moment involved Lucas Ridgely, not Rafferty O'Connor.

Her hands shook as she unfolded the cloth, and she stared at the cotton print until her vision blurred with tears.

"What am I going to do?" she whispered.

Abandoning the fabric, Meghan sat down in a nearby chair and bent forward to cradle her head in her hands.

"I'm in love with a man who wants to bed, but not wed me."

Twenty-one

"Why can't ye come to Somerville next Saturday?" Rafferty scowled at his fiancée as he pulled the carriage to a stop before Patty Rhoades's boardinghouse.

Meghan sighed. "I told ye that I've been working for Mrs. Gibbons. I promised to alter two gowns for her."

"Work on them in the evenings."

She shook her head. "I cannot. 'Tis my position now. I'll not lose it." She shot him a look of irritation. "I'm earning a living, O'Connor. What else would ye have me do? Quit me employment here and work at the powder mill?"

He shook his head. "We'll need evera bit of our resources for our cottage after we're married." He studied her with speculation. "Ye've been saving yer money, haven't ye, Meghan? Perhaps I should hold onto it for ye."

She shook her head. "I've been saving it fine, Rafferty O'Connor. I don't need ye to keep it." What she didn't leave on account at the mill, she'd stashed beneath her mattress at Patty's. Why was she uncomfortable with the idea of spending her money on a cottage with Rafferty? She'd known all along that she'd be sharing his home some day.

Lucas Ridgely invaded her thoughts. Since she'd begun work at the house, she'd seen him daily and her love for him had grown . . . while her feelings for Rafferty had . . . changed.

"I'll be here next Saturday as usual, Meghan."

She bristled. "No, Rafferty."

Her fiancé's hands tightened on the horse's reins. Studying his whitened fists, Meghan had the feeling that Rafferty would like to reach over and shake her. "I'll be ready a week from Saturday," she told him. She didn't suggest he come to visit her before then, although he could have if he'd wanted badly enough to see her. But she was irritated with him, and something had happened between them the previous evening that had scared and appalled her and made her want to put some distance between them for a long while.

Last night, Rafferty had kissed her, but he'd tried to touch her breasts, too, and—God help her—she'd struggled. She hadn't wanted Rafferty's touch. She hadn't even wanted his kiss, let alone for him to paw at her the way he'd done! Rafferty had been furious with her, but she didn't care.

"Good night, Rafferty." She climbed down from the carriage. As usual Rafferty made no move to help her as Lucas did. Which was just as well, she thought, given the way she was feeling at present.

"Aren't ye going to kiss me?" he asked angrily.

Meghan ignored him as if she hadn't heard as she walked to the door of Patty's boardinghouse.

"It's been over four months since yer da died, Meghan," he said. "It's high time we marry!" He'd shouted his last words, which sounded too much like a threat to Meghan.

With a loudly muttered curse that made Meghan's face flush with anger, Rafferty flicked the reins and drove the carriage away.

Meghan stood on the porch before entering the house. *I can't marry him,* she thought.

"Meghan? Is that you?" Patty came out of the kitchen with a warm smile of greeting that died upon seeing the young woman's face. "What is it?" she asked with concern.

Tired, Meghan shook her head. "It . . . it's not something I can talk about yet."

Patty didn't appear offended. "Well, you come into the other room and join us. We're about to taste a new cake receipt I've tried."

"Thank ye, that'd be nice," she replied, one corner of her mouth lifting in a slightly crooked smile.

But after she'd taken several steps, Meghan felt as if her limbs were leaden. She was tired of worrying about her life. She'd not slept in Somerville, not with Miss Doddleberry's snores, which had been horrendous with an infection of the woman's nasal passages.

"Patty," she called softly. "I think I'll go up to bed, if you don't mind. I'm not feeling up to cake, I'm afraid."

The woman nodded with understanding. "You look to need sleep." Her gray gaze held concern. "Go on up then," she said. "I'll make your excuses to the others."

Meghan murmured her thanks and then made the long, arduous journey up two flights of stairs. In her attic room, she undressed, lay on the bed, and closed her eyes. Her muscles throbbed. Her thoughts spun with images that confused and disturbed her. The memory of Rafferty's behavior as he'd tried to fumble beneath her bodice to fondle her breasts made her shudder with revulsion.

Don't think of him. She thought of Lucas's kisses instead . . . how they made her feel warm and fuzzy inside . . . not chilled and . . . unclean.

"I can't marry Rafferty O'Connor," she whispered into the dark attic room.

It no longer seemed to matter about Lucas's offer to make her his mistress. Her decision was based on her feelings—or lack of—for Rafferty alone.

I've enough money saved to pay Rafferty for me voyage and me clothes. Somehow I'll pay him back for Da's passage, too. But I'll not stay and marry him, simply because I'm grateful for what he's done.

Suddenly, she remembered Lucas's words. *"It's not gratitude I want from you, Meghan . . ."*

He wanted her still. And Lord help her, she wanted him and loved him.

She'd have to be content to live alone.

By the time Saturday evening came and she'd joined the others at the dinner table at Patty's, Meghan felt edgy. Now that she'd made her decision to end her betrothal to Rafferty, she valued her employment as a lifeline. Fortunately, Flora Gibbons seemed to have a great deal of work to keep her busy, but what would happen once Mrs. Gibbons ran out of things for her to sew? Would she be allowed to return to the mill?

"Is Rafferty coming tonight?" Susan asked pleasantly.

"I hope not," Meghan replied without thinking.

Susan stopped and regarded her friend with surprise.

Meghan flushed as she realized that everyone at the table was staring at her. "Have ye forgotten that I've work to do at Mrs. Gibbons's?"

"Oh, yes, you told me, I forgot."

But Meghan thought she'd heard disappointment in her friend's tone, so she cornered her alone after dinner to question Susan about it.

"Ye don't like Rafferty O'Connor, do ye," she asked as she found Susan in her room. The young woman seemed hesitant to answer as she stood at the window, gazing out into the night. "Susan, please . . . tell me."

Susan turned to regard her with a sober expression. "No, I can't say I have a liking for the man."

Meghan raised her eyebrows. "Why?" She'd never given thought to how her friends felt about her fiancé. She'd been too busy struggling with her own mixed feelings. Did they all feel the same way?

"You don't seem angry," Susan said with a glimmer of surprise.

"No, I . . ." Meghan's voice trailed off, and she looked away. "How can I be angry when I feel the same way?"

Susan's startled gasp brought Meghan's head around. "You don't care for the man, but you're going to marry him?"

Meghan grabbed her friend's arm as she heard voices from the stairs. "Please," she begged, "not so loud. I don't want the others to know yet."

The woman blinked. "Okay," she said, as she regarded her friend strangely. "Now would you please explain?"

Meghan had to smile. Susan sounded excited that she was the one whom Meghan had chosen to confide in. "I've decided not to marry him," she admitted after a brief hesitation.

"You have!" Susan burst out.

Meghan hushed her, and the young woman apologized to her friend.

"Aye," Meghan said. "He is . . . well—changed. It's been over two years since we became betrothed, but he and I hadn't seen each other for most of that time." The voices outside the room receded as the women went back downstairs.

Her thoughts turned inward with old memories. "He seemed a different man when Da was alive. Rafferty was full of ambition . . . of life. He had such wonderful plans, ye see." She came out of her reverie with a smile for Susan. "I've never met a more solid and dependable man as Rafferty O'Connor—except Da, of course." Something twisted inside her as she recalled the months of struggling to find food. "When our potato crop failed us again, we went hungry. Many of our people gave up hope. Children sickened and died . . . men and women, too . . ." She felt her throat tighten. "We'd been eating roots, berries, and cabbage leaves, but soon they'd disappeared."

She turned pain-stricken eyes on her friend. "Do ye know what 'tis like to see the people ye've known and loved all of yer youth naked and filthy, when they weren't dressed in rags? To watch a mother cling to her dead child, both of them looking like skeletons?" Meghan choked back a sob. "Dear God, I hope to never see or know the likes of such again. Every day I pray for those who stayed behind, knowing that if it hadn't been for Rafferty O'Connor, I'd still be there just like the rest of them . . . sick or dead . . . and with the *Sasanaigh* uncaring as long as they continued to take our grain."

"Oh, Meghan . . ." Susan's eyes filled with tears as she caught Meghan's hand. "I'm so sorry."

Meghan tried to smile. "There was Rafferty, ye see," she said with a soft expression. "He never gave up hope that our lives could be better. He was fighting angry, he was. Swore no Sax'n was going to lay him low. He'd find a way to get to America, he said." She released a shuddering sigh. "He promised to send for us—me and Da—once he had the funds." She paused. "And he did."

Susan's features reflected her understanding of Meghan's current situation. "You're grateful to him."

"Aye." Meghan dabbed at the corner of each eye with her finger. "I'm grateful to Rafferty O'Connor, and when I began to have doubts about us, I kept remembering my gratitude." She closed her eyes. "But is gratitude alone enough for a lasting marriage?"

Susan shook her head. "No," she said. "Although there are some who have married for less."

"And were happy?" Meghan probed with the intensity of needing to know.

"Perhaps," the other woman said. "But I know I wouldn't be," she added.

"No," Meghan agreed. "I think I wouldn't be happy either."

"So you've decided to break your engagement."

Meghan nodded. Break, she thought with a pang. Would she be breaking Rafferty's heart when she finally told him?

"You feel terrible about it," Susan said as she gave Meghan's arm a gentle squeeze meant to comfort.

"Aye. Wouldn't ye feel the same?"

Susan's mouth firmed. "About Rafferty O'Connor? No."

Meghan stared at her, shocked. "Why?"

"Because he's treated you appallingly, Meghan McBride. You've been so busy being grateful to him that you've been blind to his behavior toward you!"

"I—" Meghan bit her lip. "Ye are right," she said with a tired sigh.

"When will you tell him?"

"He'll be coming for me next Saturday. I suppose I'll tell him then."

"No," Susan said. "You must tell him before that. Why suffer another week of worrying when you can get the deed done with sooner?"

"I guess I could go Sunday evening."

But Susan shook her head. "We can go on Monday. It's the easiest day in the dressing room, and I'll be able to leave early." The woman's lips twisted. "I suppose there's one good thing to working there."

"We?" Meghan said as she realized that her friend had included herself.

"You don't think I'd let you travel to Somerville alone, do you?" Susan replied, and Meghan experienced a rush of affection for the girl. "Quick goodbyes are always best. I'll wait in the carriage for you."

Aye, Meghan thought. *Quick goodbyes are always best.* Her heart thumped with pain. Then why couldn't she follow that advice when it came to Lucas?

Because although she knew that the time spent in his company was a long farewell to the man she loved, she wanted to experience . . . to have something to remember . . . for those lonely nights when finally she'd be left all alone.

Rafferty gripped the jar of licorice drops fiercely, before he slammed it onto the counter. "Damn her," he muttered. He had an ache in his loins for Meghan McBride that had become obsessive.

He'd wanted her from the first signs of her budding womanhood, but he'd done the honorable thing and waited, because she was the daughter of his best friend. He'd been nervous when he'd asked her to marry him, surprised when she'd agreed.

"Ye're dragging yer feet, Meggie love," he said with a sneer. "I'll not be put off much longer!"

Alicia Somerton had become whiny of late. Apparently, someone else had seen him leaving the Somerton residence at an unusual hour and had mentioned the fact to her husband Michael. She'd managed to allay Michael's suspicions with the excuse of Rafferty having delivered some supplies. Her husband had seemed satisfied with her answer, but Alicia was now nervous.

Although she found Meghan annoying, Alicia wanted Rafferty to marry his fiancée soon.

"I'd hate for Michael to learn about us, darling," she'd purred as she'd stroked his chest after the last time they'd been together. "You and I are good together—you're so creative—but until you and Meghan are safely married, I think it best if we suffer a separation."

His anger roiled in his gut until he recalled the pleasurable satisfaction he'd felt with what had followed their conversation . . . in Alicia's bed.

He enjoyed his employer's wife. Who wouldn't relish bedding a lust-inciting, earthy wanton? As much as he loved to futter Alicia, he knew she was right to part company for a while. But without Alicia to sexually excite and appease him, his yearning for Meghan had increased to an agonizing, stiff bulge beneath his trousers.

His shaft got hard just thinking about Meghan's breasts. His hand cupped his crotch to ease the throbbing. He closed his eyes and saw himself sucking her nipples as he thrust between Meghan's open thighs.

The bell on the shop door rang, and he glanced toward the entrance. Mrs. John edged inside, her gaze noting him before sliding away.

Rafferty squeezed his crotch before releasing himself. It was early morning, the wrong time for what he had in mind, but he didn't care. "Good day to ye, Mrs. John," he said. "Top of the mornin' to ya."

The woman's head bobbed as she nodded. She looked as if she'd skitter away at the least little provocation.

"Can I help ye with something?" He came from behind the counter, his trousers taut over his pulsing cod.

"I . . ." She glanced down his length and, with a small gasp, looked away.

Rafferty came to her quickly, encircling her shoulders with his arm. "No need to run, Mrs. John." His breath rasped as he stared at her breasts. Such small breasts to nip and bite and rub hard with his hands, he thought. He imagined the breasts belonged to Meghan. "Ye look lovely this day," he said hoarsely.

"Please," she whispered.

He spun her to face him. "Please, Mrs. John?" He grinned as he studied her quivering mouth. "As I pleased ya when I turned a blind eye to yer husband's debt?"

Fear flashed in her eyes, but she didn't pull away.

"I hear yer boy's sick, Mrs. John."

She nodded.

"I've a new candy treat in stock. Perhaps the boy would like one?"

Mrs. John swallowed and shook her head, and he tightened his grip on her shoulders. "Not even a wee one?" he asked.

"Yes," she breathed.

His gaze rose to her hair, and he lifted a hand to stroke the brown strands. "Good." His fingers slid down her face and throat, and then hovered for a heartbeat over her bodice. "Now how much did ye say ye had to spend?"

"I . . . I don't—"

"No need to fret, Mrs. John," he purred. "We're friends, aren't we? *Good* friends, I'd even say. I'll give ya the candy for yer boy."

Mrs. John inhaled sharply as he cupped her breast and began to worry the tip with his finger to make the nipple harden

"Thank you, Mr. O'Connor," she said meekly.

"You're quite welcome, Meggie," he said. And he released her to lock the store entrance.

Twenty-two

Lucas came into the sitting room and paused inside the doorway to study Meghan. The young woman was bent over her sewing, her features taut with concentration. *She looks tired,* he thought. Something wrenched in his gut as he noticed how slowly she plied her needle. When she turned to grab a new piece of thread, he saw the dark circles under her blue eyes.

He'd been gone only a week. Why did it seem as if he'd been gone for several?

Because you missed her, a tiny voice inside him whispered, giving him a jolt.

Seeing her again was a feeling unlike any other. He felt alive and at peace . . . and what? In lust? No, he realized with a frown, because he was concerned that Meghan was overworked. There was more to his feelings for her than lust. He cared for the woman. And it was that thought that frightened him, because like his father, it made him vulnerable to pain.

Meghan sighed and paused in her stitching to arch and stretch her back muscles. She grimaced, stood, and turned at the waist. She froze as her gaze collided with Lucas Ridgely.

"Meghan."

"Lucas," she breathed, "you're back."

He nodded as he approached. "You look tired." He stopped when he was within a few feet.

"I'm all right." She hadn't felt all right, Meghan thought, until just a moment ago when she'd realized that he'd returned. A pain lodged beneath her breast bone. "Did your trip go well?" It was crazy, she knew, but she'd been more than a little upset to learn that he'd gone back to Kent County without telling her a word.

"Beth's leg is healing nicely. The doctor—"

"Your sister was injured?" she asked, unable to contain her curiosity.

He frowned. "My aunt didn't tell you?"

She shook her head, and the furrow between Lucas's brow deepened. "I told her to let you know," he told her quietly.

Her heart rejoiced. "I guess she didn't think it was important for me to know."

He narrowed his eyes. "I specifically mentioned *you.*"

Meghan could see the muscle along one side of his jaw tick as anger lit up his dark eyes. She shrugged to make light of his aunt's mistake.

Suddenly, Lucas's features softened. "Did you think I'd forgotten you?" His voice was soft, tender, filling Meghan with a longing so poignant it made her want to cry out and confess her love for him. But she didn't speak.

"Meghan?"

"Aye."

"Oh, Meghan . . ." He touched his hands to her temples and threaded his fingers into her hair. "I couldn't possibly forget you . . ."

Dangerous, she thought. Although she knew she should be objecting to such attention from him, she allowed him to pull her closer, to tenderly kiss her closed eyelids . . . and slide his lips over her nose to fasten with sweetness on her quivering mouth.

"Don't stop." Her words came unbidden as his head lifted, but she'd spoken her thoughts . . . her desires.

With a groan of hunger, Lucas recaptured her mouth in a searing contact that made her tingle all over, that caused her blood to flow hotly and her toes to curl.

He pulled away with a growl of frustration. "You're killing me by slow degrees, Meghan McBride," he whispered. "I want you. You want me. Why won't you come to me?"

Mortified, Meghan stared at the floor with flushed cheeks. *"Please . . ."* she choked out. *"I can't."*

"Because of Rafferty." The irritation in his tone sounded so unlike him that her gaze snapped upward to read his face.

"Because of *me*, Lucas," she said evenly. "I'm a good Catholic woman. It's not me habit to leap into bed with any man!"

He blanched. "And I'm any man?" he asked.

"No, but—" She spun and put a distance of several feet between them. She stopped and faced him. "I believe in the sanctity of marriage."

"Love . . . marriage," he said darkly. The mockery in his expression hurt her. "I've seen the consequences of a so-called happy marriage."

Sudden insight struck Meghan like a lightning bolt. "Your parents are not happy?" she guessed.

He appeared taken aback, before his face became unreadable. "My father married my mother for love," he said with an underlying hint of disparagement in his tone. "God knows why she married him."

Impulse urged Meghan closer to him. She touched his arm. To her surprise, his muscles beneath his shirtsleeve felt tense and hot beneath her fingertips. "I think I understand."

"Do you?" He regarded her with a derision that stung.

She released him and went to sit and gather her sewing. "I'm not unfeeling, Lucas," she murmured after several silent moments had passed. She hoped she'd hidden her pain well.

His silence continued. Meghan forced herself to work as tension filled the quiet. She felt her muscles contract with each throbbing pulse beat.

"I know," he said suddenly.

His two simple words were uttered with such tenderness and feeling that Meghan had to swallow against a lump as she regarded him with bright eyes. His admission hadn't come from him easily, for to admit that he believed in her was to admit that he might care.

"Have you and Rafferty set a date to be married?" he asked in a low voice.

She shook her head as she bent low over her work. Lucas felt a burst of pure joy. Why did he have the feeling, though, that there was something she wasn't telling him? His joy faded, and his stomach knotted.

"Ah, well, there's plenty of time, I guess," he said easily. Too easily, he realized.

"Aye," she murmured without looking up from her lap.

He studied her while she continued to ply her needle. She created neat, even stitches as she tacked a length of lace on one of his aunt's gowns.

Suddenly, he realized that it was Sunday, and Meghan shouldn't be here. "Why are you working today?" he asked. He recalled how tired she'd first appeared to him and wondered if his aunt had become too demanding of her.

Meghan seemed to have difficulty forming an answer.

"Is my aunt working you too hard?" he demanded sharply.

She blinked up at him. "Oh, no! Mrs. Gibbons has been wonderful. 'Tis just that . . ."

"Yes?"

"I want to finish. I fear that your aunt will run out of things for me to do. I need to start back at the mill," she said as if reluctant to confess. "I don't want to lose me position there."

"Didn't I promise you that wouldn't happen?" His growl of anger clearly startled her.

"I know, but—" She bit her lip, and again he sensed something odd in her manner. "Promises can't always be kept," she said softly. He saw her throat work as she swallowed.

"I see." He was annoyed, for he didn't see at all. Surely, his aunt needed to keep Meghan on as seamstress.

He softened his tone when he saw that she was upset. "It's good to see you again," he said, and was pleased to see her blush.

" 'Tis good to see ye, too."

"Is it?" he probed, wanting to know the truth. He didn't wait for her reply. "Good, for you'll be seeing a lot more of me now."

He was disappointed when his declaration brought no visible signs of reaction from her.

His trip home to Windfield had disturbed him, not because of his sister's injury—Beth was healing well—but because of a woman whom his parents had thrust at him . . . someone they'd approved for his wife. But the attractive Valerie Bain had held no interest for him. The only woman he wanted in his bed and his life, he realized, was sweet Meghan McBride.

He'd always known he'd be expected to marry, but he'd hoped to put off the horror for some years yet. His parents wanted his wife to be of the same social standing as they . . . someone with breeding, money, and class.

Meghan, born of Irish peasant stock, met none of his parents' expectations.

He'd vowed not to marry for any reason other than business. Valerie Bain certainly fit the bill nicely, only Lucas was loath to settle down. The woman his parents had chosen for him was, by all appearances, smart, attractive, and intelligent. All traits he admired in a woman.

But Valerie Bain wasn't Meghan, and therefore, he didn't want her. He'd been polite to Valerie, but he'd made it clear that there was no future for them. His mother had been not only disappointed, but furious with him. His father . . . well, because of his own experiences, James Ridgely was more inclined to side with his son.

I'm obsessed with Meghan, he thought as he continued to study her. And until he'd had her in his bed and his life for a while, he'd didn't want to even think of another woman.

So, he would find a way to bed Meghan McBride before she wed her Rafferty O'Connor. He owed it to himself . . . and to Meghan to show her what she'd be missing if she married a man who didn't physically move her.

"Alicia."

"What, Rafferty?" Alicia Somerton regarded the man she'd found the most sexually stimulating to date . . . besides Michael, who no longer seemed to be interested in her. It wouldn't do for Rafferty to know it, however; for although he made her scream and shudder with ecstasy, she didn't trust the man not to use her weakness for him against her. "What do you want from me now?"

He gritted his teeth as he grabbed her from the chair. His grip on her upper arms was cruel, but there was about him a look that titillated and teased her. "Ye're denying me your bed?" he growled.

She arched an eyebrow with disdain. "Perhaps you just don't interest me today, Rafferty."

"No?" His green eyes gleamed with intent, and she struggled to be free, loving it when he used his strength to subdue her. "You don't like it when I do this . . . ?" He bent his head. "And this?"

He kissed and bit her neck, and then released her when she moaned, before he took her to the bed and proceeded to show her who was the master of sexual games.

"Say it, Alicia," he demanded after he'd taunted and teased her with his kisses and intimate caresses. He hovered between her legs, ready to make her shatter into a thousand bright lights.

"Yes, Rafferty," she cried, arching up, inviting the ultimate connection. "I want you."

"And?"

"Take me, you bastard, before I rip your eyes out!"

With a ragged laugh, he buried his shaft between her thighs. He thrust deep and hard only a few short times before Alicia cried out. Then, he drove home one more time, before he shuddered and spilled his seed.

"Thank you, Rafferty," Alicia said politely after she'd regained her steady breaths.

Rafferty lifted himself on his elbows, and his gaze caressed her love-swollen lips and whisker-burned breasts. He smiled with satisfaction. "Yer pleasure was mine, lass."

Twenty-three

The next day Lucas went directly to George Simmons's office. He hadn't mentioned it to Meghan, but there was still the matter of Mathew Phelps.

George rose from his desk to greet him. "Lucas," he said, "you're back."

After murmuring an appropriate response, Lucas took the seat before Simmons's desk. "Mathew Phelps," he said. "What did you learn?"

The mill foreman leaned back in his chair. "The man's innocent, it seems. No one would come forward to substantiate the woman's story."

"So you think Meghan lied?" Lucas said, unconsciously using her familiar name.

The man nodded. "It appears so. Under the circumstances, there was nothing for me to do, but leave Phelps with the weavers."

"Is it possible that the workers are afraid to come forward?"

"Why would they be afraid? I haven't threatened to dismiss them if they told the truth."

"But did you tell them that?"

The man looked uncomfortable. "Well, no, but I'm not known as an unfair man, Lucas."

Lucas's expression softened. "I know that, George, but I just can't believe that all the workers would follow Meghan's lead if there wasn't something else here . . ."

"Perhaps she's a persuasive person," George suggested.

"And then again," Lucas said, "perhaps Mathew Phelps is."

The foreman looked angry. "I'm tired of worrying about the incident. We can't tolerate such nonsense from the workers. We pay decent wages for a good day's production."

"I realize that, George." Lucas rose to his feet. "But if Phelps did misuse his position to proposition our women workers, don't you think it will affect the workers and their production? Who'd want to work for a man who threatens to fire them if they refuse to meet his personal needs? At the first opportunity of other employment, they'll be gone."

"We are the best employers on the Brandywine," the foreman insisted.

"Not if we allow Phelps to remain in his position, if he's guilty." Lucas opened the office door. "By the way Meghan McBride wants to come back to the mill."

George Simmons scowled. "I'll keep on the matter, but keep her away from here until I get a chance to question the women further."

Lucas's smile held no humor. "If you'd like me to handle this, I will."

"I'll handle it, Lucas," the foreman insisted.

"Hurry and get it over with," Susan urged in a loud whisper. "I want to get back to Patty's before it gets too dark."

Meghan nodded and climbed from the carriage. They'd arrived at the Somerville Company Store only moments ago. Her knees shook as she walked up the two store steps and pushed on the shop door.

The sound of the bell made her jump, and she

blinked to adjust her eyes. Rafferty was nowhere to be found, and Meghan realized with a frown that he must be working in the back room.

She hesitated for only a second. *Oh, well,* she thought, *better to tell him where no one could overhear.* Her gaze swept the shop's interior as she crossed to the counter and circled it to reach the stockroom entrance. The door was slightly ajar, and she heard sounds that confirmed that someone—Rafferty—was indeed working in the back.

She shoved on the door. "Rafferty—"

Meghan gasped, and then shock held her immobile. Her fiancé was inside the storeroom all right, but he wasn't alone. She stared for a moment at Rafferty with his pants about his ankles, his bare ass bobbing as he humped the naked woman sprawled across a large sack of grain. Horrified by what she'd seen, Meghan cried out and ran blindly from the room in a wild search for the exit.

Rafferty cursed as he recognized Meghan's voice, but he was too consumed by his lust to do anything but finish what he'd started. With a jerk of his hips, he gave a guttural groan and then fell gasping onto the woman beneath him.

"I think she's left," Katie Jones commented, her tone thick with satisfaction.

Fortunately, it was this particular woman he'd chosen to futter that day, Rafferty thought. No outraged virgin or unwilling wife. Katie was neither embarrassed nor concerned by what had just occurred. The woman had given as much as she'd gotten, and this was the third time this week he'd enjoyed her charms.

Despite Katie's protests, Rafferty scrambled off her nude body, hefted up his pants, and ran to the front door after Meghan.

"Shit!" he muttered as he saw the carriage disappear over the crest in the road.

Katie came up from behind him and pressed her naked form against his length. "It's too late now to worry about her." She rubbed her breasts against his bare back. "Come back inside, Raff." She slipped away and went into the store.

"Damn, she'll not forgive this," he said, cursing himself for forgetting to lock the door.

But then he followed Katie, locking the door behind him, before he continued toward the stockroom.

"Meghan, what happened?" Susan asked.

Meghan could hear the concern underlying her friend's voice as their carriage sped down the coach road. Devastated by her discovery, she slapped the reins, urging the horse faster until the vehicle tilted dangerously as it barreled around a curve.

Susan cried out with fear, and Meghan tugged on the reins to slow the animal to a safer pace.

"Godalmighty, McBride!" her friend said angrily. "Will you tell me what happened, before you get us both killed!"

Eyes blurring with tears, Meghan took a second to gather herself before answering. "Nothing," she said, glancing briefly at her friend.

Susan had raised her eyebrows. "Nothing?"

The tears that she'd thus far managed to keep at bay fell as she heard the scorn in Susan's answer. "Rafferty was busy," she admitted, keeping her gaze fixed on the road. The conveyance moved at a leisurely rate of speed now, and Meghan was glad, for she could barely see for her tears.

Why did she feel so terrible about what she'd seen

when she had come to break off her betrothal to Rafferty?

Because ye trusted him, she thought. And despite the change wrought in him by recent years she'd always believed him to be honorable and good.

She shuddered as she recalled what she'd seen and heard. Dear God in heaven, Rafferty had been rutting like an animal!

"I'm sorry," Susan said, reminding Meghan of her friend's presence. "He was so angry with you that he didn't say a word after you told him," she guessed.

Meghan's laughter was harsh. "I didn't get the chance to tell him," she said. "He was too busy fornicating with another woman to realize that I was there."

Susan's horrified gasp brought a twisted smile to Meghan's lips.

"It wasn't a pretty sight," the Irishwoman said.

"Oh, Meg . . ." Susan's hand on Meghan's shoulder offered the comfort of friendship.

Meghan's smile became genuine as she turned back to stare at the roadway. The sun had set fully within the last few minutes, and it was dusk . . . the time when eyes could be tricked in what they were seeing. The tree-lined lane was full of dark shadows. Meghan was careful as she steered the carriage to negotiate another curve in the winding road.

"Ye should have seen them, Susan," Meghan murmured. "They were lying across a brown sack. It probably contained flour or something."

"Ugh!" Susan exclaimed. "Remind me never to purchase anything from the Somerville store!"

Meghan nodded, her lips twitching as she fought back a reluctant smile. "Rafferty's pants were . . ."

"Off?" Susan encouraged.

The Irishwoman shook her head. "They were down about his feet. I think he eventually realized that someone—maybe even I—was there, but he couldn't—" Meghan stopped as amusement suddenly seized her. "He couldn't . . . stop!" She made a sound as she choked back a laugh. She exchanged looks with her friend, and the two burst out laughing.

"Good God, he must have been startled to learn that you had come in," Susan gasped, wiping the tears of mirth from her eyes.

Meghan's laughter had softened to chuckling. "Aye. I think he wanted to say something, but he had to finish what he started!" Her laughter that followed quickly transformed from a sound that was genuine to something forced and overly loud.

Susan stared at her friend, and an awkward silence descended inside the carriage when Meghan finally caught her breath.

"I'm sorry," Meghan whispered.

Her friend grabbed hold of the reins, firmly taking control of the carriage. "Don't be. Rafferty was your fiancé, even if he is a son of a sorry bitch."

A garbled sound escaped Meghan's throat. "I should be glad it happened. Now, I don't have to feel guilty for changing me mind about him."

"Yes," Susan said softly. "Now you're free to find someone you love, someone you deserve."

No, I'm not, Meghan thought. *I love someone else, a man who doesn't share me dreams for the future.* And though it would be wonderful to belong to Lucas for a time, she needed forever, not a few short months.

"Rafferty deceived me." The pain of it still hurt, for they'd been friends before they were betrothed.

Susan regarded her with sympathy. "I know," she said, her attention moving back to the road. "But would you have rather married him, before you found out . . . for that's surely what Rafferty must have intended."

"*Damn him.*"

"Aye, 'tis true," Susan said, mimicking Meghan's Irish brogue.

The porch lantern was lit as they passed Patty's on their way to the Gosiers. The two women thanked Susan's floor overseer, Mr. Gosier, who was glad to see his carriage returned safely. Then, Meghan and Susan headed home.

A flurry of excitement greeted them at the door.

"Meghan," Betsy exclaimed upon seeing her roommate, "there's a man here to see you."

Meghan's heart gave a thump. *Rafferty?* No, she thought. It wasn't physically possible for Rafferty to have reached Gibbons Mill before her.

Patty's face appeared flushed as she came out of the kitchen. "He's asked for tea," she said. She swung her surprised gaze on Meghan. "Meg, he asked to drink tea in *my* kitchen!"

Lucas. Meghan knew it instinctively, before anyone mentioned his name. Heat rushed along with the rush of her blood. "Lucas Ridgely?" she asked, her voice unusually high.

"It's him, all right," Priscilla said as she came up from behind Patty. "Said he's come to see you, Meghan."

"Go," Susan urged. "Go and see what he wants."

With heat in her cheeks, Meghan moved toward the kitchen on unsteady feet. She stopped in the doorway and studied him. Her heart slammed in her chest to see him sitting there in Patty's kitchen, looking larger than life and more handsome than a man had the right to look. He sat at the table, talking with James, Patty's eldest son, who was perched on the chair across from him

James spotted Meghan first. "Here's Meg now." He stood, and Meghan's throat went dry as she watched Lucas rise, slowly unfolding his long legs.

"That didn't take too long now, did it, Meg?" James said.

Lucas's dark gaze gave Meghan a jolt as he studied her from across the room. "Where did you go?" he asked in his deep voice.

"She went—"

"I went to the store," she said quickly, while she shot James a telling look.

"The store?" Lucas intoned. His look told her that he didn't believe her.

She glanced away. "In Somerville."

He nodded then, seeming to accept that answer easily enough. But as he continued to watch her with hawklike eyes, she saw a frown settle upon his brow. "We need to talk," he said.

Meghan shifted uncomfortably and flashed James a glance. The boy's gaze was alight with curiosity.

"All right," she said, realizing that there was no way to avoid it. "James—"

"I understand," the boy said.

"Thank ye," Meghan whispered.

James's scowl became a smile, and an admiring light entered his brown gaze. "For you, Meg, anything."

And she gave a fake laugh, sensing Lucas's displeasure at the exchange.

James left, and no one else entered the kitchen. Meghan and Lucas were alone.

Meghan stood within a few feet of the door, feeling vulnerable. She wondered if Lucas could see that she'd been crying recently, and she prayed that he couldn't tell. Her prayers went unanswered.

"You look like hell."

She averted her glance briefly. "Thank ye."

His lips twitched slightly. "Sit down, Meghan, before you fall down. I'll not bite, you know."

"Do I?" she retorted, regaining some of her spirit

as she moved to take the seat that had recently been vacated by James.

"Full of fire, Meghan McBride—it's what I . . . love about you."

The word *love* seemed to hover in the air between them, and the tension that followed told Meghan that Lucas had meant it figuratively, not literally.

She swallowed hard. "Why are ye here?"

"What?" he said. "No pleasant idle chitchat over a cup of tea first?" He hesitated, and Meghan was shocked to realize that whatever Lucas had to say had to be difficult.

"What?" she gasped. "What is it?" Was he here to fire her? To tell her that no one admitted to Phelps's behavior and that he and his aunt had decided that she—and not Phelps—should be the one to leave?

"Meghan . . ." He seemed reluctant to continue.

"*Lucas, please.* You're frightening me."

Finally her fear penetrated through his discomfort. "Will you walk with me?" He glanced toward the door. "Your friends are nice, but I don't want them to hear this . . ."

Stifling the urge to scream, Meghan nodded.

" 'Tis cold out," she said.

He smiled. "Get your cloak." His eyes fell upon her old shawl. "You do still have the cloak?"

"Ah—aye," she confessed. "But I left directly from work, ye see, and—"

His dark eyes lit with warmth, and her thought vanished with her reaction to him. "I'll wait while you change your gown, too, if you'd like," he said with understanding.

She nodded and left, hurrying up the stairs to her bedchamber. When she returned, he was still at the table, only he'd been rejoined by James and the women of the house.

IRISH LINEN

He stood. "I explained to Patty that my aunt needs your assistance."

"I see," she said. Did his aunt need her assistance? She had changed from her work gown to a clean dress and had her cloak over her right arm.

Lucas took the heavy forest green cloak and gently lifted it over her head. Meghan could feel her burning cheeks as she adjusted the garment over her shoulders. "I'll be back soon," she told her friends.

"I'll have her back within the hour," Lucas promised, and the two left the warmth of the house for the cold outside.

Twenty-four

The night air was chilly, and Meghan drew up her hood as she walked along the road beside Lucas. Stars filled the sky, and the moon was a bright crescent against the jet backdrop.

Lucas was silent as their footsteps crunched on the top frozen layer of earth, but his thoughts were anything but calm. He had something unpleasant to tell Meghan and he wasn't sure how to start. "Meghan—"

She looked at him, her blue eyes glistening with emotion, her body poised as if she'd shatter at the littlest provocation.

He caught his breath. "I have something to tell you, and I—"

"Are ye firing me?" she interrupted in a choked voice.

Lucas jerked to a standstill. "No," he said, and was shocked that he hadn't understood her fear. "This isn't about you . . . well, it is, but only because it concerns your fiancé."

"Rafferty?"

He could sense some of her tension leave as he nodded. "Yes, Rafferty O'Connor. Your fiancé."

She glanced away and started to walk again. He saw her shoulders stiffen, and he wanted to know desperately what was going on in her mind. "What about him?" she asked.

IRISH LINEN

He halted and grabbed her arm, turning her gently to face him. Because of his interest in Meghan, he'd done some checking on her fiancé and what he'd found disturbed him greatly, so much so that he felt that he had to tell her.

"He's old enough to be your father!" He'd been shocked when he'd learned that Rafferty O'Connor was a middle-aged man.

Meghan gazed up at him with luminous blue eyes, and something kicked in Lucas's gut. "Aye," she murmured. "I know."

He made a sound of disgust and looked away, but he didn't release his hold on Meghan's arm. "Of course, you know, but what I want to know is why? *Why would you tie yourself to a man over twice your age!*" He was furious—damn it, but he couldn't help it.

She reacted in kind. "I'm not tied to a man twice me age!"

"Then what are you if you're not tied to him? You're engaged to be married—that's the same thing!"

Jerking from his grasp, she started back to Patty's. "I don't need to listen to this," she cried.

Lucas grabbed her and spun her to face him. "Don't you understand? I'm only thinking of you!"

Meghan stared at his taut features, at the wild light in his dark eyes; and against her better judgment, she felt herself respond to him.

"I want you to be happy, Meghan," he rasped. "It was difficult enough when I thought your fiancé to be a young man, but . . ." His voice trailed off.

She gazed into his ebony eyes, and a trembling started at her nape and frissoned outward, enveloping her limbs and midsection.

"Meghan," he said, leaning toward her.

"I'm not tied to him," she whispered, swaying forward. Her breath quickened.

"You're betrothed," he pointed out. His mouth was only a hair's breadth from her lips as she shook her head.

"I . . ."

Her confession ended before it had barely begun when Lucas took her mouth in the lightest of kisses. Her head swam at the pressure. As he deepened the contact, Lucas pulled her into his embrace. His hardness met her soft curves, and heat shot up her length from wherever their bodies touched.

She heard the labored sound of Lucas's breathing as he left her mouth to rain kisses down her throat. She arched her neck instinctively, shivering not from the frigid night temperature but with the pleasure of his touch. Lucas ignited a fire that burned hotly within her, and from his shuddering response as he lifted his head, she knew that he was caught up in passion, too.

His eyes seemed to glow in the darkness. He shifted his hands from her waist to her shoulders. "Meghan, you must listen to me. Rafferty O'Connor is not the honorable, trusted man you believed in."

She closed her eyes briefly on a wave of pain. "I know."

The hands on her shoulders tightened. "You know?" he asked, sounding skeptical.

Meghan felt drawn into the depths of his glittering dark orbs. She saw first his tension reflected in his gaze . . . and then his surprise.

"You know?" he repeated with a narrowing of his eyes.

"I saw for meself this day," she admitted. The pain of Rafferty's betrayal was still raw and must have been evident in her tone, because Lucas's look softened and he began to stroke her upper arms in a caress obviously meant to comfort her.

"What happened?"

IRISH LINEN

The gentleness in his voice was nearly her undoing. Tears sprang to her eyes, blinding her. He cared, she thought. He cared whether or not she'd been hurt by her fiancé. *Former fiancé.* Meghan shivered.

"Come," he said, turning her to walk beside him within the circle of his arm. "Let's find a warm place to talk."

They were silent as they continued over the thin layer of icy earth. Lucas brought her to the mill house, and he told her as he released her that she'd be warm soon. He inserted a key, and she heard it click as he turned the lock. Then, he urged her inside and to wait while he lit an oil lamp. Within seconds, it seemed to Meghan, Lucas had a lamp burning, and he was taking her through to Mr. Simmons's office. And everything had gone a little too smoothly for Meghan's peace of mind.

"Were ye planning to bring me here all along?" she asked, her stomach tightening.

Lucas, who'd gone to Simmons's chair, glanced at her with a dark look. "Is that what you think? That I planned to bring you here to seduce you?"

She stared at him a long moment, noting his handsome features . . . the hint of pride in his firm jaw, the commanding glitter in his cobalt eyes. There was a sensual curve to his masculine mouth that made her heart race each time she looked at him. Her question sounded ridiculous even to her now that she thought about it.

Did she really think he'd resort to such secretive measures to seduce her in such an unromantic place as George Simmons's office?

"No," she admitted softly. "I don't believe ye'd planned to bring me here."

His grin lit up the tiny room, brighter than the oil

lamp, and her body reacted with a jolt of joy. "Now the smokehouse perhaps," he teased.

She laughed at the image. After the matter with Mathew Phelps, she was surprised that she could joke about such things. "And ruin yer clothes?"

A smile lingered about his lips as he regarded her with warmth. "You've a point, Meghan McBride." His eyes gleamed. "I'll have to think on this for a while."

Meghan inhaled sharply at the underlying promise in his tone.

Suddenly, the amusement in his expression was gone. "Tell me what happened today," he urged.

The flame of the oil lamp flickered, and the dancing light highlighted and softened Lucas's rugged features. Meghan felt drawn to the man with a strength that frightened her. He was most dangerous to her like this . . . when he was attentive and caring, anxious to listen to what she had to say.

She was uncomfortable standing. She glanced about for somewhere to sit, and Lucas immediately came around the desk with George Simmons's chair for her. She sat gratefully at his invitation, for her knees had weakened and begun to fail her. Lucas perched himself on the edge of the foreman's desk, which discomfited Meghan because of having to look up at him.

This man has shown you nothing but kindness, she reminded herself. Meghan forced herself to relax.

"Meghan?" he prompted when she still hadn't said a word. His regard was full of tenderness as he straightened away from the desk and found another chair.

Finally, she felt comfortable with their eyes level. "I told ye that I went to the store in Somerville," she said, "but what I didn't tell ye was why I went . . ."

Meghan then told him of her decision to break her engagement to Rafferty, how she'd noticed that he'd changed over the last two years.

"Changed?" Lucas asked. "In what way?"

She bit her lip and looked down. Meeting Lucas's gaze—although she glimpsed no censure—distracted her, for Lucas filled her mind with other thoughts . . . forcing her from the subject at hand. "Rafferty seemed . . . angry all the time."

Lucas watched the play of emotion on Meghan's face and read more into her words than she was telling. "He seemed angry," he said, encouraging her with his tone.

"Aye." She inhaled deeply before releasing the breath on a ragged sigh. "He gets angry at the littlest thing."

Her hands twisted in her lap, and he covered them with his own. "Did he hurt you?" he asked, keeping his voice light and steady, although he knew he'd blow up with anger if he learned Rafferty had done something to injure Meghan. As things stood now, he wanted to find the bastard and severely throttle him.

"No . . ."

He felt the tension start to leave him, but some of his anger remained.

Then, Meghan told him about her visit to the store. He listened with horror and mounting disgust for Rafferty O'Connor, while she described in detail what she'd witnessed early that evening in the back room.

"I ran outside to the carriage, and then Susan and I left in a hurry." She paused. "I didn't want to see or talk with him," she said. Then, her mouth formed a wry smile as she confessed how she'd grabbed the horse's reins and sent the vehicle barreling down the road at a dangerous speed. "Susan brought me back to me senses," she finished.

"Thank God," Lucas said. "You could have been killed . . . the both of you."

Meghan looked ashamed. "Aye. I must apologize to

Susan . . ." Her voice trailed off, and the room was silent.

She's no longer betrothed, Lucas thought.

The silence continued, and he searched Meghan's expression, needing to know her thoughts. "What will you do now?" he asked gently.

She met his gaze. "I'm not sure," she said.

Meghan was grateful for Lucas's question, because she felt that he wasn't pressuring her to come to him at a time when she was most vulnerable. It was frightening to imagine a future on her own. But at least she had her employment, she realized. And the people at Patty's.

Unless Flora Gibbons released her from her employment, she'd be content to live and work here for a long while yet.

But what if seeing Lucas—and loving him the way she did—made it too unbearable for her to stay at Gibbons Mill? What would she do then?

And then there was still the unresolved matter of Mathew Phelps. With Lucas gone, she'd been unable to discuss what had happened. It'd been weeks now. She knew from her friends that Phelps was still working at his position on the weaving floor. Why? "Lucas—"

"You like working for my aunt, don't you?" Lucas asked suddenly.

She nodded and grew wary of his motive for questioning her. He'd leaned forward in his chair time and again as she'd told her story, but now his presence in the room seemed large and threatening to her.

As if sensing this, Lucas sat back in his chair. "Then you can continue to work for her at the house," he said. He stood and held out his hand to help her rise. "Your friends will be wondering what happened to you. I promised to get you back within the hour, and I'm afraid it's much later."

IRISH LINEN

But Meghan, who had tensed at his suggestion, dug in her heels and refused to go. "Wait! Why would your aunt keep me on at the house?" She frowned. "It's the matter with Phelps, isn't it? Ye don't believe it happened, and Simmons doesn't want me back at the mill." When he didn't immediately answer, she said, "Did he question the other workers?"

Lucas nodded and started to walk back. Anxious to learn more, Meghan had no choice but to keep up with him. "And?" she asked.

"Not a single woman would corroborate your story," he said solemnly.

Meghan halted. "No one?" she breathed.

He shook his head. "I'm sorry, but George Simmons had no choice but to allow Phelps to remain."

"I see," she said. She stood for a long moment, wondering why no one would come forward to tell the truth. Had Phelps gotten to them first with new threats? Why didn't they stay banded together? Because of fear? And what of Mari? She'd seemed so sure that they'd all been doing the right thing. "Mari Bright," she murmured, making a mental promise to speak to the woman to find out why everyone had kept silent.

"Excuse me?" Lucas said.

Meghan realized that she'd been mumbling. "I was just thinking," she explained. And as a new thought took hold, she couldn't keep it silent. "Why did the women stop production then? Did anyone say?"

Lucas frowned. "I don't know," he said, as if disturbed that he hadn't thought to ask. Suddenly, he smiled. "Don't concern yourself, Meghan. You've a position with my aunt's house staff. I'll handle things at the mill."

She stiffened. "Suppose I don't want to continue to work at the house?"

He narrowed his gaze. "It's a good position. Why wouldn't you want it?"

"Because I won't keep employment meant to control me behavior, Lucas Ridgely. I liked me job in the weaving room. It's good pay for good work."

"But I'm paying you twice the amount to stay at the house!"

"Exactly!" she snapped. "You're paying me, aren't ye? It's ye, and not your aunt that's seeing to me wages. Like I said, I won't be still and see the injustice of that man's behavior going unpunished."

"Vicious little wench, aren't you?" he said tightly, incensed by her stubbornness.

"If Mathew Phelps is allowed to remain with all those innocent women workers, then it'll be because of ye! And then I can honestly say that you're no better than he is!"

Angry with each other, man and woman said nothing more as they walked back to Patty's, and Lucas deposited Meghan at the door. Only then did Lucas speak, and it was only to wish her a crisp good night.

Inside Patty's foyer, Meghan felt shaken and slightly off balance. She was free of Rafferty and she'd just exploded in anger, risking her job—her only source of survival. Lucas had been furious with her when he'd left, but then she was mad that he didn't believe what was happening between Phelps and the workers at the mill! It was hard for her to accept that she'd actually allowed Lucas to kiss her! Why wouldn't he accept her word?

She thought back over their conversation. Lucas had listened intently to her concerns about work . . . as if he cared. He had kissed her, but he hadn't insulted her by asking her to be his mistress, although he'd learned that she had broken off her betrothal to Rafferty.

IRISH LINEN

Yet, she'd accused him of being like Phelps. Her mouth tightened. He was like Phelps! She hadn't lied, and Lucas knew it! She had a right to be angry! If Lucas allowed that lecherous man to stay at the mill, then as far as she was concerned, Lucas was as guilty of wrongdoing as Mathew Phelps!

Twenty-five

A week had passed since her disagreement with Lucas. Every day she'd hoped he would come to the sewing room to tell her that he was wrong and had fired Mathew Phelps, but he'd stayed away. If he had learned the truth and done something about it, he was still too angry with her to let her know. None of the women at Patty's had been able to tell her a thing. Rumor had it that some of the women were being called down to George Simmons's office, but no one on the other floors knew whether or not that was true. Then, she heard from one of Mrs. Gibbons's housemaids that Lucas Ridgely had left Gibbons Mill to return home to Kent County.

Meghan's anger faded as her spirits plummeted. *I should be glad he's gone. I could never have a future with him,* she thought.

The sewing room seemed particularly hot and close to Meghan this day. She had trouble breathing through her nose, and her chest felt tight as she pulled in each lungful of air. By the end of the day, her head hurt so badly that she begged Patty's forgiveness for avoiding supper and went directly upstairs to bed.

"Oh, the poor dear," Priscilla exclaimed after Patty had told those at the supper table that Meghan wasn't feeling well.

Meghan's roommate pushed back her chair and stood. "I'll check on her."

"Eat first, Betsy," Patty said. "You must keep up your own strength. Meghan will be all right for another half hour." She ladled out a bowl of soup and set it before the young woman. "Perhaps I should speak to Mrs. Gibbons," she murmured as she dipped the curved spoon into the porcelain tureen.

"I wouldn't if I were you," Susan said. "Meghan won't thank you for it. She's proud, and she needs the money. If she's too sick to work, she'll tell the woman herself."

"I suppose you're right," Patty said with a sigh after hearing the others agree.

Betsy smiled. "Of course, we're right."

"You can't help but worry about her, though," Susan said. "She hasn't been the same since she broke her engagement."

Priscilla shuddered. "If that man comes back to this house one more time, I'll . . . box his ears!"

"We've managed to put him off twice already. We'll handle him again if we need to," Patty said.

Betsy snorted. "The man must be mad to think that Meghan will take him back . . . even if she hadn't realized that she didn't love him."

"Love never entered into her relationship with Rafferty," Susan said with conviction. "She wanted a man she could trust, and she thought she could trust her father's best friend."

"Well, he proved her wrong, didn't he?"

"Yes, he did, Betsy," Patty agreed, and then she added softly, *"Thank God."*

"Well, the next time he comes I think we should let him see her. Perhaps he'll leave her alone after she looks him in the eye and tells him to go to hell."

"James!" his mother said.

"I think he's right," Susan said. "She left the store so quickly that day that they've never actually exchanged words."

By the next day, Meghan felt worse instead of better. The throbbing in her head had intensified, and the ache was centered behind each eye. Her limbs were stiff and sore. The sewing room spun each time she made a sudden move. She was gasping and dizzy when she stumbled outside at midday for a breath of air.

She went home to Patty's for a brief period of rest, and the woman exclaimed with concern as Meghan entered the house and stood swaying on he feet, her face white.

"You must lie down, Meghan," she said. "I'll send James to speak with Mrs. Johnson."

"No," Meghan protested as she plopped down onto a kitchen chair. Mrs. Johnson was the head housekeeper at the Gibbons's residence, and the woman had never taken a liking to Meghan. It was only after a comment from Mrs. Riker that Meghan understood why. Mrs. Johnson didn't like the Irish. When asked why, Mrs. Riker didn't have an answer, but it became clear to Meghan in her dealings with the housekeeper that the cook was right. Meghan had worked hard to give the woman no cause to complain. And she wouldn't start now. "I'll finish the day," she insisted. "I'm sure I'll feel better after a rest."

Patty's mouth formed a frown, but Meghan couldn't summon the energy to care about her landlady's displeasure.

Meghan had some time before she had to go back to work—one of the benefits of working at the big house. After forcing down a bowl of broth at Patty's

IRISH LINEN

insistence, she went upstairs to her room to lie down for a while.

"Wake me in an hour please," she asked Patty. She lay on her bed and promptly fell asleep.

Patty spoke to her son after dinner. "I want you to go tell Mrs. Riker—*not Mrs. Johnson*—that Meghan is too ill to come back to work."

"But Ma—"

"James," she scolded. "Do it!"

"Yes'm," he murmured, and then he left to obey his mother.

"She'll be angry," Betsy said, coming up behind Patty as the woman watched her son run across the road.

"I know," Patty replied softly, "but it's for her own good." She met the other woman's gaze. "It's like she doesn't care if she lives or dies."

"Ah, no, Patty," Betsy said, shaking her head. "Meghan cares. She's just tired and ill . . . and unhappy."

It was Mrs. Gibbons herself who responded to James's message. Patty answered the knock, and her eyes widened as she saw who stood at her front door. "Mrs. Gibbons!"

"How's Meghan?" the woman asked, accepting Patty's invitation to enter. "I happened to be in the kitchen when your son came in to say that Meghan's sick."

"Meghan's sleeping. I'm afraid she's very ill." Patty took the woman into the parlor and gestured politely for her to sit in a comfortable armchair. She sat across from her and shifted uncomfortably. "Mrs. Gibbons, Meghan doesn't know I sent James. She wanted to return to work, but I—ah—well, she's too sick!"

Mrs. Gibbons looked outraged. "Why, of course, she shouldn't be working if she's ill. I'd planned to speak with her this afternoon anyway." She leaned forward in the chair. "I'd like to make Meghan's position in the house a permanent one . . ."

"You want Meghan to continue to work at the house?" Patty asked.

Flora Gibbons nodded. "She'll get an increase of wages, of course. I know she enjoyed working in the weaving room, but—well, I could really use her to make clothes for the servants. If she wants, I'll see that she has her own loom at the house. Do you think you can convince her to stay?"

Patty grinned. "I'll do what I can," she promised. "And my name's Patty."

"Flora," the woman offered her the same courtesy. She extended her hand. "Thank you, Patty," she said as Patty accepted the handshake.

"No, Flora. It's I who thanks you . . . for Meghan."

When Meghan woke up, it was dark outside, and the attic bedchamber was lit by the soft glow of a burning oil lamp. Realizing that it was late, she sprang to sit upright, her heart pounding.

"Betsy," she gasped as she caught sight of her friend seated on the other bed, "why did no one wake me?" Her head swam, and she cupped it until it stopped reeling.

"There was no need," Betsy said with sympathy. "You've lost your job at the mill."

"Oh, God!" Meghan cried. The worse had happened, she thought, just as she'd feared. "What am I to do?"

Betsy rose from her bed and sat down on the edge of Meghan's. "Don't fret, Meghan. It's all right."

Meghan focused her tear-filled eyes on her room-

IRISH LINEN

mate and friend. "Me money won't last forever. What happened? Did Mr. Simmons fire me?"

"Mrs. Gibbons did."

Meghan made a choked sound and started to cry. She felt miserable. Everything in her world had gone wrong. Rafferty . . . Lucas . . . and now she'd lost her employment again. "Oh, Da," she sobbed. "I've done it now!" She missed her father fiercely. She'd promised not to cry, but she couldn't stop the tears.

"Meghan. Meghan, listen to me!"

She felt Betsy's arms surround her, and she vaguely heard her friend urging her to listen, but Meghan couldn't stop crying. How could she find other employment when she felt ill? And why did she feel so sick?

"Meghan, you're not to worry—*do you hear me!*"

Betsy's anxious tone penetrated past Meghan's misery. Meghan blinked several times and saw the tension in her friend's face.

"Meg, you're still employed." Betsy had enunciated each word loudly and carefully to be understood.

The young Irishwoman sniffed. "I'm still employed?"

Betsy nodded. "Mrs. Gibbons made your position as seamstress permanent."

"Her seamstress?" Had she heard correctly? Mrs. Gibbons wanted her to work in the big house?

"Yes," her friend assured her. "It's good employment with good wages, Meg. According to Patty, it's all Mrs. Gibbons's idea. She came to ask you herself, but—"

Meghan became alarmed. "Oh, no. Patty told her I was sick? What must she think of me?"

Betsy shook her head as her lips formed a gentle smile. "Meg, she obviously thinks enough of you to want you on her household staff." She brushed back Meghan's hair from her wet cheeks. "You're to start again on Monday."

"Monday! But that's six days away!"

"Don't sound so alarmed. She's paying your wages while you recover."

Meghan stared at her friend with amazement. "Truly?"

Betsy laughed. "Truly. Oh, and Meg? Did I forget to mention that she's giving you an increase in pay?"

As the carriage pulled up in front of his aunt's house, Lucas had the most insane desire to find Meghan. It was late, in the middle of the night, which was why he felt the urge was insane.

His aunt didn't expect him back from Philadelphia until tomorrow, but once he'd completed his business there, he'd found he wanted desperately to go back to Gibbons Mill. The feeling became so powerful that he finally gave in to it. He roused the livery man where he'd stabled the horse and carriage. Then he paid the fellow and had the vehicle readied for travel.

Lucas thought of the machinery he'd ordered in England and knew his aunt would be pleased. The new roller printer and power loom had arrived safely and would be delivered to Gibbons Mill within the next three days. He had paid the man at the shipping office a great deal of money to see that the equipment was transported safely.

His aunt's house was dark, and he had to wake up Stephen, the stable boy, who accepted the duty of settling the horse in without complaint. After apologizing for the hour with a generous tip to the young man, Lucas headed toward the house and his room. He paused for a moment to stare down the lane to the house where Meghan ate and slept. Emotion surged through him as he remembered her smile and the way it lit her beautiful blue eyes when she was amused or pleased.

Lucas scowled. She'd had little enough to smile about lately, but he hoped to remedy that. He thought of the extra item he'd purchased while he was away and pictured Meghan's pleasure when she realized that the sewing machine was hers to keep. She was a talented seamstress by hand; he could imagine what she could do with the newest in modern machinery.

He turned and climbed the porch steps. The door opened as if his aunt's houseman, Richard, had been waiting for him all along. With another murmured apology for disturbing the servant's rest, Lucas bade the man good night and then climbed the stairs to his bedchamber.

Lucas's thoughts returned to Meghan as he began to shed his travel clothes. She could leave Gibbons Mill with her machinery. With her talent and drive, she'd be able to work and live anywhere.

He threw back the bed covers and climbed into bed naked. Pulling up the blankets, he lay on his back and stared at the ceiling.

He didn't want Meghan to go, he thought. He wanted her to stay where he could see her. He wanted to change her mind about being his mistress.

He wanted to love Meghan with his body until he or she got tired of the arrangement. Would he ever tire of her? he wondered. Lucas smiled. He didn't think he'd ever grow tired of the lovely Irishwoman with a voice like a songbird and eyes the color of a clear summer sky.

The next morning Lucas thought he was dreaming when he was awakened by the sound of Meghan's voice. He rolled over, tugging the covers over his head, and willed his imaginative mind to stop. Then, he heard her again, and he sat up as he realized that he hadn't been asleep at all. Meghan was here in the house.

The door to his room burst open suddenly, and she backed into the room, struggling with her arms full of clothing. He started to rise to help and then thought better of it, because his dreams had made him hard and ready for her. The last thing he wanted to do was to frighten or shock her.

A maid entered seconds later, carrying a sewing basket.

"Just put it over there," Meghan said, unaware of his presence. She faced the other wall . . . and he wasn't supposed to be home.

The maid happened to glance toward the bed and gasped softly when she saw him. Lucas flashed her a mischievous grin and held his finger to his lips, instructing her to keep silent.

"Rachel, what's wrong?" Meghan said without looking up as she sorted through the pile of clothes. "Did I forget something? Cook's apron perhaps?"

"No, Meghan," the girl said in a strangled voice. "Mrs. Riker's apron is there."

Meghan flashed the young maid a frowning look. "Rachel—"

"I have to go now." Rachel shoved the sewing box into Meghan's hand and then glanced toward the hall.

"Oh, oh, of course. I'm sorry to keep ye. I should've guessed . . ." Meghan blushed. Certainly, the girl had work to do, and she'd been keeping her from her duties!

The girl left, and Meghan set the sewing box on the desk next to the garments that needed mending. *I'm in Lucas's bedchamber.* She could feel him as surely as if he were home and in the same room.

She had chosen this room to work this day, for there was a loose hem on one of his drapes and several of his garments to be mended.

Her gaze caressed the oak desk where she'd laid her work, and she pulled out the chair to begin.

"Still, why did Rachel act so strangely?" Meghan wondered aloud, recalling the girl's look of fear. "Is there something about his room that scared her?"

"I sincerely hope not," a deep voice said from behind her.

Meghan spun, and she drew a sharp breath. Lucas Ridgely was in bed, the covers draped about his waist, exposing his bare chest. She dragged her gaze from his nakedness to hurriedly gather her things. "I'm sorry," she gushed. "I had no idea. Mrs. Gibbons said you weren't expected until later."

Heedless of his state of undress, Lucas sprang from the bed and grabbed her arm. "Don't go."

Her breath hissed out on a gasp as heat seared through fabric where he held her arm. "Lucas—" She glanced around, saw that he was nude, and spun back with a choked cry. "Please, sir!"

His chuckle vibrated in her ears as he released her to put on some clothes. "All right," he said after a few minutes. "I'm properly decent."

Meghan turned and thought that his dressing gown was far too revealing with its clinging silk to be called decent. The gown was as black as his gaze and looked as wicked.

"What are ye doing here?" she asked, looking at anything but the way his garment hung from his broad shoulders or the length of his bared calves beneath the hem.

"I was sleeping." He looked amused.

"I'm sorry." Again, she tried to gather her mending; and again, he stopped her.

"How are you, Meghan?" he asked softly. His ebony eyes caressed her warmly, and a shiver ran down the length of her spine.

"I'm better, thank ye for asking," she said, her heart thumping.

A slight frown settled upon his forehead. "You talk as if you've been ill."

She blushed and looked away. "I have been." She picked up a shirt and spread it across the pile of clothing, stroking the fabric until she realized that it was his shirt she touched. She released the garment as if stung.

Lucas regarded her silently for a long moment. "You're still sewing for my aunt," he said with approval.

She lifted her gaze to his. "Aye," she said softly. Her gaze fastened on his mouth. Then, with sudden realization, she jerked her attention away from his lips and pretended an interest in the carpet beneath their feet. "She's given me a permanent position as her seamstress."

"Good."

He'd said it with such arrogant satisfaction that her regard turned wary. "Lucas—?"

"This has nothing to do with Phelps and the mill, Meghan!"

"Thank ye for that then," she said softly.

His expression softened. "For what?"

Meghan shrugged, and this time he didn't stop her from gathering her things. She feared he'd see that she was trembling. "I'm sorry for disturbing ye," she said. "I shouldn't have come into yer room."

"You're invited to enter my room any time you desire," he said huskily. "And you've disturbed me, Meghan, on a daily basis since the first moment I laid eyes on you."

The heated look in his eyes that accompanied words laced with meaning sent Meghan scurrying from the room with a racing heart and the joy of seeing him again.

Twenty-six

He had to speak with Meghan. Rafferty stumbled as he climbed down from his horse and then gazed at the Rhoades house through blurred eyes. He was drunk, and all because of his betrothed. *Former betrothed*, he thought with growing anger.

He flung the reins around a porch post and tied a loose knot. It was late, and the residents of the village at Gibbons Mill slept. Rafferty tried the door and scowled when he found it locked. *Damn Sax'ns don't trust anybody.* He moved to check the first-story windows, cursing beneath his breath because each one was secure.

"Damn it, Meghan McBride," he shouted. "Ye can't avoid me forever!"

Mumbling obscenities, he retreated to his horse and jerked the reins from the knot. He thumped his fist angrily on the porch post.

Sounds inside the house alerted him that he'd awakened someone. Rafferty panicked. He wanted to talk with Meghan, but he knew that his way would be blocked by every other resident of the boardinghouse.

Bloody hell! he thought as he saw a light flicker through a downstairs window.

The door opened, and Patty Rhoades came out onto the porch with her eldest son James. "O'Connor, what do you want?"

"Ye've refused to let me see Meggie during the day so I've come at night, I have."

"You're drunk," she replied.

"Aye, I'm drunk," Rafferty said, "and I'm determined to stay until I speak to Meggie."

"Very well," Patty said much to his surprise. "James, tell one of the girls to get Meghan. I'm sure everyone in the house is awake now anyway."

"You're going to let me talk to her?" Rafferty asked, amazed that she'd agreed.

The woman shrugged. "If she'll see you."

The man scowled, until James came back to tell his mother that Meghan would be right down.

Rafferty's head spun as he waited for Meghan. Then, she was there on the porch beside Patty and her son. The other women in residence hovered in the doorway behind them. "I don't need an audience," he snapped.

"Girls, please. Mr. O'Connor would like a private word with our Meg."

His mouth firmed at the "our," Rafferty waited for the others to leave. Patty, however, refused to budge. "I'll not leave her alone with you, O'Connor. You're drunk."

"I'm not that drunk."

"She's staying, Raff," Meghan said quietly, speaking up for the first time.

"Meggie—"

"It's over, Mr. O'Connor," she said. "You—you were rutting like an animal that day! Did ye think to carry on yet after we were married?"

"Meggie, it's ye I want. Only ye!"

"No, Rafferty," she said, "it was never right—ye and me. Da knew it, but he didn't say anything, because he thought I wanted it."

"Ye promised to marry me!" In his frustration, Rafferty had raised his voice.

IRISH LINEN

"I'll not marry someone I cannot trust. And I no longer trust you, Rafferty O'Connor." She turned to go back inside.

"Meghan!"

She froze at his cry and spun back. "Go home, Rafferty. Maybe that woman ye were enjoying will marry ya, but I'll not have ye."

"I think you'd better go," Patty said with her son at her side after Meghan had gone into the house.

"I'm not through with her."

James's expression darkened and he took a quick step forward, only to be halted by his mother's hand. "You stay away from her, you bastard. She's too good for the likes of you!"

Rafferty cursed as he climbed onto his horse, nearly falling off the animal's other side, but he managed to quickly right himself. He glared at the door. "I'll be back to make you mine, Meggie," he shouted. "You can believe it!"

With a wild cry, he kicked his mount's sides and rode away.

"The man's too determined; he'll not leave Meghan alone," Patty said as she and James headed toward the kitchen and the women waiting there.

"The boys and I can keep an eye on her," James declared.

Patty nodded. "I think that's a good idea." A persistent man was a dangerous one, she thought, especially when the bastard was Meghan's former fiancé.

Michael Somerton stood at the window of his study, his jaw taut as he stared into the yard. An attractive raven-haired man, he looked much younger than his forty-two years. "What was he doing here this time, Alicia?" he asked. He spun to glare at his wife. "It seems every time I turn around someone mentions that Rafferty O'Connor has been here."

"Michael—"

"Damn it, Alicia!" He grabbed his desk chair and threw it against the floor. "Why is it that you need so much attention? You know I love you, yet it's not good enough, is it? Not for those days I'm forced to work late at the paper mill."

"You love me?" Alicia's face had whitened, and her voice was strained.

He could see her hands tremble as she raised them to grip the edge of his desk. The thick knot of tension inside him uncoiled, replaced by a warm surge of feeling for the woman. He loved her, he thought. Was completely smitten with her. Why else would he agonize over the pain of her infidelities?

"Of course, I love you."

"Oh, Michael." Tears filled her green eyes, making them shimmer.

His gaze softened as it caressed her face. She was beautiful; he'd never met anyone so perfectly lovely . . . and she was his wife. *His—damn it!*

Rage filled him, threatening to erupt until he saw her quivering mouth. Dear God, he loved to kiss her mouth. Did she think that because he had to work some nights that she no longer held his interest, that he no longer cared?

A shudder passed through him, releasing all his anger. He skirted the desk and pulled her into his arms. He held her a while, his chin against her hair, his heart thundering as he closed his eyes and enjoyed the warmth and sweet scent of her. He felt intoxicated as she encircled his waist with her arms. Michael kept her trembling body close until she stopped shaking. After a while, he heard her sigh and felt her arms about him tighten.

"Alicia." Soft tendrils of her blond hair tickled his nose and mouth as his breath stirred her hair. He set her back, but continued to hold her gently by her upper arms. "I love you, Alicia. If I work incessantly at the mill, it's because I'm doing it for us . . . for you." He paused to study her mouth, before he gazed deeply into her eyes. "There have been a few problems at the mill lately, but I think I've taken care of them now . . ."

"Michael, I love you."

He smiled, for he could tell by the look on her face that she was surprised by her admission. He released her arm to touch the tip of her nose. "About Rafferty O'Connor, love," he began.

"I've fired him, Michael."

"You have?" He gaped at her in shock. From what he'd recently learned, it was the last thing he'd expected her to say.

Alicia nodded. She'd rushed into an explanation. ". . . Should have checked with you first, but—ah, Michael, I found out that he'd taken my ring! You know the one that was your great grandmother's?"

"Dear God!" Michael exclaimed. "Did you get the ring back?"

His wife shook her head. "He said he sold it. He's sold it, Michael!" she wailed. "He's sold my precious emerald ring!"

"It's all right, love," Michael said, relieved that the man was gone. "Would you like me to call the authorities?"

"No!" she cried. She inhaled and then released a sharp breath. "I don't want word of this to get out, Michael. I'll look like such a fool for trusting the man to allow him to run our store. I should have known that he was too good to be true!" she exclaimed.

Michael nodded. The matter of the stolen ring could be handled later, he thought as he jerked Alicia close and lowered his head. Alicia was his and only his. He kissed her with passion made urgent by relief, jealousy, and adoration. His mouth bruised her lips; his tongue invaded past her teeth. She whimpered, but she responded with a force as equal and as powerful as the one that drove him to possess her.

His head lifted after he heard her cry out, but she wasn't upset with his roughness. Her eyes were heavy-lidded with sexual arousal, and the corners of her mouth were turned upward in a smile of love that was mirrored in her slumberous green gaze.

"I love you, Michael."

He sighed and closed his eyes, then he kissed her again with tenderness. Rafferty O'Connor was gone, he thought. And he'd make sure that from this moment on his wife needed no other man but him.

Bitch! Rafferty grabbed his belongings from his room at the boardinghouse and stomped down the stairs and out of the building.

"Mr. O'Connor!" Mrs. Pridgly exclaimed from the doorway.

He paused in the road to glare back at her. "I've been fired, Mrs. Pridgly."

"But my pay—"

"Have ye forgotten that I've paid ye until the first part of next week?" He scowled and swore as he spun back to continue down the lane.

"Fired!" he muttered. "I've done a good job for 'em. I've worked me bleeding fingers to the bone, and for what?" He threw up one hand. "To be cast aside when I no longer suited her!"

The money in his pocket would see him far. Oh, aye, Mrs. Somerton had seen that he'd been well paid for his services, with a little extra to keep his mouth

IRISH LINEN

closed. His smile was grim in the gathering darkness of dusk.

"I'll see that she gets her due," he vowed aloud. "But only after I take care of Meghan McBride, for it is she who's the cause of all me troubles."

She'd managed to avoid him thus far, but no more!

"Aye, Meggie, ye'll not put me off any longer."

Lucas was making it difficult for her to resist him, Meghan thought. Her breath quickened as he came into the room. She'd been given an area of her own . . . a small room that had been intended as a nursery, but had never been used. Flora Gibbons had explained with a wistful look on her face that she had never been able to conceive.

"But we had Lucas," she'd said, and Meghan had seen the love the woman had for her nephew. "He spent as much time here as a lad as he did at home."

Flora's words had conjured up images of a beautiful blond boy scampering about the house and yard. No wonder Lucas had his own room here, Meghan thought. Gibbons Mill was as much a home to him as Windfield.

She watched Lucas as he approached, her heart fluttering with love as he gave her a warm smile.

"Meghan," he said. "Hard at work yet, I see."

She nodded, before she glanced down at the shirt he carried in his right hand. "Have ye some mending for me?"

His grin became sheepish. "If you don't mind . . ."

She stared at him with suspicion, trying to read beneath the boyish grin. He'd brought her enough garments this past week to clothe an army, she thought. "Ye wouldn't be tearing yer clothes on purpose, would ye?" she asked, narrowing her gaze.

He chuckled. "Now why would I do that?"

She sighed and set aside the apron she was sewing for one of the girls who helped Mrs. Riker. "I don't know, Mr. Ridgely, and I—"

"*Mr. Ridgely?*" He quirked an eyebrow. "Is there some reason why we're getting formal again?"

"I work for your aunt; and so in a way, you're my employer, too," she said without pondering the consequences of her words.

"Is that so?" The gleam in his eye made her uneasy. "Good." He threw his shirt on the table and extended his hand toward her. "As your employer, I order you to take a rest." His features softened. "Meghan, you've been working too hard."

She glanced at his hand, feeling her pulse accelerate, and then lifted her gaze to examine his face. "I've hardly been working at all, it seems," she whispered, struck again by his masculine beauty.

"How can you say that," he asked with surprise, "when you've mended at least twelve items for me alone in the last six days?"

"Counting, Mr. Ridgely?" An imp of mischief prompted her to dig at his conscience and get him to confess that he'd been ripping his garments.

"I . . ." To her amazement, he blushed.

Meghan laughed. She couldn't help it. That a man such as Lucas might have torn his shirt so that he'd have an excuse to visit the seamstress—her . . . was it any wonder that she was unable to resist his charm?

"I'll not be your mistress," she said.

Something flickered in his black gaze. "Have I asked you again? I might have changed my mind."

Meghan studied him, and warmth invaded her being as she realized that he was acting to protect his pride. A man's pride was a delicate thing, she thought. And she wondered how he'd stood her rejection more than once without giving up on her. The strength of his desire for her made for a heady experience.

"Have ye?" she dared to ask. "Changed your mind?"

A flame entered his dark eyes. "What do you think?"

She swallowed. "I think that if I went down the hall to your bedchamber tonight, ye wouldn't turn me away."

"Damn right!"

She blinked, and then laughter burst forth from her lips. "And ye swear like a gentleman, too."

"There's nothing gentlemanly about my feelings for you, Irish. And I've told you, I'm no gentleman."

She picked up Nancy's apron and started to stitch again. "Ye couldn't prove that by me, kind sir," she said with her head bent low over her work. Then she raised her eyes to him. "Ye've been much more than a gentleman to me on numerous occasions now." On the subject of the behavior of a gentleman or the lack of such, Meghan asked him about Mathew Phelps. Until now, she'd avoided the subject.

"I've taken care of the matter," Lucas said, his expression darkening at the mention of Mathew Phelps.

From his look and his tone, Meghan took him to mean that Mathew Phelps had been found guilty of wrongdoing and been dismissed from the mill. She breathed a sigh of relief for all the women who would no longer have to suffer the man's presence. "Thank ye, Lucas," she said.

Twenty-seven

Smoke seeped into the attic room, waking Meghan. She sat up with a frightened gasp and glanced over at her sleeping roommate and then the door. "Betsy!" she cried. "Wake up!"

"Fire! Fire!" The call came from downstairs.

Meghan heard the alarmed cry as she sprang from bed to shake Betsy, who still hadn't moved. "Betsy! Wake up, lass. There's a fire. We must get out!" Her heart started to pump hard against the walls of her chest. Fire was not new to her. She could feel the resurrection of childhood fears, fears long buried in the years since her family's cottage burned in Ireland when she was nine years old.

As Betsy started to stir, Meghan retreated into a past filled with fear. Horrible memories returned to haunt her . . . images of bright blue and orange flames . . . sounds of her mother's wild cries as she begged Meghan to get out of their burning house. Meghan was a little girl again, escaping a back room filled with thick smoke. She could feel the heat of the fire singeing the fine hairs on her arms and legs. She could hear her father calling her name, guiding her from the searing heat. It'd been dark when she'd finally stumbled outside the house into her father's arms, gasping. And when she'd caught her breath, she'd seen that their tiny cottage was gone and her mother along with it.

"Meg! We've got to get out, Meg!" Betsy was tugging on her arm, but Meghan stood frozen, her limbs leaden, unable to move.

"Meg, *please!*" Betsy cried.

Her friend's fearful screams roused Meghan enough to get her to move. She touched their bedchamber door and found it cool, so she opened it. A thick dark haze filled the hall as the two girls felt their way down the hall toward the stairs.

"Oh, God, the smoke!" Betsy cried, and then choked on a lungful. "We'll never get out alive!"

"We must," Meghan said hoarsely. "We must!" The desire to live gave her new strength and courage. "If only we could see!" She crouched to the floor and was able to breathe easier. "Keep low, Bets!"

The two women felt and crawled their way down the stairs to the next floor. Each step they fought to negotiate was a nightmare that could tumble them into the heat-blasting inferno of the first floor.

"Help!" someone cried from a room off the hall of the second floor. "Meghan? Betsy? Is that you?" It was Susan.

"Aye!" Meghan cried. She and Betsy fell into Susan's room and slammed the door shut.

"We managed to get the window open," the young woman said, "but it's a long climb down and Priscilla's afraid."

"Where are Patty and the boys?" Meghan said as she hurried toward the open window. She breathed in a rush of fresh air, glad to escape the smoke.

"Outside, I think," Susan said. "It was James who warned us."

Once the smoke had cleared from the room, Meghan

saw that there was plenty of moonlight to light the yard and outside wall.

Priscilla sat on the bed, whimpering. Betsy perched on the edge beside her and placed an arm about the frightened girl.

Meghan stuck her head out the window and examined the distance to the ground. This wasn't her time to die, she thought. And she'd allow no fire to hurt her friends—or anyone she cared about ever again. She searched the room for a rope. There was none, but she had an idea.

"Susan, pull off yer bed blankets," she said, turning to capture the girl's gaze. "We'll knot them together and then tie them to—" She looked around the room. "—your dresser chest."

Susan stripped off two blankets while Betsy urged Priscilla up from the other bed so that they could do the same.

The chilly night air seeped into the bedchamber, but Meghan didn't feel the cold; her only concern was to get them all out of the house alive. The exterior walls of Patty's house were granite, but the interior partitions and the ceiling were wood . . . fuel for the fire.

Meghan knotted the ends of the blankets and then threw one end of the fabric chain through the window opening. The makeshift rope fell down the stone wall halfway to the ground.

"It doesn't reach!" Priscilla cried.

"It will have to do," Meghan said. "Who wants to be the first to go?" The smoke was thickening in the room as it came in through the thin crack under the door.

None of the others wanted to go first. "I'll go then," Meghan said. "I'll wait on the bottom and catch each one of ye when it's yer turn."

IRISH LINEN

Three feminine heads bobbed in unison as the women agreed.

The floor beneath their feet, Meghan noticed, was starting to get warm. A dangerous sign that the fire was spreading. She took hold of the blanket rope and swung her leg over the windowsill. Next, she tugged once on the rope to see if it would hold, and then her gaze touched briefly on each friend.

"Susan, Betsy, be ready to grab the dresser if it starts to move under me weight," Meghan said. Her heart raced as she met each of her friends' gazes.

Susan nodded, and Meghan lowered herself outside, releasing her grip on the window edge. She hung suspended, her knees and elbows bumping against the warm stone. The temperature of the granite urged her to hurry, and Meghan loosened her grasp and slid down.

When she reached the end of the chain, she gauged the distance to the ground and decided that the six-foot drop wouldn't kill her. She let go and fell.

Betsy had cried out during Meghan's final drop; Meghan experienced the bone-jarring impact through her entire body as she landed briefly on her feet and then her backside.

"Meghan, are you all right?" Susan asked.

The Irishwoman glanced up as she rose, stifling the urge to rub her behind. "I'm all right," she called up, meaning it. Her gaze went to the lower level of the front of the house. Flames shot through the windows, lighting up the yard. "You'll have to hurry," she told her friends above. "Send Priscilla first—I'll catch her."

The next moments seemed agonizingly long as they struggled to get Priscilla to hang on to the rope. Finally, Meghan lost her temper. "Damn it, lass! Do ye want to die?" she shouted.

Priscilla whimpered but she grabbed the rope and

climbed out of the window. She cried softly as she began to lower herself down.

"I've got yer feet!" Meghan exclaimed. "Now let go!"

The woman obeyed, and Meghan stumbled as she took Priscilla's weight, but both girls remained unharmed. "All right! Who's next?" Meghan asked.

Susan urged Betsy to go; and as the young woman started down, James and his brothers came to help them. "Hurry, Bets!" Meghan urged.

Susan's descent happened soon after, and everyone was all right. The girls hugged and cried, and the boys urged them to leave the area of the building.

They found Patty nearby at a neighbor's house, wrapped in a blanket, shivering. Her expression was bleak as she stared at the burning house. She smiled, though, when she saw that everyone had escaped the fire without harm. Someone handed Meghan and the others blankets. Meghan accepted hers gratefully and wrapped it tightly about her shoulders.

A fire brigade of men had formed at the other end of the house, but although they worked hard, handing buckets of water down the line to the burning porch, they were ineffective in saving Patty's home.

"Everyone's fear now is that the fire will spread to the other houses," James said to his mother. "I'm going to help the men, Ma."

Patty nodded, and all three of her sons went to help wet down the neighboring houses' roofs.

Everyone from the village had awakened and gathered to watch a friend's home burn. It was a sobering experience for the Gibbons Mill residents.

Meghan heard that someone had gone up to the big house to tell Mrs. Gibbons. Then, she heard the deep anxious timbre of Lucas's voice.

IRISH LINEN

"Is everyone all right?" he asked one of Patty's male neighbors.

Shivering with reaction more than the cold, Meghan stood behind Patty and her neighbor, Mrs. Trill, with Susan, Betsy, and Priscilla.

"Mrs. Rhoades."

"Mr. Ridgely," Patty answered in a hoarse voice. "We're all right. Everyone is all right."

"Thank God," Meghan heard him say with feeling. He stared at the burning house. "We'll rebuild for you," he said. "You mustn't worry."

"Thank you," Patty said, then she began to cry. James, returning from the brigade, pulled his mother into his arms.

It was then that Meghan saw Lucas anxiously searching the crowd. He turned in her direction. Their gazes locked, and his eyes glowed as he excused himself, pushing past Susan and Betsy to reach her side.

"Meghan," he muttered, and then uncaring of everyone around, he jerked her into his arms and held onto her trembling form tightly. "Oh, God, Meghan, I thought you had—" She felt him shudder and pressed against his chest, clutching his waist. She could hear his thundering heartbeat that matched her own. The rush of joy Meghan experienced made her head spin as she rested, cradled within his strong arms.

After a long moment, Lucas set her back and peered into her face, his ebony gaze probing. "How did you get out?" he asked huskily.

"There," she said. "Through the window of Susan's room."

"Good God," he exclaimed when he looked to where she pointed.

She smiled. "Aye, but we made it."

He nodded, and then his attention was taken by his aunt who had just come down the hill.

"Lucas, dear God, how did this happen?" the woman exclaimed.

Meghan was too busy studying Lucas to hear his answer. She gazed at his handsome face and fought the strongest desire to grab and kiss him. She'd never forget how wonderful—or right—it felt to be in his arms.

"You have no idea how the fire started?" Flora Gibbons asked her nephew.

Overhearing her, James turned from his mother's side. "We found a lantern and an empty whiskey bottle by the kitchen door."

"You think it was set deliberately?" Lucas asked with a frown.

The boy nodded, and Lucas promised to investigate the matter.

"Patty, you all must come up to the house to stay," Flora said.

"I'll take in Patty and the boys, Mrs. Gibbons," Mrs. Trill offered.

"Susan and Priscilla can stay with us!" said another woman.

Mr. Jones said that although he had three daughters, he'd be able to take one of the two remaining girls.

"Meghan will come with us then," Lucas's aunt said. "She's employed as my seamstress, so it makes perfect sense."

"Then I'll go with the Joneses," Betsy said.

The bedchamber Meghan was given was beautiful. She stepped into the room, and tears filled her eyes as she was hit by the magnitude of what she'd managed to escape.

She saw the lovely green damask draperies and the green and ivory woven counterpane on the bed, and her tears increased, forming trails down her smoke-darkened cheeks.

"My cloak," she gasped. "I've lost me beautiful green cloak." It was the color of the room that made her think of the cloak.

Aunt Flora, who had accompanied her to the room, made a clucking sound of concern. "I'm sure it can be replaced," she said.

But Meghan knew it couldn't. How could she replace an item that had come to mean so much to her because it had been a gift . . . a treasured gift from Lucas? She'd lost some money, but she didn't care.

"You'll want to get out of those dirty clothes," Lucas's aunt said.

Meghan blushed as she nodded. What she must have smelled like to Lucas while he'd held her! Then, she recalled the way he'd kept her close and she no longer thought he'd noticed or cared that she reeked of smoke.

"I'll get you something to wear to bed," Flora said kindly as she turned to leave.

Meghan touched her arm. "Mrs. Gibbons—" She suffered a resurgence of fresh tears, and her throat closed up, making it difficult to speak.

The woman seemed to understand. She gave Meghan a tender smile that brightened her dark gaze. "You're welcome, dear." She patted Meghan's arm. "Now, don't you worry about a thing. We'll take care of things for you."

Touched by Flora's caring, Meghan nodded.

She'd barely turned to look for a washstand to bathe her face when Lucas knocked on the open door. He came to her immediately and caught her shoulders in a gentle grip.

"Are you all right?" he rasped.

"Aye."

He shuddered and closed his eyes before he released her. "Good." Lucas glanced about as if to ensure that everything in the bedchamber met his approval. "I think you'll be happy here. Beth usually sleeps in this room and she finds the bed quite comfortable—" He paused when he caught her staring. "What?" he said.

Her lips quivered. "I lost me cloak. I'm sorry."

Lucas's expression softened. "Oh, Meg." He touched her cheek. "It's all right—honestly."

She swallowed and nodded, but was unconvinced.

"Here we are," Flora announced as she entered the room. She seemed unsurprised to see Lucas. She crossed the room to where the couple stood and handed Meghan a white garment. "I think this will fit."

"Thank ye," Meghan said hoarsely. She could feel Lucas stiffen beside her as if he'd just realized something unpleasant.

"You've lost everything," he said disbelievingly, as if he'd just become aware of the tragedy of the fire.

"Aye."

"No, Lucas dear," his aunt said. "She hasn't lost everything. She has her life, her friends . . . and us. I think that's plenty to be thankful for, don't you?"

Twenty-eight

Smoke clogged Meghan's throat, choking her. She sat up in bed, panicking when she couldn't see.

"Meghan! Ye must get out! Get out of the house now!"

"Mother?"

"Go, daughter!" her mother screamed.

"Mother!"

"I'm all right, Meggie. Go and save yerself. I'll be right behind . . . as soon as I can come."

Heat seared Meghan's face and hands. The fire licked at her nightdress, and she screamed, beating at the hem with her hands.

"Meggie!"

"Da!" She turned with joy toward her father's voice. "I'm here, Da!"

"Keep comin', Meg. Ye're all right, lass."

The heat was unbearable. The smoke stung her eyes, but she listened for her father's encouraging words and obeyed him. Finally, she was outside in the night air with Da bending over her.

"Where's your mother, Meggie?" he demanded while she gasped for air.

"Inside. Da—"

"No!" he cried, and her gaze followed his to the house which was entirely engulfed in flames.

Meghan started to run toward the entrance. "Ma!"

"No, Meghan." Da rasped. "Ye cannot go in, lass. 'Tis too late."

"No!" she screamed. "No . . . No . . . No!"

"Meghan!" The deep voice called her from the hells of her nightmare. "Meghan, love, wake up. It's just a dream, sweetheart. A terrible dream . . ."

Strong hands gripped her shoulders and gently lifted her.

"Lucas?" she breathed, shuddering with the horror still fresh in her mind.

"Yes, love," he said softly. "It's me." A candle burned on her bed table, and the flame flickered, casting his features in soft light. He released her. With a wild cry, she flung herself into his arms, and he immediately embraced her, pulling her onto his lap.

" 'Twas awful," she sobbed, burrowing against his chest. "Our cottage was burning, just like before." Her words were muffled against his bare skin.

"Before?" He'd been stroking her back; his hand stilled. "At Patty's?" he said.

She pulled back and shook her head. "No," she said. "Me cottage where I lived with me mother and father."

Surprise then distress crossed Lucas's face. "This happened to you before?"

She nodded, her eyes spilling tears. "Da and I—we made it out alive, but me mother—" She threw herself back against him, and Lucas held her tightly while making soothing sounds of sympathy.

He kept her against him for a long time while she cried for all that had happened in her young life. She mourned again for her mother and father. She sobbed for the hurt she'd known at Rafferty's betrayal.

Meghan felt safe within Lucas's arms, her wet cheek against his chest. As she hiccuped through the last of her tears, she became conscious of the warm, sleek skin and muscles of Lucas's bare chest . . . of the strong legs that cradled her within his lap . . . and of the wonderful feeling of her arms wrapped about him with her hands at his back. A tingling began at the base of her neck and spread.

"Lucas," she whispered.

He set her back to study her. What he saw must have mirrored his own thoughts, for he groaned and fastened his mouth to hers. She responded instantly, wildly; she'd wanted this kiss . . .

Sensation shot through to her breasts, making them swell and her nipples harden. Lucas cupped her head as he worshiped her mouth and nibbled on her lower lips.

"Open your mouth," he whispered.

When his lips touched hers, she obeyed immediately, moaning softly as he explored the inside of her mouth with his tongue. She imitated his actions, wanting to give him pleasure, and he made a strangled sound.

Meghan gasped as he kissed her neck and trailed his lips down her throat.

Lucas lifted his head and studied the trembling woman in his arms. "Dear God, woman, when I think of what could have happened to you in that fire!"

She raised soft fingers to his lips. "I'm alive," she murmured.

"Yes," he rasped. He kissed her and rose up to watch how her eyes dilated in the burning candlelight. His desire for her was thick and urgent, but he hadn't come to seduce her, only to hold and comfort her.

Her wild cries hadn't awakened him, for he'd already been awake. He was unable to sleep with his thoughts of her. She touched him in a way that no other woman ever had before.

He knew he should leave, but he couldn't find the

will or the energy. "Meghan, I should go—" He started to pull away.

"No, Lucas," she said. "Please stay . . . I need you." She reached out for him. Her warmth and sweet scent radiated toward him, pulling him in.

A shudder passed through him. With a guttural exclamation of need, he bent, recapturing her mouth, and the pulsing heat that gathered blood between his thighs filled him until his whole body burned and hummed with feeling.

Meghan closed her eyes as she felt the passion in the man who held her and experienced a growing urgency of her own. She slid her hands over Lucas's chest, loving his sleek hardness, the heat of his skin. She welcomed his intermittent kisses, murmuring her pleasure as he alternately paid attention to her neck and her mouth. She loved his strength, his passionate tenderness.

Her breasts grew hot and full as they pressed against her soft cotton nightgown. Warmth and a strange budding sensation tingled and throbbed in the most secret intimate area between her legs.

"Lucas!" she gasped as he began to slowly untie the ribbons on her nightdress.

He stopped and searched her gaze, apparently encouraged by what he saw for his fingers went to the button below the tie. After he had undone two buttons, he lifted her from his lap and stood her on the floor before him. His ebony gaze glowed hotly as it caressed her length before settling on her breasts.

Meghan trembled as he settled his hands about her waist. The warmth of his fingers seared her beneath the fabric. She held her breath as he pulled her close and leaned forward to capture her breast with his mouth. Stars flashed behind her closed eyelids, stars and bright colored lights swirling about in a wild frenzy. *"Lucas."*

He released her breast and leaned back, gazing up at her with heavy-lidded passionate eyes. A pleased curve formed on his sensual lips. "Sweet," he murmured. "So sweet . . ."

She shivered as he bent to lavish attention to her other breast. Moisture gathered low, and she arched her back as she recognized the need there for Lucas's touch. "Please, I—"

"Sh . . . sh . . ." he soothed her, shifting her back so that he could rise.

Meghan swallowed hard as he rose to his full height. His trousers rode low on his waist, and her gaze fell to his flat belly and then lower beyond the button closure. Prickles of awareness heightened her desire as she took note of the fabric taut over his thigh muscles. And then her interest followed down the length of his legs to his bare feet.

Lucas had remained still while she studied him. When she lifted her eyes to meet his glittering gaze, she felt her cheeks warm, embarrassed that he'd noticed her appreciation of him.

"Touch me," he said.

Her blood flowed with excitement as she brushed trembling fingers against his smooth, flat stomach. She felt his muscles contract, heard his sharp intake of air, and his reaction encouraged her to be bolder. Her hands grazed his nipples with their thumbs. Recalling her pleasure, she captured a male tip with her mouth.

Lucas cried out, clutched her head, and then tugged her away from him. "You're killing me by slow degrees," he gasped.

Meghan blinked up at him, her blue eyes wide and uncertain, as she released him as if stung. Tenderness seized hold of him, tempering the heat of his desire. He wanted to give her pleasure.

"We must go easy, love," he said softly.

A sigh shivered from her lips. "Tell me what to do . . ."

Emotion gripped him hard at her unwitting confession of innocence. He wanted to be the one to show her the joys of womanhood . . . and she was giving him the honor. Her gift humbled him.

"Trust me?" he asked.

She nodded without hesitation, and he felt a feeling close to love.

He was gentle as he sought the hem of her gown and eased it up over her belly and breasts, and finally off her head. Her hair was a soft cloud of dark auburn about her shoulders. He felt like a nervous, untried youth as he combed the silky strands down her neck and back.

He caught his breath as he studied her breasts, the tiny tight buds in full womanly mounds of white flesh . . . breasts made for kissing . . . touching. Flesh meant for tasting with lips and tongue.

Her belly was flat, her hips perfectly formed. The curly nest of hair shielding her femininity was dark and beautiful against the white skin of her abdomen and thighs. His gaze caressed her legs. *Lovely,* he thought. He reached out to stroke one, and she jerked at the simple touch.

"Open my trousers, love," he said.

She hesitated for only a second, and then he trembled as she undid the buttons. He heard her surprised little gasp as his desire burst free of cloth and constriction. But then it was he who made a startled sound as she encircled him with her hands.

The simple innocence of her warm, soft fingers caressing him nearly sent him over the edge.

"No, love," he said. "Not yet." He grabbed her hand, not without gentleness. "I want to pleasure you, and I love the feeling of your hands on me too much."

Meghan's smile lit up her blue eyes. "I love your hands touching me, too."

Her admission surprised him, and then he realized why he cared for this woman. She was genuine and good.

He stepped out of his pants. "Come here, Meghan."

He held out his hands, and she went to him, pressing against his naked length. He kissed her hard and then swung her into his arms before he lowered her on the bed.

"I'm going to kiss you everywhere," he said. "Frightened?"

"A little."

"Don't be."

She nodded. "All right."

Then while she lay across the white rumpled sheet covering the feather-tick mattress, he pressed his mouth to her forehead and then trailed a thorough path lower, kissing and nuzzling her, until he reached her soft belly.

He raised his head. "Meghan—"

"Aye, Lucas," she said. "I trust ye."

Then he tasted beneath the damp curls, and she moved and whimpered as he felt her desire surge and threaten to burst free. He loved it when she shuddered; and when she stiffened and cried out, he closed his eyes and fought down his own rising passionate tide.

"Okay, Meghan, now we fly together," he said, as he covered her with his length. He wanted to be inside her so desperately his muscles strained with the need.

Lucas parted her legs and positioned himself for entry, pausing as he prepared to thrust past her virginity . . . for there was no denying that Meghan McBride was a virgin.

"Lucas?" He heard her uncertainty, her surprise that he hadn't moved.

"Remember the joy, Meghan, as you've just felt it. It will hurt at first, but then the joy . . . the feeling will be all the greater." From somewhere came the realization that once he'd fully claimed her, his life would be forever changed. He pressed closer.

Meghan embraced him, closing her eyes as he touched her opening. She gasped as he inserted the tip of his penis, and then she cried out softly as he went deeper, pushing gently against the thin membrane of innocence.

"Meghan, I don't want to hurt you."

She clutched his shoulders, her fingernails biting into his skin. "You'll not hurt me," she gasped, and he saw that she was aroused, not frightened as he'd feared.

"Oh, love," he growled before he reared back and thrust hard.

Her sharp inhalation of breath made him pause with his staff buried deep. He could feel her pulsing softness. She felt so good . . . so damned good.

"Are you all right?" he asked with concern.

"Aye." Then, she began to move, and he made a choked sound as he lifted his hips and rocked forward in a rhythm that teased and raised the level of his desire. He had to hold back a moment while he fought for control.

Meghan cried out as Lucas filled her time and again. The world spun and her whole body started to shudder with ecstasy. *I love you, Lucas,* she thought. She stroked and fondled him from back to buttocks as he continued to move against her. Lucas groaned, his muscles tensing, and Meghan experienced the wet warmth of his seed. She gasped and stiffened as he brought her to the peak of pleasure again.

She loved him. She held him tightly and smiled.

Twenty-nine

Meghan woke up and stretched. Her lashes fluttered as she reached across the bed linen. "Lucas?"

The bed was empty beside her. She opened her eyes and sat up quickly. He'd left her! Her heart thumped wildly as she recalled the dark hours she'd lain willingly within his arms. Why did he leave?

Then, she recalled the servants. It wouldn't do for them to know that she'd allowed Lucas into her bed. She smiled. Lucas was being thoughtful again.

Her gaze fell on the hearth in her room, and she shuddered, recalling the fire. She felt chilled and rubbed her arms. Everything she owned was gone. Her clothes and belongings, even her only pair of shoes! All that was left was her smoke-stained nightdress.

Meghan rose, naked, flushing as she caught sight of her discarded borrowed nightgown and recalled when Lucas had removed it from her with tenderness. A tingling heat invaded her abdomen at the memory of Lucas's hands on her breasts . . . his mouth everywhere. That time with him had been glorious! If she never knew what it was to have a husband, at least she'd had this.

I love him. Tears filled her eyes as she realized that she couldn't stay, for when the time came that Lucas no longer desired her, she'd be devastated. Better to leave now, she thought, before the pain became unbearable. But how could she leave when she had nothing to wear?

A lump rose in her throat, making it difficult to swallow. She grabbed the night garment from the floor and slipped it over her head, glad to see that the gown wasn't ripped or damaged in any way. Then she opened the door and peered into the hall, hoping to see one of the upstairs chambermaids, but she saw no one.

She shut the door and leaned back against it, closing her eyes. *Now what am I to do?* She opened her eyes, saw a dresser, and went to rummage through the drawers, hoping to find something more modest to wear than a bed gown. Although the garment adequately covered her from neck to ankle, it was still meant for sleeping.

The top two drawers were storage for bed linens and blankets, and the rest of the drawers were empty. But before Meghan had a chance to fret, her attention was drawn by a knock on the bedchamber door, and she answered it. It was Rachel, one of the housemaids.

"Mrs. Gibbons sent me with some garments for ya," the girl said.

"Oh, thank ye," Meghan said. "I was wondering what to wear."

The maid smiled with sympathy and handed her an armload of clothes. "There are a few extras there as well from me and the others." When Meghan would have protested, Rachel said, "We've got everything we need, Meg, while you've got nothing."

Meghan blinked back tears as she murmured her thanks. "I've got friends, it seems," she said.

Rachel nodded. "Do you need any help?"

The Irishwoman shook her head. "I'm sure I can manage. Thank ye."

The girl started to leave. "Well, then, if you need

anything, you let one of us know." She paused. "I'm sorry about the fire, Meghan," she said after Meghan had thanked her again. "But at least no one was harmed."

"Aye."

"I wonder who wanted to hurt Patty."

Meghan stiffened. "The fire was deliberately set?" It was the first she'd heard of it.

Rachel told her what she'd heard from James about the lantern and whiskey bottle he'd found near Patty's back door. When the girl left, Meghan suffered a strong feeling of foreboding. She recalled Rafferty's vow to get even with her. Dear God, could Rafferty O'Connor have done such a thing? There was a time when Rafferty had a terrible weakness for whiskey, but that was a long time ago, so long ago that she'd been a child. She'd forgotten about it, because Rafferty no longer drank. But he'd changed so much, and she wondered . . .

Meghan recalled Rafferty's occasional outbursts of anger and shivered. *Oh, Lord, don't let it be Rafferty who did this.*

She dressed in a servant's gown and went downstairs to eat. When she saw the servants hard at work, she felt guilty for having slept so late.

Mrs. Riker seemed unconcerned when she glanced over and saw Meghan. "Meghan, you're up." She gave her a smile.

"I'm sorry for sleeping in," Meghan began.

"Of course, you should sleep! You've had a terrible night." The cook's expression was sympathetic. "Come and sit, dear, and I'll give you some breakfast."

"But Mrs. Gibbons—"

"Said you're to take it easy today, Meghan," Mrs. Riker assured her. "Both she and Mr. Ridgely left specific instructions to see that you're well cared for while they're gone, and I aim to follow them."

"Gone?" Meghan's heart tripped. Lucas had left without telling her again.

Mrs. Riker wiped her flour-coated hands on the skirt of her apron and put water on the stove for Meghan's tea. "The Mrs. and her nephew had to go to Philadelphia."

"Oh." At least, Lucas hadn't returned to his home in Kent, she thought. Meghan watched Cook set a plate filled with cinnamon buns before her. Then Mrs. Riker went about preparing eggs.

"Please," Meghan said, "there's no need to trouble yerself."

"It's no bother, Meg," a kitchen girl said. "Mrs. Riker loves fussing, don't ya, Mrs. Riker?"

The older woman shot the young maid a look. "Get back to work, girl." But her expression was soft and her eyes kind.

"Have ye heard how Patty Rhoades and the others are faring?"

"I spoke with Peter this morning, Meg," another girl said, referring to Patty's middle son. Meghan learned that the young woman was Mrs. Trill's daughter. "They're all fine. Shaken, but glad to be alive."

"Aye," Meghan murmured with a shiver, recalling the fire. "We're all glad to be alive."

The morning passed quickly for Meghan, as she went to see Patty and her sons. But by the afternoon, Meghan was having doubts about staying in Gibbons Mill. Everyone had been wonderful and kind to her, but then they didn't know that she'd given herself to Lucas.

Guilt began to gnaw at her conscience. She had lain with a man outside the bonds of marriage. She'd sinned, but—God forgive her—she loved Lucas

Ridgely, and it was impossible for her to be properly penitent.

Meghan became more nervous and ridden with guilt with each new hour of the day. When asked, Mrs. Riker had confessed that she didn't know when Lucas and his aunt planned to return. It could be tomorrow, she'd said. Or could be as early as this evening.

Despite orders to enjoy a free day, Meghan went back to her sewing, for she needed something to keep herself occupied. But she learned that busy hands still left a mind to think and worry. Several times during the course of the day, she'd found herself getting up to check the time on the mantel clock in the sitting room. On each occasion that someone opened or closed a door during the day, Meghan's heart would race until she learned that the noise hadn't been created by the returning aunt and nephew. Only then would her heart slow, and her breathing flow easier.

Meghan had worked herself into such a state by bedtime that she felt shaky as she undressed. She'd convinced herself that to stay at Gibbons Mill wasn't a wise thing to do after all . . . not since she'd responded so wantonly to Lucas's experienced touch.

Experienced, she thought with pain. How many women had Lucas taken to bed? Had he kissed and caressed them like he had her? Had he cried out the way he had with her when he'd finally found his satisfaction?

She went to her bedchamber window and peered out into the February night. It was cold, but fortunately there was no snow. Her gaze rose to the sky, and she judged from the look of the cloud-hazy moon that it would snow soon.

Should she leave now and chance it? And if she left here, where would she go? She owned nothing . . .

not even the clothes on her back . . . not even the shoes on her feet.

Her eyes stung as she turned from the window to examine the lovely room. She could be happy here if not for her feelings for a man who only desired her.

He'd left for Philadelphia without telling her. If things had changed between them, he would have left a note—something!—if he loved her . . .

Love! She made a face. Lucas lusted for her; he'd never professed to love her. *Did ye forget what he wanted from ya from the start?* He'd been honest; she couldn't find fault with him for trying to trick her.

Meghan threw back the bed covers and climbed onto the feather-tick mattress. Lucas's scent still lingered on her pillow, and she could almost feel him beside her, touching her again. The pain was bittersweet.

Tomorrow she'd speak with Patty. Patty would know where she could go, what to do, Meghan decided.

Then she recalled Patty's devastation upon seeing her house burn. No, she couldn't bother Patty.

Mari Bright. Mari had been a friend to her from the first day, Meghan thought. She'd ask Mari if she knew where a woman could start a new life.

He was anxious to see her again. Yesterday morning, it had nearly killed him to leave her room. He'd risen before the sun and lingered for a long while just studying Meghan as she'd slept. The wealth of tenderness he'd felt toward her had amazed him. He'd never known he was capable of experiencing these feelings. He'd looked at Meghan and experienced a rush of warmth and happiness that he choked up just thinking about it now.

Lucas glanced at his aunt on the carriage seat across

from his. To his surprise, he found her watching him with a speculative gleam in her dark eyes.

He questioned her with a smile. Inside, he felt quivery and vulnerable; it was both exciting and frightening for a man who'd never been in love before. He decided then what he must do about it.

"You seem anxious to get back," Aunt Flora said softly.

A jolt passed through him. "Why do you say that?" he asked, managing to keep his tone light.

His relative smiled. "Son, it wasn't hard to figure out when you woke me at five, hurried me to breakfast, and then bullied that poor Mr. Abernathy into loading the wagon at six."

Lucas shrugged as if he thought nothing unusual in his actions. "If it wasn't for Mr. Abernathy, we'd have had the new machines by now. I paid that man good money weeks ago to see that they were delivered . . ."

Flora raised an eyebrow. "I suppose that might be true—"

"Are you angry that I disturbed your night's sleep?" her nephew asked with amusement.

"Are you saying I'm irritable?"

He chuckled at his aunt's sharp tone. "Darlin'," he soothed, "you're never irritable, irritating perhaps, but never irritable."

His aunt scowled. "Whatever—or whoever—is calling you back to Gibbons Mill," she said, "I hope she realizes how impossible you can be. Charming perhaps, but impertinent and impossible."

Lucas grinned. "I'm sure George Simmons appreciates me just fine."

Flora's undignified snort told him that she didn't believe for one second that it was business calling him back. "I hope *she's* worth it," his aunt murmured, making his amusement fade.

IRISH LINEN

Lucas looked away. *Oh, she is, Aunt Flora,* he thought, recalling Meghan's loving response. *She is worth it enough to me that I plan to marry her.*

He stifled a niggle of misgiving that his family wouldn't love or accept the woman he'd chosen. A poor woman. A woman of Irish birth.

They'd accept her, he vowed, because he loved and wanted her.

Marriage to Meghan seemed like a wonderful, exciting adventure. She wasn't his mother, and he wasn't his father. He and Meghan would stay happy together for the rest of their lives.

Marriage could make a person happy, couldn't it? "Aunt Flora?" he said.

She glanced away from the window to meet his gaze. "Yes, dear?"

"You were happy with Uncle Walter, weren't you?"

Her soft smile was all the answer he needed. "He and I were very happy together." Suddenly, she frowned. "What is this all about, Lucas?" Enlightenment entered her dark eyes. "Nephew, not every marriage is like your parents'."

"Lord, I hope not," he said with great feeling.

Her regard intensified. "Are you thinking of getting married?"

"Perhaps."

"Someone I know?"

"Perhaps," he said with a smile. When she tried to question him further, he refused to answer. Instead, he called up to the carriage driver to pick up the pace for home, and his excitement grew as he looked forward to seeing Meghan again.

Thirty

"Where is she?" Lucas said as he burst into the kitchen. He caught Mrs. Riker's gaze. "Where's Meghan?"

"Why, I don't know, Lucas," the cook replied. "I haven't seen the girl since first thing this morning, when she told me she was going to visit Mari Bright."

"Mari Bright?" Panic had swelled within his breast moments ago when he'd returned to the house and found Meghan absent. No one had seemed to know where she'd gone.

"She's one of my employees," Aunt Flora said as she entered the room during the last part of the conversation. "Why do you need Mari?"

"He's looking for Meghan," Mrs. Riker said. "I told him she'd left to see Mari, but that was early this morning. I'm sure she should be back by now."

Lucas caught his aunt's sly look as he passed her to exit the room. "I'll check the mill then."

"Lucas!" his aunt called.

He froze and turned, expecting to see her censure. "Yes?"

"Try the Smiths, two houses down from Patty's. She may have gone there to see Susan. Although she rooms with Betsy, I've noticed that Meghan and Susan are close."

Lucas raised his eyebrows over the fact that his aunt

knew so much about the woman who was only her seamstress.

And then he knew. His aunt had guessed about his feelings for the young Irishwoman and had learned all she could about Lucas's choice.

"She's been through a great deal," Aunt Flora said in a quiet voice.

He nodded. "I . . . care for her."

"So she's the one." Was that a disapproving frown that touched Aunt Flora's lips for just the briefest second? She stared at him. "Lucas, we need to discuss this later," she said.

"There's nothing to discuss," he said. Anxious to find Meghan and ask her to be his wife, Lucas then left his aunt abruptly.

He found Susan easily enough at the Smiths, just where his aunt had said. The young woman seemed surprised that Lucas hadn't passed Meghan on his way, because the Irishwoman had just left her.

"Is she all right? Do you know where she went?"

Susan shook her head. "I thought she was going back to the big house. She seemed upset when she left, but she wouldn't tell me why," she said, her glance evading his.

"Susan, please—" he pleaded. "I'm worried about her."

"She and I were talking about the fire," she said, "and I mentioned how Priscilla had been through a lot lately. First at the mill and then the fire."

"At the mill?" he asked.

The young woman nodded. "With Phelps. He's bothered her just like he had Meghan."

Lucas felt his chest tighten. "Why didn't she come forward?"

Susan gave him a look. "Because Priscilla is petrified of him, that's why!"

"I'm sorry," he apologized. "But why would Meghan become upset?"

"It wasn't learning about Priscilla and Phelps that bothered her," she began. "It was hearing from Mari Bright that Mathew Phelps was still working at the mill. Only he'd been moved down to the second floor." She met his gaze with a look of blame.

"We couldn't fire him," he said. "No one would come forward; we had no proof."

Lucas realized that Meghan wouldn't only be hurt but she'd be angry to learn about Phelps that way. He was relieved that Meghan was still here, but for how long he had no idea.

"I think Meghan went that way." Susan pointed in a different direction than the way he'd come.

He started to hurry away, only to be called back by Susan.

"Mr. Ridgely, what is Meghan to you?"

"She's a friend," he said with a sad smile. "And more if I haven't ruined things between us."

Then, he turned from the sight of Susan's shocked expression to follow the path Meghan had taken. The day was clear. Miraculously, it hadn't snowed although the previous night's sky had looked threatening.

He rounded a bend and frowned when he couldn't see Meghan ahead. Had she become so angry that she'd left Gibbons Mill? The house was directly before him; yet, there was no sign of her glorious auburn hair and lovely figure.

He started to run the rest of the way and nearly tripped when his foot hit an iced patch of ground. Muttering, he righted himself and glanced about. He didn't think Meghan could have made it back to the house. But where could she have disappeared?

Terror invaded his chest. Rafferty O'Connor, he thought. Had the man kidnapped Meghan? His fear

IRISH LINEN

grew as he recalled the conversation he'd had with James Rhoades on the night of the fire. James had confided in Lucas that he suspected Meghan's former fiancé of setting the blaze. He told Lucas of the man's persistent attempts to see Meghan, and their successes in keeping him away from her. What disturbed Lucas most now was the memory of the boy telling him of the night when they'd been awakened by a noise and hurried outside to see that someone had been about the house.

"Meghan," he whispered. He clenched his fists. He'd kill the bastard if Rafferty touched even one tiny hair on Meghan's head.

Then he heard a sound . . . a choked sob that made him change direction toward the smokehouse.

And there he found the woman he loved, huddled on the frozen ground, her arms wrapped around her body protectively, her head bowed as she cried softly.

Lucas felt like he'd been kicked in the gut. He rushed forward. "Meghan!" he gasped, hunkering down beside her.

She gave a startled little scream as he took her by surprise. Then she blinked several times as she gazed at him, focusing as if she couldn't believe her eyes. "Lucas?" she said hoarsely.

He gave a jerky nod and grabbed her arm. "Are you all right?"

She gasped and drew back. "Ye didn't fire him!" she said. "Ye lied to me! Ye didn't dismiss Mathew Phelps!"

"Meghan—"

"No," she hissed, "don't lie to me again."

"I said I'd handled it, and I had. Simmons moved him to a floor where we employ mostly male workers. No one from the weaving floor would come forward and tell us the truth. We couldn't dismiss him without proof!"

"I'm proof!" she said, scrambling to her feet. "What is it? Can't ye believe an Irishwoman? Is that it? Or is it because I'm from a poor family, unlike yours?"

"I'm sorry, Meghan," he said. "I believed you, but my hands were tied." He closed his eyes on a wave of pain. He didn't want her to find out this way. He would have told her eventually. It had been his intention to keep an eye out and try to trap Phelps into arranging his own hanging.

Meghan caught her breath as she studied his bent head. "Lucas?"

"Marry me, Irish. Marry me and stay with me forever."

"Excuse me?" she gasped, her eyes widening in shock. Had she heard him correctly? Did Lucas actually propose to her? "But I thought ye didn't want to marry," she said.

He caught her other hand and clasped both of her palms gently within his fingers, rubbing her skin, making her tingle. His ebony gaze was bright with feeling, and there was a look of tension in his features that she found endearing in that he appeared extremely vulnerable at that moment.

"Marry me, Meghan," he pleaded. "Tonight. Tomorrow. In two weeks. Whenever you want. Just say you'll have me for your husband."

Meghan took one look into his misty black eyes and she was lost.

"Oh, God," she whispered shakily.

"Does that mean you will?" He released her hand and sat back on his haunches.

"Ye really believed me?" she asked, and he nodded. "Oh, God, we're not right for each other. My background is so different. I'm a working woman, Lucas, while ye—"

"Marry me, Meghan."

"Oh, God. Oh, God . . ."

"Is that a yes?" he said with some amusement.

Meghan threw herself against him, tumbling him to the ground. She peered down into his face with eyes full of love for him. Throwing caution to the wind, she kissed him. "Aye, Lucas Ridgely, I'll marry ye tonight and again in two weeks if ye want . . . whenever and for how many times ye'll have me, I'll willingly say 'I do.'"

Thirty-one

Lucas bundled Meghan against him and headed to the big house. "Let's say we'll marry in three weeks," he said. He paused in his footsteps and turned her to smile down into her blue eyes. "We'll have a big wedding."

Meghan's heart tripped. "Lucas, it isn't necessary to spend money on a big wedding. I'd be happy if it was just the two of us."

His eyes lit up with loving warmth. "I know you would, but it wouldn't be right." He tucked her against his side, and they continued toward his aunt's house. "We'll have to keep our engagement a secret for a while, love," he said after they'd taken a few steps.

Meghan stiffened within his arms. "Why?"

A knot formed in her stomach. Was it because he realized that his family would never accept her as she was? She couldn't forget that spinner Catherine Brown's cruel remarks about her and Lucas. It was true that she was well beneath his station and that she'd never be woman enough to hold his interest. And she doubted his family would want her as Lucas's wife.

"Because it wouldn't be proper for the people here to know before my family," Lucas explained gently.

Despite her misgivings, Meghan nodded her agreement. "All right, I can wait if ye can." Lucas's answering smile was enough to give her goose bumps.

He paused on the porch steps. "Meghan, the other night—" A bright passionate flame lit up his black eyes.

Meghan felt herself blush as she met his gaze. "I know, Mr. Ridgely." Her stomach did a flip-flop as she realized that in three short weeks she'd be a Ridgely, too. Meghan Ridgely. She smiled. She could certainly get used to the name.

With a heated look at her, Lucas opened the door and gestured for her to precede him. "Remember, love, not a word to anyone."

"I promise," she said. It made perfect sense for his parents to be informed first. But what about Aunt Flora? "Lucas, your aunt—"

He shook his blond head. "Not yet, I'm afraid, Irish."

And so for a little while, Meghan would have to keep her joy to herself. Lucas wanted to marry her. He hadn't declared his love for her, but he must care, she thought. Besides, she hadn't told him she loved him either.

She stifled a silly grin as she greeted Lucas's aunt, who seemed glad to see her as the woman inquired politely how Meghan had fared since the fire.

Meghan thanked the woman for all the wonderful clothes, blushing slightly because she'd chosen to wear one of the servants' garments instead of an expensive gown. But she was still an employee, and unless there was a special occasion, she would act and dress like an employee of Flora Gibbons. She knew she'd eventually have an occasion for taffeta.

I'm going to marry this woman's nephew. She wanted to share the secret. The man she loved wanted her to be his wife. But would it work? Would he still want her if his family disapproved, which they were bound to do?

* * *

Gifts began to arrive at Meghan's room daily. Because she'd lost everything in the fire, no one thought Lucas's generosity strange. It began with a gown of blue satin with white lace trim and pearl buttons. The garment was beautiful, but like the taffeta gown, the satin garment was unsuitable for a house servant. When she expressed her pleasure, but made mention of that fact, Lucas smiled and told her to wear it when his parents arrived on the fifteenth of February.

Meghan tensed, nervous with the prospect of meeting the Ridgelys. "Lucas, I've never worn a gown like this."

"Did you try it on?" he asked.

"Aye," she admitted, "and it fits perfectly, but—"

He grinned. "It's yours, love. Now as my future wife, there are things you must learn—like how to accept gifts from me."

She sighed, not unhappy but uncomfortable with the idea of accepting gifts.

That night she recalled his words and wondered with dismay what else Lucas expected her to learn as his future wife.

Three days later, Meghan was alone in the kitchen. It was late; the servants had left or gone to bed. Lucas had cornered her for a few seconds early in the day, asking her to meet him there. It would be the first time they'd have private time together since he'd asked her to marry him.

Meghan could hear the thundering of her heartbeat as she stood in the dark room, listening for his arrival. The tall case clock in the foyer chimed the hour; it was 2:00 A.M.

IRISH LINEN

Would he come? she wondered, afraid that he'd overslept or changed his mind.

"Meghan."

She gasped and spun toward the back of the room. She hadn't heard him enter, because he'd come from the pantry.

"Lucas!" she gasped. "I didn't know ye were in there." He must have been there for some time, she realized. He carried a plate filled with food in each hand.

His smile took her breath away. "I know you didn't. I've been watching you for the past fifteen minutes."

She swallowed. "Why?" It was disconcerting to learn she'd been watched without her knowledge, even though the one who had done the staring was the man she loved.

"Come into the pantry, Irish." He waved toward the door.

She grabbed her candle from Mrs. Riker's worktable and followed him into the back room, her pulse racing as she wondered what he had in mind for her.

He led her into the pantry, stopped near the rear wall, and handed her the plates. "Hold these for a minute."

While she held on to the plates filled with cakes, Lucas slid aside a crate and a huge barrel of flour. The noise made by his actions sounded loud in the quiet of the night. When no one came to investigate, Meghan decided that the volume of sound had been magnified by her concern with their being discovered.

Once the barrel was rolled aside, Meghan could see a small hidden door "What is it?" she asked, narrowing her gaze as she wondered whether or not he expected her to fit through the door opening.

"It's my escape door." He grinned, his teeth flashing in the candlelight. "The room behind it was originally built as a priest hole, but I used it as a hiding place when I was a boy . . . usually when it came time for my parents to take me home to Windfield." His smile became softly reminiscent. "It worked, too. No one could find me, but my aunt knew that I was safe, so she would convince my parents to let me stay one more week after promising to see personally that I got home.

"Once my parents had reluctantly agreed to let me stay, I would come out of my special place from another door behind the house. I'd suddenly appear as if I'd been oblivious to their calling me."

Meghan listened, fascinated by his tale of youth. "And did ye get to stay?"

He nodded as he caressed her with his gaze. "My aunt had made my mother promise, you see, so neither Mother nor Father would dare go back on their word. Their word was as good as gold coin."

Lucas looked down at her hands holding the plates. There was no place for her to put them, and Meghan could see by his mischievous twinkle that he'd realized it, too, and was about to take advantage of the situation.

She felt the tingle of anticipation at her nape travel down her spine as he loomed closer, his gaze fastened on her mouth.

"It seems like forever since we've been alone," he said, exciting her with his words.

"Aye," she breathed.

"I'm going to kiss you, Meghan. Don't you spill our cookies now."

Her nod was solemn, but a tiny smile began to form on her lips.

With a groan, Lucas bent and kissed her over the two piled-high plates. It was a brief kiss, but the contact made Meghan dizzy with happiness, because Lucas seemed as moved by the experience as she.

"Come," he said. "I didn't bring you here for this."

She was disappointed. *Then why did ye bring me here?* Now that she knew Lucas wanted her for his wife, she wanted—needed—to lay intimately within his arms again. But how does one ask without seeming like a wanton? She'd have to wait for Lucas's lead, she thought.

"I wanted you to see my private place . . . the one I had as a boy," he said, touching her heart with his desire to share what had been special to him. "I mean to share everything with you," he murmured, thrilling her.

A lump rose to her throat as she became blinded by emotional tears. "Thank ye, Lucas," she whispered.

His answer was a sheepish smile and an extended hand toward her.

She gave him a look and held up the plates. He laughed, took the plates and found a place for them that she'd overlooked.

A week later she thought back to that night and wondered if it had really happened or if it had all been a dream. Lucas had taken her into his room, which was small, damp, and had a dirt floor, and he'd begun to tell her other stories about his experiences as a boy at Gibbons Mill. They'd shared cookies and drank water from fancy glasses. Meghan regarded the time as one of the most wonderful she'd ever enjoyed, for Lucas had opened up to her, telling her a great many things. She, in turn, had told of her early years, and he'd listened, his expression tender, as she'd spoken of her mother and father. And he'd held her in his arms when she'd cried.

They'd shared no physical intimacy that night, but

a stronger, more intimately emotional bond had been formed, Meghan thought.

But the Lucas she'd seen since then seemed like a stranger. His little gifts kept coming to her room daily, but there seemed to be a thread of purpose in the choice of them now.

This week she'd received a jeweled hair comb, a gold bracelet, and a pair of fancy shoes. These items differed from Lucas's early gifts in that they were expensive and of little practical use, not serviceable and functional as the cloak he'd given her to replace the one she'd lost or the sewing machine that she'd marveled over and quickly learned to use.

Meghan knew that she should be happy that her fiancé was wooing her with tokens of his affection, but she would rather have received the gift of three words. A sincere "I love you" would be his three greatest gifts to her.

But she would have to be happy with jewels, she thought miserably. Lucas cared for her, but love? No. She must be content that he desired her enough to want her for his wife.

Please God, allow me to make him happy. She was of poor Irish stock, while Lucas was a wealthy, upper-class Delawarean. Were his expensive gifts hints that she should learn to become a proper, socially acceptable wife? Meghan frowned. She knew she was right; Lucas was trying to mold her into something—someone—she could never be. The question was what was he going to do when he learned that she could never be anything more than she was—a woman born from poor Irish stock.

"Meghan." Flora Gibbons entered the sewing room and went directly to where Meghan sat at her sewing machine, making a new shift for Rachel. "I'd like you to try on this bonnet. It's a lovely hat, but I'm unable to wear it anymore." She lowered her voice conspiratorially. "It's much too young-looking for me, but not for you, dear."

The bonnet was made of straw with a large brim. A huge ostrich feather stuck out of a band of artificial roses, and there were pink satin ribbons attached to be tied under the chin.

Meghan regarded the hat doubtfully, but Lucas's aunt insisted upon setting the bonnet on the young woman's head herself. The Irishwoman felt like a small child again as Flora fussed over the correct placement. Meghan sat silently while Flora straightened the brim and ensured that the ribbons were tied just right, until finally the older woman seemed satisfied.

"There," Lucas's aunt said as she straightened. She regarded her handiwork with a critical eye. "Oh, yes, it looks quite lovely on you, my dear. Here . . ." She helped Meghan to rise. "Come and see how perfect it is for you."

Meghan allowed herself to be dragged down the hall to Flora Gibbons's bedchamber where she was thrust before a cheval looking glass. The bonnet was beautiful, although a bit fancy for Meghan's taste.

"What do you think?" the woman prompted.

Peering at her reflection, Meghan didn't feel right in taking it, which was clearly what her employer had in mind. "I think 'tis grand, but—"

"It would go splendid with your new blue gown, wouldn't it?"

Meghan studied Flora's mirror image as the woman smiled over Meghan's shoulder. How did her employer know about Lucas's gift? The blue gown was the one that Lucas had intended she wear to meet his parents.

"Mrs. Gibbons, I can't take this . . ."

Flora waved her hand. "Nonsense, dear. You must. I simply insist." She paused to lovingly touch the bonnet's brim. "My late husband gave it to me, Meghan," she said softly. "I'd be pleased if you'd wear it."

Fighting emotion, Meghan couldn't refuse. How could she say no when she was offered something that obviously meant so much to Lucas's aunt?

Ye're going to marry him, girl, an inner voice said. *Get used to it, Flora is his aunt; it's all right to accept the gift.*

"Thank ye, Mrs. Gibbons. 'Tis lovely—truly." She blinked back tears. But the woman's kindness only emphasized in Meghan's mind her failings as Lucas's future wife.

Flora nodded. "You're welcome, dear. Now," she said, turning, "I also have this wonderful book of poetry." She moved to a dower chest and searched inside. "Ah, here it is! A collection of works by Robert Browning!" She closed the lid and approached Meghan with a book, smiling. "I know the most perfect poem for you to memorize. We'll have to work on your pronunciation, of course, but . . ."

The rest of Flora's words were lost to Meghan when she realized what Lucas's aunt was doing. She was going to tutor Meghan in the fine art of being a woman of higher class.

"I think 'Bells and Pomegranates' is the best piece, but 'A Soul's Tragedy' is good, too. It's up to you, Meghan, after all, you'll be the one to recite it!"

Pain choked Meghan's throat. "How did ye find out?" she rasped. She'd never felt so hurt before, because someone thought she wasn't good enough as she was. Lucas, she thought. It was because of Lucas. "Did Lucas—"

"No, Lucas didn't say a word," the woman said, regarding her with kind eyes. "But it was easy for me to guess." She laid her hand on Meghan's shoulder. "I know my nephew better than his own mother does. I've seen how he looks at you and . . ." Her features were soft. "I knew."

Meghan felt a little better once she'd learned that Lucas hadn't told his aunt of their relationship. "Mrs. Gibbons—"

"Aunt Flora," the woman insisted.

"Aunt Flora, I don't know if I can be what Lucas needs."

The woman was quiet for so long that Meghan realized that she'd tapped into Flora's own feelings. "Of course, you can," Lucas's aunt said carefully, "because you already are."

Then why don't ye sound convincing? And why are ye both trying to change me? Meghan wondered. She glanced at the book and then the older woman, and a dawning light entered Flora's gaze.

"This isn't for Lucas, my dear," his aunt said. "Well, in a way it is, but only to get past his mother." Her lips firmed. "My sister is a snob, you see." Then her expression warmed. "But my brother-in-law James will love you."

Meghan blushed. "Will ye tell him ye know?"

"Lucas?" Her employer shook her head. "Lucas will tell me himself in his own time. In the meantime, we'll help things along a bit. Agreed?"

Determined to make Lucas a good wife, Meghan said, "Aye, agreed." The two women shook hands.

From that time on, Meghan met with Lucas's aunt for a brief period each day to learn "Bells and Pomegranates" by the poet, Robert Browning. She also practiced walking and talking properly. She was taught how to dress and how to breathe—or not breathe—while wearing a corset.

Never having owned such a garment in her entire life, Meghan hated the feminine contraption almost more than she'd hated going hungry in her homeland. But for a while each day, she wore it—to please Aunt Flora . . . and for Lucas.

Her instructional meetings with Flora she kept a secret from Lucas, although it bothered her to keep silent. She loved her fiancé so much; she wanted to share everything with him.

Each time she got frustrated with trying to learn proper lady's comportment, she'd remember the night when Lucas had taken her into his hiding place and the emotional closeness they'd shared.

Meghan recalled the one time she and Lucas had shared a bed, and she ached with the desire to lie with him again. The physical pain intensified with each day of celibacy. Lucas thought that since they were engaged they should wait until after the wedding before they again became intimate with each other. Meghan thought him sweet for being honorable, but she wanted to scream with frustration that they shouldn't wait. What difference could a few short weeks make when they were bound by promises to become husband and wife?

Tonight, she thought, *I'll ask him.*

The opportunity to speak with him privately came when Flora Gibbons retired early, leaving Lucas and Meghan together alone in the sitting room. It had been Flora's idea that Meghan join them; Flora had wanted to entertain them with a poem piece by Elizabeth Barrett called "The Cry of the Children." Shortly after they'd collected in the room, however, Flora had pleaded a sudden headache and taken herself off to bed.

Lucas stared at Meghan seated across the room from him with a look that told her that he still wanted her.

IRISH LINEN 317

As she held on to that burning glance, Meghan was glad that his interest for her continued to hold true. With no caresses and only the briefest kiss these last few days, she'd begun to wonder if Lucas's desire for her had waned.

Apparently not.

"Come here," he said.

Her blood rushed as he patted his lap.

"Your aunt—" she began.

"She'll not come back. Couldn't you see how tired she is?"

Couldn't ye see that yer aunt was acting so that we could be alone? She rose and approached him on trembling legs. She'd wanted so badly to be close to him that her thoughts and her body were responding wildly as she neared him. She chose to sit beside him on the sofa. He raised his eyebrows and reached over to tug her into his arms.

"I've missed you," he said, his words whispering like a caress across her lips.

"Ye've been busy." She gasped as he nibbled on her neck. Closing her eyes, she cupped his head, her fingers entangling in his soft, golden hair as he shifted her onto his lap. "Lucas . . ."

His mouth trailed a heated path to the collar edge of her gown, grazing lower to moisten a fabric-clad breast.

Meghan moaned as he blew into the cloth, heating her nipple and making it rise, before moving to its twin.

"I want you," he said thickly.

"Aye," she whispered. "Love me."

Lucas gently set her off his lap and onto the sofa beside him. "I can't," he said with a raw look in his eyes and a twisted smile. "I promised to wait."

Here was her chance, she thought. "Why, Lucas? Why do we have to wait?"

He seemed startled by her question. Then he continued to study her, his lips forming a more genuine smile. "Soon, love. I'm anxious, too."

"Are ye?" she thought, not realizing that she'd spoken aloud until she saw his expression change.

"Of course, I am." He cupped her face with both hands. "Look at me."

She raised her lashes and regarded him uncertainly.

"Do I appear to be content to keep from touching you? Look at me, Meghan. Even now, I can hardly keep my hands still."

And Meghan realized that he spoke the truth. His hands had been caressing her—and still were—back and forth the length of her upper arms. "Oh, Lucas."

They kissed. Briefly.

"There's a child to consider, love," he pointed out. "We must wait to ensure that our child is conceived within wedlock. Now, come." He rose and helped her to stand. "I'll walk you to your room."

He paused at her door and eyed her solemnly. "I think you'd be interested to know that we fired Mathew Phelps today. Your friend Priscilla came in to talk to us, and after she did, so did several others. It's as I thought, they hadn't come forward before now, because they were afraid."

"Why did Priscilla change her mind?" she asked.

"I think you'll have to speak to your friend Susan about that."

Meghan smiled, pleased with her friend and the man who stood before her for doing the right thing. "I love you," she said on impulse.

Her only answer was a deep, long kiss that left her dizzy and gasping for breath. When he kissed, her doubts about their marriage disappeared, only to resurface later.

Two days later, afraid to face being a failure as Lucas's wife, Meghan was packing her belongings to leave Gibbons Mill.

Thirty-two

It was the evening before the Ridgelys were due to arrive in Gibbons Mill. Meghan had had a trying day. She'd begun her courses only that morning, and her abdomen hurt. And she felt particularly clumsy.

Earlier, when she'd met with Aunt Flora to try on her blue gown with all the proper undergarments, Meghan had felt so restricted by her corset that she'd nearly fainted. And her new "quality" shoes hurt her feet.

She couldn't remember the poem she'd practiced daily to recite to Lucas's parents. Flora had been extremely patient, but Meghan had recognized the worry in her dark gaze.

Lucas had been charming and polite today, as always, but she'd sensed tension within him. He was obviously concerned whether or not she'd be able to win his family's approval.

She could never be anything more than a simple peasant girl from Ireland. Which was why she realized she couldn't stay here.

The house was dark. Fortunately, there was a full moon to light up Meghan's way as she left. She picked up her small pack with one servant's gown, a clean shift, and an extra pair of stockings. The cloak that Lucas had given her to replace the green one was red and had a hood just like her other one. She recalled

IRISH LINEN

with a sad smile how Lucas had apologized when he'd given her the cloak. There hadn't been a green cloak available in all Philadelphia, he'd told her, but he'd hoped she would accept this bright red one. Meghan had accepted his gift, because the wish to please her had come from his heart. She would treasure her new red cloak forever.

Meghan put the cloak over her simple muslin gown and glanced about the bedchamber one last time through a haze of tears. She thought she'd go to Philadelphia and find Bridget, who was living there with her cousin Sean. When she'd visited Mari Bright that other morning, she'd been unable to bring herself to discuss leaving the area with her friend. And she'd decided that she didn't really want to leave—then.

A note for Lucas lay on her pillow. She could have left earlier, for the household had been asleep for some time, but she'd struggled over the right words. Finally, she'd carefully written what was in her heart. The missive was short, but she'd said what she had to say. She'd told him she loved him, but that she could never be the wife he needed. She asked him not to be angry with her for leaving.

As Meghan left silently down the stairs, logic waged a battle with her emotions.

It would be all right if she stayed. Surely, Lucas's parents would love and accept her.

Don't be daft, lass! Why would Aunt Flora go to so much trouble if she thought ye'd be willingly accepted into the Ridgely family?

Lucas would marry her even if his parents hated her.

But with the pressure from his parents, Lucas will soon hate ye, too . . . after a while.

"But I love him," she whispered.

But he's never declared his love for ye.

But he asked her to marry him.

Guilt, lass. He's bedded ye against his better judgment, taking advantage of ya after the fire when ye were most vulnerable. She couldn't forget how Aunt Flora thought she needed lessons to be a proper wife to Lucas. She couldn't put aside the fact that they had been raised differently in different classes. Lucas was of the upper class while she was well beneath him.

She would never measure up; she would shame Lucas before his family and friends. It was that last argument that kept Meghan going out the front door and into the cold mid-February night.

Clutching the ends of her hood with one hand and her satchel of clothes with the other, Meghan left Gibbons Mill and headed toward Philadelphia.

Beth and his parents were due to arrive, and it occurred to Lucas that Meghan might be overly anxious this morning. After going to the kitchen to get his fiancée a cup of tea, Lucas went upstairs to her room.

He'd been anxious and concerned himself these last days. He loved Meghan so much that he wanted his mother and father to love her, too. Not that it would alter his feelings for her if his parents didn't take to his bride-to-be. But his concern was for Meghan, who could be hurt by his family.

Meghan was genuine and sweet. On the night of the fire, she'd given herself to him without reservations or guile. It had been hell for him these past weeks keeping his distance from the woman he loved. But today, he thought, the wait would be over. Finally, he would tell his parents and then the world just how much he cared for his "Irish."

He'd tried to express how he'd felt for her these last weeks. The little gifts he'd given her had been his way

IRISH LINEN

of telling her that he'd always be there to love and care for her.

It was his concern for her feelings that had prompted him to buy her the blue gown. He preferred to see her in a dress of plain linen, for her Irish features were beautiful enough without adornment of any kind. But as he'd recalled his sister's delight in pretty things, he'd worried that Meghan would feel out of place or insignificant in Beth's and his parents' company without a gown as expensive or as well made.

Lucas smiled as he reached Meghan's door. His betrothed could stitch a gown better than any of his sister's. In fact, he'd be willing to wager that Meghan would have preferred and enjoyed sewing her own gown.

He knocked and waited for her to answer. He could picture her inside the room rousing from sleep, her blue eyes slumberous, her dark red hair tousled about her smooth white shoulders. She'd be wearing that white bed gown his aunt had given her—for modesty's sake, of course, in case one of the servants entered without knocking first.

A frown settled on Lucas's brow as he stared at the closed door. Surely she must have heard him. He wondered if she was all right.

Poor thing, she'd seemed tense yesterday, probably from worry over meeting his family.

His face softened. He'd have to assure her that his family would love her. His mother might cause a scene, but he would explain to Meghan beforehand about Mary Ridgely's penchant for the dramatic.

"Meghan," he called, thinking she might not want to see one of the maids right now. He no longer cared if the servants saw him at her door. She was his betrothed, and he had a right to bring her a cup of tea.

Everyone would know soon enough about their relationship.

A scowl formed on his features when Meghan still didn't come to the door. He reached for the doorknob and turned, relieved to see that the door was unlocked.

"Meghan, wake up, love," he teased as he entered the room.

Sunlight streamed in the window and fell across the empty bed. Lucas froze. The bed looked like it hadn't been slept in, and it was too early for the chambermaid to have been in . . . unless Meghan had put the linens to right herself.

Lucas's gaze fell on a folded sheet of paper propped against Meghan's pillow. He approached the bed with a growing sense of dread. He unfolded the parchment and began to read. The letters were printed carefully as if she had written the words with great care. It read:

Lucas,
 I can never be the kind of wife you need. I love you—always. Please don't be mad at me, because I had to go.

Forever yours in my heart.
Meghan McBride.

"No, love, no," he whispered. Lucas closed his eyes as raw pain ripped through him, making his heart bleed. "Aunt Flora!" he shouted. "Aunt Flora!"

His aunt came hurrying down the hall. "What on earth is it, Lucas—" She halted in the doorway, her gaze fastening on the note in Lucas's hand and then the unmade bed. "Oh, no," she said. "This is my fault."

"Yours?" he said, astonished.

She nodded. "I'd been tutoring her to be a proper wife, because of Mary . . . I'm sorry."

"No," he said, "it's not your fault at all. The blame

is mine. If she'd believed in my love, then she wouldn't have run."

As he stared at the note, he realized that he hadn't told her he loved her—not in so many words. And he vowed that if it took him till his last dying breath, he'd find Meghan McBride . . . if only to tell her that she was everything and all to him.

"Why do ye want to go to Philadelphia, lass?" Mrs. Garrity asked. "Why not stay with us?"

Meghan smiled at the Irish couple who'd appeared like a gift of God when she was hungry, tired, and frozen to the bone. Their thick Irish brogue had sounded like home to her, so she'd been easily persuaded to accept their offer of spending the night. They'd taken her into their home, fed and warmed her, and when they'd found out her destination, offered to take her to the Pennsylvania city themselves.

"I'm grateful for the offer, Mrs. Garrity, but I'm meeting a friend there." And their home in northern Delaware wasn't far enough away from Gibbons Mill, she thought. She'd find her former cabin mate, Bridget, if it took her days . . . months. Meghan shivered. She didn't want to think what she'd do if she couldn't find the girl.

"We're almost there, Meghan," Mr. Garrity said as he handled the reins to his horse-drawn wagon.

Meghan glanced ahead and saw the masts of several tall ships beyond the roof lines of many buildings. *Philadelphia.* She had made it, thanks to the Garritys. She didn't think she'd have made it if they hadn't found her huddled by the side of the road under a tree, trying to get warm, clutching her small bundle of meager possessions with numb hands. Fortunately, she hadn't been sitting there long when they'd come.

She had fought the urge to rest for hours, aware that she'd feel colder if she stopped. But now she was here.

The city of Philadelphia was noisy and bustling with merchants, patrons, and residents going about their work despite the cold winter temperature. Mr. Garrity pulled the carriage into a livery at the edge of town.

"I've me business to handle," he said, "but I'll see ye safely first to yer friend Bridget. There are people here who've no liking for us Irish."

"Oh, but that won't be necessary—" Meghan began.

"No bother, lass," he assured her.

"No, Mr. Garrity, I appreciate the offer, but I'd rather go alone." She flushed, for she hadn't wanted to hurt his feelings, but she couldn't allow him to know that she had no idea where Bridget lived.

Meghan thanked the Irish couple, embracing each one with tear-bright eyes.

"Lass, we'll be here till tomorra morning," Mr. Garrity said. "If ye need anything—or if ye should change yer mind and want to stay with us for a while—meet us here at the livery at eight o'clock."

Meghan nodded, overcome with emotion at the man's kindness. "Thank ye," she said. "Thank ye, both." Then she said goodbye and hurried away before the urge to remain in the safety of their home overruled the need to make it on her own . . . away from the man she'd left behind.

"Where are you going, Lucas?" his mother asked. "We've just arrived."

"I have to leave for a while, Mother." Lucas flashed his father a look that pleaded.

"But why?" Her voice sounded whiny.

"Mary," her husband said. "We weren't due to arrive until late this afternoon. Lucas has . . . business to at-

IRISH LINEN

tend." James Ridgely met his son's gaze. "Important business, I'd say."

His mother continued to complain, but her words were lost on Lucas, for he hurried from the house toward the stable. Traveling alone by horse would be faster than a carriage, he decided. He'd already been to Somerville and back, but he'd had no luck finding Meghan there. Rafferty O'Connor had left the area shortly after the fire, Lucas had learned while there, and Lucas was concerned that the man was out there somewhere . . . and so was Meghan. It frightened him that Meghan might face her former fiancé alone . . . even though there was no proof that Rafferty was the one responsible for the blaze.

He mounted his aunt's fastest horse and headed toward the Pattersons. Maybe, just maybe, he thought, Meghan had stopped to stay at the inn. But a few hours later when he arrived, he learned that the Pattersons hadn't seen her.

Lucas left behind two concerned people and continued toward Philadelphia, a place where a woman might find work and lose herself in the crowd. He worried about the dangers of the city to a woman—the pickpockets and thieves . . . and the drunken men looking for someone like Meghan to entertain them.

Meghan wandered the streets for hours. She'd asked every single person she met, but no one had seen nor heard of Sean and Bridget Cleary. She hugged her pack under her cloak and wondered what to do.

The Garritys were still in the city. She could always go back to them. *No*, she thought, her eyes burning. She couldn't abuse the couple's generous nature. They had done so much for her already.

Rafferty's ring was at the bottom of her pack. She

didn't know why she'd kept it. James had found it in the ashes from the fire, and he'd given it to her because it held value. Now, Meghan was glad that he had, and that she decided to keep it, for whatever unknown reason. She could sell the ring and have money to take a room.

She stifled the feeling of guilt that she hadn't returned the ring to Rafferty, that she hadn't allowed him to speak with her since that day. But she'd felt too betrayed, too upset, to see him.

But why had she slipped the ring into her pack? Had she planned to sell it all along perhaps?

Surely she'd be able to find a buyer for the ring in such a big city. She took out the circlet and studied it. The green jewels shimmered and winked as she turned it in the sunlight.

A heavy hand settled on her shoulder, and she gasped and spun, her eyes widening in startled shock. "Rafferty!"

He reeled drunkenly. "Hello, Meghan me girl." He held out his hand. "I believe that ring belongs to me."

Thirty-three

"What ya gonna do with 'er, Micky?" the unkempt man said as he glared across the room at Meghan.

"Oh, I've plans for me Meghan." Rafferty leered at her, and Meghan shivered. "Plans that will make us rich!"

"What kind of plans, Micky?" Ned Wiley looked at the Irishman stupidly.

"Be quiet, fool! I'll tell ya later." His green gaze raked Meghan with a wicked look from head to toe. "I wouldn't want to ruin me surprise, would I?"

"Ye're a bastard, Rafferty O'Connor," Meghan spat. She was tied to a chair at her hands, waist, and ankles. She'd never had a chance to run from her former fiancé, for there had been another man with him—the slow-witted Ned Wiley, who asked questions incessantly. From what she'd heard from the two men's conversation, there was apparently a third man.

"Now, Meggie love, what would yer da say?"

She struggled against her bonds, trying to rise. "He'd kill ye if he were alive!" She had seen that Rafferty's hand was burned, and she knew that it had been him who'd started the fire at Patty's. But she kept silent.

"Well, darlin', your da's not alive, is he? So I've nothin' to worry about." Rafferty turned to Ned.

"Keep an eye on her, Neddie boy. Don't touch 'er and don't let anyone else near 'er. Got that?"

Ned bobbed his head vehemently. "I got it, Micky."

"Good boy," Rafferty said, and the "boy" beamed.

"Rafferty," Meghan called as he started to leave, but he ignored her. "Rafferty O'Connor, I'm not finished with ye!" she shouted.

He stopped near the door, stiffening before turning around. "Apparently ye were finished with me, weren't ye, *love?* Ye wouldn't speak to me these last weeks. And then when ye finally did, ye wouldn't listen!"

She glared at him as if unafraid, but she was frightened of Rafferty O'Connor. He wasn't the same man from the County of Cork. He wasn't the man she'd known as her father's friend. *He may have tried to murder me!*

Meghan was relieved when her former fiancé left. What did he plan to do with her? As she studied her dim-witted guard, she recalled Rafferty and that naked woman. *Oh, Da, what's happened to him?*

Ned Wiley sat at a table and was shoving bread into his mouth faster than he could chew it. Meghan watched him with disgust. The man caught her staring and paused with half-chewed food hanging from his lips to offer her a hunk of his bread. Although she was hungry, she eyed the bread in Ned's dirty hands and then she shook her head, deciding that she'd rather die than eat the man's offering.

The man shrugged, uncaring whether she ate or not, and went back to eating his simple meal, washing the bread down with a tankard of ale.

Meghan closed her eyes, believing she was safe for now. Ned was obviously stupid enough to follow Rafferty's instructions to the letter, so she had nothing to fear until Rafferty or that other man—whoever he was—returned.

Her thoughts went to Lucas. He would have found her note by now. Was he furious with her? Hurt?

Oh, God, she'd never meant to hurt him! She loved him, and it'd been foolish, she realized, for her to leave. She'd braved more difficult trials in her life than meeting Lucas's family. Why hadn't she stayed and married the man she loved?

Trapped in a run-down building with an idiot guard and her hands tied, Meghan decided that it no longer was important whether or not Lucas returned her love. He was a man of his word. He would have married her whether or not his parents approved of her, whether or not anyone approved, because he wanted her.

She recalled the tenderness in his expression when he gazed into her eyes . . . the sweet caress of his fingertips against her skin. He had looked at her with something in his gaze . . . even if he didn't love her, he had cared.

Why didn't I stay?

Keeping her gaze on Ned, Meghan worked to break her wrist bonds, but she was unable to free herself, only rub her skin raw. *God, please let Lucas come . . . even if it's to get angry with me. Please let me see him one more time.*

The door to the room burst open, and Meghan gasped. The third man in Rafferty's little group of hoodlums was none other than Mathew Phelps. Meghan began to pray harder.

"Well, well, if it isn't the weaver, Meghan McBride," he said with a sneer. "Thanks to you I lost my job. I sure hope I find that you're worth it." He approached her, his eyes gleaming wickedly, his intent plain.

"Touch me, and you'll be sorry," she cried.

But Phelps only laughed and reached out to fondle her.

"Phelps!" Rafferty barked as he came through the door. "Hands off till I have her first!"

Meghan breathed a sigh of relief and closed her eyes. She prayed that she'd escape before either man could lay a hand on her.

Lucas had searched Philadelphia for two days with no sign of Meghan. He would have given up the notion that she had come here long ago, if not for the Garritys, whom he'd stopped to question on his way to the city. Their small house was located off the main road, and Lucas had gone to the door with little hope—after so many unsuccessful attempts with others—that the Garritys would have seen Meghan. But to his surprise, Mr. and Mrs. Garrity had not only seen his Meghan, but they'd taken her in for the night. Mr. Garrity had expressed his concern for the young woman. She'd been worn out and clearly unhappy with—he suspected—no real place to go.

"She said she was going to visit a friend," Mrs. Garrity said. "Bridget, I believe the lass's name was, but I'm afraid I can't remember her last name."

Lucas had searched his memory. "Cleary," he murmured. "Bridget Cleary."

"Oh, so there really is a friend then," Mr. Garrity said.

"But I don't think she knows where Bridget lives," Lucas replied after he'd nodded. "But I'll find her. If there's a God in heaven, I'll find her."

"We're glad to know that someone is looking for Meghan, but may we ask the reason why?"

"She's my betrothed, Mrs. Garrity," Lucas said, "and I love her. I'm afraid she may have thought I didn't care, but I'll make sure she knows," he added with determination. "I want her home with me."

The couple looked relieved to know that someone cared for Meghan McBride, and they wished Lucas God's blessing for success in finding the young Irishwoman.

But now after two long days of asking questions about Meghan and whether or not anyone knew the Clearys, Lucas was frightened and at his wit's end.

"Meghan, love, where are you? Think of me . . . let me know."

Then it suddenly occurred to him that he looked out of place in some of the seedy parts of the city. He stopped a poor-looking soul on the street and offered the man coin and his own clothes in exchange for the ragged garments the man wore.

The man stared at the shiner in Lucas's hand and then at the well-dressed gentleman, and when he realized that Lucas was serious, the fellow was quick to agree.

The stranger left with Lucas's good clothes, a grin, and a gold eagle in the pocket of his new waistcoat, the ten dollars more money than he'd ever possessed at one time. Lucas headed into the bowels of Philadelphia, wearing smelly old clothes that were a size too small for him.

"Slavery!" Meghan gasped.

"Aye, love, I'm afraid since ye didn't want me to husband, ye'll be pleasing other men for the rest of yer dear sweet life." Rafferty smiled. "There's a white slave trader who specializes in female goods . . . and although I've yet to experience how good ye are, I could, at least, assure him that ye are a female—and a lovely one at that."

"Bastard!"

His grin became a scowl. "So ye've said, and yer name calling's beginning to get tiresome."

Anger made Meghan dare to taunt him. "Why are ye here, Rafferty O'Connor? What happened? Did yer employer find ye with yer trousers down!"

"Bitch!" Rafferty drew back his hand and slapped her hard across the face. Meghan's head reeled from the impact as he addressed Phelps. "Hold in yer tongue, lad. Ye can have a taste of her soon after I've tried her."

"I told ye I'll not let ye lay a hand on me!" she vowed, shaken.

Rafferty laughed, and his cohorts chuckled with him. "Now, lads, how de ye suppose she plans to stop us with her hands tied?" He looked away, dismissing her. "Matt, I need ya to come with me. We need to make arrangements to leave this city as soon as we get our money." He shot Ned a look. "Watch her, Neddie boy, but don't touch her." And then Rafferty left with Phelps, confident that Ned would obey his order.

"Ned," Meghan called softly after the two men had gone. "Would ye untie me hands? They hurt me."

Ned stared at her and then shook his head. "Can't touch."

"Just the rope, Ned."

He hesitated as if deciding. "Nope."

Meghan cursed beneath her breath as she closed her eyes. It'd take a miracle for her to escape her present predicament.

Lucas waited in the shadow of a brick building and watched the old grogshop across the street. According to Slim-Eye, a pickpocket he'd caught trying to lift his pouch of coin, there were three men and a woman holed up in the room above the shop. One of the fellows was an Irishman. Slim-Eye had seen the woman go in several days ago, but he'd never stayed to see if she came out.

He knew he was crazy to follow such a pathetic lead, one given to him by a petty thief, but Lucas was desperate. He'd watch every building in Philadelphia if he had to—he loved Meghan that much.

It had been four days that he'd wandered the city, looking for his beloved, and at times—like now—he wondered if he'd ever find her. He asked himself whether or not she could still be alive, and then he'd thought that he'd surely feel it if she were dead.

His family must be frantic, he thought. Although he'd managed to send word to his aunt's telling her that his "business" had delayed him, his mother would be beside herself that he wasn't there.

If he didn't find Meghan by morning, he'd have to seriously consider going home. He had some affairs to be put in order, before he came back and continued his search for Meghan.

The door next to the shop entrance opened, and Lucas tensed. Two men exited; one was an Irishman and the other—*Good God, Mathew Phelps!* The Irishman spoke to his friend, and Lucas strained to hear. He couldn't make out the words at first, until the men began an argument, and the Irishman's voice rose along with his temper. Then Lucas heard the one word he'd wanted so badly to hear. *Meghan.*

Dear God, he'd found her. Or at least he'd found Rafferty O'Connor, he'd wager. The man was middle-aged with Irish features, sandy brown hair, and a stocky build. The same description had been given to him by his friend, Robert Somerton, Michael's brother.

His heart began to beat faster as he waited for the two men to disappear down the street. "Thank you, Slim-Eye," Lucas murmured as he hurried across the road toward the building. He was actually glad now that he'd let the thief go, that he hadn't punched the man senseless as he'd threatened.

The shop, it appeared, had been closed down for some time. Lucas stared at the groggery before pushing open the door beside it. The action didn't make a sound, which was a miracle, Lucas thought, considering the deplorable condition of the wood.

There was a narrow corridor with a long flight of stairs to the second floor. Lucas studied the steps and decided that they appeared solid enough. He set his first footstep carefully, his breath quickening as he wondered what or who he was going to find above.

He stopped on the second to the last step and listened. Lucas heard voices, one of them Meghan's. *Oh, love, thank God!* He stuck his hand in his pocket and slipped out the weapon he'd confiscated from Slim-Eye, the knife that the thief had attempted to turn on Lucas when the man was caught. Lucas cradled the knife handle in his palm and stepped onto the top landing, grateful when the floor didn't squeak beneath his worn boot heels.

"Ned, please. I promise I'll behave if ye untie me arms." Meghan bit her lip. Her cheek throbbed where Rafferty had struck her, and she had to relieve herself. Although her need wasn't urgent, she didn't want to wait for Rafferty's return and the embarrassment of his amusement as he stood guard over her and watched. "I've got to use the necessary." She blushed, because it was true.

"Can't," Ned said. "Can't touch."

"But I have to relieve meself!" she cried on a note of desperation. "Would ye rather I go here . . . in this chair?"

The idiot regarded her with alarm. "No. Ya must wait. Micky will be back soon."

"His name is Rafferty. Rafferty O'Connor!"

"Micky," Ned insisted. "Said to call him Micky, so I call him Micky."

"Do ye do everything he tells ye to do?"

The man nodded.

"Why?"

He looked surprised by the question. "Because Micky said to. And Micky knows a lot."

"Micky doesn't know everything, Ned," a deep male voice said.

Meghan's heart leapt as Lucas stepped into the room. She offered God a silent prayer of thanks.

"Love," Lucas said, his ebony gaze roaming over her hungrily. His expression grew dark with anger when he saw her bruised face. "Are ye all right?"

She nodded, tears pooling to blur the wonderful sight of him.

"Ned, untie her," Lucas said with authority.

Ned had risen, and he regarded the stranger warily. "Can't. Micky said."

"Ned," Lucas boomed in a loud, angry voice, "I said to untie her. Micky sent me. I'm in charge now."

Meghan saw Ned's confusion and then finally his understanding.

"I have to touch her," Ned said, looking uneasy.

"Just her hands, Ned," Lucas warned.

The man nodded. "Just her hands," he promised.

Meghan exchanged looks with Lucas, and she saw that he was startled by how easy it'd been to manipulate Ned.

Still, they had to get away quickly, before Rafferty and Mathew Phelps returned.

Ned freed her hands within seconds, then he started to untie her waist.

"Ya from the slave shop?" Ned asked innocently.

After a startled look, Lucas stared at the slow-witted man and silently fumed. "Slave shop?" he said. He nodded. "Yes."

Ned seemed to accept Lucas's reply as truth and stood back once Meghan was freed.

Meghan shot up from the chair and ran into Lucas's arms. "Oh, God, Lucas. I thought I'd never see ye again!"

"I love you, Meghan McBride," he said huskily.

"Hey," Ned said, puzzlement in his expression. "How can ya love her when ya don't even know her?"

"But I do know her, Ned."

"Ya do?" The man blinked. "Ya know the slave man," he said to Meghan. "Well, that's a strange thing to hear . . ."

"Ned, I want you to sit in Meghan's chair," Lucas said.

"Why?"

"So you'll be comfortable."

The man bobbed his head jerkily. "All right."

Lucas held Meghan tightly against his side, his arm about her waist. He kissed the top of her head before he let her go. "Get out of here, love," he ordered. "Run across the road and wait for me behind that large brick building."

"But Lucas—"

"Go, Meghan."

She started to hurry and then stopped short at the top of the stairs.

"Going somewhere, lass?" Rafferty came up the stairs with his knife drawn.

"Lucas!" she cried, warning him.

Rafferty struck her with his fist, throwing her against the wall.

IRISH LINEN

"Ned," Lucas growled in a last-ditch effort to gain Ned's cooperation. "Micky was going to cheat you!"

The man blinked, confused. "Cheat me?"

"Ned, take him," Rafferty commanded as he came into the room. "Phelps, bring Meghan over here."

"Ye'll never get away with this!" Meghan vowed, struggling against the man who held her arms. She kicked back with her heel, and Mathew cursed as she made contact with his shin. Then, the man twisted her arms until she screamed.

"Meghan!" Lucas exclaimed, but he couldn't go to her. Ned had listened to Rafferty and was circling to get Lucas's knife. As far as Lucas could tell, Rafferty's only weapon seemed to be the one in his hand.

"Ned, here," Rafferty said, and he threw the weapon near the idiot man's feet.

Lucas heard it clatter as it fell; he scrambled for the knife first and grinned as he caught hold of the handle. Triumphant, he turned to confront the foolish Irishman who'd given up his weapon and drew a sharp breath to see that Rafferty had a second blade, which he now held to Meghan's throat.

"Give Ned the weapons, Ridgely."

Lucas blinked. "You know who I am?"

Rafferty's smile was evil. "Aye, everyone in Somerville was only too happy to tell me that it was ye who brought Meghan from the ship. Meg is a beautiful woman. Stands to reason that ye'd be attracted to her."

His green gaze fastened on Meghan with regret. "But ye, lass—I wouldn't have thought ye'd betray me so." He pulled back the blade as he retreated to some memory in his mind. "Dermot was me best friend."

Meghan caught Lucas's eye. "I know," she said softly, not wanting to bring him back to the present.

"I loved the man just like I loved ye, Meggie." He

closed his eyes. "Ye were so good. I had to have the others, don't ya see? I was waiting for ya to marry me, Meggie . . ." His face darkened. "And then ye seemed to change yer mind."

Ned stared at the Irishman, his mouth open, his expression blank. Apparently, he'd forgotten Micky's orders to take Lucas's knives.

Lucas gauged the danger of the third man. His eyes then met blue ones and Meghan nodded in silent understanding. They had one chance and now was as good a time as any.

"The man is from the slave ship, Micky," Ned said suddenly.

"He is not, you fool!"

Ned's eyes narrowed as Rafferty started to call him names. Clearly, the slow-minded man didn't like being told he was stupid.

"Now, love!" Lucas cried.

Meghan kicked back and high at Phelps, while Lucas lunged toward Rafferty, knocking the man down and struggling for his knife.

Ned watched without moving, because no one had given him the order to fight.

The whole episode happened in a matter of minutes. When Rafferty started to rise then, Ned suddenly decided to take action.

"I'm not stupid!" he said angrily. Ned grabbed the Irishman and hit him in the jaw. Phelps, whom Meghan had kicked in the groin area, lay on the floor, groaning and clutching his private parts.

Lucas handed Meghan a knife and told her to hold it on Phelps. "If he moves, cut him," he said.

With a grin, Meghan crouched next to the injured man and held the knife blade between the man's thighs.

Then, Lucas ordered Ned to tie up Rafferty and his

friend, while Lucas held the other two knives, preparing to use them on either of the two felled men, if needed.

"I did it," Ned said, rising to his feet with a smile.

"Good man," Lucas said, and Ned beamed. Lucas then took out his money pouch and handed three coins to Ned. "Run and get a copper, Ned. Micky and his friend are bad men. If you hurry back with the law, I'll give you this bag of coins."

Ned's eyes gleamed. "For me? I'll hurry," he promised, and they could hear his hurrying footsteps on the stairs. He tripped once, yelled up that he was all right and hurrying, before he continued.

When the three men were taken care of, Lucas turned to Meghan. "You left me." His expression was dark, angry.

Meghan's eyes filled with tears. "I know. I'm sorry."

A smile replaced the scowl on his face. "I love you, Meghan. Don't ever leave me again." He opened his arms, and she ran into his embrace.

"I promise, Lucas. I promise I'll always love ye and be there whenever ye turn around."

And they kissed, ignoring Rafferty's loud curses.

Meghan responded with all the love she felt. The magic had returned. She was back in Lucas's arms.

Epilogue

June 1848

Lucas sat on the front porch of his Windfield estate house, waiting for his lovely wife to join him. He and Meghan had been married four months this day, and still, every time he saw her he felt himself respond to her like a lovesick boy.

Their life was good, and he would see that no one would bother or harm Meghan again. Rafferty O'Connor had been arrested for not only kidnapping Meghan, but for stealing the Somerton emerald ring. Mathew Phelps was in jail as well on numerous charges, including assaulting a young child. Believing the man harmless, Lucas had given the slow-witted man Ned a job on Windfield. Ned worked well helping Jack in the stables; he listened carefully and followed all of the groom's instructions, and everyone was pleased with his work.

"Mr. Ridgely?"

He turned toward the sound of a prim-sounding voice and spied Meghan framed in the open doorway. She was outfitted in a low-cut fancy gown of deep crimson, her hair pinned up with flowers woven into the confined curls. She wore white gloves and jewelry at her throat and wrists. As she approached, she walked with her back straight and a cool demeanor. She looked the perfect lady, his aunt's lessons having done their job. But her polished act didn't belong to his Meghan. It belonged to women like his mother or Valerie Bain. He didn't want a woman like his mother or any of her peers. He frowned with disapproval. He wanted the Irish girl who'd chased him across the lawn last night and rained kisses across his face after toppling him to the ground.

"Your mother and father are coming to tea this afternoon," she announced.

"Why are you dressed like that? You don't have to change to please my mother," Lucas growled. His mother had accepted his marriage to Meghan with amazing good grace. His father loved her, just as Lucas had predicted he would, while Beth . . . it made Lucas nervous how well Meghan and Beth got along together. He was sure that someday the two would be up to mischief against him, and he wouldn't stand a chance.

"Dressed like what?" Meghan's lips curved when his scowl deepened. "It's a special occasion," she said, and the sun shone in her smile and in the bright sparkle of her beautiful blue eyes. "I've news to tell—"

"So you felt you had to dress up for my parents?" Lucas asked with a frown. His parents had moved to the house where Lucas himself had been living for several years. It had been his father's idea, since Lucas had taken over full reins in the running of the plantation. His mother hadn't objected—another miracle, Lucas had thought at the time.

Lucas regarded his wife, noting her strange, almost dreamy look. "What news?" he asked.

"I'm with child," she said softly. "Our child."

"You're—" He stared at her blankly, unsure if he'd heard her right.

Meghan studied her husband's dumbfounded expression and suddenly worried that he might not be pleased. She'd been so excited herself when she'd realized that she was three weeks late, that she'd assumed that Lucas would be happy, too.

Her lips quivered. "Lucas?" Perhaps he didn't want her child of low birth. Her old doubts resurfaced, making it difficult for her to breathe.

He had closed his eyes, and now he opened them again, revealing all the love and awe he felt for her. "We've made a baby together?"

Relieved, she nodded and smiled.

He reached out and tugged her onto his lap. "Have I told you I loved you lately?" he said huskily.

She grinned down at him. "No. It's been . . . oh, a half hour or more. Too long for me to go without hearing the words."

"I love you, Mrs. Ridgely," he said solemnly.

Meghan trembled as she encircled his neck with her arms. "I love you," she gasped.

She thought of her new life here in America. She had nothing to worry about now that Rafferty and Phelps were locked away.

"Mr. Ridgely!" she cried as he began to nibble at her neck and then lower. "My gown! What will your parents and Beth think if it wrinkles?"

"Sorry," he said. "Teatime with the family has been cancelled. We have business to attend this afternoon."

"But the baby—"

"Ah, the baby," he said with satisfaction. "Our baby will not leave you, just because you haven't told my family." He paused to smile. "Mother will be a nuisance once she finds out, you know. She'll believe you've presented her with a grandchild just to please her." His voice became a soft whisper. "She'll love you all the more for this."

"Lucas, I—"

He kissed her. And he rose with her in his arms and carried her up the stairs to their bedchamber, calling out to one of the maids to tell his parents that teatime was cancelled for today, and that they were invited to come tomorrow at precisely four.

Then, in a room lit by the sun shining softly through the window, Lucas gave his wife an afternoon of wild kisses and tender caresses . . . and he gave her time and time again the three greatest gifts a man could give to his wife.

"I love you." He told her he loved her with words . . . with his body as they joined . . . and eternally with all of his heart.

Author's Note

Most of the Irish immigrants who came to America during the Great Famine entered the United States in New York or Boston. Only a fortunate few managed to arrive directly in Philadelphia. The Irish in Philadelphia were the lucky ones, for their opportunities for employment were greater. While many households advertised that they wanted to hire Protestants only, it was still a fact that the Catholic Irishwomen were in demand as domestics. But life for the Irish immigrant was different in New York and other cities, where he faced prejudice. Shop windows and other places of employment held signs that read NINA—"No Irish Need Apply."

The Irish were more often than not treated like slaves, but their good humor and their willingness to work hard helped them to rise above the prejudice until finally they were accepted in American society.

Meghan McBride was fortunate to arrive in Philadelphia on the *Mary Freedom* and to find kind people who employed her. Rafferty O'Connor's experiences were much different, however. His struggle against prejudice hardened the once idealistic man until his drive for success was fueled only by his anger, bitterness, lust, and greed.

About the Author

Candace McCarthy lives in Delaware with her husband of over 21 years and has a son in college. She enjoys writing and feels that a part of her is missing during the times she's not creating stories. "I love romances especially," she says. "Reading or writing a romance novel is reexperiencing those first moments when you first realized you've found love." Candace is the author of eight other published romances, among which are *Heaven's Fire*, *Sea Mistress*, and *Warrior's Caress* for Zebra Books. She considers herself fortunate to have a loving family, good friends, and her writing; and she thanks all the wonderful fans who've read her books. Candace loves hearing from her readers. You may write her at: P.O. Box 58, Magnolia, Delaware 19962. She also has a website on the Internet. The address is: http://www.comet.net/writers/candace

DON'T MISS THESE ROMANCES FROM BEST-SELLING AUTHOR KATHERINE DEAUXVILLE!

THE CRYSTAL HEART   (0-8217-4928-5, $5.99)

Emmeline gave herself to a sensual stranger in a night aglow with candlelight and mystery. Then she sent him away. Wed by arrangement, Emmeline desperately needed to provide her aged husband with an heir. But her lover awakened a passion she kept secret in her heart . . . until he returned and rocked her world with his demands and his desire.

THE AMETHYST CROWN   (0-8217-4555-7, $5.99)

She is Constance, England's richest heiress. A radiant, silver-eyed beauty, she is a player in the ruthless power games of King Henry I. Now, a desperate gambit takes her back to Wales where she falls prey to a ragged prisoner who escapes his chains, enters her bedchamber . . . and enslaves her with his touch. He is a bronzed, blond Adonis whose dangerous past has forced him to wander Britain in disguise. He will escape an enemy's shackles—only to discover a woman whose kisses fire his tormented soul. His birthright is a secret, but his wild, burning love is his destiny . . .

Available wherever paperbacks are sold, or order direct from the Publisher. Send cover price plus 50¢ per copy for mailing and handling to Penguin USA, P.O. Box 999, c/o Dept. 17109, Bergenfield, NJ 07621. Residents of New York and Tennessee must include sales tax. DO NOT SEND CASH.

FROM AWARD-WINNING AUTHOR
JO BEVERLEY

DANGEROUS JOY   (0-8217-5129-8, $5.99)

Felicity is a beautiful, rebellious heiress with a terrible secret. Miles is her reluctant guardian—a man of seductive power and dangerous sensuality. What begins as a charade borne of desperation soon becomes an illicit liaison of passionate abandon and forbidden love. One man stands between them: a cruel landowner sworn to possess the wealth he craves and the woman he desires. His dark treachery will drive the lovers to dare the unknowable and risk the unthinkable, determined to hold on to their joy.

FORBIDDEN   (0-8217-4488-7, $4.99)

While fleeing from her brothers, who are attempting to sell her into a loveless marriage, Serena Riverton accepts a carriage ride from a stranger—who is the handsomest man she has ever seen. Lord Middlethorpe, himself, is actually contemplating marriage to a dull daughter of the aristocracy, when he encounters the breathtaking Serena. She arouses him as no woman ever has. And after a night of thrilling intimacy—a forbidden liaison—Serena must choose between a lady's place and a woman's passion!

TEMPTING FORTUNE   (0-8217-4858-0, $4.99)

In a night shimmering with destiny, Portia St. Claire discovers that her brother's debts have made him a prisoner of dangerous men. The price of his life is her virtue—about to be auctioned off in London's most notorious brothel. However, handsome Bryght Malloreen has other ideas for Portia, opening her heart to a sensuality that tempts her to madness.

Available wherever paperbacks are sold, or order direct from the Publisher. Send cover price plus 50¢ per copy for mailing and handling to Penguin USA, P.O. Box 999, c/o Dept. 17109, Bergenfield, NJ 07621. Residents of New York and Tennessee must include sales tax. DO NOT SEND CASH.

Taylor-made Romance from Zebra Books

WHISPERED KISSES (0-8217-5454-8, $5.99/$6.99)
Beautiful Texas heiress Laura Leigh Webster never imagined that her biggest worry on her African safari would be the handsome Jace Elliot, her tour guide. Laura's guardian, Lord Chadwick Hamilton, warns her of Jace's dangerous past; she simply cannot resist the lure of his strong arms and the passion of his *Whispered Kisses*.

KISS OF THE NIGHT WIND (0-8217-5279-0, $5.99/$6.99)
Carrie Sue Strover thought she was leaving trouble behind her when she deserted her brother's outlaw gang to live her life as schoolmarm Carolyn Starns. On her journey, her stagecoach was attacked and she was rescued by handsome T.J. Rogue. T.J. plots to have Carrie lead him to her brother's cohorts who murdered his family. T.J., however, soon succumbs to the beautiful runaway's charms and loving caresses.

FORTUNE'S FLAMES (0-8217-5450-5, $5.99/$6.99)
Impatient to begin her journey back home to New Orleans, beautiful Maren James was furious when Captain Hawk delayed the voyage by searching for stowaways. Impatience gave way to uncontrollable desire once the handsome captain searched *her* cabin. He was looking for illegal passengers; what he found was wild passion with a woman he knew was unlike all those he had known before!

PASSIONS WILD AND FREE (0-8217-5275-8, $5.99/$6.99)
After seeing her family and home destroyed by the cruel and hateful Epson gang, Randee Hollis swore revenge. She knew she found the perfect man to help her—gunslinger Marsh Logan. Not only strong and brave, Marsh had the ebony hair and light blue eyes to make Randee forget her hate and seek the love and passion that only he could give her.

Available wherever paperbacks are sold, or order direct from the Publisher. Send cover price plus 50¢ per copy for mailing and handling to Penguin USA, P.O. Box 999, c/o Dept. 17109, Bergenfield, NJ 07621. Residents of New York and Tennessee must include sales tax. DO NOT SEND CASH.